LITTLE
SISTER

LITTLE SISTER

A JAMES PALATINE NOVEL

GILES O'BRYEN

Published by Thomas & Mercer, Seattle

www.apub.com

Amazon, the Amazon logo, and Thomas & Mercer are trademarks of Amazon.com, Inc., or its affiliates.

ISBN-13: 9781503951945
ISBN-10: 1503951944

Cover design by Lisa Horton

Printed in the United States of America

To Emma

Part I

Chapter One

In Eversholt Street the weird girl who'd been following him hailed a black cab and scrambled in. She was tall and big-boned, and agitation was making her clumsy. James Palatine watched intently, hoping to recognise her: a student of his at Imperial College, maybe, or one of the academic office staff? Her overstuffed canvas courier bag snagged on the taxi door, so she had to turn and yank it in behind her. James caught a glimpse of a pale, angular face with high cheekbones, a wide mouth, and hair that had been frizzed and dyed a bleached orange, though both the curls and the colour were growing out. She reached for the strap and slammed the door shut, and the cab rattled its way back into the flow of traffic.

Who was she? She had none of the studied anonymity of a trained operative – and besides, a professional wouldn't just give up and drive off in a taxi. Stalker? Lunatic? Or just confirmation that five years in the cyber surveillance business had left him sufficiently paranoid to make even shambolic young women seem threatening?

Over the last week James had seen her in Camden, Bloomsbury and Pimlico, where he'd been to visit his accountant – something he did strictly once a year so it surely couldn't have been a coincidence. Whenever he caught sight of her, she was fidgeting with something:

checking the contents of her pockets or reaching down to tug at a sock. She always wore the same clothes – a baggy, plum-coloured sweatshirt printed with an American university crest, skinny black jeans and green canvas pumps that looked brand new – and always carried the black courier bag that appeared to contain a collection of small paving slabs. She shouldn't have been as conspicuous as she was, but there was something discomposed about her – as if following James Palatine was an irritating chore she wished she'd never agreed to but could not now abandon.

Three days previously he'd seen her watching his flat from the open space used by drunks and defecating dogs on the other side of Camden Road, and he guessed she'd be going there now. Approaching from the south five minutes later, James circled round to the entrance on the far side and knelt on a patch of meagre grass behind a holly bush. The girl wasn't hard to spot. She'd sat down on a bench and was peering over the back through a screen of dusty foliage that separated the park from the pavement. The front door to his flat was directly opposite, on the other side of Camden Road. It was just after five, and the air was smeared with exhaust fumes from the line of rush-hour traffic heading north. She shifted back and forth along the bench, trying to get a better view.

A gang of five teenage boys wearing sweatshirts and baggy jeans had congregated not far from her bench: two of them were engaged in a histrionic dispute, aiming extravagant shoves and kicks at each other while the rest looked on. The older of the two, who sported a black baseball cap with a gold badge, paused to look over his shoulder at the girl. Early twenties, James guessed. Too old to be hanging out with a bunch of schoolboys. He'd torn the sleeves from his sweatshirt to show off his gym-honed shoulders. He beckoned to a tall boy with loose, ropey limbs wearing a white Nike headband, who turned to stare at the girl. A sly, predatory stare.

The girl leaned down and rubbed the heel of her left foot. The courier bag sagged beside her. It was obvious that she was in danger of being attacked. James felt oddly responsible for her, as if he'd invited her to run round after him and get herself mugged. He focused on the older man and the one in the headband, saw how they held their arms away from their bodies as if to accommodate the slabs of muscle beneath their hoodies. James could have guessed the weight of each of them to within five pounds and neither was as big as he thought he was. They and one of the other boys were armed: their hands, twitching compulsively over a cargo pocket or a section of waistband, were as good as pointing out where they kept their blades. The other two were negligible. James calculated distances, assessed the obstacles the girl would face if she decided to run. *The more you see, the less you surprised.* So Sam Hu Li, his t'ai chi instructor, would be telling him. *Know everything, expect nothing.* With Sam, the line between wise and glib was easily crossed.

The one with the muscular shoulders moved in among the others and said something, then led them over to the bench. James stood up and started across the park. Headband sat down on the bench, threw a lanky arm around the girl's neck and clamped one leg over hers. James saw her flinch and struggle, but Headband tightened his grip, forcing her head down into his groin.

'Bitch wants to suck my dick.'

Shoulders sat on the other side of her and started to go through her bag with an air of casual entitlement.

'Let me go, shithead!'

Despite being strangled by Headband's grip, she managed to sound angry as well as frightened.

'Yo, EJ! Man comin', bruv.'

EJ – he was the one searching her bag – looked up and saw James.

'Let the girl go. This is over. Walk away,' James ordered. He positioned himself at the end of the bench, with EJ and Headband

and the girl in front of him, the rest grouped to his left. Headband relaxed his hold and the girl was able to lift her head. She caught sight of James and looked appalled.

'The fuck you lookin' at?' EJ demanded.

'The girl and I are walking away. Don't try to stop us.'

'Fuck you, wasteman.'

'Stand up, move away from the bench,' he told the girl. She jabbed Headband with her elbow, but he held her hard.

'OK, I'll buy the girl off you for twenty quid. If not, I start picking on your boys. You're the boss, you decide.'

He continued to stare at EJ, seeing the usual overcharged mixture of front and fear, at once insubstantial and dangerous. Some hint of intoxication, probably skunk, but not recent. EJ stood up, took a step towards James and began to bounce on his heels and weave from side to side like a boxer, hands up, biceps pumped. His bloodshot eyes had the petulant, vindictive look of a man who has never got beyond thinking he's been hard done by and someone ought to pay for it. But there was also a flicker of unease: James was supposed to retreat and he hadn't. EJ stopped swaying and lowered his right arm.

'Gi'ss the note.' He held out his left hand.

'Let the girl go.'

EJ reached round and made as if to scratch his back. The boy who had seen him first approached from James's left.

'You don't want to attack me,' said James evenly.

He moved on EJ without waiting for a reply, right hand stretching for his throat. The weapon appeared, a kitchen knife with a four-inch blade, slashing at James's arm. James swivelled from the waist and his arm was gone, leaving EJ slicing air. His left hand clamped EJ's wrist from the side. He stepped in, continuing his rotation, pushing the knife-hand on through its parabola until he had the back of EJ's upper arm braced across the point of his shoulder. He pulled back sharply, felt the arm pop clear of its socket. EJ screamed. James let him fall. The knife clattered on the path.

Headband was rooted to the bench, his arm still hooked around the girl's neck. Two of the younger ones were backing away. The one to James's left had a blade out, but his eyes were showing fear. James didn't want to let him run. He moved in sideways, watching for the boy's reaction. It came: a reluctant dart that stopped a foot from James's stomach. James feinted a kick and the blade swung down, leaving him wide open. A jab to the mouth and the boy wobbled, the knife dangling. James caught his knife-hand and twisted a half-turn, looked up to see Headband and the other three running off across the open space. The boy he'd caught was doubled over, the top of his head pointing at the concrete apron round the bench. James pushed down smoothly on the boy's wrist, twisted another quarter turn until he felt the bone crack. The boy gave a moan of surprise.

EJ was sitting on the bench cradling his bicep, his face grey with shock. 'Broke my fucking arm,' he said.

'Frontal dislocation of the shoulder. Get to A&E, you'll make some junior doctor's day.'

James turned to look for the girl. She was heading for the gate. He ran ahead of her and turned.

'I saved you from a mugging and now I'll probably be prosecuted for assault. You can't just walk away.'

'I didn't ask you to beat them up, did I?'

She looked down and started to fasten the buckle on her courier bag.

'You think I should have let them get on with it?' said James. 'Come to the pub over there and I'll buy you a drink.'

She turned to look at the place he'd indicated. She didn't seem to be able to make up her mind what to do, so he took her elbow by way of a prompt. She shook her arm away.

'You don't have to steer me, I'm not a five-year-old.'

* * *

Clive Silk stepped from the lift into the lobby of the seventh-floor executive office suite of MI6's Embankment HQ. It was 5.15 p.m. The PA stationed at the reception desk saw him coming and called through to tell Sir Iain Strang that he'd arrived.

'Do you want to take a seat, Clive? They're not quite ready yet.'

'Who's in there?'

'Oh, just Sir Iain and Nigel. Coffee, tea?'

Clive shook his head and walked over to the seating area, modular blocks of foam rubber upholstered in purple fabric arranged around two glass coffee tables. The decision as to which module to sit on was so trivial that for a moment Clive couldn't make it, and found himself swerving from one to the other, until he finally came to rest next to a threadbare weeping fig. A vacuum cleaner whined from the corridor behind him. He set his briefcase on the table, and pulled out a report entitled *The Theft of the Grosvenor Systems IPD400: Preliminary Findings*. He'd sent it in shortly before eleven the previous night. Clive was an officer in MI6's Strategic Projects Department. Eighteen months ago he had been discreetly seconded to the Grosvenor Systems board so that he could monitor development work on the IPD400 – or Little Sister as it was known by the wags at Grosvenor. Which was not to say he was in any way responsible for the thing going missing.

The door to Sir Iain Strang's office opened and Nigel de la Mere, Sector Chief for North-West Africa, stalked out. He was a tall man, narrow-shouldered but heavy around the bottom and thighs; his dusty-looking hair stuck up from his head, making him look permanently surprised. He was dressed in black needlecords and a plaid shirt. He came over and sat on the outer edge of the purple module next to Clive's, squashing the foam rubber so badly out of shape that he had to brace one knee against the floor to stop himself falling off.

'Heads up,' he said, leaning in close so that Clive could see the pale mottling on his cheeks and smell stale coffee on his breath. 'Fair amount of blood on the carpet but I think we're through the worst. Don't be tempted to make excuses for yourself, is my advice.'

'Sir Iain's blaming me for this?'

'You do seem to have taken your eye off the ball.'

'That's absolutely not true. It was never in my remit to— '

'Only came out for a pee, Clive.'

De la Mere levered himself upright and hurried off. Clive leafed apprehensively through his report and now saw that the entire thing could be read as just that: making excuses for himself. On his way back, Nigel paused. His boyish, club-bore's face looked strangely eager.

'Do a lot of nodding. You'll be fine.'

Another ten minutes had passed before the PA trotted over and told Clive he could go in. He walked to Sir Iain's office, knocked and heard a bark from within. Nervousness had drained the strength from his arms so that he couldn't open the heavy door more than half way and had to sidle round it. The Director-General of MI6 was watching him from a chrome and leather sofa. Nigel de la Mere sat beside him in a matching armchair, his hands folded behind his head in a display of lofty detachment. The view of the Thames beyond was curiously flat, as if it might actually be a backlit photograph that could be changed with a flick of a switch to a vista of the Himalayas or a street-scene in Shanghai.

'Clive Silk, our Grosvenor mole, reluctant paddler in that slurry pit of ineptitude.' Strang's full, leathery lips formed the words with scornful precision. 'Sit here, next to me.'

His accent was Manchester Grammar, carefully preserved through years of contagion from Whitehall's Oxbridge riffraff.

Unwilling to meet Strang's gaze, Clive's eyes wandered over the Director-General's office, which looked as if it had been inspired by a corporate furnishings catalogue, then once installed, zealously protected from the sullying effects of human occupation.

'Can I just say how much I appreciate the opportunity to work with you on this,' Clive blurted out. He hadn't fully resolved to speak and his voice sounded shrill. He cleared his throat and continued: 'I hope my inside track on Grosvenor's processes will be helpful— '

'Unless you're planning to give me a blowjob, Clive, I think we might start. I've read your report, but please strain my credulity once more by explaining what the fuck happened.'

Clive had always dismissed Strang's reputation for being foul-mouthed as office tittle-tattle, and was disconcerted to find it was true. He turned to a random page of his report to cover his embarrassment, and started again.

'One of the Grosvenor finance officers offered to import the inventory data from the warehouse into the accounting system, so they could use it to value Grosvenor's assets,' Clive said, trying not to gabble. 'Once he had administrator access to the warehouse system, he deleted the UNDER EMBARGO tags from the entry for the IPD400. Anyone who looked at an inventory print-out would think it was OK to sell.'

'And within a matter of days the confounded thing has been shipped off to Claude Zender in Morocco,' said Nigel de la Mere. 'Which is not a coincidence.'

'Please tell me there's more to it than that,' said Strang.

'The paperwork was in order.' Clive couldn't think what else to say. 'The internal paperwork, I mean.'

His mouth was dry, but he couldn't even summon the nerve to pour himself a glass of water from the jug on the table in front of him.

'I put copies with my report.'

'I saw,' said Strang. 'The authorisation-for-release box is labelled "Operations Director", but it's been crossed out and someone's written "Logistics Manager" instead. Why?'

'Oh, yes, the Operations Director had a car accident on the way in to work. Not hurt— '

'I really don't give a fuck. Hit and run?'

'I'm not sure.'

'I am. Nigel, see what the plods can dig up. So, some dick-in-a-suit pisses all over the inventory, the post-boy slaps down his big rubber stamp, and the greatest British military invention since the longbow gets trolleyed out of the back door and into the hands of the panto villain from Marrakech.'

Clive thought it prudent to confine himself to a nod.

'If that turns up in your memoirs, Nigel, I'll have so many briefs up your arse you'll be shitting horsehair for the rest of your days. Dick-in-a-suit went back to the States forty-eight hours before the IPD400 shipped out, correct?'

'Yes. Said his mother was dying.'

'Background?'

'Harvard Business School, accountancy, two years at Lockheed, four months at Grosvenor.'

'What about the Grosvenor Sales Director who did the deal with Zender?'

'Natalya Kocharian. She's from Kiev originally, though her father's Armenian. Worked at Gazprom in Moscow, then GE.'

'And on a KGB training course in the northern steppes she had a brief fling with an ageing he-man called Vladimir Putin?'

Clive attempted to laugh at his superior's wit, but the noise came out like a yelp stifled by a cough. 'She was vetted, of course,' he managed to say. 'A career woman – highly rated at Grosvenor.'

'Get her file over here and have it properly checked. The IPD400 walked out of the Grosvenor warehouse, then what?'

'It was added to a consignment due out of Northolt in late morning,' said Clive, feeling relieved that he'd reached an episode in the narrative for which he couldn't be held culpable. 'Routed via Paris, arrived in Casablanca about nine p.m. It was in Zender's warehouse on the Boulevard Moulay Slimane by midnight.'

'It cleared customs in three hours?'

'They get more from expediting shipments for Zender than they ever see in their wage packets,' said de la Mere.

'Then Zender transferred the IPD400 straight on to his client?'

'Yes,' said Clive. 'I mean, arms brokers never hold on to things longer than they have to. I'd say he was in possession of the IPD400 for twenty-four hours at most.'

'And who did he sell it on to?' de la Mere asked.

'He wouldn't reveal that.' Clive glanced at the faces beside him and realised he was expected to say more. 'Confidentiality agreements, a duty of trust to his clients, that sort of thing... Not that a man like Zender needs any excuse to keep something secret.'

'Your thoughts on who his client might be?' asked Sir Iain Strang.

Clive looked over at de la Mere. Neither of them spoke.

'This is why I get such a thrill out of the intelligence business,' said the MI6 chief. 'Supercharged professionals at my beck and call, intellects fizzing, theories clamouring to be heard. Who's down as the end user on the export licence?'

'Some tribal leader with a nominal role in the Mauritanian government,' said de la Mere, 'name of Makhlani.'

'You can bulk buy them from any self-respecting stationers south of Tangiers for fuck's sake. I thought Mauritania was on the proscribed list?'

'Depends who's lobbying. I'm having him checked now, but I think we can assume that Makhlani isn't the proud owner of a brand new IPD400.'

'What leverage do we have over Claude Zender?'

'Rather less than he has over us,' said Nigel.

Strang gave an irritated snort. 'Well, thank you, underlings, for placing the cock-up naked before me in all its throbbing majesty. Now we have to retrieve the IPD400 from Zender's anonymous client while simultaneously pretending nothing's happened. Nigel, you run this one. Clive, confine yourself to the Grosvenor end of it. Clear?'

Clive nodded and glanced over at de la Mere. The sector chief, who was waiting to meet his eye, favoured him with a patronising nod.

'Regarding your report,' Strang went on. 'I see that you call it *The Theft of the IPD400*, whereas the truth is that Grosvenor sold it. From such a flaccid start, it's hard to see your list of action points yielding anything other than a bout of anxious foreplay followed by an apologetic withdrawal. But the gist of it is, you're going to leave everything to Ms Kocharian. What chance does she have of bringing Zender to the table?'

'Surprisingly good,' said Nigel de la Mere. 'The special offers she makes to favoured clients are said to be irresistible to any man with blood in his veins.'

'So this over-promoted callgirl gives Claude Zender a tit job and we get the IPD400 back?'

When neither of them replied, the MI6 chief gripped the edge of the conference table and squeezed so hard it looked as if he might shortly come away with two fistfuls of polished oak. His hands, Clive noticed, were those of a butcher, big-boned and thickly covered with pink flesh. Strang released the table and ran both hands over his sleek black hair.

'Clive, handle Ms Kocharian. Explain that I want her to suck Zender dry. Nigel, draw up a list of candidates for ownership of the IPD400. Take note that the operation to lift it was expensive and sophisticated – we're not looking for a trio of holy warriors in a Cairo bedsit. You may as well get New York on to dick-in-a-suit, though I predict he'll turn out not to exist. Then see what access we have to Zender's financial arrangements.'

'Zender's USP is that he's a big fat dead end. It'll be hard to get past his minders.'

'Good thing we're spies, eh?' said Strang. 'The more people who find out that we've lost the IPD400, the less likely we are to get it back. Nigel, you have the list of those who know it's missing – put the fear of hell into everyone on it, and make sure it doesn't get any longer. No horsetrading with other intelligence agencies, especially not our American cousins. I expect us to find it before the lubricious Ms Kocharian – when we do, tell no one. I want the IPD400 under my control until I've decided what to do with it.' He paused to make a note on the pad at his side. 'All that said, we need to tell James Palatine.'

'You think it's safe to trust him with this?' said de la Mere.

'He built the fucking thing, maybe he knows some way to track it down. Maybe it talks to him in his sleep. Remind me what he calls us.'

'The Playpen,' said Nigel.

'Cheeky cunt. It's a risk but we'll have to take it – because our only other angles of attack are Clive's floozy, a phoney accountant and your big fat dead end.'

* * *

The Lamb and Flag was an unreconstructed hellhole on the ground floor of a seventies office block. James Palatine followed the girl into a dank interior that might once have been decked out in cream and raspberry, but was now almost uniformly beige. A bored-looking woman of about forty sat at the bar smoking; her only customer was an old man in a tatty yellow shirt with an empty beer glass on the table in front of him.

'Brandy?' James asked the girl.

'Coke. Thanks.'

Early twenties. A well-brought-up girl from a well-off family.

James went up to the bar. The bored-looking woman waited until there could be no possible doubt that James wanted to buy a drink before laying down her cigarette and lumbering over. He ordered a scotch for himself, took the drinks to their table and waited while the girl produced a rubber band and tied back her hair, gathering the dyed section into a large, frizzy orb and smoothing the rest tight over her scalp. There was an air of determination in her brisk movements and stern expression – a girl who knew her mind and wasn't going to be argued with – but it was all a bit too brittle and calculated.

'I thought you were going to kill those boys.'

'You saw the knives? I couldn't take any chances, with you there.'

'Oh, so it was all just to save me?' Her light blue eyes glittered with indignation. 'It seemed like you enjoyed it.'

Was it so obvious, even to this girl who knew nothing about him? The man – he wasn't a boy – whose shoulder he'd dislocated, that was justified, certainly. He wasn't so sure about the other one.

'I suppose I should say thank you,' the girl said.

'My pleasure, apparently. Next time I'll give them a nasty pinch, see how they like that.'

Perhaps she heard the self-recrimination in his voice. Her features relaxed and she permitted the corners of her wide, shapely mouth to lift in a conciliatory smile. They talked on, but after five minutes of listening to her guarded answers, all he'd found out was that her name was Sarah and she was a student at SOAS, the School of Oriental and African Studies.

'All right Sarah, I give in. Why are you following me?'

'I'm not,' she said, much too quickly. 'If anything, you're following me, so I don't— '

'You are. Tell me why, or I'll follow you and find out for myself. Among my various accomplishments, following people is second only to breaking their arms.'

The threat seemed to disconcert her. An internal debate was taking place and she wouldn't meet his eye. He bought her another Coke and they sat in silence for a while.

'I was hoping to bump into you,' she said finally. 'Only not like this.'

'You didn't set yourself up to be mugged? Then what?'

'I was supposed to find out everything I could about you, then see if we could meet up – as if by accident.'

'*Supposed to* in what sense?'

'I was… I guess it doesn't matter if I tell you straight out.' She paused to re-tie her hair. 'I'm in the Islamic Society at SOAS – I converted to Islam a year ago.' She tossed her head, as if accustomed to this announcement being the prelude to an argument.

'You don't cover your head, though,' said James.

'I did for a while but I found men stared at me more so I stopped. Allah, praise Him, expects men to behave modestly, too.' She gave James a look that suggested she'd already found him wanting in this regard.

'Anyway,' said James, 'you joined this society.'

'Yes. There's a man who comes to our meetings – he runs a charity that looks after Muslim victims of Western tyranny. It's such important work – I did some leafleting for him.'

'You have to follow people around before thrusting leaflets at them?'

'Ha ha. He said they were trying to get in touch with you, but you never replied to their emails.'

James couldn't remember any such approaches, but that didn't mean there hadn't been any. His Imperial College email was a vast and largely uncharted territory. 'What's this man's name?'

'Hamed. He said your work contributes to the oppression of Muslims. He wants to try and persuade you to stop.'

'So you told Hamed you'd arrange to bump into me?' said James, trying to keep the incredulity out of his voice.

'Yes.' She looked relieved that her story was out. 'He said it was the best way of getting to you – it's not the sort of thing I usually do.'

'Good, because to be honest, you're not that good at it.'

She looked down and tried to pout. She wasn't very good at that, either. 'So will you? I mean, come to one of our meetings and talk to Hamed?'

'I'm not helping to oppress Muslims,' said James, wondering if in fact, in some obscure way, he was. 'What's the charity called?'

'Children of Islam.'

'Is it a registered charity? They have a website and so on?'

'No, Hamed says all the money they raise must go straight to the victims. He's very passionate about it.'

'I wonder who else he's going to get you to pursue round London,' James said – but then decided it would be unfair to tease her. However improbable this Hamed's story, it was clear that Sarah believed it. There didn't seem to be much harm in her, anyway – and for all the spikiness and ingratitude, he found that he rather liked her.

'I'll need your phone number, in case I end up in court opposite two nice young men with their arms in slings.'

She found a scrap of paper and a pen in her courier bag and they swapped numbers. When he dialled hers, a phone rang in her bag.

'Actually, it belongs to Hamed,' she said. 'Mine was nicked and he said I could use it until I get a new one.'

'Charitable of him.'

She stood up suddenly, as if exchanging phone numbers had been the sole purpose of her mission.

'I have to meet someone.'

'You don't want to start converting me right away?'

She heaved the courier bag onto her shoulder and shot out of the pub without replying. The old man in the yellow shirt raised his glass and nodded vigorously at James.

'Go after her, mate, lovely gel like that.'

*   *   *

The ten-year revenue growth chart for Grosvenor Systems – 'the UK's leading supplier of surveillance systems and solutions', as it styled itself, although most of its revenues came from arms brokerage – had one striking feature: for the first seven years it depicted an incline so smooth and gentle as to be almost undetectable; then three years ago it had turned sharp left and followed a dramatic upward trajectory – to the point where, at the end of the previous financial year, turnover could be seen to have doubled since the month when the upturn began. Something momentous must have happened in the life of Grosvenor Systems to cause such a radical shift in its serene progress into the new millennium. Something had: Natalya Kocharian.

Nat liked the revenue growth chart very much. She updated and circulated it regularly, and had recently overlain it with a second line showing a parallel rise in the company's market value. On the day when the 2005/06 accounts were published, she appeared at work carrying a large black tote bag with the revenue chart printed on one side, the share price on the other: the lines that illustrated progress prior to her arrival were in grey; thereafter, shocking pink and studded with diamantés. The latest sets of numbers filled the first slide in every in-house presentation she ever did, and those of her colleagues who did not benefit from the Grosvenor Systems Performance Related Remuneration Scheme were mightily bored of it. For the rest, its appearance was the cue for an agreeable bout of mental arithmetic. While Nat told them about the new contracts she had won, the market sectors opening up before her, and the competitors sent skulking off to the world's least profitable backwaters, her colleagues calculated their bonuses. And when they had finished, they fell to admiring the smattering of freckles across their sales director's pink-flushed cheeks, or the way her upper lip would not quite close over her teeth. Or they tried to catch, without being caught, the captivating animation in her lovely green eyes.

Nat had been summoned to a 6.30 p.m. meeting with the Grosvenor chairman, Sir Peter Beddoes, and her prowess as a sales director was not on the agenda. Beddoes was a tall, skinny old bird with watery eyes and a neck liberally adorned with turkey-wattles of scaly, purplish skin. She counted him as one of the quite large number of men who dangled from her little finger, but this time the pencil skirt and promising smile were met with a look of prudish gravitas.

Clive Silk, who sat on the Grosvenor Board under the title Head of Innovation, was also there: cautious, slippery Silk who had so far resisted Nat's attempts to engage him in a little light banter of the kind she was accustomed to regard – with good reason – as irresistible. She thought he must be gay, despite the evidence of a wife and teenage daughter.

The meeting was to discuss what Beddoes insisted on calling the 'potentially disastrous disposal' of the IPD400 prototype. Nat had already told him everything she knew about it in a succession of emails that she now wished she'd written with a little more care.

'It was marked as AVAILABLE FOR IMMEDIATE SALE and I immediately sold it,' Nat protested at the start of the meeting. 'What's wrong with that?'

'You knew this was a highly sensitive item,' Clive Silk told her. 'It was negligent of you not to query the change of status.'

'First it was secret, then it was for sale: it's called the product development cycle,' came Nat's retort.

At this, Sir Peter Beddoes compressed his lips, causing the lines around his mouth to arrange themselves in an arsehole-like way. Nat seldom saw these two men together outside of corporate jollies, and they presented a tricky challenge. She couldn't play the power-struck little ingénue to Beddoes, while also plugging away at the husky siren act that she'd judged most likely to bring Clive Silk to heel. Her inclination was to flirt with Beddoes and leave Silk to sit and spin; but she'd always been suspicious of the Head of Innovation, who seemed to have more authority at Grosvenor than his job title warranted. And since it now appeared that her feisty defence was not going to have the deterrent effect she had hoped for, Nat sat in demure silence while the two men admonished her, Clive Silk delivering what sounded like a well-rehearsed script, while Beddoes knitted his brow in the manner of a schoolma'am with an untidy piece of homework. It was most unpleasant.

'Lecture over, then,' Beddoes said finally. 'You know how much we value your work here, Natalya. If we didn't – and I make no bones about it – we wouldn't be having this meeting and you wouldn't have a job. It's not just the IPD400 – all our development projects are under the spotlight. We can protect ourselves only if we play by the rules, and I won't have the future of Grosvenor Systems put in jeopardy because a member of senior management can't see the bigger picture. Clive?'

'Thanks, Peter. Next step, Natalya, get on and sort this out,' said Clive Silk. 'Your man Zender is the priority – do whatever it takes to bring him to the table.' He directed at her a look at once full of meaning and overlain with matronly disapproval.

'It was you who introduced us, Clive, so— '

'Why didn't you pitch the IPD400 to anyone else, by the way?'

'Zender's offer was pre-emptive,' said Nat, having prepared this answer in advance. 'He always pulls out if he suspects there's an auction going on.'

'I wonder if you could have got more for it,' said Silk. Nat's jaw bulged with the effort of not responding to this slight. 'But that's irrelevant now. You have our authority to buy the IPD400 back for the thirteen million you sold it for, plus a five per cent sweetener for Zender and his client. Any higher and you'll have to get back to me.'

'You're on good terms with Zender,' said Beddoes, 'that's the critical point. Time to call in some favours, so to speak?'

'He's a client, he doesn't owe me any favours.'

'If we don't get the IPD400 back, never mind your job here, you are potentially in serious trouble,' said Clive Silk, looking pleased to be able to deliver the threat. 'I've taken advice and it seems that as directors of Grosvenor Systems, we could face legal proceedings.'

'I'm not on the board, Clive,' said Nat. 'But I can see it would be awful if you went to prison over this.'

'That's hardly likely,' said Beddoes, his normally patrician voice disrupted by a querulous wobble. 'The final point is that you are not to discuss the loss of the IPD400 with anyone— '

'Other than Claude Zender, of course. And everyone else who already knows about it?'

'I shouldn't need to tell you this,' said Clive Silk, 'but I've come directly from a meeting with the Director-General of MI6. He's taking personal responsibility for throwing a cordon of silence round the loss of the IPD400, and I'd strongly advise you not to be the one to break it.'

Was that a hint of a squeak in Silk's bland voice? The chaps are scared, Nat thought. She was greatly cheered.

'My very first need-to-know secret,' Nat said, the semblance of contrition beginning to fray. 'Just to be clear, is it secret that we sold it, or that we want it back?'

Silk glared at her, his pale lips pinched with irritation.

'Discretion is required, Natalya,' said Sir Peter quickly. 'Clive, how much time do we have?'

'Our first deadline is a JIC briefing in three days' time – we'll need to provide a full update. There's talk of a COBRA meeting, if things go critical.' Silk glanced at Sir Peter, then at Nat, for evidence that they understood the import of these references to the highest echelon of the state security apparatus.

'Let's hope that's not necessary,' said Beddoes obligingly.

'Shall I write the JIC report?' said Nat brightly. She was thinking that if an acronym could take human form, it would look just like Clive Silk.

'No,' said Silk. 'I will.'

'Then I'd better go and get Little Sister back,' she said, her expression as polite and chastened as someone who felt neither could possibly manage. 'Unless there's anything else?'

'Keep in close touch, Natalya. Until we have the genie back in its bottle, the scrutiny is going to be rather uncomfortable – for all of us.'

Nat stood up and started for the door. A little swing of the hips will do no harm, she judged. There was not much point in being so appealingly petite if you didn't use it to put men off their stride when they were being obnoxious. She arched her back slightly as she walked and then, a yard short of the door, turned suddenly. Beddoes' eyes were levelled at her bottom, as expected, but Silk was shuffling papers in his lap. What a prick!

*   *   *

'I wouldn't mind having something to say to your colleague Nigel de la Mere,' said Sir Peter when Nat had gone. 'You know he was here this afternoon? Told me he could be ironic about Little Sister for a maximum of seven days before turning vicious. Seemed to me to be in a thoroughly bad mood already.'

The arrangement by which Clive Silk had been foisted on him by MI6 was a source of annoyance to the Grosvenor chairman, and he frequently grumbled to Clive that it was as well they'd called him Head of Innovation because no one, himself included, knew what Clive actually did.

'I'll be handling the Grosvenor end of things from here on,' said Clive. References to his primary role as an officer of MI6 usually gave him an agreeable sense of superiority. But Nigel de la Mere hadn't bothered to tell him that he'd called on Beddoes; and Clive couldn't now ask what had been said without drawing attention to this slight.

'Oh. Good.'

'Best to let me deal with Natalya.'

'What, on the grounds that you're immune to her charms while I am the proverbial putty?'

'I didn't say that. But Sir Iain is all over this one, and Natalya Kocharian is key to our strategy.' Clive paused, then said: 'He wants you to call James Palatine – thinks he may be able to help.'

'I'd rather Palatine never found out about this,' said Beddoes. 'Every time I meet him I have the feeling he's working out the quickest way to kill me. Do you get that?'

'Better call him now.'

'You always were a cold fish, Clive,' said Beddoes, eyeing with dislike Silk's square, doughy face with its self-absorbed expression. 'I wonder what Sir Iain will do with you next?'

*   *   *

It was seven when James left the pub. His flat was two minutes' away, but he had nothing much to go home to; and his legs were restless, his head bustling with half-formed theories about the enigmatic Sarah. Arriving on Camden Road, he decided to walk to the private lab he'd set up for himself in Southwark.

James only ever crossed London on foot, and spent many hours loping through its jumble of backstreets, parks, precincts and housing estates. He could do the five-mile route from Camden to Southwark on automatic, leaving his mind unoccupied: this was the state he sought when he needed inspiration. He'd spend hours worrying at a problem in the lab, then finally give up and go home, furious that he'd wasted the evening on an abject defeat. After ten minutes of hard walking, it seemed the solution would drift out of the night air and settle on the outskirts of his consciousness, waiting to be let in.

His encounter with Sarah had all the hallmarks of a clandestine approach – and one which obeyed the first rule of such operations: make sure the people at the business end know as little as possible. So who was Hamed? The answer did not seem to be blowing in the wind that evening. The plane trees in the squares south of the Euston Road had shed leaves the size of a man's hand which spun and rattled on the pavement, scrabbling at his feet as he passed. High above, the empty boughs flailed against a darkening sky. He stopped for a bowl of noodles in Exmouth Market, then headed on towards the river, reaching the footbridge from St Paul's to Tate Modern just as a fine, drenching kind of rain began to fall. A punk girl leading a tubby little dog with a red bandana tied around its neck approached and started to spin him a line. James stopped her mid-flow and handed over his change. The fingers that picked the coins from his hand were long and graceful. The brown Thames churned behind her. The tide was coming in hard and a dirty white dinghy with an underpowered outboard was struggling downstream, slapped about by a succession of stubby waves. James stopped and watched it for a while, willing the boat to defeat the dull might of the water. Its bow kept disappearing as it plunged into the gullies between waves, then leaping up again as if startled by something it had seen.

* * *

Nat swept down the stone steps at the entrance to Grosvenor's Mayfair HQ and hailed a cab. Clive Silk can kiss his precious IPD400 goodbye, she thought. I'm not fucking getting it back for him.

'Hard day at work, love?' asked the cabbie.

'Garrick Street,' said Nat, and slammed the dividing window shut. The galling truth was that the accusation of irresponsibility levelled at her by her male colleagues was not entirely baseless. When news had got out that James Palatine was building a surveillance device for Grosvenor Systems, the reaction from her government and military clients had been dramatic. Barely a week later, Tony Schliemann, Chief Procurement Officer for the Signals Intelligence Directorate of the National Security Agency – Grey Tony, as he was known – had turned up in London and summoned her to the Intercontinental for cocktails. Speaking with the queasy mix of ingratiation, self-importance and menace that was the NSA man's trademark, Grey Tony informed her that any attempt to sell the fruits of Dr Palatine's labour to anyone other than himself would be treated as a threat to US national security.

'I'm going to set aside the procurement hat, if you will, and don the avuncular Stetson,' he concluded. 'There's plenty of good business out there for a smart young woman like you, but this isn't it. Some real heavy hitters have taken the field, and even I'm staying out on the boundary. Forgive the sporting metaphor. But you understand what I'm telling you?'

Yes, Nat thought, resisting the temptation to slap the avuncular Stetson from his well-groomed head, you've promised Little Sister to some people even more important than you and you're terrified you won't be able to deliver the goods.

In the ensuing months, the queue for Palatine's creation, whatever it might turn out to be, became so long and so fervent that Nat imagined herself retiring to Monaco on the commission from its sale. But when the IPD400 was finally delivered, nearly eighteen months later, Grosvenor immediately placed it under embargo. Nat assumed this was because it didn't work.

All things considered, she reckoned she'd been pretty astute to unload the IPD400 promptly when the embargo was unexpectedly lifted. Claude Zender marked it on the Grosvenor sales inventory print-out she'd sent him and made her an offer so generous that it should probably have made her suspicious. But anyway, she'd accepted it. Unlike her government and military clients, Zender wasn't forever mired in a swamp of sign-off procedures, and she was mindful that the embargo could be reimposed just as quickly as it had been lifted. When he asked her to fast-track the deal, she did so without asking unnecessary questions. Because she was good at her job.

If she hadn't been their best chance of getting it back, Nat was sure they'd have fired her outright. Brash, beautiful, foreign-sounding, female: she ticked every wrong box on the list. Even now, if they thought they could dodge prosecution by blaming the over-promoted bimbo in sales, it wasn't difficult to see which way the chaps would swing.

The cab stopped on the corner of Garrick Street, just by Nat's private drinking club. It was called Softly Softly, and it fulfilled all her requirements in a bar: busy, glamorous, faintly seedy. If you wanted a drink, a line of coke and some male company for the night, it was the perfect place to be.

*   *   *

James took the stairs to the sixth floor, unlocked the front door…
And the loneliness he always felt when he came here rushed out to
greet him.

Citygate was a big, purpose-built block that was only five years
old, though the modish, stripped-down look had already revealed
itself to be merely cheap. He'd bought the place with cash, using
an assumed name – because what he'd needed at the time was not
a private lab but a bolthole, and underground bunkers stuffed with
survival rations and girdled with high-explosives were in short supply. Once the need to hide had passed, he'd set up his computing
equipment in the kitchen and, sporting a high-vis jacket to keep
the caretaker at bay, spent several mornings delving around in the
ceiling of the underground car park until he'd adapted the cabling
infrastructure to give himself enough bandwidth to satisfy the needs
of a small office block.

He checked the routines he'd left running, inspected logfiles,
re-started processes that had stalled. The kitchen was dark, animated
only by the scrolling screens and the hectic whiff of fans running
at full pelt as the chipsets parsed away a torrent of bits. Soon after
setting up the lab, he'd been struck by the unwelcome insight that
spending time in Citygate was like finding yourself inside the pale
beige shell of a giant desktop computer, complete with ducting, air
vents and white noise. His wet coat draped over the ungenerous
radiator and his shoes standing in a spreading puddle of water were
the only visible signs that this space ever had a human occupant.

He was a bachelor at thirty-two, uncomfortably aware that this
probably couldn't be ascribed to misfortune any more. He seemed
to attract the sort of women who thought men were emotional
simpletons. In his most recent relationship, he realised now, he had

played the role of emotional simpleton to the point where the girl in question had decided he was a bore and left him. Sometimes it felt as if emptiness were his default state. There were his postgraduate students to turn to, plenty of whom seemed willing to slip into bed with him. But after repeated experience of this form of solace, James was coming to the dispiriting conclusion that he was regarded not so much as an eligible prospect, but as a trophy that was not all that difficult to win.

No curtains, either. It wasn't cosy.

The walk across London had done nothing to settle his mind.

It seemed like you enjoyed it, Sarah had said. If you need to fight, you fight with precision and force, he should have replied. Instead, he'd felt ashamed.

Who was Hamed? Go to the next meeting of this Islamic Society and find out.

He pulled out his cellphone and dialled Sarah's number. The call was connected but no one answered. He heard light breathing, then a pointed cough.

'Who am I talking to?'

'You should not have called this number.' A man's voice, Middle Eastern accent, soft but full of authority.

'This is Sarah's number. I want to speak to her.'

'No, it is not. Please do not call again.'

'She gave it to me earlier. I tried it in front of her.'

There was a pause.

'You should not have approached her. You have put her in a difficult position. A dangerous position.'

'Are you threatening her?'

'I cannot be expected to protect this girl.'

'Why did you get her— '

The man had already hung up.

Hamed.

Sarah must have gone straight from the pub to meet him, and he'd reclaimed the phone he'd lent her. James went online and checked which network was handling the number, then telnetted into the exchange and waited while the access control software checked his credentials. He'd been on the list of super-users for several years – it was wonderful what doors were flung open once you'd been identified as a friend by the first line of defence. He spoofed the system into thinking that someone was ringing her so that it would respond with the ID of any cellphone masts capable of connecting the call. Three masts picked up the roaming signal – one strong, two much weaker. He brought up the geo-locator query engine, keyed in the IDs and cross-referenced. The phone was in Wembley. The area capable of delivering the signal spectrum he was looking at was roughly half a mile square, but most of it was occupied by a park and an industrial estate. That narrowed it down to two or three streets.

Sarah's phone was a Nokia 6282. He checked its specification at the Nokia developers' site. It was GPS-enabled, but the UK version didn't come with the locating software installed, so he'd have to upload it to the SIM – that would require an OK from the user, and he wasn't sure he could circumvent it. Anyway, GPS didn't work well indoors. He'd use the three masts instead, calculate the angles between them and the cellphone, and the fractions of milliseconds it took for the signal to transmit. He started to log the data.

The principle was sound, but the ether was always full of noise: any drifting pocket of damp air or swirl of diesel smoke could disrupt the passage of a data packet as it whisked from phone to mast. He waited impatiently while the measurements accumulated, then started to collate, discarding obvious anomalies and applying a Kalman filter to smooth out what remained.

In half an hour, he had drawn two curves – one for the angles, one for the latency – which mapped the most likely location of

Sarah's phone. He cross-referenced, then used the results to re-run the raw numbers, adding in new measurements as they appeared in his log. Twenty minutes later the results of his calculations stabilised.

Got you. Number 28 Ashington Road.

What next? Tracing a cellphone signal was an interesting challenge, but now it was done, James found himself asking sternly why he should be responsible for rescuing Sarah from whatever danger she might be in. Those in charge of his professional development as a military intelligence officer had repeatedly accused him of being impulsive, of behaving as if he could set the world to rights by diving in head first with his eyes shut – a particularly foolish form of egotism, apparently, and quite inappropriate for an officer of the British Army. They had a point: the consequences of his less well-considered actions had usually been both unintended and bloody. Anyway, if Sarah was in trouble, it surely wasn't because he had made a call to her cellphone and conducted a wholly uninformative conversation with a stranger called Hamed.

James felt a little cheated by this bout of conscience. He made himself a cup of instant coffee and watched TV for half an hour before checking the trace again.

Wembley. Hamed hadn't moved, or called anyone. Nor had he turned off Sarah's phone. Careless.

The ten o'clock news came on. There'd been a terror alert at Stansted Airport and the Home Secretary was pontificating about the need to take pre-emptive action to safeguard national security in the context of the global terror threat. He talked about getting the right balance between freedom and safety – as if he knew just what the right balance was, but had only now decided to establish it. It was over a year since the July bombings, but the mantra hadn't changed. Be alert but not alarmed, the minister advised. What was that supposed to mean? What if, in your alert state, you noticed something alarming?

James checked again. Wembley.

He watched an American sitcom that didn't make him laugh. Wembley.

He swept up all traces of his visit, then logged out of the exchange. He washed up his mug and went to put on his damp shoes and coat. It was nearly midnight and he was hungry. He would spend the night here now, not sleeping much, but fretting over this odd girl who had elbowed her way into his life. *I cannot be expected to protect this girl*, the man had said, as if he were fed up with being asked.

And since you're in the mood for a bit of aimless worrying, James thought, as he strode towards the kebab shop on Southwark High Street, why has Peter Beddoes' PA at Grosvenor Systems rung three times over the last two hours? Sir Peter didn't usually seek out his company – James had the impression he made the old man nervous. It could only be about Little Sister, and that could only be bad.

Chapter Two

The man Nat had brought home from Softly Softly the previous night left for the City at six, which saved her the trouble of throwing him out at eight. He was handsome in an identikit kind of way, but his eyes were always on the lookout for a mirror, and his buttocks seemed to be held in a permanent sculptural clench. After breakfast she went into Grosvenor and searched through her folder on the IPD400 prototype.

In among the thickets of technical documentation, she found the press release they'd issued in April 2006, just over five months ago:

> Grosvenor Systems today announced that it has taken delivery of a prototype of the IPD400 (Internet Protocol Detector, version 4.00). The IPD400 is a monitoring and intercept system capable of untraceable real-time infiltration of secure data networks. This breakthrough technology has the potential to revolutionise the surveillance of terrorist organisations, organised crime syndicates, drug traffickers, money launderers and other criminal enterprises, as well as of hostile governments and their intelligence networks.

In the same folder were copies of the reactions it had elicited. 'Grosvenor's IPD400 is a spymaster's wet dream,' the *Economist* had declared, 'like having the entire intercept capability of GCHQ packed into a square metre of clever circuitry with a carry handle on top.' And a blogger had written: 'From multinational corporations to government departments and the military and intelligence communities, anyone who thinks their secrets are safe had better think again.'

No wonder the spooks are salivating, Nat thought. She flipped through the briefing papers that had been prepared when the investment was signed off: development pathways, risk assessments, mitigation scenarios, and enough budgets and schedules to launch a mission to Jupiter. In among the i-dotting and t-crossing, she found a document that covered the life and career of Dr James Palatine. It was more extensive than usual, because he'd been designated a level 4 risk, only one rung short of the no doubt terrifyingly perilous summit.

While researching his doctoral thesis at UCL, she read, *Palatine came to the attention of the intelligence establishment.*

He took a commission with the Intelligence Corps, and spent much of his time on assignments with the SAS in the Middle East and Kosovo. As well as training in combat and survival to the level required for an SAS secondment, he attended courses in surveillance and counter-surveillance, explosives and artillery. He also studied Arabic and is said to have an exceptional facility for languages. Palatine endured a fractious relationship with his senior officers and intelligence service liaisons, frequently questioning orders and proving resistant to the disciplines inherent in a military career. He is reported to have shown exceptional courage and cool-headedness in combat situations, but his detractors point to an aptitude for violence that is alarming even for a serving soldier. Despite successfully completing assignments that could probably not have been carried out by any other operative, he is now regarded as unreliable.

Nat remembered him from a Grosvenor conference he'd been paid to attend: tall, rangy, with wolf-like grey eyes and an arrogant manner. He'd been standing in a group of men who seemed to be keeping their distance, as if instinctively aware that proximity to Palatine would do them no favours and might possibly be dangerous. When it was his turn to speak, he'd presented a single slide, which read:

INFORMATION THAT IS 100% SECURE IS 100% USELESS.

As soon as information was shared between two people, he'd explained, it became insecure; but unless it was shared, there was no point in having it. He had then, to Nat's annoyance, delivered a lecture on the ethics of eavesdropping, warning that, if the objective was to liberate the world from the threat of terrorism, data monitoring would prove to be a red herring: the only solution was to eradicate poverty, war and oppression – most of which, he asserted, originated in policies devised by western politicians intent on serving only the short-term interests of a powerful elite. As he spoke, Nat, who spent most of her working life feeding these men's overweight egos, set aside her irritation, the better to enjoy the spectacle of their baffled and indignant faces.

Feeling a little fluttering resurgence of the interest he'd aroused in her at the time, she skimmed the rest of Palatine's biography. Born 1974. Mother died in a cycling accident when he was fourteen. Father, a doctor, became a recluse – addicted to opiates, apparently – and left care of his son to various au pairs and boarding schools. A long list of cups and caps (though not quite as long, Nat decided, as the list of accolades she'd collected during her own school career). After leaving the army, he was offered a fellowship at Imperial College, where he founded a discipline called DAIMS, which stood for Data Acquisition and Interpretation on a Massive Scale – *a constellation of innovative technical solutions which have transformed the once intractable problem of accurately searching the world's data communications for evidence of hostile activity.*

My god, thought Nat, the things people do for a living. She opened her email and sent Clive Silk a message, copied in to Sir Peter Beddoes, with contact details for half a dozen of her most sluggish clients.

'These are my top prospects right now,' she wrote. 'I'm expecting them to sign deals to a minimum value of £4.2M over the next few weeks. Don't let them off the hook!'

On her way out, she dropped in on Sir Peter and told him that time was of the essence and she was taking the late afternoon flight to Marrakech, where Claude Zender was based.

'Well done, Natalya. Report daily, if you wouldn't mind. I'm sorry this thing has blown up— '

'I don't think Zender's going to co-operate,' she interrupted, finding that she could not bear to observe the wistful expression she brought to her chairman's drooping features for a moment longer. 'Can you keep Clive off my back, Peter? You understand how these things work, but he really doesn't.'

* * *

Green slime, as Intelligence Corps officers were known to the rest of the military, didn't usually see much combat; but in January 1999 Captain James Palatine had been assigned to a 'no-contact' operation with an SAS unit in Kosovo which turned bad. The things he had seen and done still slopped through his dreams. It was as if some stinking dungeon in his psyche had been breached and its inmates allowed to run amok. Afterwards, they'd offered counselling, but even the word had sounded feeble in his ears, like throwing an inflatable duck to a man drowning in sewage. He'd left the army and retreated to the lab; and, drawn by the idea that fighting might be an art rather than a compulsion whose depths he dared not plumb, he'd taken up t'ai chi.

He could turn up at his master's gym whenever he liked, and Sam Hu Li would make time for him, though he might have to work alongside 'my paying students', as Sam pointedly called them. It was two years since the Korean had charged James for his services.

'You still come see me?' he observed one day. 'I did something wrong. I put it right. For free!'

He emphasised the words *For free!* as if they must be a source of amazement and delight, the sort of thing James would want to tell his friends about. Whenever the opportunity arose, Sam would introduce James as, 'My charity student. A very sad case.' Time had not dulled the pleasure this tease brought him.

Sam's gym was a former boxing establishment in an unloved area of Kentish Town, sandwiched between a bedraggled dirt football pitch and an Edwardian council block. James elbowed open the double doors and saw Sam in the middle of the empty room, completing a form. Beneath his feet, a hundred and twenty square yards of sprung oak floor gleamed with the lustre of a racehorse's rump on a hot summer's day. The floor was Sam's obsession: every morning at seven he got down on hands and knees and buffed it with a wad of threadbare dusters; and periodically throughout the rest of the day, he would glare with great loathing at the chipboard ceiling, which was blotched and stained with the story of a long succession of floor-threatening leaks.

It wouldn't do to interrupt Sam's form. James walked over to the cotton rag-rug that served as a changing room and pulled on a tracksuit, then watched his teacher cycle through the sequence of movements that composed the form. Sam moved so slowly it was as if he were recalibrating time itself in order to accommodate the degree of precision he required. Finishing the form, he stood motionless for a moment, then looked up.

'Charity student, you are welcome!'

Sam was a lightly built man in his early fifties with a shock of thick black hair, forthright brown eyes and a forbidding expression that disappeared when he smiled.

'Begin, please.'

James had completed barely thirty seconds of the form before Sam began his critique.

'How ugly your arms are today! Your belly won't be still and your legs are like stepladders, clack-clack-clack. Stop. Push hands with me.'

Pushing hands is a discipline beloved of practitioners of 'soft' martial arts, those that aim primarily to manage and deploy the flow of energy, or *chi*. Practising with a master of the classic soft art, t'ai chi, is a disconcerting experience. With a few subtle movements that originate deep in his core, he corrals the student's chi for his own ends, exploiting the loss of balance that results when a move the student initiates dissipates into nothing, or one he anticipates never takes place. As he worked with Sam, James found himself tottering like a puppet. His pushes were really Sam's pulls, and his pulls were like leaning on a rope tied to thin air.

They practised in silence, enjoying the companionable synchronicity of their movements, then stopped and bowed to each other.

'I am a better teacher for teaching you.'

'Good of you to say so, Sam.'

'But a poorer one.'

'Master Sam Hu Li fails yellow belt in humour,' said James.

Sam roared with laughter and slapped him on the back. 'Maybe you say the jokes, I do the laughing,' he said.

James didn't know if the t'ai chi had done anything to help round up the ghouls of Kosovo and lock them in again. He still felt like a man who'd volunteered to have himself shackled to a desk – for his own good and everyone else's – but at least he hadn't killed anyone for the last six years. And today's session with Sam had brought some comfort. You're right not to go chasing after this Hamed character, he told himself as he left. The fight in the Camden park was a one-off, and you saved a girl from being assaulted – what could possibly be wrong with that?

* * *

Having got back from the Grosvenor office at midday, Nat was reclining on her aquamarine velvet sofa and wondering what to do when she arrived in Marrakech. An incurable optimist, she didn't doubt that she could get the IPD400 back: the combination of Grosvenor's money and her own persuasive charms would prove irresistible to Claude Zender. But what was in it for her? Nothing… Except a black mark against her name and the commission on this and several other excellent deals she'd recently struck absent from her pay-packet.

The beauty of this affair, it dawned on her, was that MI6's insistence on absolute secrecy had a side-effect Clive Silk and Sir Peter might not have considered: it gave her carte blanche to do whatever she pleased. Claude Zender had never in his life revealed anything to anyone without being extravagantly paid for it, so who could say where the IPD400 might end up next, and who would know how it had got there?

She opened a bottle of Tokaji Aszú and took it out onto the balcony. Her apartment was on the top floor of a Modernist block in Highgate and looked west over Hampstead Heath – a charming view in sunlight, though today the slopes of Parliament Hill lay flat under a uniform mass of low cloud and the bathing ponds around the near perimeter had the colour of tarnished pewter. Still, she needed the fresh air, and the wine. A moment of decision was upon her.

Yesterday's meeting had reminded her that the chaps at Grosvenor had a place for her, and she was in it. At their precious board meetings, she'd found out from Sir Peter's PA, they made smirking reference to her sexual generosity and amused themselves by trying to guess which of Grosvenor's clients she had slept with. To which the answer was, in fact, very few – most were the sort of men who seemed to have landed up in their lucrative and monotonous careers like fat cherubs descending on a fluffy cloud, and even flirting with them was dull work. Not that she cared what the Grosvenor men thought of her: Nat enjoyed sex and in her view people made too much of a fuss about it. Besides, she wasn't a woolly-minded north London feminist, but a tough, ambitious girl from Kiev. On the Gazprom trainee scheme in Moscow, you either crossed your legs, frowned and did the same job for thirty years; or you wore a short skirt, smiled and took it from there. London called for a more covert style: Nat favoured sleekly tailored outfits with an invitingly soft or lustrous finish; and a touch of the uniform never went amiss. But still, whether played with scarlet lipstick or slub silk skirts, the game hadn't changed.

Nat wasn't sure how much further it would take her. And an idea was taking shape – a daring idea that was thrilling to contemplate, even in its infancy. She spent a moment calculating how rich it would make her, then decided that, although she could probably do this alone, it would be good to have an ally. Someone strong, resourceful and trustworthy. Someone with whom she could happily share her eventual triumph. Someone like her older brother Nikolai.

Nikolai Kocharian made a living smuggling cigarettes into Western Europe and stolen cars back East, and was the perfect man to have at your side when contemplating a course of action somewhat adrift from the straight and narrow. Nat called him in Kiev and explained what had happened.

'End result,' she concluded, 'I'm ordered to get the IPD400 back. If I want to keep my job, which I don't.'

'You must not say that, Natalya. Why did they not want you to sell this weapon?'

'It's not a weapon, Niko, it's an intercept device. The key thing is, they're ready to spend nearly fourteen million sterling to get it back,' said Nat, knowing that her brother liked hearing big numbers.

'You want me to help you, huh?'

'I'd feel much safer with you there, Nikolai. People might see I'm in trouble and try and mess me around. And you're really the only person... ' she tailed off appealingly.

'I'll look after you, little one. This guy you sold it to is in London?'

'You're a star, darling Niko, I knew you wouldn't let me down. He's in Marrakech.'

'Marrakech?'

'Morocco. It's a fabulous place, you'll love it,' Nat lied. 'It'll be like a holiday. You'll get a winter tan and all the girls will be after you.'

'All the girls are already after me. Jesus, Nat. Africa!'

'Just a few days. A couple of weeks at most. Please?'

Nikolai said OK and gave a brotherly sigh; she said he was her hero and made a succession of affectionate noises. With the recruitment of her brother successfully completed, Nat felt her idea simply could not fail. Yes, there was planning to do, detail to work out. No doubt she'd encounter obstacles that would demand all her strength and intelligence. She couldn't at present imagine what they might be, but anyway, what were obstacles for if not to be overcome? She poured herself another glass of wine and ordered a taxi for Heathrow. Most people in her position would have been cowed by the censure and the threats, the ominous directives emanating from the upper reaches of government, but she, Natalya Kocharian, had sensed an opportunity. It was this mindset that distinguished her from the herd.

*   *   *

Sarah's phone was still signalling from Wembley when James got back to Citygate soon after eleven. Seeing it blinking away made James realise that his resolve to leave well alone was weakening with every hour that passed. Soon, the battery would die and the trail would go cold.

He went to Imperial College and discussed progress on their current project with his research partner Hugo Vanic, an anxious, kindly Slovenian who had once been James's doctoral supervisor, but was now very much his junior. It soon became known that Dr Palatine was in at last, and a queue of visitors formed outside his lab, most of them bearing paperwork he was supposed to have dealt with months ago. At two-thirty, he sloped out of the building and walked back to Southwark. There'd been two more calls from Beddoes' office and he decided he ought to return them.

'James, many thanks indeed for getting back to me.' Beddoes sounded like he was already on the wrong side of a bottle of claret. 'There's something I need to talk to you about – can you come in to the office, say Thursday?'

'No. What for?'

'Oh. Not ideal to talk about it over the phone. How's your schedule for next week?'

'Fully booked,' said James. 'Is this about the IPD400?'

'Yes, I'm afraid it is.'

When James didn't reply, Beddoes cleared his throat and said: 'Well, I suppose you ought to know. It's gone AWOL from the warehouse. Bloody awkward business.'

James squeezed his cellphone so hard that the battery compartment cover popped off in his hand.

'You don't know where it is?' Even asking the question made him feel sick. 'Was it stolen?'

'Not as such. James, I don't want to say any more over the phone. Can I put you through to my PA? She'll clear the diary— '

James hung up, walked over to the window and stared out at the concrete-framed oblong of brown water that, in Citygate parlance, qualified as a view of the Thames. Grosvenor had somehow managed to mislay the prototype he'd completed barely three months ago. The news hit him like a long-expected act of retribution. On first conceiving the project, he'd indulged himself with the fantasy that his device would be used to expose wrongdoing. He imagined dissembling politicians sent skulking back to their families, City fatcats denounced as cheats and thieves, tyrants exposed as tyrants and torturers with no place to hide. But had he ever really believed that? One of his assistants had christened the device Big Brother, to which James had objected that there was nothing Orwellian about the project – it was primarily a theoretical challenge that sought to demonstrate how the boundaries between software and hardware might be moved so as to better expose the power of the microprocessor to the fluidity of a bespoke programming language.

'We could call it Little Sister,' the lab assistant had replied.

James didn't like that any better, but the name stuck and now seemed disturbingly apt. Responding to a triumphant press release issued by Grosvenor's marketeers, an article in the *New Statesman* had described him as 'a textbook example of how well-meaning scientists end up playing stooge to the forces of oppression'. The implication of nerdy naivety rankled. Because it was true. Little

Sister would not be used to hold the powerful to account – it would simply make them more powerful.

There was one minor cause for optimism: his Grosvenor contract specified that none of the technologies he developed could be patented, and that all he need deliver was a proof of concept – a working prototype rather than a device which could be put into commercial operation. As far as James was concerned, that gave him licence to bury Little Sister inside the digital-security equivalent of several cubic metres of reinforced concrete which only he knew how to penetrate. There had been a number of frosty meetings on the subject, but James knew that their association with 'the most radically innovative computer scientist of his generation', as their PR people liked to call him, was Grosvenor's trump card. However commercially idiotic the terms of his contract, they'd always been careful not to fall out with him – no doubt mindful of the fact that whenever the markets were reminded of the collaboration, their share price ticked pleasingly upwards.

The IPD400 could not be operated without him, even if it did fall into the wrong hands. Had that already happened? It would surely be pig-headed not to connect its sudden disappearance with the equally sudden appearance in his life of a gullible twenty-year-old girl and her sinister handler. If only he had not been so wary of getting himself into trouble! At least he was one step ahead of them: Hamed could have no way of knowing that he had traced him to 28 Ashington Road – no one outside the intelligence community knew he had super-user access to the cellphone exchanges. It gave him a priceless advantage.

So use it. Pay Hamed a visit. Tonight.

The decision sent a tremor through him, like a hunting dog that feels a hand on the clip of its leash. *You haven't felt that since Kosovo.* The mere possibility of hunting this man down was making the blood dance in his veins. *A snapped wrist and a dislocated shoulder less than twenty-four hours ago – isn't that enough?* An aperitif, something to whet the appetite. It looked like the years of t'ai chi had been a waste of time after all.

*   *   *

He arrived in Wembley just after dusk, bought latex gloves and gaffer tape, headed for Ashington Road. A short street that whispered of fearful conformity. Narrow terraced houses with PVC windows clamped shut. Cars squeezed into squares of concrete out front.

There was a dim glow from the fanlight set into the front door of number 28, but no lights in any of the rooms. No dustbins by the gate. He walked on. Television screens flickered through net curtains, a faint smell of turmeric laced the damp air. A dog started barking as he passed a backyard behind an end-of-terrace house, its front paws scratching at the low wooden paling that fenced it in. A Doberman with a sharp, neurotic bark that didn't stop until he was half way down the next street. The garden that backed onto number 28 belonged to a low block of flats with a short alley on one side – the original section of terrace had probably been demolished by a wartime bomb. A useful escape route. Was that why Hamed had chosen this house as his base? It was a common enough sight in a London street.

You should watch the house for at least an hour first.

There was no obvious vantage point and already the tension was getting to him, the muscles of his chest and shoulders drawn tight as steel hawsers. He re-entered Ashington Road, walked up the short path to number 28, rang the bell.

No answer.

He rang again, then rapped on the door. Footsteps in the street behind him: a woman wearing a full burqa hurrying past. Silence.

He ran round to the alley by the flats, thinking he had flushed Hamed out. If so, his quarry had gone.

He crossed the patch of grass behind the flats and climbed the fence into the garden at the back of the house. There was a low-built rear extension with a half-glazed door. A strip light on in the kitchen, its drab, bluish glow illuminating the uneven line of paving stones at his feet. He stood by the back door and waited, listening, watching for signs of movement.

He pulled on the latex gloves, stuck strips of tape over the pane of glass to deaden the noise, then elbowed it in and reached inside for the latch. It turned, but the door was deadlocked. He picked out enough glass to get his hand in and feel around for a key. It was hanging on a nail hammered into the door frame.

The kitchen was a dismal place: badly fitted wood-effect units, a small fridge with rust spots on the door, grey vinyl flooring curling at the edges. Cooking oil, a bag of rice and two tins of sweetcorn beside the cooker. He moved swiftly through the rest of the house. In the front room, a dark brown wing chair stood in front of a portable TV on a low table. Gas fire, oatmeal carpet. Smell of damp plaster. Inhabited – just. A grimy bathroom off the narrow stairs, two bedrooms at the top. In the one at the back was a single mattress and a duvet with no cover. A computer was set up on a frayed offcut of the oatmeal carpet next to the mattress. James moved the mouse to wake the screen. A command line blinking in a black DOS console, asking which drive to format. What had the man been trying to hide? He'd known enough not to simply delete – computers don't delete files, they just detach the metadata that the operating system uses to locate them. A re-format would make information on the hard drive much harder, perhaps impossible, to retrieve. But it seemed the computer had more than one partition and he'd neglected to specify which. Because he'd seen James patrolling the streets and had left in a panic? Compounding his carelessness, he'd left a Hotmail account open.

James sat on the mattress and started to look around.

* * *

He was there for two hours, wondering when he would be interrupted by the sound of the front door opening, footsteps on the stairs. But Hamed didn't come back.

Hamed was taking instructions from someone who liked to garnish his emails with the verbal mannerisms of a devout Muslim – Insha'Allah's and Masha'Allah's aplenty. It all sounded a bit routine to James, but he was no expert. Hamed's messages were addressed to 'Honoured Sheikh' or 'Most Learned Sheikh' or 'Beloved Sheikh', but the honoured, learned and beloved one's replies were unsigned. James was referred to as the *kufr* – the unbeliever.

The *kufr* was undertaking work that was potentially of great value to their Holy Cause, and the Sheikh intended to secure James's services – *by any means necessary*. The first step was to collect information about his habits, his working practices, his amorous proclivities and the state of his finances. Hamed complained that he did not have the resources for such delicate work. This provoked a torrent of sanctimonious rhetoric to the effect that he was to do the work of Allah with a willing heart and not place obstacles in His way – Hamed should remember how many others had already given their lives in the Holy Cause. It didn't sound much like charitable work.

Hamed had submitted several reports about James's doings over the previous week, but they seemed to have discovered very little about him. The locations where Sarah had seen him were duly noted, along with the fact that he'd withdrawn money from various cashpoint machines, and bought a copy of *The Week* in a Camden newsagent. He had not met up with anyone who could be identified as a sexual partner. There was no mention of the encounter between himself and Sarah the previous day.

The most recent communication said there had been a 'highly significant development', and summoned Hamed to a meeting on Thursday 25 September in Oran, Algeria. He was to wait in the Café Mouloudia in Avenue de Lamur at 10.00 a.m., where he would be met and taken to the rendezvous. The man who came for him would wear a black BMW logo baseball cap to identify himself.

The day after tomorrow…

He was being sized up at the behest of an irascible sheikh with an unspecified interest in how his work might further some unspecified 'Holy Cause'. The man doing the job had ballsed it up so badly that his target was actually sitting in his bedroom reviewing the assignment and wondering what the *significant development* was and whether this meeting in Oran might just be something he ought to attend. Simultaneously, Little Sister had disappeared from the best secured warehouse in Europe. Who were these people?

He looked in the document folders and recycle bin, but found nothing of interest. He ran a series of wildcard searches to see if Hamed was storing personal data in a hidden folder. No. Nothing about the Children of Islam, either. He downloaded an application that would allow him to identify files that had been deleted and removed from the recycle bin. All he discovered was that Hamed's nights were filled with fantasies about teenage boys of Teutonic appearance. There were dozens of them hidden away in the recesses of his hard drive.

James set the drive to re-format, completing the job Hamed had started so that if he came back, he'd think James had drawn a blank. Café Mouloudia, Avenue de Lamur, Oran, Algeria. You want to know who's following you, follow them and find out. More than likely, you'll find Little Sister waiting at the end of the rainbow.

Walking back to Wembley tube station, James told himself what a foolish idea that was. *Hand this over to Her Majesty's Secret Intelligence Service, let them sort it out.* Except that he didn't trust the Playpen – and his opinion of its importance and efficacy was the exact opposite of those who played in it. He didn't trust them to do the right thing, or even to do the wrong thing well. A 'cultural attaché' would be dispatched from the consulate to monitor the rendezvous in Oran. This office junior would trot along to Avenue Lamur towing half a dozen Algerian DRS agents in his wake. Lo and behold, the meeting would be cancelled and that would be that.

Alternatively, if they did stumble upon Little Sister, they'd be constitutionally unable to resist the temptation to pretend they hadn't. The residents of the Playpen had been furious— no, *incandescent* when they'd found out they couldn't get their hands on it, and if an opportunity now arose to hide the prototype in an SIS vault, the Playpen would take it.

Of course, whoever had taken the IPD400 would never be able to get it running. He was sure of that – wasn't he? But suppose he'd made an error? Suppose they defeated the layers of security by some fluke he hadn't properly covered off? No one would know. They'd never get caught. The definitive principle of the IPD400's modus operandi was that it was untraceable: it spirited itself into your network like a light breeze flitting through a brake of trees, and left behind no stray bits or bytes, no toolkits or phantom users, no telltale humming in the wires, no inkling that it had ever dropped in and had a look around. It gave you free rein to violate the digital sanctuaries of anyone you pleased, while remaining yourself inviolable.

He called directory enquiries and asked for the number of Air Algérie.

Oran… Wasn't that the place where, at the end of the War of Independence in 1962, the entire population of Europeans had been massacred? A fine place for an autumn break.

Chapter Three

Nat lay on her back on the bed in her suite at the Riad des Ombres and surveyed the expansive dome of tawny belly beside her. It was a good thing the beds in this place were eight feet across or there wouldn't have been room for her. She had her hands clasped behind her head so that her breasts stood up plump and irresistible, although Claude Zender couldn't see them because he still had his eyes closed following the seismic tremors of pleasure she had just recently caused to rumble through his body. But if he did choose to glance over at her breasts, he would see how lovely they were.

It was exciting to play the courtesan to the legendary Claude Zender, whose fortune was said to rival that of Donald Trump and whose network of influence took in heads of state, police chiefs, warlords and corporate powerbrokers from here to Cape Town and beyond. Every arms trade in Africa passed at some point (and sometimes several) under his attentive nose, and Nat had originally succumbed to his elaborate seductions as a matter of good salesmanship. Then, over time, she had grown fond of him. Half fox, half jackal in business, he was a great big fussy bear in bed: enthusiastic about every detail of their lovemaking, full of demonstrative growls, snorts and howls, sure of his own pleasure and attentive to hers. Nat felt beautifully warm and invigorated; her thighs tingled.

'My dear Natalya, that was very fine, very fine indeed,' announced Claude Zender. 'And now we shall have an enormous pot of tea and a tray of pastries, offering a prayer to any god you please that it is not Tigana's day off. His *ghoriba aux amandes* is the second best reason for visiting the Riad des Ombres.'

'And what is the first?' asked Nat, because when a man is lining up a compliment it is always best to feed him his cue.

'Why it is you, Natalya, as you very well know!'

'It's good to hear that you don't prefer a nest of honey to a taste of fanny,' Nat told him with dignity.

'Ah ha,' Claude bellowed in delight. 'And I taste it still! What a priceless treasure you are, Miss Kocharian, what delicious wit. I swear nothing Tigana could compose will ever come near!' And reaching over with one vast arm, he pulled her on top of him and wrapped her in a voluminous embrace.

Nat squirmed, luxuriating in the sense of being the merest little creature in his massive arms.

'Hold tight, Claude, if I fall from here it will be the end of me!' she exclaimed.

A thunderclap of laughter erupted from the belly beneath her and it felt so funny that she began to giggle too. It was a relief to be here in Marrakech, on her favourite bed in the whole world, bouncing around on top of this absurd, wobbling mountain of man! Tears were streaming down Claude's cheeks; and the more he laughed, the more the reverberations tickled her. For a moment, they were beyond control.

'Natalya, please, you are crushing me flat as a crepe,' Claude managed to gasp, setting himself, and her, off all over again.

Nat rolled off him. Claude heaved himself into a sitting position, wiped his eyes, threw a glass of water down his throat, and reached for the phone to order his tea. Nat pulled on a dressing gown and went to run a bath. The one in her suite – a sunken oval rendered in pink terracotta and a good seven feet in diameter – took nearly an hour to fill, even allowing for the great volume of water that would be rendered superfluous by the bulk of Claude Zender.

'Eh bien, veuillez expliquer à Monsieur Tigana que c'est Monsieur Claude Zender qui a commandé ces délices, hein? Il va me préparer les pâtisseries les plus fraîches, les plus légères, les plus douces, j'en suis certain… Très bien, à tout à l'heure.'

'I see you've already started to enjoy your cakes.'

'And you are preparing our bath. Is there time in this world to sample all its pleasures, I wonder?'

'What a poetic old man you are, Claude.' She wrapped her hands behind his neck and kissed the leathery folds of his forehead, then batted away the large hand that was trying to reach inside her bathrobe. She went out onto the loggia, where a low sofa and table were set. Her room was on the second floor, and looked out on to a small garden of coarse grass, ornamental cacti and oleander swamped with ruby-coloured blooms. Zender followed.

'Not like that,' she said. 'You'll frighten the monkeys. Put a bathrobe on – there's one hanging on the door.'

The oversized arms broker, more or less decent, padded out onto the loggia and lowered himself into the sofa beside her.

'Enchanting,' he said complacently. 'But you haven't yet told me to what unforeseen circumstance I owe the intoxicating delights of your company. Your last visit to Marrakech was a mere six weeks ago, as I recall, and you fleeced me quite disgracefully with various odds and ends from the Grosvenor scrapyard. I wonder you have the gall to show your face here again.' He spoke amiably enough but, as usual when business was being discussed, his eyes had the serenely rapacious look of a crocodile resting its long chin on a muddy riverbank.

'Everything Grosvenor sells is of the highest quality, as your clients expect. And no one knows better than me how demanding they are, Claude, because no one gets told it as often as I do. Anyway, I had nothing else to do so I came out here. I love Marrakech in autumn.'

'You speak English better than the natives,' Claude replied. 'And yet the vowels will sometimes growl their allegiance to Mother Russia – it is most alluring. You are at a loose end, you say?'

'Mother Ukraine,' said Nat. 'If you want to know, Grosvenor have suspended me. I'm on probation.'

'Mais non, Natalya. They would not be so foolish.'

A monkey swung from a sprawling oleander onto the stone balustrade at the end of the loggia, sending a cascade of petals down to the lawn below. A second joined it, and the pair of them squatted side by side to watch the humans talk.

'It's good of you to be cross, Claude, but you know I've never really been one of them. I'm their secret bit on the side, terribly exciting and naughty – and easy to dump when things get difficult.'

'They are even more idiotic than I imagined. Really I should be delighted that I won't have to do business with you any more, for you are a remorseless tyrant who has several times nearly ruined me. But I am not. Your successor will be some foully charming Old Etonian. In your honour, I will refuse to deal with him. I suppose they have some reason for biting the hand that feeds them with such unfailing generosity?'

Having learned the delicate art of being partial with the truth from the man beside her, Nat judged that this was an appropriate moment to put it to use.

'The Foreign Office sent back one of our end-user certificates and asked for clarification,' she said. 'They've been going on and on about it, and now Sir Peter says Grosvenor have to show they are taking it seriously.'

There was a knock at the door. Nat went to answer it while Claude drummed the fat fingers of both hands on his fat knees. She returned with two boys carrying their tea. As soon as the monkeys saw the boys' uniforms, they fled back into the oleander tree. One of the boys carried a glass jug filled to the brim with boiling hot water and packed with sprigs of fresh mint. He poured the tea from an extravagant height into two rose-coloured glasses in silver holders and the sweetly scented vapour drifted on the air. The other boy put down a silver platter of pastries. Claude's eyes assessed them expertly.

'So there is a fake EUC on file?' he said after the boys had gone. He picked a pastry from the platter, regarded it briefly with a wistful expression and delivered it into his mouth. 'Oh, this is quite *superbe*. I beg to know if there is any such thing as a genuine one.'

'Not in the pile they're looking at: they all have Monsieur Claude Zender down as agent.'

'What a dreadful tease you are!' said the man in question, who had a morbid fear of bureaucrats – and especially of their archives and filing cabinets. He laughed unenthusiastically and chose two more sweetmeats from the platter.

'Don't be so paranoid,' said Nat, sipping her tea and looking closely at him, the better to enjoy his discomfort. 'No one wants it to become public knowledge that we sell arms using dodgy EUCs, especially not with an international criminal mastermind like you appearing in all the paperwork.'

'You misrepresent me in every imaginable respect, Natalya. And you are quite spoiling my pleasure in these exquisite sweetmeats.'

She studied him for a moment, then said: 'Claude, this business has got me thinking there's more to life than Grosvenor Systems. I'm putting a deal together, and I'm hoping you'll help me.'

'That seems unlikely,' said Claude.

'I'm not trying to sell you something, so there's no need to be stand-offish.'

He gave her a sceptical look before carefully blowing a little excess icing sugar off the crown of a whorl of pistachio and honey, opening his great jaws far wider than was necessary, and popping it in.

'One of the items on that EUC was some sort of a hacking device. It's called the IPD400 – you remember the name?'

'I believe I do, yes.'

'It turns out it's a prototype, and we don't really know if it works. To tell you the truth, Grosvenor are a bit embarrassed about it.'

'I should think they are,' said Claude. 'Now I learn in such unwelcome detail how thoroughly you have duped me, Ms Kocharian, I am astonished that you are back here asking for favours.'

'Shortly after I sold it to you, another party was in touch asking if they could buy it and offering me a small margin over what you paid.' Nat reeled off the lie without a tremor. She didn't want Zender to know that Grosvenor were trying to retrieve the IPD400 in case he was tempted to sell it back to them direct.

'And what has all this to do with me, Natalya? You think I keep the thing under my bed?'

'I'm suggesting I take this piece of junk off your client's hands and sell it on to mine. I told them it was only a prototype but they don't seem bothered. So, you get a nice cut and walk away.'

'How nice?'

'A hundred and fifty thousand.' Nat knew that the opening price was the critical number in any negotiation, and spoke with an air that suggested the figure had been predicated by fate itself.

'Sterling?'

'US dollars,' she said sternly.

'And in return, I help you to a sum of – let's see, assuming you didn't leave your negotiating skills on your desk at Grosvenor, your *small* margin will be somewhere in the region of twenty per cent?' Nat issued a brisk laugh by way of rebuttal. 'Which means, if I remember my figures correctly, that there is a profit for you of two million, six hundred thousand pounds sterling. And you propose to buy access to these riches for a hundred and fifty thousand US? A fine way to treat an old friend.'

Claude Zender frowned, causing the fringe of close-cropped hair along the outskirts of his scalp to bristle like the hackles of an angry mastiff.

'There are other ways of finding out who you sold it to, Claude. And the IPD400 is a dud, don't forget. Already your client may be sharpening his dagger and cursing the wicked Swiss unbeliever who sold it to him.'

'A charming image, I must say. Even if the wretched thing is little better than a satellite dish with a fancy laptop attached, that isn't my fault. My client asked for it, *eh bien*, I procured it. An offer to buy it back will arouse suspicions in people inclined to be suspicious, and what will I tell them? That a beautiful woman has set her heart on it?'

'Let them think what they like.'

'I never allow my clients to think what they like. All kinds of erroneous suppositions might occur and I would be out of business in a trice, perhaps also dead. No Natalya, what you propose is out of the question. Pretending to a valued client that I have sold them something worthless in order to help you re-sell it for a quite disproportionate profit? And for a mere quarter of a million sterling? Inconceivable. Ugh!'

Claude contrived to quiver with indignation at the monstrous betrayal Nat had proposed.

'I said a hundred and fifty, and it was dollars. You expect me to believe this man-of-principle act?' said Nat, affecting a huff. 'You wouldn't know a principle if it came down from heaven and sat on your knee! You're the richest man in Africa, yet all you can think of is your precious cut. And I might not even have a job any more.'

She got up abruptly from the sofa, pulling her bathrobe tight.

'I suppose I should have known you wouldn't help.'

Nat ran quickly to the bathroom and slammed the door behind her. A perfect start, she thought. Water vapour scented with eucalyptus was swirling off the huge bath so that every surface glistened behind a tissue of mist. She wiped the mirror with her sleeve and allowed the bathrobe to slip from her shoulders so that she could admire the reflection of her slim, half-naked body, lit by the generous warmth of the early evening sun. She began to imagine the deal she was planning already complete and a sum equivalent to ten years of Grosvenor bonuses taking up residence in her bank account. Claude would have Little Sister packed up and ready for dispatch within a fortnight, she predicted. For the moment, he could sip his tea and consider his options at leisure – or at least for as long as he could manage to hold at bay the distracting thought that Natalya Kocharian was lounging naked in the bath next door.

* * *

Café Mouloudia occupied a section of Avenue de Lamur devoted to high-end clothes stores, although they hadn't yet succeeded in displacing the mini-markets that occupied every other corner. James had arrived late the night before and booked in to the Sheraton. In the morning, he took a cab to one end of the Avenue, then got out and walked. He found Café Mouloudia, then turned into a small hotel that was almost opposite. He took a room on the first floor which had French windows with white cotton neatly pinned over the lower panes, giving on to a tiny Juliet balcony. He set a bentwood chair a few feet back from the window and sat down to watch. It was ten now – an hour to go. He'd done forty minutes of t'ai chi that morning, but still there was a low thrumming in his bones, as if he'd been plugged into the mains overnight.

It was a gentle autumn day, the sun slowly warming the air, the cool of night lingering in shade. Above the line of buildings opposite, a band of chalky cloud was forming against the pale, pink-hued blue of the sky. You couldn't see the sea from here, but you could smell salt and rust and hear muted booms from the loading gear down at the port. Café Mouloudia did a modest trade.

Hamed's email had said he'd be met by a man wearing a BMW logo baseball cap, but so far the only customers were a frail old man and his vigorous wife sitting side by side at a table on the pavement: she smoked a cigarette and kicked her pointed leather shoes at a stray cat, while he studied a long and complicated pools coupon through a magnifying glass. James stretched in his chair until it started to creak and he realised it was about to snap in half. The Kosovo feeling was back, the feeling he'd had when heading out into hostile territory to do something deniable. Something unspeakable. Exhilaration and dread bubbling in the gut. You're going soft, he told himself. This isn't a war zone. Then a man James thought might be Hamed turned up.

The man sat at a table on the other side of the entrance from the old couple and looked around him. He was plump and wore a dark blue suit, cream-coloured shirt and gold-framed sunglasses. He seemed at home, although his demeanour had an oddly reluctant quality – much sighing and leaning back and looking down his nose. He didn't look dangerous – but then the truly dangerous ones seldom did. The waiter came out with a glass of water and a menu, and the man gave his order without looking at it. He produced a cellphone and started to jab at the keypad, then a moment later tossed it down on the table and folded his arms.

Five minutes passed and he was served a cup of coffee. He sugared it copiously, then as he took his first sip, a tall man in black trousers and a red shirt arrived. Approaching the café, he pointedly adjusted the BMW logo baseball cap on his head. Hamed nodded and stood up. The two men shook hands, then moved off down the street.

They were no more than fifty yards away when James reached the pavement outside the hotel. He waited until the gap was nearer a hundred, then followed. They turned right and James hurried to the corner in case they turned again. They were ambling along together, the tall man's hands gesticulating as he talked. They entered a district of seventies apartment blocks with stairwells at either end and covered walkways leading to the front doors. Mats and rugs lay over the parapets to air and James heard snatches of conversation, the tap of a broom. He started to feel conspicuous, but before he could decide whether to hang back further, Hamed and his companion crossed the road and entered a narrow street of older houses on the other side. There was nowhere at all to conceal himself if either of them turned round; but the street curved away to the left, and as soon as they left his field of view, he was able to follow.

He heard a scuffed footstep. Someone behind him. He slowed in the hope that the person would pass and offer him some cover, but they hung back. He quickened his pace, then bent to tie his shoelace and took a look behind him. The street was silent, empty.

He walked on. Suddenly Hamed and the other man were thirty yards away, entering a doorway on the left. They only had to turn round to see him, but they kept their eyes ahead. James looked back again, listened. A pair of seagulls shrieked at each other from the rooftops. Then... A faint *slap-slap* on the polished cobbles? He stood close to the wall of the house beside him and waited. No one came.

He ran to the place where Hamed and his companion had disappeared: a large wooden door with iron straps and hinges. The latch disengaged with a click and he felt that it was not locked or bolted. He pushed the door open and stepped into a dingy courtyard with a paved stone floor and rough rendered walls, barely six feet across, lit by a square of sky four storeys above. He heard the babble from a television, then voices talking somewhere on an upper floor. To his left was the door to the ground-floor apartment; ahead was a concrete staircase.

He crossed to the stairs and climbed the first flight, then turned on to the second. The conversation was clearer now. He reached the first landing, and heard a muffled knock behind him, as if someone had pulled on a leather glove and tapped on the big wooden door.

That was the third time. It was all wrong. Everything. How many warnings did he need?

Again he heard the voices, quite distinct in the hushed building. If there was someone below, blocking his exit, then he'd have to get past him anyway, whether or not he found Hamed and the man in the BMW cap. He carried on up, reached the third floor. A doorway covered by a rippling plastic strip curtain. The voices came from beyond it, talking French with throaty North African accents.

'Go inside, please Dr Palatine.'

He swung round to find a small man with close-cropped hair pointing a semi-automatic at his chest. A shemagh wrapped round his face. No tremor in his hand and his eyes said he would shoot.

'All the effort you've put into following me,' said James. 'I don't think you want to kill me.'

'I do not want to kill you, no. Inside.'

A hand pulled the strip curtain aside and a large figure emerged.

'Je peux vous aider, Etienne?'

He was James's height and fifty pounds heavier, but all James saw was that he was young and had a look of excitement in his eyes.

'Get out of the way,' the man with the gun hissed through his shemagh.

James moved fast on the big man in the doorway, who shot out a fat fist to stall the attack. James caught him by the wrist and used the momentum of the punch to pull him off balance. He bent at the knee and swung the man round until his bulk stood between himself and the gunman, then dropped his shoulder into the man's ribcage and hurled him across the landing. The man in the shemagh tried to dodge but the big man knocked him sideways before spinning head first into the concrete wall. James ran for the stairs. The gunman swung the barrel of his weapon up into his face. James parried and the blow thudded into his shoulder. The gunman jabbed at James's eyes and he drew his head back, swept his left arm across to deflect the extended fingers. He felt a fingernail catch in the corner of his eyelid, but the late parry worked in his favour – the man had expected to get to James's eyes and didn't have another move. James closed in tight to neutralise the gun, smashed his forearm down into the bridge of the man's nose. He staggered back and James kicked him in the stomach. He hunched over and James swung the side of his fist into the man's temple, saw his eyes wobble and roll.

The strip curtain rustled behind him. He turned. Another man. In his hands, a weapon that looked like a toy gun.

The wired barb twitched between his ribs.

Taser. In a flash he felt the scrubbed lino floor of the training camp outside Kettering cold on his cheek. *Who's first for the big jolt?* Smelled vomit. Went into spasm. The jangle of voltage searched his spine. *You won't like it, lads.* Like someone plucking at the nerves with a pair of pliers. Laid out prone at the top of the stairs. The need to move not getting translated into movement. The spasms dying away now, but not the paralysis.

He watched the third man put down the Taser and pull a sap from the inside pocket of his jacket. He walked over to James, crouched, then raised the sap above his head with ceremonious care. He too was wrapped in a grey and white shemagh. A copious beard bulged beneath it, black hairs sprouting over the hem below his cheekbones. James screamed silently at his limbs. One knee started to straighten. An oily perfume wafted over him. This had all happened much too easily. Much too easily. He was going to get slapped with a pound of ground lead: hard and on the temple, by the look of it. Yes, that was probably how it went.

*   *   *

The Kocharians hailed from the outermost of seven twelve-storey apartment blocks in rust-streaked concrete plonked on the malnourished eastern fringes of Kiev. Four apartments on each floor, forty-eight per block, 336 families in total. About fifteen hundred people, the young Natalya had worked out, looking down from their ninth-floor window over blocks one to six and the lumpy grey outline of the city beyond. Their road was called Pyrochova Street, and it ended at the bus-stop outside Block 6, as if exhausted by the effort of reaching even that far. In order to turn round and take passengers back into the city, the drivers liked to accelerate their buses into a tight circle, careering over the patch of rough ground at the end of the road with the springs compressed and the battered oblong body heeling over in a pathetic parody of vehicular agility. In winter, when the circles they inscribed got churned into ditches full of brown ice, they carved new ones, until, from Natalya's vantage point, it looked as if the road itself had spewed out huge concentric loops of braided mud.

The Block 7s had to negotiate this quagmire to get to the bus stop. Natalya's mother would berate the drivers, demanding that they stick to the road and perform a proper five-point turn, as any self-respecting bus driver would. It didn't make any difference. The 7s were at the bottom of the heap and would just have to put up with it, or find an apartment in Block 6.

Natalya and Nikolai had been born on the ground floor, and it had taken the Kocharians three years of bribing and sweet-talking the caretaker just to get up to the ninth. Then their father had gone back to Armenia – to visit his brother, he said, though he never returned. With him went any chance of moving further up the Pyrochova Street hierarchy. Nat remembered thinking that she didn't want to live in Block 6, nor Block 1 for that matter, nor even in the city centre that smelt of damp newspaper and exhaust fumes so thick you could taste burnt oil on your lips. She had other ideas – most of them based on detailed study of a copy of *Vogue* she'd stolen at a Sunday flea market. She asked her mother what she had to do to live in London or New York, and her mother said, 'You must learn English and work at your books, my little dumpling.' Her mother was a teacher and this answer was to be expected.

Nikolai had taken a less reputable approach to his career – and here he was now, standing in the passport queue at Marrakech Airport, looking every inch the gangster from Kiev: aviator shades, golfing blouson, Gucci jeans and cream leather deck shoes. He even had an aluminium attaché case swinging from one hambone fist. Despite that, he breezed through immigration and swept past the trestle tables in the customs hall as if arriving at the premiere of his own Hollywood blockbuster. When he saw Nat, he raised his arm in salute, took off his sunglasses and hugged her mightily.

'My little Natalya, I am happy to see you. What happened to your hair?'

Since moving to London, she'd worn her honeycomb-coloured hair short, to show off the graceful curve of her neck, but her brother always forgot.

'It's lovely to see you, too, Nikolai. And how handsome you look. What have you got in your briefcase? Diamonds? Cocaine?'

'I couldn't decide, so I got you some of each.'

It wouldn't be the first time she'd had such gifts from her brother, and Nat felt a moment of alarm. But Nikolai was by nature a cautious man. He might cultivate the cheerfully belligerent manner of a stereotypical East European gangster, but he would never try to smuggle anything past anyone he hadn't paid off first.

They found a taxi and set off for Marrakech. After a short while, her brother became taciturn, and she realised that he was fretting over the driver's fatalistic approach to navigating the traffic, swaying through junctions at a constant thirty miles an hour and enjoying a richly humorous discourse with those who swerved to avoid him.

'Why is everyone hooting all the time?' said Nikolai to his sister. 'There's no point. How far to the hotel?'

'Maybe half an hour.'

'Shit. I'm hungry. All I had on the plane was a yoghurt and some crackers. Everything else was dog food. And most of the passengers looked like terrorists.'

'You mean there were Arabs on the flight?'

'Right. And all the cabin crew were poofs.'

When they approached the outskirts of town, Nat wound down the window. It was early evening, the food stands were firing up, and the scent of harissa and charcoal drifted on the air. She loved Marrakech. The heat caressed her skin, the carnival of smells relaxed her, and the cheerful swirl of noise was sweet relief from the portentous grey hush of Grosvenor's London office. The taxi slowed to walking pace where the current of cars, motorbikes, scooters, bicyclists and people driving goats or riding donkeys had formed a complicated eddy and subsided into a general impasse that was being worked out by way of an elaborate concatenation of honks, shouts, shrieks, curses and cries. Several wonky towers of plastic crates rose from the back of the truck next to them, and through its slatted sides Nat could make out the figures of two men smoking and playing cards. Further down the road she saw a girl of seven or so in a yellow dress and pink flip flops with a three-foot-long branch of dates dangling above her head, and a boy leading a donkey with a flagon of water in one pannier and a TV in the other.

'We're stuck,' said Nikolai.

'Arrêtez ici un petit moment, je vous en prie,' Nat told the driver.

The taxi pulled over and was quickly surrounded by boys eager for whatever business this foreign lady might bring. Nat looked the nearest boy in the eye and gave her order, along with a ten-dirham note. The chosen one elbowed his way back through the crowd. She gave another twenty to the oldest-looking boy and gestured to the rest. 'À partager, compris?'

'Oui, merci!'

The boy returned with water, barbecued chicken and aubergine fritters wrapped in a paper towel.

'You eat that kind of dirty food, you are asking to get sick in the stomach,' Nikolai informed her.

'Don't be silly, I have it every time I come to Marrakech. Here, I got this for you.'

'No way.' He paused. 'How come you give money to those kids, huh? Makes them think they can beg all their lives,' he said self-righteously, as if he had hit upon the root cause of all indolence north of the Sahara.

'It's what you do here, Niko. It's what makes it OK for you to be rich and them to be poor. You'd better get used to it.'

Nat's hotel, the Riad des Ombres, was in the old town, five minutes' walk from the main square of Marrakech, the Djemaa el Fna. She had reserved a room for Nikolai on the quiet, cool side of the building, but all her brother noticed was that the TV was too small. They went down to the pool in one of the two courtyards, and the swim washed away his rebellious mood.

'I've been learning French,' he told her. 'Bonjour mon soeur, comment vous allez vous?'

'*Ma* soeur. And for your sister, you use *tu*.'

'For my little sister,' said Nikolai, 'I use one hand to keep her away from the edge and the other to drown her.'

He placed a meaty palm on top of her head and did so. Nat screamed obligingly. It was mean of her to criticise. Learning languages was Nikolai's hobby. He said that Russian was no good for business, unless you liked doing business with drunks. Therefore, he must learn English, German, and now French. It wasn't obvious to Nat how his linguistic accomplishments would assist him, since his business style was to sit in silence with his arms folded, occasionally shaking his head and grimacing.

She said she'd take him to a French restaurant so he could practise. After sufficient steak, chips and beer to allow him to feel as a Ukrainian man should after his evening meal, Nikolai became convivial to the point where a gullible observer might have thought him cosmopolitan.

'What's he like, this Zender?' he asked.

Nat hesitated. 'He's clever, charming, forty-something, I guess. He's only interested in money, so I feel like I know where I stand with him. The most obvious thing is that he's fat.'

'Fat?' said Nikolai. Most of his male friends were fat, or well covered as they liked to say. It testified to their affluence and virility.

'Not like you. He's huge, must be nearly two metres tall and easily a hundred and thirty kilos. Greedy, too. He hangs out at a café called Zizou's which he says has the best pastry chef in the world. In the evening he goes to the Casino des Capricornes and finds rich people to play poker with.'

'A pig,' said Nikolai.

'A very powerful pig. He knows everyone, taxi drivers, businessmen, city officials and politicians, the chief of police. The whole of Marrakech wants to do him a favour, and for anyone who doesn't he probably has the number of a hired killer in his cellphone.'

'So when do we see him?'

'Not for a few days... Nikolai, I have to make a trip. To LA – I fly out first thing tomorrow, back Thursday.'

Nikolai's face took on an expression intended to inform his sister that she was taking a liberty. 'You're leaving me in fucking Morocco,' he said testily. 'Great.'

'You can stay here and relax, get a feel for the place.'

'I don't want a feel for the place.' He paused. 'Anton and Mikhail are coming out – be good to have them around.'

'Must they?'

'Be a holiday for them, right?'

In Nat's eyes, Mikhail – a former state-sponsored weightlifter who never quite made it into the Olympic squad of his native Bulgaria – seemed to have been designed expressly to stand stock still and go red in the face. An impressive sight, but all wrong for Marrakech. Anton was a cut-price gigolo who fancied himself a great deal more than anything about him warranted.

'Don't cause any trouble, Nikolai, I don't want to get back from LA to find the three of you slurping mutton fat in the local jail.'

* * *

She took him back to the Riad and kissed him goodnight, then went to bed herself and slept contentedly, as she nearly always did. Next morning, she ate a large breakfast and met up with her friend Jamila, the wife of the owner of the Riad des Ombres, who had offered to drive her to the airport. The two women had spent many happy hours in each other's company: Nat regaled Jamila with tales of London high society, which in truth she knew nothing at all about, while Jamila repaid her with vivid portrayals of the scurrilous lives led by the great and the good of Marrakech. It was an altogether comforting relationship.

Nat chatted with Jamila until they reached the highway, then called Zender and told him she'd been summoned to London.

'Grosvenor have checked their revenue projections and realised their mistake, I surmise,' he said. 'You will be re-instated as soon as they have worked out a way of doing so without further humiliating themselves.'

After listening to more in this vein she told him he was cutting out and hung up.

'I'll never know what you see in that greedy *maloof*,' said Jamila. 'And you, beautiful enough for a prince!'

'In fact, he does make me feel like royalty. I don't believe he has ever missed an opportunity to pay me a compliment.'

'My advice is this, Natalya: you must take him by some tender part – I leave the choice to you – and squeeze as hard as you like. It will remind him who is boss.'

'Now I know why your husband is so red in the face,' said Nat, and the two women laughed without restraint at the thought of their wincing bedfellows.

They reached the airport just before ten. Nat checked in and went through to the departure lounge, then put in her call to Grosvenor. She'd been delaying as long as possible because she hoped to get away with speaking to Sir Peter Beddoes, who disliked early starts.

'Hi Nat,' said the chairman's PA. 'Clive wants to speak to you. Shall I put you through?'

Nat reluctantly agreed. It was too soon in the game to be evasive.

'I managed to meet with Zender,' she told him. 'He said getting the IPD400 back was impossible. That could be a negotiating position – I'm not sure yet. The five per cent sweetener won't be enough, anyway.'

'It seems more than generous. Has he told you who has it now?'

'Obviously not. He just said he'd have a word with his client – and only because it was me who asked.'

'It would help to have a name, Natalya. Please work on that.'

'I'm a sales director, Clive, not a secret agent.'

'Keep your ear to the ground – Marrakech is always full of chatter.'

'Actually, it's not. What have you found out your end?'

'If we turn up anything relevant to your line of enquiry, I'll let you know. Do we have a time-frame for Zender's approach to his client?'

'He said he'd call on Thursday.'

'Is that the best you can do?'

'Yes, Clive, it is.'

She hung up, thinking it had been smart of her to get riled. All right, not exactly smart, since she hadn't intended to... But if she suddenly became docile towards him, Clive Silk would get suspicious – not a good thing, given that she was sneaking off to LA for four days behind Grosvenor's back.

Chapter Four

James was moaning. Moaning again. Or still moaning. His mind slopped around like a seagull in an oil slick. His limbs were clods of meat.

He realised why he'd woken. He was going to be sick. He pitched his head to one side and held it there as the bitter juice swamped his nostrils.

When it was over, he gurgled gently, trying not to draw the filth into his lungs. He swallowed and it felt like he had a garden hose jammed down his throat. This wasn't the first time he'd vomited, but he couldn't remember the others.

It came to him that he could open his eyes. Soon. Soon, he would have to open his eyes.

*   *   *

His room was made of breeze blocks outlined with irregular squidges of mortar. Small and square, with one corner walled off. Concrete floor. He was lying on his side on a thin foam mattress covered in canvas, still trembling from the shock of coming to. To his left was a door made of orange-stained pine. Whoever had installed the light switch hadn't straightened it up before screwing it to the wall.

He tried to raise his head and sheets of light flared and crackled behind his eyes. It felt like someone had pounded a Champagne cork into the canal of his left ear. The outside of the ear was raging hot, probably infected by the puddle of congealing vomit in which it lay.

Opposite his mattress was a small window covered with a square of yellow cotton. Iron bars on the outside of the window cast stripes of shadow which bent and rippled as the cotton billowed in and out. It was soothing to watch – as if the room were breathing. Wafts of hot air circled him like empty thoughts, like ideas you couldn't catch hold of.

Eventually he persuaded one of his arms to bend at the elbow and lever itself up where he could see it. There were puncture marks, brown and yellow bruising. A drip had been inserted into the back of his hand.

James contemplated the billowing yellow curtain for a further, indeterminate length of time, then decided he ought to move. He stretched out his legs and his torso and allowed his head to roll back. He waited, eyes shut, for the jangling inside his skull to slacken. His ear popped and creaked. He thought of water for the first time since coming round. He would not last long without water – maybe just a few hours. A wave of self-pity clutched at his throat.

The walled-off corner… He could perhaps make it to the edge and look round. He began to wrestle himself off the mattress. Some cruel alchemical transformation had made sludge of the air and given the concrete floor the contours of a ploughed field. He allowed himself to roll onto it and tried not to cry out.

Later, he hauled himself up onto hands and knees. His head swung between his arms. The feel of his kneecaps scraping across the concrete kept him going. It was a long way, and he lay down and rested many times.

Near the corner, he stretched out on his front until he could see round. No door, just a narrow room with a squat toilet, a sunken plastic tray with rests for the feet either side of the drain, covered with a film of reddish dust. A fat blue plastic hose emerged via a butterfly tap from the base of the wall beyond. James craned his neck round and his eyes followed the hose. It ended six feet up in a shower head attached with a twist of wire to a hook screwed into the wall.

He dragged himself over and turned the tap. With a polite cough, the water flowed, brown and tepid. He found the place on the floor where the stream landed and set his head beneath it. The water spattered over his face and slipped away down the toilet. He put his fingers to his head and found a band of swollen tissue the thickness of a banana stretching from his left temple round to the back of his skull. A sap's doing.

He crawled out of the shower room and lay on the floor. The effort drained him and he felt sick again. He realised he could smell food – a plate of cornbread and dates on the floor by his mattress. The bread was speckled with black dots and it took him a moment to see they were ants. He watched them marching under the door, like a length of pulsing black wire. There was a droning noise in the background – a generator. He heard a dog barking, then a yelp.

He lay still until he felt strong enough to move, then heaved himself back to the mattress. As well as the mess his own body had made, the canvas was stained with a blotch of plum brown fading at the edges and overlaid with a swirl of greenish yellow. It looked like someone had bled to death from a gut wound. However, it was dry. Probably happened years ago. He lay down and slept.

* * *

71

His bruised head and infected ear woke him every time he moved, but there was not much difference between asleep and awake. The generator bawled and babbled in the background. The drug-induced stupefaction would not loosen its grip. In a moment of clarity he remembered that he'd been trained for this before one of his SAS ops: CAC, the course was called, Conduct After Capture. *Make your captors believe that you do not pose any threat,* he remembered. That shouldn't be difficult. His brain fogged up again and he closed his eyes. When he opened them, there was a hand on his shoulder.

'Dr Palatine?'

A woman's voice.

'How are you feeling? I am a doctor. I will examine you.'

He flicked his eyes open and saw the woman's outstretched hand.

'I... I... What will you do with me?'

'I must look at the contusion.'

James raised his hand to his temple, as if discovering the injury for the first time. The doctor was European, with a sallow complexion and a small, square face framed by short-cropped light brown hair. She spoke English as if it was hurting her nose. James really wanted to ask, *Are you the evil doctor who doped me up?* Instead he stared at her stupidly.

She produced a torch and looked into his eyes, then spotted his burning ear – tsk tsk! – and inspected that too. She promised him painkillers, antibiotics and a clean mattress.

'I can't sleep,' he said miserably.

'Sure. Some diazepam also. Please, you must eat this food.'

He moved his jaw up and down as if trying to speak and reached after her in mute supplication as she moved away. There were two guards in the doorway, watching intently yet with a great show of being bored by this fuss over a sore head. The one in charge was in his late forties, with a broad, curved back and an angular face that was dark from the sun and heavy with stubble. The other was a large, slope-shouldered man, barely into his twenties, with small eyes and a sparse collection of wiry black hairs sprouting from his chin. Some kind of skin disease had left pale blotches across his cheeks. Both wore threadbare army fatigues of a faded khaki, belted at the waist. Behind them was an enclosed yard, across which James could see a row of four doors identical to his below an oblong of blue sky. A flock of scrawny sparrows tumbled in the dust.

When the doctor had gone, James sat up, lowered his feet onto the floor, and discovered that he could stand. And walk, after the fashion of an infant, or a very old man. He flipped the switch by the door and the light bulb in the ceiling came on, trembling in time with the throb from the generator. He looked at the ant-infested bread and dates, but didn't feel capable of eating. He went over to the window and, cautiously, keeping to one side of the opening, lifted the yellow curtain and looked out.

Twenty yards in front of him was an arc of coiled razor wire, shafts of sunlight shearing off the barbs. Beyond it, a high mesh fence stretched for several hundred yards before curving round to the left and dipping out of sight. Beyond the fence, an undulating desert landscape pockmarked with wizened scrub. There was a guardpost just visible to his right: a shack with boards nailed to the corner posts and a corrugated iron roof. A square of canvas had been fastened to the roof to form an awning, under which three guards sat in white plastic patio chairs. Unlike his guards, they wore blue overalls. Their weapons were propped up against the shack – automatic rifles, two M16s, the other James couldn't identify at this distance.

Then he saw the dogs, four of them, inside the razor wire, large, rangy creatures with long jaws, well cared for, fit and alert. They were sniffing over something out by the wire, but one of them must have seen the curtain move or smelled him because it raised its head and stared, then cantered across the dirt towards his window, head lowered, hackles raised. Something like a cross between a Ridgeback and a greyhound: a fine-looking animal, if you didn't intend crossing its patch some time soon. The other dogs followed and they stood twenty yards from his window. He let the curtain fall. That set them off, and their heavy, metronomic barking jarred the clear morning air.

He tottered over to the shower room and wrestled himself free of his clothes, then sat under the fitful trickle of water. He used his T-shirt and some water to clean his ear, then washed his jeans and boxer shorts and hung them from the blue plastic pipe to dry.

He sat naked below the yellow cotton curtain, irregular puffs of air cool on his wet shoulders. His brain seemed to be functioning again – or at least, it was cranking away in some dogged semblance of acuity. *You should not have entered the house in Oran*, it told him. *You knew there was someone behind you.* How far had he come since then? A journey complicated enough to justify knocking him out with a liquid cosh so powerful it had nearly killed him.

A few minutes later, he heard a key in the lock and the door was pushed open. There was a moment's silence when they saw him, then sharp disagreement outside. A woman tittered. He didn't move. His guards were escorting a tall woman and a girl, dressed in black with their heads covered, carrying a fresh mattress and a mop and bucket; but evidently they wouldn't enter with this naked man inside. It was a quandary for the men. After a minute's discussion, during which the levity of the females and the irritation of the guards increased in equal measure, the older of the two men shoved the mattress into the room and dragged the old one out. He came back and handed James a plastic cup with two ibuprofen and a penicillin capsule.

*   *   *

'Wake up. Eat now!'

It was dark outside. The older guard put something on the floor, then the door banged shut. There was a warm, rich smell. He turned over and saw a plastic dish containing a red and yellow stew and a steel spoon. Next to it were two ibuprofen, two diazepam, a penicillin capsule and a slice of melon. Room service. *Your evening meal will be served with a complimentary portion of fresh fruit.* Laughter pattered in his stomach. He examined the food for several minutes, allowing his appetite to wake. Then he clambered over and ate. It felt strange, as if his body had forgotten what to do. When he had finished, he tucked the diazepam into the hem of the yellow curtain, took the other pills, and went to sleep.

*   *   *

Nikolai Kocharian's first day in Marrakech had started badly. Resolving to at least set eyes on Claude Zender, he'd taken a taxi to Café Zizou – a gruelling journey that entailed a twenty-minute trip to the outskirts of town and a short hurtle round a section of ring road, followed by a tortuous navigation of countless narrow, foul-smelling streets. At last he'd found himself standing under a pink awning decorated with a motif of a pirouetting flamingo; but despite peering through the window of Café Zizou for several minutes, he'd seen no one who resembled the enormously fat arms dealer. A waiter had then come out and asked him if he'd care to sit down at a table. Ignoring Nikolai's firm refusal, the waiter had persisted – to the point of actually trying to surround him with pieces of café furniture. Nikolai had become angry and found he was clenching his fists. He'd walked quickly away and, realising he had no idea where he was, entered a bank to ask for directions – only to discover that the Riad des Ombres was less than two hundred yards away.

He'd spent the rest of the day drinking beer, prodding suspiciously at the various meals he ordered from room service, and failing to locate the European sports channel promised by the entertainments menu on his undersized TV. And brooding. This was Natalya's fault. First she'd dragged him to Marrakech, then she'd abandoned him while she went off on some mysterious errand on the far side of the world.

Yet Nikolai could not find it in his heart to be cross with Natalya. Rather, he was terribly impressed that she could conjure up a trip to LA as if it were no more bother than popping to the shops for a newspaper. He was proud of the business he had built – the wretched riffraff of sly bureaucrats and putty-headed thugs who occupied his working life had last year helped him to a profit of nearly two hundred thousand euros – but it was nothing to what Natalya had achieved. While divisional boardrooms wilted before the violence of her intrigues and the immanence of her sexual charms, back in Kiev, Nikolai bored his gang brothers with news of her ascent into the upper echelons of London's business community. And when she sent him a link to the *Arms Trade Gazette* report announcing her appointment at Grosvenor – complete with a photograph of her standing proprietorially outside the grandiose stone façade of the company's Mayfair offices – he printed it off and stuck it on the noticeboard beside his desk, where it had the miraculous effect of dispersing the smell of urine and petrol that rose up from the cold warehouse below.

Natalya's exemplary career now seemed to be at risk. Nikolai wasn't quite sure why, but he did not like the sound of Claude Zender. Here was a man who paid off policemen and taxi drivers, hung around at a casino and had the number of a hired killer in his cellphone: such men belonged in his world, not his sister's. He wished he could meet the fat arms dealer face-to-face and inform him that Natalya was not to be messed with. In Kiev, a threat from

Nikolai Kocharian would have been enough. But in Marrakech, nobody knew anything about him. Zender might use his police contacts to have him arrested. The phrase *slurping mutton fat in the local jail* resonated unpleasantly at the back of his mind.

Perplexity was an unfamiliar state of mind for Nikolai Kocharian, and eventually he could bear it no longer. It was six o'clock. He took a taxi from the line outside the hotel and asked for the Djemaa el Fna.

'You have a guide, sir?' the driver asked.

Nikolai shook his head.

'Please, sir, I find you very good guide. Very good.'

'No. And take me straight there because I know the way, OK?'

'You get good carpet, sir, good quality, cheap price.'

'Just drive the fucking car,' Nikolai told him, thoroughly disgruntled and already regretting his decision to leave the Riad. The square was empty apart from a handful of tourists being pestered by two young men leading lethargic monkeys on chains, a row of orange-juice sellers and a crowd of boys playing football with a semi-deflated plastic ball. The dust spurted up at their heels as they ran. A huddle of old women in black dress stood by the area where taxis drew up on one side of the square. They shuffled rapidly over as Nikolai got out, and the boys stopped their game and ran to join the ad hoc queue. The women cuffed and jabbed them with their elbows to keep them at the back. Nikolai had been preparing for this. Taking his cue from Nat – how smart that girl was! – he distributed the change from his pocket with gracious *Voilàs!* until there was none left, upon which he yanked the lining of both trouser pockets out and waggled them like a pair of supernumerary ears.

'Plus de monnaie!' he announced.

The boys ran off, shrieking 'Plus de monnaie! Plus de monnaie!', and even the solemn faces of the crones broke into smiles. Heartened by the reception of his few words of French, Nikolai crossed to the far side of the square and followed a steady stream of people into the souk.

The maze of alleys swirled with unfamiliar smells – spices sharp and sweet, peppers and aubergines still warm from the fields, the chocolatey scent of wood and leather as he entered a quarter given over to the sale of shoes and bags. Small boys tugged at his shirt; shopkeepers batted them away and took him by the elbow, urging him to examine the kaleidoscope of wares crammed into the narrow booths behind their wooden chairs.

After half an hour of wandering he came to an area full of carpet emporia, milling with anxious tourists and eager guides. He entered a shop and was seized by an old man who sat him on a kelim-covered stool and served him mint tea from a small silver pot. He was thirsty and, setting aside his reservations about the cleanliness of the water, the pot and the old man's hands, drank off several glasses in succession while the carpet-seller heaved acres of rug over to him, holding up fingers to indicate the prices. Nikolai sipped his tea and looked unimpressed. He knew how to bargain. It was pleasant in the shop, with the little man cajoling him and the scent of mint in his nostrils. Eventually he saw a rug small enough to carry home.

'Deux mille trois cent dirhams,' said the man, 'so very cheap, yes!'

Nikolai produced a bogus laugh and shook his head.

'Deux mille trois cent,' the man repeated. 'You buy. C'est un tapis de toute qualité, voyez, fait à la main en village du Sahara.'

They bargained amiably for a few minutes, then Nikolai had an idea.

'Je suis ami de Monsieur Zender,' he said. 'Vous savez Monsieur Zender, sans doute?'

The old man looked at him, startled, then hung his head and backed away behind a screen at the rear of the shop. Seconds later, a man of about Nikolai's age with a full beard and large belly tenting his blue robe stood before him.

'I must say I am so much sorry,' he said, looking nervously at Nikolai. 'I did not know you as friend of Monsieur Zender's, you did not say. Then I would have served you myself. I am so much sorry, Monsieur… please, I do not know your name?'

'Sartorius,' said Nikolai, giving an alias he sometimes used back home.

'Monsieur Sarshooz, of course. May I please offer fresh tea?' He snapped his fingers at the old man, who picked up the tray and carried it off behind the screen.

'You are liking your visit to the City of the Seven Saints, Monsieur Sarshooz? You stay at La Mamounia, where Monsieur Zender entertains his friends?'

Thrown by the reference to the seven saints and never having heard of La Mamounia, Nikolai pretended to examine the rug the old man had laid at his feet.

'I am much sorry to ask you this questions,' said the man. 'My uncle says you like this beautiful rug. You have very fine eye, I think. It is two thousand dirhams to buy. For you, I give it as a gift.' He beckoned to a boy lurking at the back of the shop, who rolled up the carpet and started to wrap it in brown paper and string.

'Thank you,' said Nikolai, alarmed at the success of his subterfuge. 'I'll pay for it. I didn't come for a free gift. Here— ' He fumbled a wad of dirhams from his pocket and thrust them at his benefactor.

'Please, Monsieur Sarshooz,' said the carpet-seller, bowing rapidly. He took the rug from the boy and held it out. Sweat had formed at his temples. 'Please say to Monsieur Zender that you came to the shop of Abdellatif Choukri and family and he showed you all hospitality, and you will please pass to him my great respects and my great hopes for eternal friendship.'

'OK,' said Nikolai, taking the rug and hurrying from the shop. He'd made a bad mistake, he now realised. Zender would want to know the identity of this man who was pretending to be his friend. He looked back over his shoulder as he walked from the souk, already convinced he was being followed.

Chapter Five

James sat upright, heart lolloping. Someone was shouting orders outside. A hard, rancorous voice that rapped against the walls of his room. His sleep had been dream-heavy and confused. It was light, and it took him a moment to work out that this was dawn, that the sun was up. He settled his heartbeat with a few slow breaths, then made his way round to the narrow, barred window. A group of fifteen or so blue-overalled guards had gathered on a patch of open ground beyond the razor wire. The three from the guardpost were walking over to join them.

Another man strode into view – a man of colossal stature dressed in smart black fatigues, face dark beneath the long peak of a military baseball cap. As he approached the wire, the four dogs bounded over and swung their long tails. The big man roared at the trio from the guardpost, and they broke into a jog. Then he marched to the front of the gathering, stood with legs akimbo, arms folded over the slab of his chest. The other men sidled away, leaving a space around him.

The three guards hurried past James's window. He heard a series of guttural cries behind him. He went over to the door: there was a strip of sunlight showing at the top. He pulled himself up and squinted through into the enclosed yard, where he saw the top of a man's head, weaving from side to side. A long, heavy blade with a shallow curve now rose slowly into his line of sight, followed by the hilt and the man's hands wrapped around it. The sword was still for a second, then sliced down. The weaving began again. The man was slightly built and seemed to compensate for his lack of stature by taking exaggeratedly large strides. He swept the sword around him in a series of grand parabolas, now dipping to a crouch, now rising on tiptoe, now spinning so that his black *bisht* swirled around his knees, revealing a pair of baggy cotton pantaloons beneath. As he moved in and out of view, James saw thin black hair swept back from a short, slanting forehead, and a glistening beard that covered his cheeks right up to the sockets of his eyes: the beard of the man who had Tasered and sapped him in Oran.

He went back to the window. Standing to one side of the crowd of blue-overalled men, conspicuous in his sand-coloured fatigues, was the younger of his two guards; there was no sign of the other. Suddenly everyone turned to watch four more guards arrive. They were leading a chubby, middle-aged man dressed in a crumpled dark blue suit. Their commander boomed an order at one of the men standing near him, who produced a video camera and started filming. The big man then nodded at the escort and they began to hustle their prisoner out into the open.

The man in the suit was barefoot and walked clumsily in the stony sand. One of the guards shoved him sideways into the guard on the other side, who threw him back. The first guard stepped away so that the prisoner fell to the dirt and both guards used their boots on him, with no particular force but in the casual way a boy will kick a discarded drinks can. When they picked him up again his head twisted rapidly from side to side, then he turned and started to stumble towards the watching men. A guard caught him and spun him round.

'Wrong way, fat bitch!'

As the prisoner's face turned towards the sun, James recognised the man he had seen waiting outside the café in Oran – the man called Hamed, who had recruited Sarah and set up the house in Wembley. His eyes squinted out of a face darkened by dirt or bruising, and James saw in his abject demeanour the desperation of a man whose instincts are telling him to run but who knows himself incapable of anything more than the most pathetic evasion.

They brought him to a patch of ground thirty yards or so from James's window and kicked his feet away, then pulled him by the hair into a kneeling position and tore off his jacket and shirt. The guards stepped away and looked back at their commander in the military cap. He turned and – it seemed to James – stared directly at his window. Then he shouted in a voice that rumbled like an underground rockfall:

'Mansour! The prisoner is ready!'

Mansour was ready, too. He rushed into view from the left and along the arc of razor wire, gripping the sword in both hands, the curved blade pointing back over his shoulder. The dogs cantered alongside him, barking and snarling from behind the barbed coils.

'You filthy, lazy, useless queer!' he screamed in Arabic as he pranced towards the kneeling figure, sword now raised high above his head. 'You foul yourself with your unspeakable lusts so you cannot do Allah's sacred work, then you beg for mercy like a slut. You are weak, weak, weak!'

He stamped around, brandishing his sword and charging his victim with all manner of depravity.

'Now you must die, like the dirty whore that you are.'

Hamed folded over and started to squirm in the dust.

'Get up! Will you not even die with dignity?'

Two guards stepped in and yanked him back up into a kneeling position. Mansour moved forwards and set himself to strike, but Hamed again fell sideways and lay prostrate.

'Up! It will be worse for you if you do not face me like a man!'

Again the guards positioned him for execution, but again he fell before Mansour could swing his sword. He made as if to slash at his victim on the ground, but then thought better of it and beckoned furiously to the guards. Hamed cowered, the fat quivering at his dirt-speckled waist, then stretched out on his back as the guards approached to drag him up.

The ceremonial execution was in danger of descending into farce. But before the guards could seize their victim's arms again, he shouted out, in a surprisingly strong voice:

'What is it, Mansour, am I spoiling your show? What will people say if you cannot carry out an execution properly? I may be an old queer, but at least I'm not a fraud— '

Mansour rushed in and hacked wildly, scattering the guards. The blow cut into Hamed's shoulder, and he jerked sideways and screamed, a howl of shock that sent a shudder through the watching men. Mansour struck again, two blows in quick succession which sliced into Hamed's back and clanged audibly against the bone of his ribs. Still he jerked and rolled, screeching at Mansour's feet.

The audience was agog, riveted by the spectacle of sharpened steel slicing human flesh, by the ease with which blood could be made to spill from severed veins, by the weight of cuts that could be suffered without bringing death. A fourth swipe glanced off the top of his skull and a gush of blood darkened the dust.

As Mansour prepared to strike again, a tall man of about sixty came up behind him and drew a handgun. A shot cracked out. Hamed's head jolted and his body went into spasm. Mansour spun round with a shout of rage to find the tall man's gun pointing at his belly.

'I congratulate you, Mansour, on your resolution in the face of such behaviour. We cannot force people to die as they should. You may wish to return to your room to pray.'

Mansour stood for a moment, breathing heavily. The man with the gun was very calm, his gaze fixed on Mansour. He wore a smarter version of the sand-coloured uniform worn by James's two guards, and had enough chevrons on his shoulders to suggest an officer of high rank. The executioner dipped his head a fraction at the officer, who lowered his gun and placed it in the pocket of his jacket, keeping his hand on the butt. He stepped over to Mansour, put an arm round his shoulders and steered him out of sight.

James watched the guards intently. They seemed subdued. The men who had led Hamed to his death stood with their backs to the body, as if it were nothing to do with them.

'Dismissed! Back to your posts!' ordered their statuesque commander.

He aimed a blow at the nearest guard, who ducked to avoid it and hurried away. The rest followed, heads bowed before the big man's basilisk gaze.

* * *

James spent the day sleeping, doing t'ai chi, and trying to keep his mind from circling back to the execution they'd staged outside his window. For his benefit, he had to assume. A strip of sunlight from the gap above the door inched across the concrete floor, so fiercely white it seemed it might at any moment start to smoke. His guards brought food at midday. It was odd, James thought, that they wore soldiers' uniforms, unlike the blue overalls of the other guards, and that they were the only two who watched over him. He extracted a piece of goat-meat and laid it out to dry in the shower room, then hid the steel spoon. The younger guard failed to notice it was missing when he collected the bowl, and James spent an hour meticulously working the last inch of the handle into a tight hook. He'd need another, but it could wait until a few more meals had come and gone. He took the antibiotics they brought him, but the ibuprofen he hid with the diazepam in the hem of the curtain.

The afternoon wore on, and the sense of isolation and confinement yawned inside him. *You'll suffer mood swings*, the CAC instructor had lectured. *Despair, rage, euphoria at any sign of hope. Develop a routine. Exercise, meditate. Keep yourself on an even keel.* He kept telling himself they would not kill him, and the image of Hamed's bloodied, twitching body kept reminding him how it would be if they did.

The strip of light from above the door was replaced by an elongating bar of hazy yellow from the window. It crept over his mattress and started to spread up the wall. At least I'll always know what time it is, James thought. There was no breath of air now, and the yellow curtain hung motionless, thin as tissue paper before a blazing sky.

* * *

'You come! Come!'

The older guard was standing in the doorway. He carried a Beretta Tomcat in a holster on his belt. The younger man had an AK47 which looked several thousand rounds past the end of its useful life.

'Come now!'

The guard grabbed James by the arm. He was strong with an iron-hard grip, but he couldn't pull James to his feet with one hand. He released him with a hiss of impatience, handed the Tomcat to his fellow guard, then took James's arm with both hands. *I could have the pair of you laid out cold in less than twenty seconds*, James thought. The younger guard had jammed the handgun into his waistband and was holding the AK47 up like a trophy. Did he have any idea that at close quarters an automatic rifle is rather less useful than a shovel?

Make your captors believe that you do not pose any threat.

'Don't hurt me,' James whined, cowering and shielding his head as the older guard propelled him through the door. They followed a concrete path down a short passage in one corner of the yard and arrived at a steel gate. The older guard whistled and they stood and waited while one of the blue-overalled men came and unlocked them – a task he completed with an insulting lack of urgency. The razor wire was fixed to the wall on either side of the gate, forming a corridor that led to the compound beyond. The four dogs loped over and stood stock still, watching until they had cleared the wire and moved on into the compound. James kept his head down and breathed steadily: the sooner the dogs learned to ignore him, the better.

When he looked up, he saw a set of buildings that wouldn't have looked out of place on an army base outside Aldershot. Ahead of him was a two-storey barracks with the rim of a satellite antenna projecting from the roof. Behind it was a cylindrical water tank mounted on an iron frame. Over to his right, separated from the barracks by a fifty-yard square of roughly laid concrete slabs, stood a larger building – an administration block of some kind, he guessed, full of offices and function rooms. It had a set of double doors shaded by a slab of concrete on steel poles. Above the doors hung a black, red and green flag he didn't recognise.

The whole of the compound occupied perhaps twenty acres of packed dirt and sand. Beyond the barracks to the south was a fourth building, a big modern warehouse with ridged steel sides. There were two guards out front, reclining under a yellow parasol – they looked like they'd just looted a homewares store and decided to take a nap on the way home. Behind their backs, rendered fuzzy by the steel links of the perimeter fence, the dun-coloured desert pulsed irritably in the early evening heat.

They led him past a concrete bunker and on towards a door in the end wall of the barracks. A woman was standing outside, scraping out the remains from a large enamelled pot, and three men in blue overalls were playing cards at a plastic table. They stopped to stare at James and his guards, and one of them made a jeering remark. The other two laughed and slapped the table. His guards ignored them and took James through the door and up steel stairs to the first floor. He heard music – a melancholy female voice accompanied by a dance beat – and the sound of a shower running. Through an open door, he glimpsed coils of wiring spewing from the ceiling, half-empty bags of sand and cement, and a steel table with a set of new office chairs shrouded in plastic. The door at the far end of the corridor had been dust-proofed with a thick layer of felt around the inside of the frame. His escort banged it with the flat of his hand and after a moment James heard the click of a lock and three bolts being slid back. The door swung open. The older guard directed him inside, then slammed it shut behind him.

*   *   *

'Good evening, Dr Palatine. My name is Rakesh Nazli. May I welcome you to my lab.'

A tall man of about his age, in a clean white T-shirt, jeans and brown leather mules. He had plump, acne-scarred cheeks, a delicate mouth and large brown eyes with milky whites that gleamed in the semi-darkness. Jet black hair was drawn back from a sloping forehead, ending in short, glossy curls at his collar. He was handsome, in the placid, well-fed manner of a second-rate Bollywood film star.

'Please, sit down. I hope you're being looked after OK?'

An American accent with a hint of Ivy League condescension, the weary drawl of someone accustomed to being the smartest person in the room. James took the proffered white plastic chair and sat.

The room was lit by the evanescent glow from an array of monitors and a dim bulb under a dirty white plastic shade which hung over Nazli's desk. The only window had been adapted to house an air-conditioning unit that shuddered ineffectually – the room was hot.

His host locked the door, tossed the key into an open drawer of his desk, then settled in a grey upholstered swivel chair. James studied the contents of the drawer: notebook, pens, cable adapters, and what looked like the handle of a screwdriver.

'I guess your journey over here was not too pleasant?' A hank of hair fell forward over one eye and Nazli swept it back, then tugged his small, fleshy nose between thumb and forefinger.

'I've been paralysed by a Taser, sapped and drugged to the point of coma,' said James. 'And one of the men who arranged it was butchered outside my window. Not pleasant doesn't do it justice.'

'It was necessary to bring you here, and this was the way that was found, I guess. You have a shower and other facilities?'

'He lay in the dirt while your friend Mansour hacked at him with a sword. And you ask me if I'm happy with my shower?'

James was conscious that the soles of his feet were pressing the floor, that the muscles of his legs and back were poised and his mind was clear: the state Sam Hu Li taught him to seek when preparing to attack.

Don't. Not yet.

'I'm just saying that if there is anything you need for your personal comfort, you must please let me know.'

Why was Nazli prattling about his personal comfort? James gripped his chair seat until its sharp plastic edges cut into his fingers.

'This has come as a shock to you, of course. Let me kick off by explaining the setup here.'

Go on then, thought James, you explain and I'll hold on to this chair. Not that it needed much explaining. It was a computer science lab, the sort of room in which he'd spent much of his working life. There was a Sun server, worth a minimum of twenty grand depending on how it was configured, half a dozen desktops arranged on steel racks, and two routers sprouting thickets of cabling, some of it fibre optic and fat as an index finger. Nazli gabbled on about software architectures, bandwidth and throughput, and James succeeded in suppressing the compulsion to kill him.

'We have a GEC 7000 satellite dish on the roof,' his host was saying. 'So you see, we are pretty well provided for.'

Who was paying for this stuff? The GEC would provide a reliable satphone link but was excessive for a lab this size – capable of locating the data equivalent of a needle in a haystack, as well as hoovering up the haystack itself and sending its secrets cascading down into Nazli's den.

'No cabling, unfortunately. We rely on the good heavens above.'

Nazli grinned the tentative grin of a man who believes himself to have been witty but isn't sure. His teeth were not as white as the rest of his face suggested they should be. He jabbed his finger upwards at the rooftop antenna, in case James had missed the point. James couldn't muster a sufficiently miserable quip to offer in return. His desire to find out what grand scheme was gestating in this sultry little room was making this chit-chat hard to endure.

'What's it all for?' he said when Nazli's smile had faded. 'Who set you up here? And where is here?'

James looked into Nazli's eyes for some sign that an illuminating response might be assembling itself within, but there was none. Instead, Nazli reached beneath his desk and produced a large bottle of fluorescent orange soda with a plastic cup over the cap. He set the cup on his desk, filled it carefully to the brim, then drank.

'I can't answer any questions, Dr Palatine.'

'Then what? We just sit here staring at each other?'

'You are here to help me configure and operate some technology we have acquired.'

James thought back gloomily to his phone call with Sir Peter Beddoes. 'You have Little Sister.'

'Little Sister? That is your project name for the IPD400?'

'Reminds me what a rotten thing it is,' said James.

'A play on Big Brother, of course.' Nazli looked delighted with himself. 'Yes, our job is to get *Little Sister* operational. When the work is done, you'll be paid and taken home.'

'That isn't what happened to Hamed.'

Nazli reached for his stray lock of hair and smoothed it neurotically with his fingertips. 'That had nothing to do with this project.'

'How about I smash Little Sister to bits and strangle you in your chair? They'd kill me then, right?'

'They have no reason to want you dead.'

'They?'

Nazli pinched his nose.

'From what I've seen, *they* are the sort who enjoy torturing their victims until the blood runs from their eyes.'

Nazli adopted the manner of a man being unfairly harangued. He returned his orange soda to its place beneath his desk and stared down at his notebook. One leg was pumping up and down on the floor. The atmosphere in the little chamber was suddenly unbearably cloying.

'You'd better show me you really do have it.'

Nazli went round behind the array of racks. James stood quickly, stepped to the desk, reached into the open drawer and closed his hand over the screwdriver. Nazli emerged backwards, dragging a wooden crate reinforced at the corners and tied with steel bands. James moved in behind his host's back, easing the screwdriver into the pocket of his trousers with the heel of his hand.

'Need a hand?'

'Please, sit down.'

Nazli lifted off the lid, reached in and heaved out an aluminium case with ribbed sides and a black handle on top. He lowered it gingerly onto the table and straightened it carefully, fussing over its alignment like a man positioning a new television set.

'Recognise this, Dr Palatine?'

He bloody well should recognise it. He'd made the case himself, adapting it from one made for an old 35mm movie camera. He could disarm each of the security devices embedded in the system to prevent unauthorised use. He knew every micron of circuitry by heart, and could explain both the theoretical and practical details of every solution that had been engineered to every technical obstacle encountered during its design and assembly. He could describe its operation, its capabilities and limitations, its most ingenious features and its ugliest fixes.

'I hope you didn't pay too much for it,' he said. 'It doesn't work.'

'It's a prototype, of course. We know there will be issues to address.'

'That's what they told you, is it?'

'You yourself have said that the technology is proven,' said Nazli. 'So has Dr Vanic.'

'A lot of money was spent. It was expected.'

Nazli walked over to the door and banged hard with the flat of his hand. 'I have kept you too long. The doctor said to take it easy for the first day.' He turned and shouted through the door: 'Salif! Younes!'

Footsteps along the corridor, then a knock. Nazli unlocked the door. James remembered another thing from the Conduct After Capture course: *Demand to be treated with respect.* He stared hard into his host's pretty-boy eyes.

'Get me a toothbrush, will you, Rakesh? Oh, and I'd like a complimentary portion of fresh fruit with every meal.'

Chapter Six

Magda Podolski liked nothing better than lunch at Ivan Kaminsky's with a fellow businesswoman. From its fourth-floor terrace one could hurl bucketfuls of hot scorn at the parade of yacht-gawpers on the harbour front below, and bucketfuls more at the objects of their gawps, lounging expansively on their polished teak decks, the desire to appear insouciant fighting a losing battle with the desire to show off. The terrace, Magda explained, was high enough that one could enjoy the sight of some blonde trophy pursing her lips like a cat's ass because she wasn't being treated as lavishly as she would have been if, say, she had been ten years younger and married to Brad Pitt, while remaining beyond reach of the yowling noise made by overfed hick-spawn campaigning for a Big Mac. She carried with her a pair of compact binoculars so that she could scour the promenade for choice examples of either tendency. She was doing so now.

'Uh oh, here we go, bratz alert code red!' she bellowed. 'Can anyone tell me how she can sit in a force six wind with her hair absolutely stock still. That's not a hairdo, that's hair architecture. It's fucking hair engineering!'

Magda was a former detective with the Washington Police Department who'd gone private when the challenge of defending all women, all homosexuals and all Poles from the accumulated wit and wisdom of DC's finest lost its relish. For a while, she had worked in corporate espionage, 'snooping for creeps and creeping for snoops' as she called it. Grosvenor had hired her to unsettle a fledgling surveillance systems outfit that looked like winning a Mexican government contract they were after. She did better than unsettle it: she unearthed documents written by their head of software testing that showed they had faked the data needed to achieve legal compliance and they went out of business altogether. Soon afterwards, she decided to milk the rich saps of the West Coast instead, and within two years, she and her team were turning over $20 million a year.

While Magda watched the harbour, Nat told her about Grosvenor. Magda put down her binoculars and swelled with outrage. She wasn't a beautiful woman, but there was majesty in her rhomboid nose and broad-set brown eyes.

'A girl like you should be running Grosvenor, not playing attaboy with the likes of Clive Silk and Sir Peter whatever the fuck his name is.'

'Beddoes. Look, darling Magda— '

'*Darling* Magda? I spy a curveball.'

Nat laughed, but it had been a mistake to open her appeal that way. She'd always been better at dealing with men than women.

'Sorry, I'll give it to you straight. Remember Tony Schliemann?'

'Grey Tony? Grey hair, grey suit, grey skin, grey eyes, grey mind. Chief Procurement Officer for the SigInt peepers at the NSA? How could I forget him?'

'You were working for San Hui and they beat us to the kill on an NSA tender I'd been working on. Their technology was three years out of date and their pricing was twenty per cent off. So how come they got the gig? You found out something about Grey Tony and San Hui used it to get the contract. Am I right?'

'For the sake of the argument, sweetheart.'

'Good. Tony owes me one and it's payback time. He's going to help me give Grosvenor the finger and set up on my own.'

'How long do we spend in jail if you get caught?'

'We won't. Tony wants this deal and there'll be a long round of back-slapping if he gets it. But I need to keep my name out of it. No one can know how he pulled it off and no one can know who helped.'

'You want to plug his mouth with my San Hui dirt. And this earns you how much?'

'Magda!'

'OK, this earns *me* how much?'

'You tell me: what do I have to pay to get Grey Tony wriggling beneath my heel?'

'Hold that thought, girl, it's doing me good! OK, so I already have the evidence filed away at my lawyers' – no need to run a new investigation.'

'Money for nothing.'

'Not quite,' she said, tapping the table with a perfect oval of crimson-varnished fingernail. 'If San Hui hear about this, they will be pissed. Tony is already pissed. He'll guess where this information has come from and he's not going to take it well.'

'He knows you did the San Hui work?'

'Sure he does. The Koreans are complicit in a corrupt procurement, so he's safe from that quarter. But you blindside him with this stuff, he's going to start wondering what kind of retirement will be provided for him by the private gated community of San Quentin State Penitentiary. And he'll be thinking, how can I hurt that Podolski bitch.'

'Maybe it's too risky.'

'I didn't say that.' She thought for a moment. 'One time use only – you get your deal, that's it, you unpin Grey Tony from your stiletto and the story is dead. The file stays with my lawyers.'

'Agreed.'

'For the information, and the risk: sixty grand.'

'Christ, Magda, I thought you were doing me a favour? Make it ten, will you?'

'I *am* doing you a favour, sweetie, I'm slapping a sign saying "Shoot here!" right in the middle of my big ol' butt.'

'What about this: if Grey Tony comes through, I'll give you one per cent of the deal value.'

'Points are good, but you have to tell me what the deal is worth.'

'I don't know yet. North of three million.'

'Nothing up front, same risks. If it doesn't come off, nothing at the end of it, either. Five per cent.'

'That's a big slice of pie for a bit of old paperwork. Two, that's it.'

'Three and you have Grey Tony writhing at your feet.'

'Deal.'

Magda popped the caviar and sour cream smothered blini she had prepared for herself into her mouth and reached across the table to shake Nat's hand.

'Mr Anthony R. Schliemann. The R stands for Randolph by the way. Randy Randolph? His sort are prime red-light bait, but Grey Tony is just *too* grey. I get to work and find out that Tony has a hunting lodge in the Sierras, complete with several square miles of bear'n'salmon-infested wilderness. He even has a collection of vintage Ansel Adams prints to hang between the dead animal heads.'

'Ansel Adams?'

'Photographer, classic Americana and they don't come cheap. Also, he has an ex-wife to support – no kids, but— '

'You sure? There's a photo on his desk – boy and a girl in the back of a convertible.'

'No shit? The douche keeps a picture of someone else's kids on his desk. Creepy. Whatever, you can't buy Tony's lifestyle on a government salary. Payola? Too obvious – and you take a kickback, the supplier has you by the balls forever. Tony wouldn't like that. I was getting nowhere, so I asked a financial whizz friend what she would do if she wielded a multi-billion-dollar budget and wanted to make herself a nice bonus. It goes like this, she said. You're about to give a fat contract to a quoted company, you buy their shares, award the contract, the shares get marked up, jackpot. Now we're into Tony's game. He's using proxies and offshores, but I know who to pay and San Hui have deep pockets. Pretty soon I find out that Tony is going the other way, too: he uses CFDs to bet against the share prices of companies he *doesn't* give contracts to.'

'And CFDs are what exactly?'

'Contracts for Difference: it's a way of betting that a share price will fall, handy if you know it's going to because you're their biggest customer and you're about to give all their work to a competitor.'

'Clever old Tony.'

'He was even talking up the chances of companies he was going to shaft just so the price would fall harder. Never made much on any deal, but the drip drip drip totalled up nicely. Would it all stand up in court, with an army of attorneys stirring in several hundred pages of mumbo-jumbo to prove he didn't have the first idea what the fuck was going on? I don't know, but I established the pattern and he knew it. There's enough to get him stomped all over by a team of granite-faced internal affairs types, anyway. He'd have been White Tony by the time they'd finished with him.'

Nat laughed. She was disappointed that the stick she was going to beat Grey Tony with wasn't more substantial – a garish photograph or two would have been nice. But if this information had been used to force the NSA man's hand once, it could do so again.

'You're a genius,' Nat told her companion, who had tucked a pink napkin into her shirt collar and was cracking open the claw of a stupendously large lobster she had chosen from the tank.

'I know. When are you seeing him?'

'Tomorrow night – he's taking me to Holworthy's for dinner.'

'He's in LA?'

'Giving face-time to some lucky West Coast contractors. He was slimy as hell on the phone. I think he may be planning to make a pass at me.'

'You wouldn't, would you?'

'I might have, if you hadn't come up with the goods.'

'Another point for saving you from that!' said Magda. 'Jeez, Nat, I wish I had that sweet little body of yours, I could have made a fortune.'

'You have made a fortune,' Nat reminded her.

'Sure,' said Magda. 'Well, I wish I had it anyway. You expecting to dedicate it to a lifelong relationship any time soon?'

'Certainly not. It would cramp my style.'

Magda pointed a large finger at her. 'You are a certified grade one booty-waggling, dick-snagging harlot and I love you for it. Speaking of making passes, you know, I've got to be more fun than Grey Tony.'

Nat saw that Magda was blushing – a splendid and magnanimous blush, like a fanfare played on a giant trumpet.

'Shame on you, Magda Podolski, hitting on a defenceless Ukrainian girl so far from home,' she said.

'OK, I'll park that one. So, Grey Tony Schliemann: what's the plan?'

* * *

James snapped awake and felt the night stretching away like a dark wasteland at his back. Somewhere in that wasteland a man was kneeling while another cut the flesh from his shoulders. He sat up quickly to dispel the memory, and the blood throbbed behind his eyes.

Salif and Younes visited three times during the day: when he heard the scratch of the key in the lock, James noted the relative positions of the strip of light from the door and the square of light from the window, so he'd have some sense of the time. Already it was clear they were creatures of routine: three meals, each with its prescription of ibuprofen, penicillin and diazepam; then, just as the rhombus of fading yellow reached half way up the wall above his mattress, they arrived to escort him to Nazli's den.

'You got the toothbrush?'

James nodded. It had come with lunch – a well-used implement you would not readily put in your mouth, but a toothbrush nonetheless.

'Now I'd like toothpaste. And a book.'

Nazli flicked at his lock of hair, then reached for his orange soda.

'What is the block where I'm held actually for?'

'What should I tell you – it's just a guest wing.'

'A guest wing? Like a motel, you mean. With razor wire. And no traffic. Though in fact three trucks came and went last night. Delivering the weekly shop, I suppose?'

'Shall we get on?' said Nazli.

James had decided not to pursue the pretence that the IPD400 didn't work – there were better ways of delaying their progress, and he could easily convince Nazli that he was co-operating without actually doing anything of the kind. There were dangerous men at the compound, but the foppish tech sitting opposite was not one of them. In fact, James thought Nazli's prospects of coming through this ordeal unscathed were not much better than his own. The longer they tinkered, the better for both of them.

He removed a side panel and pointed out three rows of tiny switches attached to the rack of circuit boards. There were twenty-seven in all: until you flipped the right combination, the IPD400 wouldn't start up cleanly, but entered a continuous boot sequence. It was a crude but effective device because it looked like a software glitch: in James's experience, software techs regarded meddling with a computer's innards as a kind of low-grade sorcery.

'How long do you think it would have taken you to find that?'

There was no answer, but Nazli recorded the key in his notebook – it could be re-set in a matter of seconds, but he didn't need to know that. James booted up and told him to look away while he entered the password.

'You'll have to give it to me some time,' Nazli complained.

James thought not. The IPD400, anyway, had a double lock: enter the first half of the password and it would let you in, but most of the critical code would be disabled and the system would fail to penetrate even the puniest defences.

'Have a look around, get to know the OS and file structures. It's cut-down Red Hat, as lean as I could make it. There's a list of commands here – they'll give you a good idea of what it can do. I'll work on the Sun server – using IP-over-satellite is going to be a problem for us and I have a few ideas.'

The Sun was running a newish Solaris release with various cumbersome (and to James's mind pointless) genuflections towards a Mac-style interface. The account set up for him did not grant access to the internet – no doubt Rakesh Nazli thought that rendered it secure. He was wrong. James found and launched a copy of Emacs, a venerable and more or less ubiquitous text editor that, in the right hands, could flip every switch in the capacious conjuror's holdall that is the Solaris operating system. He turned echo off, so the screen didn't display his keystrokes, then started to type C code from memory. He found a standard compiler, instructed it to make an executable, and waited for the report. There were several errors, and he had to turn echo back on to find and correct them.

'If I run *Initiate manual trace*,' asked Nazli, 'will it then merge the results with data from auto-traces on the same address?'

'No,' said James, and explained why, simultaneously checking that his program executed correctly. It was a naughty piece of work, a keystroke logger he'd written himself: every touch on the keyboard would now be recorded until an escape sequence was entered. However, to complete the job, he needed to get the operating system to start the program before the login page, so it could capture passwords. Only a sysadmin could perform that function, so James wrote a script that, when Nazli next logged in with sysadmin privileges, would present him with a dialog box which announced: POSSIBLE DATA CORRUPTION AT SECTOR 4222000.987.9800 – REPAIR OR CONTINUE? Unless Nazli was feeling especially paranoid, he would click REPAIR. Upon which, the keystroke logger would be incorporated into the Sun server's boot routine. A few seconds later, Nazli would see a messagebox telling him: THE DATA WAS SUCCESSFULLY RECOVERED. PLEASE LOG OUT TO COMPLETE THE REPAIR. What that actually meant was: YOU JUST INSTALLED A SPY ON YOUR SERVER. NOW LOG IN AGAIN SO I CAN CAPTURE YOUR PASSWORD.

James exorcised the Sun of the evidence of what he'd been up to. The script was a weak link, but it couldn't be helped. He looked around him. On a shelf below the ranks of monitors was a pile of coiled ethernet cables. He stretched out his leg and found that he could hook them with his foot and pull them closer. When he had them almost below his chair, he said: 'Can you get the temperature down? I don't feel well and it's like a furnace in here.'

Nazli got up and crossed to the window. James picked up the cables and tucked them into his waistband. The air conditioning unit started up. It sounded like a handful of bolts in a washing machine.

'You'd think that whoever can spend a hundred grand on DP kit could afford a decent air conditioner,' James said disagreeably. 'I feel sick. I need to lie down.'

He stood up, then doubled over the coiled cables at his waist and groaned. Salif was summoned and James swayed through the door, giving a fair imitation of a man about to be sick. His guards wasted no time getting him back to the guest wing, as Nazli called it. As they crossed the compound, James surreptitiously inspected the black plastic cowlings perched like a row of hunched ravens on the roof.

* * *

Nikolai Kocharian was greeting his two favoured lieutenants at Marrakech airport. Mikhail was a man to whom the word *squat* did no justice – he looked like a cartoon version of his boss. His youth had been spent in state gyms in the company of weightlifters who were at least a rank better than him at the only thing he was good at. He wasn't exactly bitter about it, but he knew that when people looked at him they saw a low-built man with thighs of improbable girth, and he would have liked the consolation of being able to tell them, if the opportunity arose, that he had a clutch of Olympic weightlifting medals to his name.

Relative to Mikhail, Anton was tall, even elegant; but the effect was spoiled by his small black eyes and the grimace that played at the corners of his mouth. He was the fruit of a liaison between his Ukrainian mother and a Scottish production-line engineer who was working on contract at the Kamaz commercial vehicles plant in Kiev, where Nikolai and Natalya's stepfather was also employed. Anton's errant father had enough Presbyterian severity in his soul to prompt him to atone for his fling by paying for Anton to read Business Studies at Dundee University. Anton had subsequently put his business skills to work by producing and starring in a series of pornographic movies called *Bitches of the East*, and the knowledge that he was, demonstrably, a stud still made itself evident in the come-and-get-me-girls poses he struck whenever on public display.

Nikolai had told them that their trip to Morocco was a holiday, so they had dressed accordingly: Mikhail wore a scarlet CSKA Sofia football sports shirt that he had tucked into his black tracksuit bottoms in order to hide the fact that it would otherwise have hung to his knees; Anton sported cream chinos and an orange short-sleeved shirt with 'Let's Play!' emblazoned at a jazzy angle across the back. Mikhail carried a Nike sports grip, while Anton had acquired a counterfeit Louis Vuitton wheeled suitcase.

'Hello, Boss,' Anton said. 'We got here.'

Mikhail agreed by means of the quiet grunt that constituted the larger part of his vocabulary.

'Where the fuck did you get that suitcase,' Nikolai said, 'you look like a poof.'

'Louis Vuitton,' said Anton. He pronounced it carefully, *voo-it-on*.

'Do yourself a favour. Give it to the next shirtlifter who comes chasing after your skinny butt, huh?'

Mikhail chuckled, a surprisingly melodious sound, while Anton's grimace blossomed into a full-blown scowl. Nikolai slapped him on the back and led them to the taxi rank. As they drove into Marrakech, Nikolai recognised in Anton's demeanour the same mingled alarm and disgust he had felt the previous Friday on the journey into town with his sister, and it pleased him now to be able to adopt her role of cosmopolitan traveller, at ease in a thousand exotic destinations.

'You give money to the beggars here, it's normal,' he informed them.

Mikhail frowned. This was a side of his boss he hadn't seen before.

'It's fucking hot,' he observed.

'Of course it's fucking hot,' said Anton, 'we're in fucking Africa. What's the deal, Boss?'

Nikolai tapped his nose conspiratorially and pointed at the taxi driver. Anton shrugged and looked out of the window. Mikhail glowered at the driver until eventually the man looked over his shoulder. 'You have beautiful holiday in Marrakech, sir!'

Mikhail maintained his glare for a few seconds, then turned to the window and folded his arms in a meaningful way.

'You want some nice girls, boss?' the driver asked. 'I fix you very nice girls.'

'Could be— ' said Anton.

'No, we don't,' Nikolai interrupted.

'Maybe you like some boys. Real pretty boys in Marrakech, boss, look just like girls!'

'The fuck he saying?' Mikhail demanded.

'Forget it,' said Nikolai. He was thinking that maybe he shouldn't have invited these two out to Marrakech. Anton was already thinking of his dick, and when Mikhail folded his arms like that it was generally to stop himself throwing a punch.

They arrived at the Holiday Inn, where Nat had booked them a room – explaining to Nikolai that she didn't think the Riad was right for a pair of migrants from the Kiev underworld.

'Get yourselves smartened up and meet me in reception at nine-thirty,' Nikolai told them. 'We're going to the casino – there's a man who hangs around there. I need to check him out.'

*   *   *

Two hours after nightfall, James took the screwdriver he had purloined from Nazli's desk into the shower room and inspected the vent in the ceiling: a slatted plastic plate with slotted bolt-heads set a few inches in from each corner. The bolts would fasten to the black plastic cowling above, so that the two parts clamped the flat roof: undo them, and you could remove the lower plate and push the cowling aside, leaving a hole that should be wide enough to climb through. Unfortunately, he couldn't reach them. The shower room was just a few feet across, though. Climbers shimmied up narrow rock-funnels just by bracing themselves against the walls. He tried it. Maintaining the starting position was easy; moving up, less so. After five minutes' uncertain effort, he was no more than three feet off the ground. He felt ridiculous, huffing and grunting from his lowly perch. Sam would have told him that he should *run* up the wall, using the balance and energy of his chi to transform forward into vertical momentum at the point where floor became wall – no doubt informing him that only a fool would consider *trudging* up as he seemed bent on doing. Thinking of Sam's indignation brought a spasm of laughter to his stomach, and he lost his grip and fell to the concrete floor.

Five minutes later he was looking down with a certain sense of satisfaction. He wasn't going to race anyone up the north face of the Eiger, but he was learning the knack. He anchored himself with his feet, then located the screwdriver in the slot of one of the screw-heads. The blade was too small and the bolts tightly fastened – he got two of them out, but the others wouldn't budge. He reached up, forced two fingers between the slats of the vent and pulled. The plastic broke with a loud snap. Too loud. One of the dogs barked. He climbed down, went to the window and watched the dog circle and settle, then went back to the vent.

He fiddled with the stubborn bolts for half an hour, then slid down to the floor, furious at being balked in this stupid way, like some cack-handed home improver defeated by a bit of awkward plumbing. He forced himself to do a t'ai chi form, then sat and thought. There was no way he could break though the vent without setting off the dogs. OK then, set them off.

He stripped and threw his clothes on the mattress, hid the screwdriver in the toilet and went back up the wall. He anchored himself and gripped the vent on either side, then swung out. His weight ripped the plastic vent from the ceiling and James crashed to the floor in a shower of concrete chips, with the vent wrapped around his fingers.

The dogs went berserk, their howls and barks ripping through the silence. James stuffed the vent under his mattress and banged hard on the door. He kept banging until he heard his guards arrive, then leaned against the wall, rolling his head from side to side as the dogs roared beneath his window.

'Let me go!' James shrieked. He barked in demented imitation of the dogs. He raised his voice a pitch and screamed: 'Let me go you bastards!'

The older one, Salif, wrestled James onto the mattress while his partner hovered, AK47 at the ready. Salif cuffed him open-handed across the top of the head. James set up a low whimper and curled into the foetal position. A gratified expression came over the younger guard's face.

'Put on clothes, dirty pig!'

Salif gestured at the clothes, but James only stared at him wide-eyed. Behind the disgruntled guard, James saw a puff of dust wafting from the shower room. *If he looks in there, he'll find debris all over the floor.*

'Let me go, you shits!' he yelled again, and the dogs responded in kind. Then he turned onto his back, took hold of his penis and began to masturbate.

Younes sniggered. Salif couldn't leave quickly enough. 'Dirty hamada!' he snapped as he slammed the door. James heard Younes yammering excitedly – *Did you see that ramzi with his zep out? He fancies you for sure, Salif!* – heard Salif's furious response, heard their footsteps as they walked back to the guardroom.

* * *

He waited for an hour, then dressed and went back up the shower-room wall. He eased up the two remaining bolts until they were clear of the ceiling, then slowly pushed the cowling aside. He went back down and collected the broken vent and the debris from the floor of the shower room. The top end of the bolts was latched, he noticed, with a small steel projection you swung in place over the inner rim of the cowl to clamp it in place. Probably made it easier to fit – certainly made it easier to remove. He wrapped everything in his T-shirt and deposited the evidence of his night's work on the roof.

He levered himself half way up through the narrow opening and checked the guards at the main gate. They had their backs to him – and their postures suggested they were asleep. A generator growled and stammered from somewhere behind the barracks. As for the dogs, noise might disturb them, but they were used to his scent by now.

He pushed himself up the rest of the way and lay down on the roof. A breath of cool air caressed his shoulders and he shivered. The sky was pitch black and studded with stars to every horizon. He allowed himself to savour this moment of triumph, then started to plot lines of escape, over the dog run to the razor wire and across the dark areas of the compound to the perimeter fence. There were lights strung around the barracks and the warehouse, but the administration block was illuminated only by an iron lantern that cast a baleful yellow halo over the double doors beneath the flag. The rest of the building was in darkness, a black void excised from the glittering sky.

What was this place, with its excellent cook and mannered little doctor, its cohort of guards and their black-capped commander, its unlimited supply of white plastic patio chairs? Nazli, Mansour…

And what about the dignified old officer who had brought the beheading to a merciful close? None of it made any sense. But one thing was sure: he was not going to be set free at the end of his stay with a holdall full of cash and a goatskin of water to tide him on his way, whatever Nazli believed.

He was about to go back down and re-fit the broken vent when he heard footsteps. A light came on in the enclosed yard behind him. He pulled himself towards the edge of the roof until he could see over: Mansour, wearing his *bisht* and a shemagh. He strode towards the centre of the yard, stopped and gazed up at the sky. He threw up his arms in a gesture of theatrical exultation and started to mutter some incantation. Then he seemed to change his mind, and went and unlocked the door to a room in the south-east corner of the yard.

Not good enough for a berth in the barracks, thought James, feeling a grim pleasure at the discovery that the inept executioner was housed here in the guest wing, with nothing but a cheap wooden door to protect him.

Chapter Seven

When James turned up for his session with Nazli the next evening, his host showed no signs of knowing that the Sun server had been hacked. James told him to carry on familiarising himself with the IPD400's operating parameters, then logged in to the Sun using the access-restricted account Nazli had set up for him. As soon as Nazli turned his attention to the IPD400, James swivelled the Sun monitor aside so his fellow tech wouldn't see the screen if he glanced up. That done, he launched his keystroke logger – and there was Nazli's sysadmin password, neatly trapped. *khwar1zmi*. Interesting choice, thought James. A ninth-century Persian mathematician, populariser of the decimal system, whose name had been adapted to form the word *algorithm*. He logged out of his low-level account and re-logged in to Nazli's, then created a new account called sysadmin_old. It wouldn't arouse suspicion – computers are littered with file-names suffixed with '_old', geeks having a morbid fear of deleting things that may turn out to be better than their replacements.

'I can't get these commands to execute,' Nazli said.

James was beginning to find his companion's whines and grumbles unendurable. Apparently Nazli didn't like working on his own; and it was becoming increasingly obvious that his knowledge of the techniques in which James specialised was not profound. James stood and looked over his shoulder.

'You can't tell the system to sidestep a procedure and then wait for its outcome.'

'Show me.'

James did so, then returned to the Sun and started to browse the vast collection of logfiles to which the sysadmin account gave him access. He soon found something that interested him: a cache of files with a CDElog suffix. Anonymous enough, unless you happened to know that they were put there by a piece of software called Centuries Deep.

Centuries Deep was a so-called 'lean-profile' encrypted communications package, used mainly by multinational corporations (and, to their shame, Her Majesty's SIS) for sending sensitive data across a multi-site network. 'Lean profile' was a joke. It was a monster of a program that muscled itself self-importantly to the front of every resource queue like a nightclub bouncer in need of a toilet. It was also fiendishly complex to install, demanding decisions on every aspect of its operation but wording them so incomprehensibly that *Select default* was the invariable choice for any technician wanting to complete the job before taking retirement. But the default settings logged all communications sent and received by the system, turning a Centuries Deep installation into a comprehensive and wholly pregnable repository of so-called 'secure' information. The fact that he'd been able to install a keystroke logger on a CDE-protected machine was further testament to its general shoddiness.

A loud sigh made him jump. Nazli had tipped back his chair and was staring at him thoughtfully.

'I'm comparing the configs with the new settings,' he said. 'It makes sense to use the XML.'

You approve, James thought. *What an honour.*

'Any luck your end?'

'There's a low-level conflict, and the workaround's not pretty.'

'We should look at it together, see if I can bring some fresh thinking to bear.'

MIT, James thought. Nowhere else do they teach arrogance to such an advanced level.

'I must have the password for Little Sister.' Nazli's voice came out unnaturally loud and toneless.

'No.'

Nazli reddened and started to go through his repertoire of tics, concluding with a soothing cup of orange soda.

'I have to show progress. I can't even turn it on,' he said, the familiar griping tone returning to his voice.

'Are they threatening you?'

'No, not at all.'

James thought that was a lie. 'Tell them to wait. Get technical.'

It was an unwelcome development, but James was impatient to return to the CDE logfiles: finding them was like being reunited with an infuriating classmate and realising that everyone has their purpose in life. Centuries Deep was probably logging every single item of communication that went in or out of the compound. He started to copy the logfiles to a server belonging to the Pixelite Design Company in Mexico City on which – amidst the terabytes of rejected drafts of designs for soft drinks cans and pizza leaflets – he'd secured for himself anonymous access to a couple of gigabytes of storage space. The stream of bits stampeded up to the rooftop satellite dish, but there was so much data James didn't think the process would complete before the guards arrived to take him back to his room. To cover for that, he knocked up a script that would carry on the good work for twenty minutes at 5.00 a.m. every weekday morning for the next five days.

He checked on Nazli: jiggling his knee and copying something into his notebook – good for a few more minutes. James opened a random selection of the CDE logfiles:

[BEGIN] CONFIRM RECEIPT OF CONSIGNMENT 4500HLE98097
DATED 03.09 DELIVERED 05:40, HANDOVER POINT B. [END]

[BEGIN] UNABLE TO SUPPLY ITEM 89008. SUBSTITUTE 89016-B
IDENTICAL MODEL WITH IMPROVED SIGHTS. YOUR ACCEPTANCE
ASSUMED UNLESS WE HEAR BY 00:00 TONIGHT. [END]

[BEGIN] REF ANEMONE, NO SIGNIFICANT ACTIVITY TO REPORT.
[END]

Most of the messages implied a commercial organisation of some
kind – the last thing he had expected. The phrase 'improved sights'
was suggestive of the arms trade. He thought of the military-
industrial corporates whose expensively groomed executives took
out consultancy contracts with him and Vanic, his partner at
Imperial College: such organisations were perfectly indifferent
to strictures of ethics and the law where a chance to enlarge their
already swollen fortunes was at stake, but their skulduggery was
the kind usually fronted by lawyers and accountants. It was surely
absurd to believe that a BA or a Lockheed might have arranged the
abduction of an eminent British scientist. And what was Anemone?
A stubborn customer? A service that wasn't working? James checked
more messages but found only a morass of cryptic references to
inventory numbers and logistics: whoever used this network was
being very circumspect, especially considering they'd paid Centuries
Deep to protect them from prying eyes.

Nazli had now regressed to fidgeting like an eight-year-old
watching the classroom clock. Any minute now he'd stand up and
come over. But if this baffling desert compound was merely an outpost of a powerful organisation, it wasn't Nazli he should be worried
about. Anyone might be watching. Perhaps Centuries Deep was
logging his actions right now – it logged everything else, after all.

On impulse, James committed to memory the IP address in the header of the Anemone message. Then he exited the sysadmin account and re-logged in to the one Nazli had created for him. He was annoyed that he'd left himself so exposed, but there was nothing he could do about it now. Anyway, thought James, I'm the leading expert in the entire world on this stuff. What did they expect?

*   *   *

Holworthy's was an over-starched kind of place a block shy of the ocean on Ventura. It catered for retired Hollywood elders who had their own favourite tables, checked their coiffured little dogs at the cloakroom the way others check a hat, and fussed about which mountain in Italy their mineral water sprang from. Nat had dressed soberly, but she still looked like an orchid in a cabbage patch. Anthony R. Schliemann, Chief Procurement Officer for the Signals Intelligence Directorate of the National Security Agency, stood up from a booth at the far end and held out both arms in a gesture of welcome that looked like it had been practised many times but still resolutely refused to come off.

'Nat Kocharian, welcome to Los Angeles,' he said in an unnecessarily loud voice. 'It's been too long!'

'Hey Tony, thanks for making the time.'

'Not a problem. You came all the way over to the West Coast just to see me. I'm flattered. Set yourself down and let me order you a cocktail. The martinis here are old school, just how they should be. You need to use the bathroom? It's right over there by the bar.' He beckoned to a waiter who was already approaching their table.

'A vodka martini would be perfect,' said Nat, passing up the opportunity to dash to the loo like an agitated twelve-year-old.

'A vodka martini for the lady, with a twist, no olive, and a whiskey sour for myself. We'll be ready to order in ten minutes.'

He surveyed the restaurant from a standing position, as if reluctant to accept the diminution in his presence that would inevitably occur when he sat down. He was a tall man, and wanted everyone to know it. Nat remembered him like this in meetings, always the first to get to his feet and dominate the room, making his generally predictable points with a repertoire of movements of hands, arms and shoulders that were at once wooden and mesmerising. He had the makings of a handsome face, but the deep forehead was bland rather than sagacious, his eyes were too small, and there was an area of blank skin where the bridge of his nose should have been. True to form, he wore a tailored grey suit with a broad check over an off-white shirt and slate blue tie.

'It's easy to get sidetracked by the latest fad restaurants that start up every other day here in LA and always seem to get sensational reviews,' he told her, 'but Holworthy's stands for something different: enduring quality.'

'There's not enough of that,' said Nat.

'You're so right. Ah, here are our drinks. The martini can go here.' He directed the glass to a precise point by Nat's table setting. 'And the whiskey here. Thank you. Six or seven minutes, please. Your very good health, as they say in London.' He raised his glass so high Nat had to stretch forward to bring hers level, then laughed, a sequence of dry, repetitive exhalations that sounded like a cough.

'And yours, Tony.' Nat already felt enervated by his pedantically chivalrous manner, and was tempted to launch straight into her spiel just in order to avoid having to eat with him.

'Now, the wine I ordered earlier, by email – an oh-four Montrachet which I think will stand up to most things we might choose, though not the boeuf en daube or the venison.' He pronounced boeuf as if it had no e, *boof.* 'We can order red by the glass if you decide on one of those dishes.'

114

'I'll have the crab to start with, then the turbot.' Nat put her menu down. 'So how've you been, Tony?'

Grey Tony was reading the menu, tapping each item with a busy finger and evidently too absorbed in making mental notes to offer a reply. 'Possible, maybe too sharp for the Montrachet... ' he was telling himself. Eventually, 'There, done. The char-grilled shrimp with asparagus and saffron rice, followed by the veal escalope with white truffle sauce. Now, how are Grosvenor Systems and all who sail in her?' He pulled his carefully groomed face into a smile by way of acknowledgement of his mastery of British vernacular.

'I'm taking time off from Grosvenor. Had a few family things I needed to attend to... Anyway, after three years of single-handedly kicking that company into the twenty-first century, I needed a break.'

'Their idea or yours?'

'It was mutual,' said Nat. She leaned forward and lowered her voice. 'Can you keep a secret, Tony?'

'I should damn well think so, working for the National Security Agency for twenty years!'

'Working for the NSA is a qualification for having secrets, not keeping them,' Nat retorted.

'Ha-ha, too right.' Tony's laugh was abrupt and toneless – a signal that he'd understood the joke rather than enjoyed it. 'You always had a great sense of humour.'

'About six months ago Clive Silk started pestering me, taking me out to lunch and pouring out his lovelorn soul, then moping like a teenager when I said no. Eventually I gave in, just to keep him quiet. He's really not my type, Tony, so undistinguished. Anyway, he just got worse and worse. Eventually the chairman— '

'Sir Peter Beddoes.'

'Yes, Sir Peter. He called me in and said he knew it wasn't my fault but how would I feel about a few months off, just to let Clive pull himself together. We had a short negotiation and that was that. Silk gets time to remember that he's a married, middle-aged man with a wife and dog somewhere in Surrey, and I get a nice long holiday.'

'How will they do without you? I heard you were the only person who ever sold anything for Grosvenor.'

'Almost true— '

'Maybe they want to see if they *can* get along without you,' Tony continued, without waiting for Nat to finish. 'Yes, that would figure. It's essential for all organisations to plan the succession – hell, the Agency probably has a replacement for *me* already lined up!' he declared, as if this were evidence of succession planning at its most extreme.

They paused to give their order. Tony looked as if he wanted to seize the waiter's pad and write it out himself.

'Anyway, here I am, finding out how *I* get along without Grosvenor.'

'And the answer is?'

'Between you and me, I may not go back.'

'They're good people, on balance, I wouldn't throw them over too lightly,' Tony said with the air of a man of the world addressing a wide-eyed waif. Nat gritted her teeth.

Their first course arrived, allowing Tony to fuss over the arrangement of dishes and congratulate himself repeatedly on his choice. Twice Nat caught him eyeing her stealthily, and guessed he was trying to make up his mind whether making a pass at her was worth the risk of rejection. Their plates were cleared, the main courses served, the conversation plodded on. Having endured the sight of Tony arranging his food into a sequence of carefully planned mouthfuls and then tidying his plate with exasperating fastidiousness, Nat finally lost patience.

'Tony, do you remember that intercept device you were always asking me about, the one built by James Palatine?'

'Dr Palatine, the computer genius with the dark backstory?'

'That's right. The IPD400.'

'A prototype – and not for sale, as I recall.'

Tony's eyes had become sharp and wary, so that Nat was reminded that this dull and even faintly ridiculous man wielded one of the US government's largest capital budgets.

'I think I can get it for you.'

For a second, Nat saw confusion on Grey Tony's face, then shock. It wasn't the reaction she'd been expecting.

'You're working for Grosvenor again?'

'Interested?'

Tony shrugged, looked over his shoulder to summon a waiter. He ordered mineral water, then rearranged his place setting.

'You were saying?' he said haughtily.

'Whenever you pretend not to be interested in something I'm selling,' said Nat, 'I get a warm feeling inside. I may be able to get you the IPD400, if you want it. Or I can start brushing up on my Mandarin.'

'These technologies go stale – I guess your Dr Palatine's work may already have been superseded. As you know, we fund a very cutting edge programme at MIT.'

'So it's a no.'

'I didn't say that.'

'Nine months ago you told me that if I found a way of swinging it past the legal embargo, I could write the cheque out myself. You had some story about turning the tables on the cyber-jedis of Beijing, discouraging them from holding any more all-night parties in US government servers.'

'You couldn't take it to Beijing, of course.'

'They don't seem to think it's past its sell-by date.'

'There are rules governing the export of sensitive technology. We in Washington take breaches very seriously indeed.'

Why doesn't he just call me Silly Little Girl and have done with it, Nat thought venomously. 'Let's forget it,' she said. 'I thought I'd ask you, since you've always been such a fan of Palatine's work. What else shall we talk about?'

Having already slipped off her shoes in readiness, Nat now gave him a playful and ever-so-slightly lingering tap on the calf with the side of her bare foot. Tony gave a start and then looked sheepish. For a man his age, he really is a wimp, Nat thought. She flashed her eyes at him and waited while he composed himself under cover of a mouthful of Montrachet.

'Of course, you were right to put this to me, Natalya,' he said without looking at her.

'I thought I should.'

'The interests of the Agency must come first, I need hardly say.'

'Always. And then your interests next, followed by mine. But I'm thinking we can satisfy everyone here.'

'Given guarantees from Grosvenor that the IPD400 actually works, there might be something to discuss here, I guess. We would need exclusivity on the technology for at least ten years.'

'You won't get either. But you do want it, then?'

'The SigInt folk might be interested in acquiring an operational IPD400, assuming favourable terms. Yes, I think I can say that.'

'I'm not exactly having difficulty finding a buyer, Tony. By the time you've put the rulebook away, I'll be on a Caribbean beach.'

'We'll look at the menu,' he said, 'and they'll bring their dessert wine list also, it's quite well thought out.'

The prospect of playing the connoisseur with the wine list seemed to restore his poise. He was playing hard to get again. Of course, he was bargaining... But the objections and indifference seemed to be coming much too easily, and Nat felt uneasy.

'Now, Natalya, let me get all this clear. This device of Grosvenor's – which you appear to be hawking round with such abandon it'll likely turn up on eBay before much longer!' He laughed appreciatively at his own witticism. 'The NSA, an agency of the government of your nation's most important military ally by far, is being asked to take its place in line. So many questions occur. Why doesn't Grosvenor turn this IPD400 into a commercial product before placing it on the market? Who sells prototypes? Why am I being offered the chance to join the fun and games over dinner with you, rather than being sent the usual stack of marketing? And lastly, why do you ask me to believe you're on sabbatical from Grosvenor while plainly doing their business?'

He sat back and folded his arms. He's not going to make a pass at me, Nat realised, though not because he doesn't want to. She'd had it in mind that this could be done subtly, a mutually profitable flirtation with the menaces merely implied. It seemed not.

'Tony, I haven't been entirely straight with you.'

Grey Tony nodded approvingly.

'I'm not acting for Grosvenor but as agent for a third party. I can't tell you who, though you'll probably find out some day – as much as we like our little secrets, we don't mind turning them into gossip a year or so later.'

Tony was staring at her coldly.

'I can broker the sale of the IPD400 and I want you to be the buyer.'

'You want me to be the buyer,' Tony repeated, his flat voice animated by an ironic inflection she hadn't heard before and his small eyes opening wide in a calculated display of amazement. 'Will you give it to me now, or are you going to giftwrap it and post it for my next birthday?'

'I can have it f.o.b. Casablanca within three weeks,' she said. 'With or without ribbons. The price is thirty-five million dollars.'

'Casablanca? Thirty-five million? No, no, wait, please. Now I'm really lost. This ground-breaking system which has Grosvenor execs salivating into their afternoon tea has fallen into the clutches of some nameless third party who has it stashed in a Casablanca warehouse? Somebody has messed up big time, I'd say.'

'You don't want to know,' said Nat.

'Correction: I *do* want to know!'

'You have an opportunity to get in at the ground floor of a surveillance revolution, Tony, and you're going to pass it up because I didn't tick all the boxes for you? You know what this thing can do. What are the big chiefs going to say when your Chinese counterparts are logging into the Pentagon every morning after breakfast?'

'Maybe you can sell arms this way in Lagos or Delhi, but not here. Absolutely not,' said the NSA man, lips tight with official disapproval. 'I'll have to call London, see if any of this checks out.'

'Don't do that, Tony.'

It was an order. She was looking him right in the eye as she said it, not smiling, not flinching.

'What's going down here, Natalya?'

'You buy the IPD400 because you want it and because it will do you good with your NSA bosses. But at no time do you ask or answer any questions about where it came from or how you acquired it. Not here, not in London, not anywhere.'

Tony gaped. She didn't wait for a reply.

'You will not reveal my involvement in the deal. You bought from a broker who has to remain nameless: that's all you will ever say.'

'You seem to have forgotten that I'm a high-ranking officer of the US government,' said Grey Tony. 'I deal on my terms, or I don't deal at all.'

'Don't get pious with me, Tony. You get the IPD400 and you keep quiet about how, that's all. We can behave nicely, like friends, or I can remind you what happens to high-ranking government officers who abuse their positions for personal gain.'

He stared at her. She could almost see the shutters being pulled down.

'I don't know what you're talking about.'

'As you've being doing for the last ten years. Remember San Hui? That was my deal, Tony, I slogged at it for six months and I should have had it in the bag. It cost me lots, time, money, status – yeah, you fucked me over all right,' Nat declared, trying to work up a head of indignation. 'But I didn't understand why. How naive I was! I made some good friends in Seoul and found out. You'd been insider trading like a Wall Street regular, and San Hui were applying the squeeze. I have all the evidence I need to have you crawled over like a rotten tree trunk.'

'You duplicitous little bitch.'

'Cheer up, Tony. Remember, you're going to do what I tell you because you want the IPD400 – and this is the only way you're going to get it.'

Grey Tony's jaw muscles bulged as he struggled to maintain his composure. Nat lowered her voice. 'Hey, you know what? If you'd said, OK, Nat, let's play ball, I'd probably be sucking you off by now.'

It was too much for Grey Tony. He stood up stiffly, folded his napkin and placed it on the table. 'Your behaviour is insulting and outrageous in the extreme. I won't listen for a moment longer. Goodbye, Ms Kocharian.'

'You have twelve hours. I'm at the Marriott.'

Grey Tony stalked out. Nat called for the check. The Montrachet was $260 a bottle. She summoned a waiter.

'I'm afraid Mr Schliemann has been called away on Agency business. Can you email this check to him at his office, please? You can use the address he gave you when he ordered the wine.'

She sashayed out and walked down to the beach. An hour in Holworthy's had made her long to feel sand between her toes.

Chapter Eight

When Salif and Younes turned up the following evening, they didn't take him to Nazli's lab but to the room by the entrance to the first-floor corridor, with the building materials and trestle table and the office chairs in their plastic shrouds. One of the chairs had been unwrapped. Laid out on the table were some things he didn't want to look at. They turned him round and pushed him into the chair and behind them James saw Mansour – and another man, sitting on a chair tapping at a laptop. Small, close-cropped hair, pale skin: the one who had followed him into the building in Oran.

Two blue-overalled guards came in. Salif and Younes stepped back, and the guards were on him, a thick forearm clamped around his throat and a fist rammed into his gut. He swung the point of his elbow back hard, felt it crack a rib. The man grunted but his fore-arm only tightened. James got both heels into the groin of the guard in front of him and unleashed all the power coiled in his thighs. The guard catapulted backwards and the chair collapsed beneath him. James swung a punch over his shoulder, felt it hammer against the skull of the man who had him by the neck. He found an eye socket with his thumb and drove in deep, feeling the eyeball slide away from his thumbnail. The guard screamed and his grip slackened.

James took hold of his forearm and twisted his trunk until he felt the man's weight shift to defend himself against the throw, then snapped the back of his head into the guard's nose and ran him backwards until he slammed against the wall. He heard the whump as the air rushed from the guard's lungs, felt his body slide down behind him, saw the other guard down on all fours, retching.

'They have much to learn. And so do you.'

Beady, weasel eyes perfectly still in the pale face. Not a tremor in the hand that held the Taser. James stood helpless, panting like a dog as the barb snickered from its perch.

* * *

Back in the chair. Ankles gaffer-taped to its legs. Wrists behind his neck, roped down tight to the back of the chair. Shirt torn off. Still twitching like a toy with a dying battery. This was it. Electricity, needles, knives. Think of something. Something good.

'The Taser is a good weapon, no?'

The man with close-cropped hair was sitting in a chair beside him, inspecting his torso. Mansour stood a little way off. His eyes shone with excitement, and the perfume from his oiled beard gave a sickly sweetness to the reek of the fight that still lingered in the room.

'I cannot ask questions about IPD400,' said the man beside him. 'Nazli cannot make you answer. So I make you answer Nazli questions. I am logical, you think?'

'Etienne, isn't it?' said James, dredging the name up from his flickering memory of the fight on the landing in Oran. 'And Mansour. What's up, Mansour, you look sick.'

'You look sick,' said Mansour, 'when we finish.'

Etienne pulled the laptop across the table, opened the lid. 'See. Some things we do.'

The first frame of a video. A man's forearm strapped to a wooden table, his fist hanging over the edge, clenched so tight it was white around the joints. Etienne pressed play. The man was pleading in a language James didn't recognise. Trying to sound reasonable when really he was terrified. Hands reached into the frame and unclenched his fist. They bound his first and index fingers together with cloth tape, then the other two. The hands grasped the pairs of taped fingers, one from each side. A kitchen knife came into view and sawed the webbed skin between them. Then they tore his hand apart down to the wrist bone while their victim's screams wheezed through the laptop's speakers.

'And for the ladies.'

A woman with her mouth clamped between two steel rods, the lips protruding like fat worms. James didn't turn away fast enough to miss the scalpel darting into shot. He sat with his eyes shut while the woman's grunts and moans conjured in his head the images he could not see.

'You get off on that, Etienne? Ça te fait jouir, hein?'

Etienne ignored him. Mansour grinned.

'How happen?'

Etienne poked a finger into an area of ribcage beneath James's left armpit. Despair pooled inside him.

'Funny. Like paper!'

Like paper. Papery thin. Drawn tight over the bones. Funny. Easily torn or pierced, ha ha. *It will always lack the thickness and elasticity of normal skin*, the consultant had said. It lacked the sensation of normal skin, too. And it had memories. It remembered the day when the bullet lashed along the groove between two ribs. Ripping, scorching. It remembered the raki-sodden doctor who slapped on a cotton pad and bound it with a single length of bandage. It remembered the infection, bulging, suppurating... The damaged flesh, now thin and crinkled like the skin on cooling milk, carried a record of every day in its over-stretched cells.

Etienne had found it. He had a pair of cheap, red-handled pliers in his hand. Blue for nice things, red for nasty things. Big jaws for bad jobs. Etienne pressed the blunt iron teeth in either side of the rib.

'Let's see.'

He squeezed the handles shut, clamping the papery skin. A sigh of misery emptied James's lungs. Etienne gripped the pliers tight and pulled the flesh away from his ribs. James's head rocked back. *Now it will tear…*

'Clack clack.'

Etienne, nodding at Mansour, making a scissor shape with his free hand. James was shuddering, grinding his jaws. Mansour went to the table. Something clattered as he picked it up. Shears. Mansour tried them. The blades rasped.

'Please,' said Etienne. He pointed at the tent of skin. 'Remind Dr Palatine that he must answer the questions of Rakesh Nazli.'

The blades crunched and the pain was nothing, nothing, nothing, but the memories jolted into life like black goblins given a scrap of meat to chew, and the scrap of meat was there, dripping a little blood over the pliers' fat jaws.

* * *

The doctor came and looked at the wound.

'Just one hole? You are lucky. The most I have seen is six. They are so difficult to treat.'

Younes watched from the door. Salif had his back turned. The doctor applied a gauze soaked in something that stank like ammonia, then left.

Clamp, pull, cut. A sharp, sticky ache in his side. The grainy rasp of the sliding shear-blades sawing in his ears. He lay awake for hours, trying to get some perspective on the horrors that churned in his head, but he could find no comfort. His point of greatest vulnerability had been pounced on by men whose viciousness knew no ordinary human bounds. Men who meant to harm him. Who had harmed others. Who would harm him again.

At last he stood up and raised his arms above his head, felt the hole beneath his armpit gape. *This is not a serious wound,* he told himself, *but stick around here and the next one will be.* He went up on to the roof, collected the broken vent, and crawled slowly round until he came to the cowling above the room furthest from the guardpost. He rocked the plastic dome gently back and forth, and soon the steel latches were loose enough to swing aside, separating the cowling from the vent in the ceiling below. He lowered himself down and removed the plastic hose from the shower, took it back up and re-fitted the cowling, using the damaged vent from his shower room. It was fiddly work. He broke into two more rooms until he had three two-metre lengths of plastic hose, which he laid out on the roof above his room, along with the undamaged vent. A little pale grey light was slipping into the sky – the job had taken him most of the night. He lowered himself into the shower room, braced himself between the walls and fitted the replacement vent. He'd managed to blank out the memory of what Mansour and Etienne had done to him – but it came back to him now. He lowered himself gingerly to the floor and studied the vent. It looked lopsided. The hole in his side screamed that it didn't want to be stretched open again, but he inched back up and straightened the plastic frame. Every little detail mattered now.

Mountbatten

MOUNTBATTEN HOSPICE
SOUTHAMPTON

```
CLERK 1           REG               ID#1
SATURDAY 26 FEBRUARY 2022   12:08 012714
1    Books £1                    £1.00
1    Books £1                    £1.00
1    Media                       £1.00

                    3 No
     TOTAL                 £3.00
     £5                        £5.00
     CHANGE                    £2.00
```

Chapter Nine

Natalya Kocharian, taking her ease in her capacious bathtub at the Riad des Ombres, balanced two towers of bath foam on her knees and giggled at herself. The terracotta plaster was deliciously soft beneath her bottom. From her recumbent position deep in the tub, she could see reflected in the mirror opposite a print of an elephant placidly hoisting a laughing child onto its back. The elephant's elegantly curved trunk seemed to sway in the drifts of steamy air. She'd flown back overnight, enjoying the pleasant sleep of someone with satisfying thoughts to wake to, and arrived in Marrakech at nine. The way she'd handled Grey Tony had been brilliant: lured, hooked, pinned in forty-eight hours flat – no room to wriggle and no chance to bite back. He'd called her precisely four minutes before the deadline she'd set, his voice about as friendly as a lump of wet rock.

'I'll buy. Eighteen million. You'll deal with Pete Alakhine in Rabat from here on. Provide him with co-ordinates for a US bank account. The transfer will be made when the goods have been authenticated by my team in Washington. This is the final conversation we will have on this or any other subject. It ends here, or your life is going to take a turn for the worse. I hope I make myself clear.'

'The price is thirty-five million US, Tony, and the account is in a location of my choosing. Please don't threaten me when you call back,' said Natalya. She put the phone down.

He rang back two minutes later. This time, there was a whiney edge to his voice. 'Don't dick me around, Kocharian. This junk you're selling is worth nothing to me. I'll go to twenty-two. This had better be on the level, or— '

'This isn't a negotiation, Tony. What you're buying can't be priced. I'll do thirty-three.'

'Thirty-three million!' Tony hissed. 'I can't just shuffle that kind of money through accounts like I'm buying a pack of light bulbs.'

'You buy light bulbs, too? I didn't know,' said Natalya.

'Fuck you. I'm not negotiating, I'm telling you, this is the absolute limit of what is possible. You want to practise your bargaining skills, go sell dead chickens in the souk.'

'OK, I'll take thirty-one, but it has to be up front. I'm not handing you a duzy – why would I when I have the real thing?'

'You say, but since I don't trust you further than I can spit— '

'You're in a foul mood, considering what a favour I'm doing you.'

There was a pause. Nat stayed silent.

'Twenty-six,' he said. 'I don't know how the fuck I can say that, but twenty-six. That's it.'

'Thirty. Up front. No verification.'

'Whatever.'

'Give me Alakhine's cell.'

Grey Tony reeled off a number.

'I'll tell him when the IPD400 is ready to ship, then you can transfer the funds. Congratulations, Tony. What a coup to have the IPD400 sitting in the labs at Langley. Stay cool and practise the line you'll spin when your NSA cronies ask how you got hold of it.'

'You have some fucking nerve.'

'Goodbye, Tony. I won't call again unless I have to.'

'Just don't.'

He'd hung up. 'Thirty million US dollars,' Natalya said out loud, arranging blobs of foam on her nipples. She reckoned she could get the thing back for twenty-six, including enough of a cut for Zender to feel he'd bested her. That left four million dollars for her. Oh boy. There was an awful lot still to do, but *Oh boy!*

In order to keep her optimism in check, she toyed with the idea that this had all gone too easily. Grey Tony hadn't exactly bitten her hand off, until she'd threatened him with Magda's file; and without his eagerness to acquire the IPD400, the deal looked a bit less like business and a bit more like crime. Still, Nat shared with her brother a view that the distinction between the two was a nicety – and this wasn't so different from ploys she'd used before, in the normal course of the arms trade. Besides, everyone would benefit from the deal – apart from Grosvenor, and they didn't deserve to.

She decided the blobs of foam made her look like a cabaret dancer preparing to emerge from a giant birthday cake. An unusually rich cabaret dancer. She giggled again.

Grosvenor... If she didn't keep up the flow of communication, they'd get restive. She'd emailed Sir Peter daily from LA, and had replies from Clive Silk as well. The tone was admonitory and impatient, but she knew that if she told them Zender was stalling, they wouldn't be able to call her bluff. Nor would they be much surprised. She picked her cellphone out of the soap dish and dialled Sir Peter's private line.

'He's not answering my calls,' she said, splashing warm water over her breasts and watching the turrets of foam slide down her belly. 'To be honest with you, I'm not sure he's still in Marrakech.'

'Keep trying, Natalya. What was that noise?'

'Oh, sorry, I'm sitting next to a fountain. Clive's putting so much pressure on me, Peter... I'm just not used to this sort of thing.'

What am I going to do if Zender says no deal and refuses to even talk about it?'

'I'll talk to Clive. I do appreciate that this isn't easy for you.'

She allowed the Grosvenor chairman to carry on in this reassuring vein while she entertained herself by creating fountain-like noises in her bathwater. Eventually he ended the call and she got out and dried herself.

The only thing now spoiling her pleasure was that she couldn't get hold of Nikolai. It was unlike him not to be around on the day of her return to Marrakech. He wasn't answering his phone, nor had he picked up the messages she'd left at reception; and no one at the Riad could remember seeing him since Tuesday afternoon, when apparently he'd ordered a taxi for the airport – to pick up his superfluous sidekicks and take them to the Holiday Inn, she supposed.

She went down to reception and got a list of hospitals and medical centres, phoned them one by one. None of them had taken in a Monsieur Kocharian, nor any anonymous East European gentlemen who matched his description.

* * *

James heard a commotion. He got to the gap above the door and saw a big man staggering around in the yard bellowing in what sounded like Russian. His face was a swollen mess and there was a sideways kink in his left knee. New guest, same warm welcome, thought James, feeling a trickle of fluid from the stinging hole in his side. His two guards stood either side of the wounded man, watching him warily. Salif grabbed the Kalashnikov and shouted at Younes, who ran off towards the passage that led out of the yard. The Russian made a hopeless lunge for the rifle, then thumped down on his backside, legs stretched out in front of him, panting hoarsely.

'You shit-eating motherfucker! I'll tear your fucking face off!'

'Get back,' Salif ordered unnecessarily. 'Get back now.'

Three of the blue-overalled compound guards arrived, the doctor trotting along behind them. The first of them ran in and swung a heavy kick into the base of the fallen man's spine. He arched backwards, trying in vain to catch hold of the man's leg. A second guard booted him in the stomach and he curled like a salted slug.

'Stop!'

The guards fell back to watch as the doctor knelt beside the prone figure and unzipped a black cloth case.

'Hold out his arm.'

They pulled the man onto his stomach. One of them pressed his head to the dirt and knelt between his shoulder blades; a second grabbed him by the wrist. The doctor was drawing fluid from a phial into a steel syringe. She slapped the skin sharply to bring up a vein before easing the needle under his skin and driving the plunger down. The man's straining torso slumped.

'You useless old woman.' The third guard spat at Salif. 'Get the key to another room.' He made clucking noises and flapped his arms at Salif, who eyed him sullenly and sent Younes on the errand instead.

They dragged the Russian into the room next to the one with the broken door. There was a brief confabulation outside. 'I advise you not to hit him again – he was brought here for a reason,' the doctor said.

She turned and marched briskly off across the yard, her incongruous white coat flapping. One of the guards grabbed his crotch and ground his hips in her direction. But the diminutive figure had already turned down the passage leading back to the compound.

*   *   *

Nat went to the Holiday Inn and there was Anton in the lobby, lounging on a grubby orange sofa and leering from beneath the fronds of a plastic palm at a group of German women gathered round a tour rep.

'Ms Kocharian, I was hoping you'd drop by.'

He was dressed in cream chinos, white deck shoes with brown tassels and a purple check shirt with the cuffs turned back. Nat ignored his outstretched hand and studied him with all the disdain he so obviously deserved.

'Where is my brother?'

'We don't know. Must have gone somewhere— '

'Gone where? I left him here, in Marrakech.'

'We went to the casino on Tuesday night. He told us to look out for a fat guy. I took the main bar and Nikolai covered the rest. I didn't see him for an hour, then there was some trouble and a lot of people left. I went and looked for him, but— '

'Where was Mikhail?'

'Keeping watch outside. He didn't see Nikolai come out.'

'Did you see the fat guy?' Nat asked uneasily.

'Couldn't miss him.' Anton paused, then leaned towards her and smirked. 'We think maybe Nikolai got lucky. With a girl,' he added.

Getting lucky with a girl wouldn't stop Nikolai sending me a text, Nat thought. 'What was the trouble at the casino?'

'I don't know, a fight or something. I didn't see.'

'Stop saying that for fuck's sake. Go to the casino and find out exactly what happened while you were lurking in the bar. Use those famous good looks to soften up one of the hostesses. I'll come and find you later.'

She sat down on the sofa vacated by Anton and called Claude Zender.

'Natalya, you are back in Marrakech, reinstated by those oafs at Grosvenor and here to peddle their trinkets once more?'

'No chance, they're still wetting themselves over the EUCs. Heard anything from your client?'

'I hear from all of them more or less constantly, a procession of grumbles as would snap the sweetest temper clean in two.'

'I mean about the IPD400?'

'Oh, that. *Rien du tout.* You will have to be patient, my dear Natalya.'

'Not my style – how long, do you think?'

'Mam'selle Patience does not ask such things, she folds her hands in her lap and emits a modest sigh. But in recognition of your tremendous zest for the deal, I will do a little gentle persuading.'

'Failing that, threats of violence can work,' said Nat, feeling suddenly oppressed by the throng of tourists traipsing round the lobby. 'Claude, there's something else I need to ask you.'

'You wish to re-purchase a further consignment of Grosvenor write-offs?'

'I came here with my brother, Nikolai – he's always wanted to see Marrakech and I needed some company. He was at the casino on Tuesday night and now I can't get hold of him. I heard there was some kind of trouble. I'm sure he had nothing to do with it, but I'm worried.'

'Good gracious, Natalya, how very sisterly of you. Quite charming!'

'Yes, all right, Claude – but have you heard anything?'

'I am sure you flatter me by supposing I see much of what goes on in this city. You know how I shun the limelight.'

'You weren't at the casino?'

'Let me make one or two enquiries.'

'Thanks, Claude, it's kind of you.'

'I can think of many enchanting ways in which the favour can be returned. Shall I find you at the Riad this evening? At seven o'clock?'

* * *

133

Later in the day James saw them bearing the unconscious Russian away on a stretcher. He couldn't stop himself hoping that Mansour and Etienne would now turn their pliers and shears on their new captive. *The most I have seen is six*, the doctor had reported, as if counting doughnuts in a bag.

Salif and Younes turned up. Younes was excited, and there was extra force behind his prods and shoves – as if the events of the day had awoken an interest in discovering how much damage the human body can endure. After a minute of telling him to leave the prisoner alone, Salif rounded on his fellow guard with a ferocity James hadn't seen before. Younes fell back, chastened. James caught Salif's eye, and the older man gave a shrug that seemed like an apology. That was odd. Salif's mood was usually bitter, and James had assumed it was directed at him. But perhaps Salif just didn't like what he was being asked to do. It was obvious that there was bad blood between him and the blue-overalled guards: when they'd arrived to deal with the wounded Russian in the yard, they'd treated him with contempt. Salif was not the kind to forget an insult.

He arrived at Nazli's den to find his host coiling back his hair and pinching his nose with more than usual vigour.

'I've been looking through the settings files and these notes— '

'You told your friends Mansour and Etienne that I refused to give you the password,' said James. He spoke quietly, in order to suppress the cold rage inside him.

'No, no… I simply said— '

'They are cutting lumps out of me with sheep shears.'

A film of sweat started from Nazli's face. *He's finally beginning to understand how much danger he's in*, thought James.

'We'll do a trial run. I need you to write a piece of code while I finish the satellite-over-IP configs.'

He gave Nazli a few curt instructions, then sat down at the Sun, logged into his administrator account and found the software that managed the satellite dish on the roof. He looked through the settings tab until he found its co-ordinates, then launched a utility that would locate them on a map. The top quarter appeared, then the rest inched down the screen. There wasn't much to look at: a featureless landscape crossed by a single road. He zoomed out until letters appeared: FREE ZONE. Perfect, he thought, I'll tell the guards at the gate. Nearest towns: Bir Lehlou to the east, and a larger place to the west, Smara. He'd never heard of either of them. He reduced the scale and more words appeared. WESTERN SAHARA. Now it was starting to make sense. A desperate place, from what he could recall, passed around colonial rulers like a desirable trinket, and eventually bequeathed to Morocco by General Franco on his deathbed. There was a guerrilla army here, fighting for independence. He scoured his memory for the name… Polisario. Their cause had been championed by US Secretary of State James Baker for a heady year or two; but eventually they'd been handed over to the care of the United Nations and left to fester in a swamp of international apathy.

So what did he have to do with all this?

James reduced the scale again. Now there were borders: Mauritania to the south and east, Algeria to the north-east, then Morocco; and finally, maybe a hundred and fifty miles to the west, the Atlantic coast. For a moment he felt dislocated, unable to reconcile this pinprick on the map he was staring at with the ugly compound and its ill-assorted residents. Needless to say, it wasn't marked. He shut the map and logged out.

'Finish that later,' he told Nazli, powering up the IPD400. 'We'll run a test. Something soft – a university intranet. You drive.'

Nazli navigated to the login page for staff at Princeton, then brought up the command line console and keyed in the command *Unlock*.

'Leave out the -r and -f switches – they'll slow it down. We don't have to be completely invisible.'

Nazli re-keyed the command and they waited.

ANALYSING TRAFFIC...

AWAITING CARRIERS...

FOUND 4 CARRIERS, ANALYSING PACKETS...

RUNNING TRACE...

James felt more intrigued by the test than he wanted Nazli to see. It should be impossible to hack even a low-security network over a satellite connection. If it worked, the prototype was much more robust than he'd expected.

FAILED 3 TRACES...

FOUND 2 CARRIERS, ANALYSING PACKETS...

They watched Little Sister snap away at the gateway to the intranet, unable to make the decisive intercept.

'Too much latency,' said James. 'Try somewhere else – we used museums when we first got it running.'

Nazli went to the Metropolitan in New York and sent Little Sister after its new prey. They watched the same sequence of procedures: carriers found and traces started, but no break-in.

'It doesn't get any easier than this,' said James.

TRACE COMPLETE, DECRYPTING...

'There,' said Nazli. 'It's latched on.'

ADAPTING CARRIER...

The main screen changed: 'Welcome to the Metropolitan Museum of Art Staff Intranet'.

UNLOCK COMPLETE.

'Result!' said Nazli. 'That is so impressive, Dr Palatine.'

'What, hacking the Met? A twelve-year-old could do it. I'd keep this out of your progress report. We'll try another site.'

He leaned over Nazli's shoulder and keyed in the IP address that he'd found in the Centuries Deep logfiles the previous day, in the header of the message referring to the mysterious Anemone. The cursor blinked for a few seconds, then a dialog box appeared:

UNABLE TO INITIATE TRACE. ERROR 16017.

That was wrong. He must have mis-keyed. He repeated the command.

UNABLE TO INITIATE TRACE. ERROR 16017.

'What does the 16017 error signify?'

What does the 16017 error signify? The words rattled in his head. He was too stunned to answer.

'James?'

'A flaw in the heuristics,' he muttered. 'I thought I'd got rid of it.'

'How often do you see it?' Nazli leaned forward eagerly, as if sensing an opportunity to earn his spurs by hunting down a bug in the IPD400 codebase.

'Too often.'

'Perhaps we can replicate it on another site?'

'I don't think we'll see it again,' said James, feeling as if he were shaking himself out of a dream. 'I need to show you how to integrate updated network stats. We'll start on that tomorrow.'

Nazli was fiddling with a personal attack alarm he'd found in his desk. *He's been given it in case I turn nasty*, thought James. *Which I might.*

'Put that thing down or you'll set it off.'

'You seem upset by this error. I guess it's more significant than you're saying.'

* * *

By seven o'clock the heat of the day had unwound. The courtyard of the Riad des Ombres was tranquil: the fountain of marble lilies puttered, and the man smoking a cigar in the shelter of the loggia opposite Natalya rustled his copy of *Le Monde*. The boy serving the tables padded round in well-worn leather slippers, a cream linen kaftan and woven cotton cap, lighting citronella candles with a box of wooden spills. The man with *Le Monde* had him hold a spill to his cigar, while he sucked and blew. Grandiose puffs of smoke issued from the side of his mouth, turning steely blue as they drifted up into the sunlight slinking over the stone balustrade three storeys above. Nat ordered a gin and tonic and it came with little silver dishes of pistachio nuts and green olives. She found herself stroking the mahogany arm of the sofa, just to feel in her palms the luxurious warmth it had absorbed from the silky, burnished air.

He's not a teenager on his first all-nighter, she told herself. *If anyone can look after himself, it's Nikolai Kocharian.*

He'd looked after her, too. He'd bought her books with the money he earned bullying people on behalf of the local gang chief – shopkeepers, debtors, anyone who got mixed up with them one way or another, which was difficult to avoid if you had any ambitions in the new world of opportunity that was ushered in by that old soak Yeltsin lurching around on top of his tank one day in Moscow. And he'd told their stepfather Dmitri that he wasn't to make a skivvy of her, or to keep her out of school so she could go into town to queue for eggs or tins of fish, or to slap her if she didn't clean up the mess he made when he got drunk. Aged seventeen, when Nat was ten and soon after Dmitri had moved in, Nikolai caught him by the throat, rammed him up against the wall of their living room so that her mother's collection of national monuments rendered in badly glazed porcelain rattled on the side table, and told him he would tear his fucking face off if he ever did such things to her, or any other things which he didn't care to mention.

'Our mother chose you, cunt-face, but we didn't.'

Nikolai had helped her… And now, here she was, the studious little girl from Kiev, lounging in the elegantly appointed courtyard of a boutique hotel in Marrakech. Would any of this have come her way if it hadn't been for Nikolai?

Where was Nikolai?

A waiter came out of the brick archway leading to the reception area at a fast trot, slippers slapping the stone flags of the courtyard, Zender's sonorous voice in effortless pursuit: 'C'est moi qui vais la déboucher, mon gars. Moi! Et soigneusement, hein?'

Zender propelled himself through the doorway, legs seeming barely to move inside a voluminous dark blue suit of a fine, smooth linen, fastidiously pressed. He saw her immediately and sailed over.

'Natalya, my dear, I am in a state of apprehension. Our friends have a marvellous bottle of burgundy, a nineteen-ninety Richebourg Domaine de la Romanée Conté, a superb wine in a simply priceless vintage.' He leaned down to kiss her on both cheeks, then whispered: 'They have no idea what a treasure they have in their cellars. A mere fifteen hundred dirhams, I beg you to believe! I have put it on your bill. One bottle only, and we must drink it immediately, before it is wasted on some passing Philistine. I have insisted that I open it myself, though the boy will probably have forgotten by the time he finds it. Pray God he does not shake it just to spite me.'

Nat laughed. 'Sit down and stop fussing. You are looking very distinguished this evening.'

'No amount of toilette could make me fit to appear beside you, Natalya, but I do my best with the satirical hand God has dealt me.'

She laughed again – though Claude's gallantry had no more substance than a soap bubble, it was nice to listen to.

'One could imagine the fate of nations altered forever by the fluent loveliness of your laughter,' Claude said. 'Charming.'

'My god, Claude, you're like a flattergram. Don't you ever stop?'

'In your company, *non*.'

Claude Zender now took to staring at the cigar-smoking reader of *Le Monde*, though the latter did not appear to have noticed. 'That man is one of al Hamra's snoops. They pursue me round Marrakech like a gaggle of courtiers who are too lily-livered even to let their faces be seen.'

Mehmet al Hamra was director of the Marrakech bureau of the Direction Genérale de la Surveillance du Territoire or DGST, the Moroccan intelligence service. She had met him when drinking with Zender at La Mamounia, and been witness to a brief but extraordinarily arch conversation between the two men. Zender's demeanour was so intensely belligerent it seemed he might challenge the cigar-smoking snoop to a duel; but then the waiter arrived, bearing a tray with the wine, two huge glasses and a basket of bread. Nervousness was making him unsteady, and when he set the glasses on the table without first removing the bottle to a place of safety, the tray wobbled and Claude sucked in his breath.

'Livrez-moi la bouteille instamment!' he hissed. 'Natalya, the bread is so you can clear the gin from your palate. A repellent drink, I must say.'

Finally, he had the bottle in his hands. 'Ah, yes,' he growled, examining the label. 'A little chill from the cellar, but it can't be helped.' He reached for the corkscrew and with a few deft movements extracted the cork.

'Shall I pour it for you, monsieur?' asked the waiter.

'Certainly not, go away. And take Mam'selle's gin glass with you. And those.' He gestured impatiently at the nuts and olives.

When the waiter had gone, Zender slipped a little of the wine into his glass and held it up to the light. 'It is beautiful, crimson suffused with amber, like stained glass at dusk. See how even the merest film where it coats the glass bears its own colour and density.'

He brought the wine to his nose and inhaled powerfully, then emptied it into his mouth, drawing in air as he did so, and sat motionless in his chair, eyes glazed with a look that could, Nat thought as she chewed diligently on a crust of bread, readily be mistaken for idiocy.

'Aaahh,' he sighed. 'Ah, yes. Nothing need be said. Nothing *can* be said. It is beyond the powers of language.'

'Hallelujah for that,' said Nat. 'Have you found out anything about Nikolai?'

'Nikolai?'

'Yes, Nikolai, my brother. I asked you about him earlier.'

'Of course. It had slipped my mind in this little moment of vinous ecstasy. Your brother… ' He took a mouthful of wine, leaned back in his chair, closed his eyes and said no more.

'Christ, Claude, you are annoying sometimes.'

She waited restlessly for the interlude of vinous ecstasy to conclude.

'I fear your brother has been arrested,' Claude said finally.

'Arrested. What for?'

'You heard there was trouble at the casino – it seems your brother assaulted someone and provoked an unpleasant scene. A broken nose, blood spilled, the casino emptied – very bad for business. I understand a girl was involved.'

'Nikolai broke someone's nose? Did you see any of this?'

'No, indeed. I am seldom at the casino these days – they have turned it into a glorified amusement arcade.'

'So now Nikolai is at the police station?'

'Thankfully, no. The incident was handled by casino security. I believe they will release him as soon as he has recovered from his injuries.'

'What injuries, is he all right?'

'Really, I do not know. It does not sound as if he went quietly.'

'I don't believe it. Nikolai isn't so stupid. And since when can you be arrested by a casino?'

'They deal with such matters the whole time, I assure you. The owners have made arrangements with the authorities that allow them to carry on their trade without adverse publicity. Equally, the police are pleased to be relieved of the burden of paperwork associated with arresting foreigners after every minor fracas. The more so because they are paid for it.'

'So where is he now?'

'That I do not know.'

'I must go to the casino immediately.' She stood up, glaring at Claude.

'I can tell you for nothing what they will say: a foreigner of the most undesirable sort accidentally gained entry to the gaming floor, got drunk, started a fight and was ejected. Please, there is no reason to be angry with me, Natalya, I simply report what I have heard. Sit down and let us talk. There is wine to drink and business to attend to.'

'Fuck business,' said Natalya. But she sat down.

'If you make difficulties, the casino will feel obliged to hand him over to the police, and then? Charges will be brought and he will end up in jail. Better to let matters take their course. The casino has no interest in anything other than a rapid and discreet conclusion.'

Nat fell silent while she digested this news. Nikolai seldom drank to excess and when he did, stupefaction not belligerence was the outcome. Nor did he *get into* fights: he started them, won them, tidied up. However, her brother did not like to see women ill treated. If Claude was right and a girl had been involved, perhaps he had let chivalry cloud his judgement.

'Have you been in touch with the IPD400's new owner?' she asked eventually.

'Yes I have, and there is the remote possibility of a deal – but it will take lengthy and elaborate preparation, or else we will scare him off.'

'What did you tell him?'

'Just as you suggested, that the IPD400 does not work.'

'And he bought it?'

'Must you taunt me with these trite Americanisms? *He bought it* implies that he believed a lie. Do I conclude that the IPD400 does work after all, and that you have manoeuvred me into deceiving a favoured client? I told you last week that I decline to engage in such duplicities. I am not entirely without scruple.'

'You have scruples? Let me know if I can help,' Nat replied. The arrival of Claude's high horse, snorting with self-righteousness, was a tactic with which she was perfectly familiar.

'You are always ready with a jibe, however unjust.'

'It's horrible to have this row hanging over us, don't you think,' Nat said, deciding it was time to remind him of the inquisition she had pretended was taking place in London. 'All those Whitehall nit-pickers snuffling over our export licences. Didn't you say the UK was one of the last civilised countries you could enter without being taken from the airport in handcuffs? You may have to cross it off your list.'

'The offending documents will be conveniently misfiled, I predict.'

'They keep asking me whether I can verify your end-users. Which I can't of course, though I do try.'

'My gratitude is boundless.'

'If you won't put me in touch with your client, why don't we just agree what I have to pay to get the IPD400 back? Go on, name your price.'

'I never name my price, it seems to upset people,' said Claude. 'But I do agree that it would be a relief to get this contraption off our hands. Already I wish I had never heard of it. Eighteen million sterling might sway my client, though it is far short of what I would expect, given the extraordinary nature of your proposal and the damage to my reputation that will surely ensue. But, as ever, I bow low before your superior negotiating skills— '

Nat interrupted: 'Twenty-five million US I might be able to do.'

'Which at today's exchange rate is the merest trifle more than I paid for it. I am curious that you think in dollars, now,' Claude observed. 'I suppose your buyer is an American?'

'Suppose all you like, I'm not going to tell you.'

He looked directly into her eyes and held his gaze.

'Claude, you look like a huge fat lizard. Stop or I'll scream and throw my wine at you.'

He stared for a few seconds longer, then threw back his head and laughed – rather unconvincingly, Nat thought. Had she actually wounded his vanity?

'Oh thou weed, that art so lovely fair and smell so sweet and so on and so forth. How in the name of all that is holy can you say twenty-six million dollars yet remain irresistible to me?'

'Do stop putting numbers into my mouth, Claude. Twenty-five gives you more than enough to play with.'

'A humiliating experience, to have an Ukrainian émigrée of almost offensive youthfulness talk one down by the best part of nine million dollars, but at least I can plead distraction in the presence of a beauty so disarming it could bring peace to the Middle East. Let us leave this difference between us and I'll bring you news when I can. And now, I am exhausted. The only thing that could possibly restore me would be dinner with you at Adela's. Let us go at once.'

'Not tonight, Claude, the jet lag's kicking in.'

'Jet lag, from a three-hour flight?'

'It was hours late and then horribly rough,' she said quickly, realising she'd told Claude she'd been in London, not LA. 'I feel like I've been round the world. Anyway, I must go to bed.'

'That enchanted place.'

'Stop it.'

'Tomorrow, then – though one of my neediest clients is in town so it will have to be late.'

'Tomorrow is perfect.'

She bent down to kiss him, then walked quickly from the courtyard, feeling his eyes upon her.

*　*　*

Mehmet al Hamra of the DGST entered his office in the Gueliz district of Marrakech, lowered the blinds, then sat down and stared across the darkened room. The air conditioning unit in the window next to his desk caused the slats to tremble and lift, spilling a pattern of pale streetlight over the worn leather inlay. He pulled open a notebook and opened it at a page headed *Mansour*.

This man was a puzzle to al Hamra. He seemed to have joined Zender's entourage about two years ago, as sidekick to the verminous Etienne. While the fat arms dealer flaunted his amiable self in the hotels and restaurants of Marrakech, these two prowled the backstreets, committing acts of appalling cruelty and striking fear into the hearts of all who encountered them. Their hold on the Marrakech underworld was such that identifying them had proved impossible. None of the many people he had bribed, threatened or blackmailed would say a word about them, let alone pick out their faces from a folder of photographs. They did not even have surnames.

Just recently, however, some subtle intelligence work on his part had revealed that Mansour was, as well as an employee of Zender's, the flag-bearer for a fledgling terrorist outfit called al Bidayat. His full name was Mansour Anzarane. Al Bidayat – the Terror Consultancy as it was known, because of its policy of funding atrocities, rather than committing them – was generating much hysteria in intelligence circles. Al Hamra thought the attention exaggerated: no one could demonstrate that they had done anything other than host a bloodthirsty website. Still, the discovery was astonishing. He'd had Mansour down as a sadist and murderer, not a zealot. And why would Zender, who was cautious to a fault, associate with a self-proclaimed terrorist? Whatever the reason, it was a chink in his armour – a mistake that might enable al Hamra to engineer his downfall.

The difficulty was how to lever the chink open wide enough to deal Zender a fatal blow. The arms dealer had contrived to make himself impregnable by providing the British SIS with intelligence on Polisario arms procurement – a subject on which Zender was particularly well informed because he managed the entire process himself. The intelligence duly found its way to al Hamra's esteemed colleagues in the Moroccan military – who in turn congratulated themselves on having a line in to the enemy camp. The information followed this circuitous route because Zender knew very well that if his Polisario clients discovered the betrayal they would not hesitate to cut his throat.

MI6 were rather sanctimonious about protecting their sources and al Hamra had no hard evidence to prove his suppositions correct. Nevertheless, he was satisfied that he had worked it out: why else would emissaries from both MI6 and Moroccan Army Intelligence drop such insistent hints that Zender was best left well alone? The arrangement probably owed its stubborn longevity as much to the thrill his military colleagues derived from dealing with the great majesty of the British SIS as to any intrinsic merit in the information supplied; nor, in al Hamra's view, could any amount of intelligence compensate for the fact that Zender was a thoroughly odious and dishonourable man, a professional humiliation to him personally, and a very stubborn and painful thorn in the side of the Moroccan state.

Mehmet al Hamra pushed the notebook aside and looked gloomily at the sofa opposite him, which served as a bed when affairs kept him late at the office – as they would tonight. He still had to complete his review of the operation to hunt down the Agadir Bomber. Eighteen months previously, someone had blown up a hotel in the seaside resort town, killing sixty-seven tourists. The police operation to catch the perpetrator had been an embarrassing failure.

He pulled the report from the drawer of his desk. As he did so an idea came to him. Since the real Agadir Bomber had eluded them, why not nominate someone else for the crime – someone who ought to be locked up anyway? And when considering possible candidates, why not concentrate on persons whose locking up might also discredit some of one's other enemies?

Mansour Anzarane fitted the bill on both counts.

Al Hamra stood from his desk and paced the office as his idea took shape. Anzarane worked for Zender and Zender worked for the Polisario. If Anzarane was named chief suspect in the Agadir Bombing, then life would become very uncomfortable for Zender: the gentlemen of MI6 could hardly continue to have even a clandestine relationship with a man who had a terrorist suspect on his payroll. As soon as this shameful fact was made known to them, Zender's untouchable status would be withdrawn. As for the Polisario, the association with Anzarane would be a political catastrophe. The UN would never allow their claim to the Western Sahara if the Polisario could plausibly be depicted as terrorist sympathisers. Their cause would be tainted forever.

The first step was to persuade those in charge of the hunt for the Agadir Bomber to name Mansour Anzarane as their prime suspect – and surely they'd be relieved to see their fiasco turned to advantage. Next, he would organise a raid on the Polisario compound in the Free Zone – under the pretext of pursuing a wanted terrorist. Once there, he could ensure (by planting it himself, which was wrong, of course, but the end would surely justify the means) that there was plenty of evidence to show Mansour had planned the Agadir Bombing with the protection and even support of his Polisario hosts. Both the internal politicking and the laying of a false trail would take some skill, but it was not for nothing that he was nicknamed the Gnome of Rabat.

A thoroughly poisonous dart that had a sporting chance of taking out at least one and possibly both of its intended targets, al Hamra concluded. He would start by allowing his counterparts in MI6 to discover that Zender's affairs were about to become disorderly – this in itself might be enough to make them sever their links with the fat arms broker. Nigel de la Mere of their North-West Africa Office was in town and would likely demand a meeting; but de la Mere was a graceless oaf and al Hamra would tell him nothing. Preferable in all ways to let the lovely Natalya Kocharian carry the message for him: her employer, Grosvenor Systems, was known to have close connections with MI6.

Al Hamra patted his stomach with satisfaction, then telephoned the man he had ordered to tail her and told him to call back immediately if the opportunity for a chance encounter with Ms Kocharian should arise.

* * *

Nat went up to her room to check her emails and change, then an hour later left the Riad by a side entrance and took a taxi to the Casino des Capricornes. As she arrived, a troupe of middle-aged women were disgorging themselves from the Holiday Inn shuttle bus – all zipped up in pastel chiffon cocktail dresses that bulged like paper bags full of wet plums. A hen night, thought Nat. They might just as well be wearing T-shirts saying *I'm going to drink too much and lose $100.*

Inside the casino, most of the guests stood clutching bowls of tokens and feeding them methodically into the ranks of slot machines, while the gaming tables were nearly empty. Nat made her way round a wall of plastic foliage and into one of the casino bars, where she found Anton deep in conversation with a large, heavy-jawed girl, all plucked eyebrows and powdered cleavage. One of his hands rested low on her waist. They were drinking Champagne. The sight of him amusing himself with the girl annoyed Nat, even though this was exactly what she had asked him to do.

'Hard at it, Anton?' she said, coming up behind him and taking both of them unawares. The girl evidently decided Nat was a rival and gave her a sulky look.

'Miss Kocharian, may I introduce you to Maria?' said Anton.

'No you may not,' said Nat in Russian. 'What have you found out?'

'I think this girl can tell us who Nikolai was with last night,' he said conspiratorially, while Maria inspected herself in a compact. 'But she's nervous. She's a sophisticated girl – I have to go carefully with her.'

'You mean you have to stick your hand up her skirt. Just get on and do it. I'll meet you back here at nine.'

She heard him say something soothing to Maria, dropping into the gravelly Scottish accent he'd picked up from his father and which he'd no doubt convinced himself sounded terribly seductive. Nat bought a pack of cigarettes and went out into the car park to smoke one, hoping it would make her feel less fractious. It didn't, so she went upstairs and ate over-cooked steak and soft chips in the restaurant. The food settled her, and she went back to the bar. Seeing Nat approach, Maria set off for the ladies room. She swung her hips a few times, then looked over her shoulder to check that Anton was watching. *You could have taken that for granted*, thought Nat... Then she remembered doing exactly the same thing while leaving Sir Peter Beddoes' office a week earlier. The insight was discomforting.

'Maria was annoyed. I had to calm her down,' Anton was saying.

'Fuck's sake, Anton, she's an early-shift casino whore. She doesn't need calming down.'

'Whatever you say, Ms Kocharian.'

'So?'

'The girl who was with Nikolai is called Aisha – she'll be here later tonight. Maria says she is very beautiful, like a cat.'

Nat snorted. 'OK, get Maria to point catwoman out to you, then come and find me at the blackjack tables.'

She changed five hundred dollars, bought herself a gin and tonic and played for a while, not really caring whether she won or lost. As she laid out her next stake, a hand reached over and placed a pile of chips next to hers on the blackjack table.

She turned and saw a small, dapper Arab in his late fifties with a speckled grey beard smiling at her.

'The gentleman wishes to play behind you,' said the croupier. 'Mam'selle is agreeable?'

Nat nodded. She was familiar with the casino custom by which one player may shadow another, and so win or lose from their hands. The gentleman in question was Mehmet al Hamra, the spy chief whose man Zender had identified in the courtyard at the Riad.

'Mam'selle is gracious,' he said. 'I have little aptitude for the game myself.'

'I hope you won't hold it against me if I lose, Monsieur al Hamra,' said Nat. She was both impressed by this man, with his urbane manner and clear, intelligent eyes, and rather nervous of him.

'Please, you must call me Mehmet.'

Nat played her hand, and won.

'*Voilà*,' he said. 'I have a poor head for cards, but my knowledge of human nature is worth a small stake. May I welcome you back to Marrakech? I don't believe I have ever before seen you in the casino without Monsieur Zender for an escort.'

'I didn't know you kept such a close watch over me, Mehmet.'

'The associates of Monsieur Zender are my particular concern, most especially in these complicated times.'

Nat played out another hand, with al Hamra again staking behind her. To her consternation, she drew a sequence of four low cards and was obliged to concentrate while she calculated the odds of the fifth breaking twenty-one. Really, she wanted to find out why she was being stalked by a Moroccan spy.

'Complicated?' she asked, calling for a card and drawing a six, which kept her tally to nineteen.

'Oh yes. Monsieur Zender's affairs are becoming disorderly. I want to warn you that to do business with him, at this moment, is inadvisable.'

'It's always inadvisable to do business with Zender. I'm used to it.'

The dealer played the house hand, went bust and paid out.

'You will make me a wealthy man, Mam'selle Kocharian,' said al Hamra. 'But please accompany me to the lounge so that we can talk without distraction.'

He led her to a booth that was only a few yards from where Anton stood posing at the bar. He gave a histrionic shrug which Nat ignored.

'It appears you are not alone?' said al Hamra.

'He's been trying to pick me up.'

'A barfly, as the English say. Shall I have him ejected?'

'No. He'll see you and think I'm spoken for.'

A waiter came and took their order. When he turned back to her, she smiled at him and saw his eyes lose their professional focus and wander over her face and down to the triangle of bare skin between her breasts. Then, seeming to call himself to order, he looked down and patted the muscular upslope of his stomach.

'The Casino des Capricornes is a vulgar place, and yet it draws commerce to our beloved town,' al Hamra said, 'and so it must be tolerated. You remember that in February last year, a terrorist bomb was exploded at the Hotel de l'Atlantique in Agadir?'

'Yes. It was horrible.'

'Sixty-seven people died, many of them French and Americans taking our winter sun. The tourist trade has not recovered. Our hunt for the bombers has been exhaustive, and at last we have made a breakthrough.'

'I'm pleased to hear it, Mehmet.'

'The complication I mentioned is that the prime suspect in our investigation is an associate of Monsieur Zender.'

'You mean he sold them something? Something they used in the bombing?'

'Very probably. The suspect's name is Mansour Anzarane, and he is known to have been a guest of Monsieur Zender's at an establishment he operates in the so-called Free Zone. I expect you know that he stores arms there – many of them no doubt supplied by Grosvenor Systems of London.'

Nat did not. The Free Zone was Polisario country, and they were sworn enemies of the Moroccan state. So how could Zender run a base there while still being allowed to live in Marrakech? Catching al Hamra's eye, she saw that he'd noticed her confusion, and she felt belittled by her ignorance.

'I can't believe Claude would associate with a terrorist,' she said. 'He's always so careful.'

The waiter arrived with their drinks. Al Hamra emptied a bottle of soda into his tumbler of brandy, took a swig, then dabbed his mouth with a napkin.

'Mansour Anzarane is a member of the terrorist group called al Bidayat,' he said. 'Sometimes referred to as the Terror Consultancy.'

'You think they were responsible for Agadir?'

'Like you, Mam'selle, I was surprised that Monsieur Zender should have dealings with such people. No doubt that was naive of me. In any event, we were able to interrogate one of the guards from the base under conditions that place the identification of Anzarane beyond reasonable doubt.'

'Mehmet, why are you telling me this?'

'Marrakech has been a commercial centre for many centuries, Mam'selle Natalya, and as a legitimate businesswoman you will always be welcome here. I personally would not wish to see you become a casualty of Monsieur Zender's impending downfall.'

There was warmth in al Hamra's eyes... He was a spy, and no doubt feeding her information that was only partially true; still, Nat could not help believing that he was also partially sincere. She thought of asking him to help her find Nikolai, but her mind was so beset with half-completed schemes and formless anxieties that she hesitated. And then he was standing up, bowing, saying, *Good evening, Mam'selle*, and walking quickly away.

'At the roulette table by the elevators. In a long black dress, next to the tall man with not much hair.'

Natalya was so distracted that when she turned to face the man who had spoken to her, all she saw was a pair of restless, melancholy eyes set in a dark, angular and quite handsome face. His words registered and she recognised her brother's sleazy sidekick. She looked across the gaming floor and identified Aisha – and experienced the frisson of envy and admiration she always felt in the presence of a woman more beautiful than she.

'I won't need you any more tonight, Anton. If Maria offers to take you home, for fuck's sake don't get rolled in some alleyway.'

Nat moved to another blackjack table near the cloakrooms in order to observe the girl more easily. Aisha had fine black hair that caressed her bare shoulders when she turned her head. Her eyes were dark and waif-like, but when she smiled, two cheerful dimples broke the flawless, concave planes of her cheeks. The contrast was very appealing, Nat thought. Maria was right, this girl was altogether feline and dainty – quite unlike the heavy-limbed blondes with big mouths Nikolai was used to. No wonder he had fallen for her.

Nat finished her gin and dropped the highball glass into her handbag. She went on discreetly observing Aisha, admiring the lithe, playful way she moved her body round her mark, brushing against him, leaning against him, taking his hand and drawing herself close. Baldy was clearly besotted, as who wouldn't be. Roulette was a game for fools, in Nat's view, and he was playing it foolishly, with large stakes on singles, doubles and fours – chosen, no doubt, by his delightful companion. Eventually, Aisha left his side and headed for the bathroom. Nat collected her chips and followed.

The girl went into a cubicle. Nat positioned herself by the sink opposite and watched the cubicle in the mirror while pretending to inspect her make-up. When she heard the bolt being drawn back, she turned and walked swiftly to the cubicle door, arriving just as Aisha was swinging it open. She got the heel of her hand under the girl's chin, fingers over her mouth, and hustled her backwards, smacking her head against the back wall. Then she kneed her sharply in the groin. Nat was small, but strong, athletic – and angry. Aisha crumpled onto the lavatory seat. Nat bolted the door, then dropped her handbag on the floor and stamped on it. She fished out the base of the highball glass, now crowned with spikes of splintered glass. She seized the girl by the hair and forced her head back.

'See this?' she said unnecessarily, holding the broken glass against Aisha's cheek. 'I'm going to slash your face open. I'm going to leave your cheeks flapping like bat wings. And you fucking deserve it.'

'No,' Aisha whimpered. 'Why… '

Nat leaned close to her ear. 'The man you picked up last night is my brother. Why did you set him up?'

'I don't— '

Nat pressed the shard against the girl's cheek and drew it down an inch. A spot of blood oozed out, almost black against her chestnut-coloured skin. The girl gave a soft wail.

'It's your job. You pick up men and get them into a fight.'

'No. My job. Yes, they make me do things. I can't say no.'

'So, you got my brother thinking he had a chance of getting into your knickers. Then what?'

'They start a fight and take him away.'

'Why?'

'I don't know, I don't. They don't tell me. Maybe money.'

'Who are they?'

'Rich men who own the casino. Please, let me go now. I don't know anything.'

'What rich men? Give me their names.'

'I don't know. I only do what they make me.'

She was talking through sobs now, her face smudged with tears. *I haven't got long*, Natalya realised, and pressed the glass splinter into her cheek. Aisha gasped.

'What happens to the people you set up? Where do they take them?'

'They do not tell me things like that. They make me get men into a fight, then I don't know what happens.' Blood had started to trickle down her neck. 'You don't have to cut me.'

'Was he badly hurt?'

'He was fighting them. The guards are big men… '

'Shit.'

Nat felt suddenly drained. She released Aisha and leaned back against the cubicle door. The girl pulled a tissue from her bag and held it to her cheek.

'He was OK, your brother,' she said through her tears. 'I feel bad about it.'

'Halle-fucking-lujah. You smiled your little smile and pointed your ass at him, then you fucked him over.'

'He is in hospital now?'

'What do you care? No. I don't know, I can't find him.'

'He was OK,' she said again.

Why was she talking about him in the past tense? Nat felt tears come to her eyes. She saw the girl watching her and realised she was still holding the jagged rim of glass. She returned it to her handbag.

'Please do not say I told you this. They will hurt me. They cut girls who talk.' She pointed to her mouth. 'One girl, they cut her lips. Now she wears a burqa always.'

Nat looked into Aisha's frightened eyes and saw how beautiful they were, deep mahogany with whites as clear as pearl.

'I won't tell anyone.'

She opened the door and Aisha slipped past. She watched her scuttle over to a sink and make a cursory attempt to tidy her hair and dab the blood from her cheek and neck. All the grace and elegance had gone out of her, she looked broken. Now it was Nat's turn to feel bad.

*　*　*

When Aisha had gone, Nat sat on the lavatory and thought for a while. Why had Nikolai been set up by these *rich men who own the casino*? Aisha said the motive was money. But casinos didn't need to rob people, and it was not as if Nikolai was in debt to them. So why?

She didn't know. Neither, apparently, did Claude Zender. He'd given his explanation with such certainty – as a matter of fact, not of conjecture – but it had not rung true. In business, it was fun not trusting Zender. They played *a game of numbers dressed up in quips and sallies* – his own expression. But this was her brother, not a consignment of fucking RPGs! She poked around among the bits of broken glass in her handbag and pulled out her cellphone. Then she remembered her promise to Aisha... If I confront Claude, he'll just shrug and deny it, she thought, and what evidence do I have? I assaulted a casino whore in the loos and she told me.

Maybe Claude knows more than he's letting on, but that doesn't mean he had anything to do with it. Mehmet al Hamra's words came back to her. Should she report the conversation to Claude, to help him evade his impending downfall? Or was that exactly what al Hamra intended, in which case might she inadvertently be helping to bring his downfall about? It was too convoluted to work out now.

She stood up, flushed the toilet and inspected herself in the mirror above the row of washbasins. *You got Nikolai into this, now get him out,* she told the tired face that looked back at her. *And wrap up the IPD400 deal while you're at it, because the sexy sales supremo act is running out of gas.* She found lipstick and a compact and tidied herself up, but even when she'd finished she still looked like a woman who's got off the bus in a bad neighbourhood and doesn't know how to get home.

*   *   *

James was sitting on his mattress at the compound, contemplating *Error 16017.*

He hadn't got rid of it, hadn't even tried. It wasn't an error. It was an alerting mechanism he'd coded under legal threats from the occupants of a certain building on the banks of the Thames near Waterloo Bridge, and it executed whenever Little Sister attempted to latch on to one of their servers. The building was the headquarters of Her Majesty's Secret Intelligence Service, SIS. More usually known by the designation MI6.

Rakesh Nazli was spying for the Playpen? The foppish, orange-soda-drinking DP tech was a highly trained and nerveless

MI6 agent, operating at the heart of an organisation that was willing to torture an innocent man and execute its own people in the most gruesome fashion imaginable? He couldn't see it. Not Nazli. But these people were skilled and devious – why did he think he couldn't be fooled? After all, there was plenty to spy on: arms dealing, theft of sensitive military technology, abductions and executions – and that was just the things he knew about.

Fooled or not, the software installed on the Playpen's servers had detected Little Sister's sly overtures; and simultaneously with the 16017 error message he and Nazli had seen, another would have flashed up on the duty officer's monitor at MI6's Centre for Internal Security:

AN ATTEMPT HAS BEEN MADE TO GAIN ACCESS TO THE SERVICE NETWORK. THE ATTEMPT WAS REBUFFED AND SECURITY WAS NOT COMPROMISED. THE ATTEMPT TOOK PLACE AT [TIME] ON [DATE]. REPORT UNDER PROTOCOL 4 RED, ATTACHING LOGFILE [CURRENTLOG]

Within minutes, CURRENTLOG would reach Head of Information Systems Julian Twomey-Smith – a talentless little time-server with a knack of saying the right thing to the right people – and within the hour he would be seeking the guidance of his boss Sir Iain Strang, Director-General of MI6. That would be a call worth tapping. How would he react? Amazed that the IPD400 had somehow ended up at a site which was the subject of an MI6 surveillance op, and appalled that said surveillance had almost certainly been compromised by, of all people, that pain-in-the-arse Palatine.

Would they now order a daring rescue, courtesy of his former SAS comrades – the Old Women as they were called, because they spent most of their time sitting by the phone? No, because Twomey-Smith would be able to identify the location of the IPD400, but not necessarily of the person operating it – and anyway, in the age of cyber-surveillance, acts of derring-do had gone out of fashion. If he'd compromised a surveillance op, they'd be doing everything in their power to salvage it. If it was something else, they'd have the shredders shredding and the non-recoverable delete routines deleting non-recoverably. Security breaches had to be plugged, and you couldn't be too fastidious about how.

There'd be a meeting – it would start within a few hours. First priority: identify the scapegoat. Next, analyse risk, discuss damage limitation, rehearse termination scenarios. There'd be a general consensus that Palatine was a nuisance and would just have to look after himself.

Part II

Chapter Ten

'Wait while I check my messages,' said Sir Iain Strang, without deigning to look up as Clive walked along behind the rank of empty chairs at the conference room table and took his place among the group at the far end. 'Lisa, would you mind?'

Strang passed his pda over to his PA, who tapped at the keypad then passed it back.

'Oh yes, you are brilliant.'

It was six-thirty in the morning and the room had an up-all-night feel to it: dirty cups stacked on trays, ties over chair-backs, sallow, tetchy faces, the sharp smell of air-conditioned sweat. It was clear that there had been several more people than now remained. They'd saved him for last, like a fresh treat to feast on before going home. Seeing that Strang was preoccupied, Clive surreptitiously inspected the other attendees: Nigel de la Mere of the North-West Africa Office; and to Clive's right, Julian Twomey-Smith, Head of Information Systems, a pink-faced man with gingery facial hair clipped in a neat oval around his chin and upper lip. When Clive turned towards him, Twomey-Smith grinned and pointed at the folder he had open in front of him.

What was that supposed to mean? Clive looked into his attaché case for something meaningful to do, but the first thing that caught his eye was a copy of his notes about Natalya Kocharian's activities in Marrakech, which were so paltry that he didn't want anyone to see them.

'That's enough diddling, we'll wear ourselves out,' said Strang, handing his pda back to Lisa. 'Julian, bring Clive up to speed.'

'You'll remember our legal team forced Palatine to write a function that alerts us to attempted IPD400 intercepts on our network?' Twomey-Smith began smoothly. 'Well, the alert went off at eight-twenty yesterday evening.'

'It worked, then,' said Clive obligingly.

'Yes. The IPD400 is heavily fortified against unauthorised use – the password function apparently includes the most deeply nested *if* statement Palatine's ever written and is impossible to decompile. There are other security features that neither we nor Grosvenor know how to detect, still less disable. So, we are safe to assume that if the IPD400 is up and running, Palatine is at the controls.'

'Nice piece of sleuthing, Julian,' said Nigel de la Mere.

Twomey-Smith's lips formed a simper inside the oval of beard. 'I looked at the routing of the IPD400 attack on our servers,' he went on, facing Clive while the others watched. 'When Zender started supplying us with intel about Polisario arms procurement, we set him up with Centuries Deep – that's the software we use for encrypting communication across distributed sites. The IP address Palatine fed to the IPD400 was generated by Zender's Centuries Deep installation – and Palatine could have found out what it was only if he had deep access to Zender's network.'

'So we know where he is? Where the IPD400 is?'

'Unfortunately not,' said Twomey-Smith. 'It's possible he's operating the IPD400 remotely.'

'Trying to get anything useful out of Centuries Deep,' Strang observed, 'is like trying to coax jism from a corpse. Nigel?'

'Palatine took a flight to Oran last Thursday. No obvious reason. Oran is one of Zender's haunts, as we know. Set alongside Julian's technical forensics, it strongly suggests that Palatine and Zender are in cahoots.'

Why wasn't I told this earlier? thought Clive. Strang was staring at him, grey eyes sharp as marbles. 'James Palatine's got the IPD400,' he said, 'and Zender helped him. You were Palatine's case officer in Kosovo, Clive, and Grosvenor is on your watch. Tell me what's going on.'

'I don't know. I didn't even know he'd left London.'

'Palatine's got at you, yes? He knows things about your jaunt in the Balkans that could ruin you, so you helped him lift the IPD400 from the Grosvenor warehouse.'

'No, that's absolutely not the case.'

'You'll have to be investigated, Clive,' said Strang. 'If I find out you're lying, I'll have your balls on toast. And I will find out, won't I?'

'Yes, of course.'

'What will I find out?'

'That there's nothing going on here.'

'I'll ask you again: have you any reason for thinking Palatine might have been planning to reunite himself with the IPD400?'

'No. I don't understand it.'

'Well fucking speculate.' Strang thrust his head forward like a hyena with the scent of young flesh in its nostrils. 'You write these clever strategy papers that have your wonk-friends at Westminster ejaculating into their Pampers, so how about applying the creative genius to a little bit of light intelligence work? Why did Palatine make off with his IPD400?'

'Money?'

'A man who makes two thousand dollars a day in consultancy fees? I doubt it,' said de la Mere. 'Besides, whatever else we may think of him, Palatine is honourable to an irritating degree.'

'Try again,' said Strang.

'Perhaps he wants to stop us getting hold of it?'

'He's already stopped us,' said de la Mere, 'courtesy of the bizarre terms of his contract with Grosvenor.'

'Is that what he told you, Clive?' Strang asked.

'No. I hardly have any contact with him now. I mean, I've seen him a few times, but he's been… dismissive.'

'Dismissive?' said Nigel de la Mere. 'You must be great pals. The last time we met, I counted myself lucky not to wind up in casualty with a broken jaw.'

Sir Iain Strang leaned back in his chair, folded his arms and looked up at the ceiling. A sigh hissed through his teeth. 'Dr Palatine is one half overpaid geek and one half psychopath,' he said. 'And didn't his mummy die when he was only little?'

'He was fourteen,' said Clive.

'Don't answer my questions unless I fucking tell you to,' said Strang. 'Nigel, when are you interviewing Palatine's partner at Imperial?'

'Had him picked up from Herne Hill a couple of hours ago,' said de la Mere. 'Dr Hugo Vanic. Timid sort, very much in awe of Palatine. I don't expect much. House was clean.'

'Palatine's flat in Camden?'

'Predictable blank,' said de la Mere.

'What about the money?'

'Nothing suspicious in Palatine's account – or at least the one we know about. As for Zender, he's a Swiss national – and as if that wasn't enough, he holds proxy accounts in Monaco and the British Virgin Islands. I have the accountancy team on it, but the man's finances have been under scrutiny for years, and his people are dab hands with the digital rubber.'

'Have we considered the possibility that Palatine is doing this under duress?' said Clive, emboldened by the fact that the inquisitorial tone of the meeting seemed to have dissipated. 'Perhaps using the IPD400 to hack a Service network is his way of alerting us.'

'Nice idea,' said Julian Twomey-Smith. 'But Centuries Deep utilises a system of session-based IPs created on the fly. Only when the handshake has been authenticated via a public-private key is— '

'Cut the wank, Julian, I feel faint,' said Strang. 'The point is, Clive, when Palatine keyed in the IP address, he had no way of knowing he was pissing on our gates.'

'I can see the reasoning. But Palatine is very resourceful... ' Why was he defending James Palatine? Strang's hard eyes would not let him think. De la Mere was watching him from beneath raised eyebrows, a caricature of scepticism. 'He must have got the Centuries Deep IP from somewhere.'

'I can tell from the constipated expression on Julian's face that he's already thinking about that,' said Strang. 'Any other ideas from the acclaimed man of ideas?'

Clive thought frantically. 'Are we assuming that Palatine hired Zender to get hold of the IPD400 for him? I do find that hard to believe.'

'If anyone spots anything in this business that isn't hard to believe, it would be sweet relief to hear it,' said Strang.

'The alternative,' said de la Mere, 'is that an unknown third party commissioned Zender to arrange both the hijacking of the IPD400 and the capture of an eminent British scientist. In the far-fetched stakes, I'd say that would be in a league of its own.'

'Your investigation has turned up fuck all, either way,' said Strang. 'But the grisly details will have to wait until we've got the IPD400 back.'

'It would help if we could enlist our American cousins,' said de la Mere, who by contrast with his colleagues seemed unperturbed by the MI6 chief's vitriolic manner. 'Or even the Moroccans.'

'We still can't,' said Strang. 'But go to Marrakech yourself. Talk to Mehmet al Hamra, see if Zender's putting out signals. I don't believe Moroccan intelligence just turn their backs while he holds arms fairs at La Mamounia.'

'I can do that,' said de la Mere, 'though al Hamra isn't known as the Gnome of Rabat on account of his forthcoming personality. He keeps tabs on the fat Swiss, yes, but Zender leads a charmed life. The Polisario intel he sells to us we pass straight on to the Moroccan military, as you know, and they absolutely lap it up – forever parading it before the UN as evidence that the Third World War is about to erupt on their southern borders. It's galling for Mehmet's people to have Zender lounging around in Marrakech, but they know he's our source so they tiptoe round him.'

'How the fuck does Zender find out what the Polisario are buying?'

'He brokers most of their deals himself,' said de la Mere. 'In return, the gullible clots let him operate out of their compound in the Free Zone, which is Shangri La for a man like Zender.'

'We shouldn't be taking sides in their interminable tiff,' said Strang irritably.

'Perhaps not, but I would go so far as to say that Zender's intel is central to our co-operative relations with Rabat,' de la Mere replied.

'A pillar of the establishment, then,' said Strang. 'Top of the guest list for embassy wife-swaps.'

'I'm told he plays backgammon with King Mohammed's private secretary.'

'If that's the sort of feeble gossip that's going in your memoirs, Nigel, you can cross me off the freeby list. When you've failed to get anything out of the DGST, find out what the special favours girl is up to. Clive doesn't seem to know – or perhaps he's just not telling us.'

'She's had a preliminary meeting with Zender,' said Clive quickly. 'I think we always knew it might take her some time to draw him in.'

'Oh, Clive, you're still here. Then we'll move on to Operation Anemone.'

Clive felt sweat break out on the palms of his hands and rubbed them furtively on his trousers, only to look up and find that everyone in the room was watching him.

'Palatine's working with Zender,' said Strang, 'so your op is compromised.'

'We don't know that,' said Clive desperately. 'Anemone has nothing to do with the loss of the IPD400, and Zender would have no reason to— '

Strang held up the palm of his hand. 'One, Anemone is quarantined. Two, you'll be investigated.' Clive looked up with his mouth open, but the Director-General of MI6 had already pushed back his chair and was striding towards the door.

'Clive, talk to Caroline.'

* * *

Caroline Hampshire was the Director of Human Resources. She and Clive sat opposite each other in a pair of undersized club chairs while she recited relevant sections of Service protocol from a blue vinyl ring binder. Clive was trying to work out from her expression whether this was a routine investigation or something more serious, but the features of her big-boned face were obscured by a thick layer of foundation and lipstick the colour of boiled lobster. Beside her was a purple African violet, bleached and wilting from too much water, set on a beech-effect occasional table adorned with a fan of SIS in-house newsletters and several issues of a magazine called *People Matters*. He started to drum his fingers impatiently on the arm of the chair, but Caroline Hampshire was not to be distracted. Her voice reeled on, its tone as neatly trimmed as a piece of suburban topiary. He found himself studying her knees, which were large and smooth, with a disconcertingly prosthetic hue. Before he could stop himself, he was imagining pushing his hand up between her thighs, guiding her to the desk and lifting the hem of her grey skirt over her large backside.

'I'll give you one of these briefing sheets, which has a full set of rules and guidelines for the quarantine procedure,' she concluded. 'An investigation *and* a quarantine all in one day. I do sympathise with you, Clive. These complex ops can cause issues on the people side of things. You understand that none of this should be taken to imply any suggestion of wrongdoing on your part?'

There was a knock and Nigel's face appeared in the glass window set in the door. He pushed it open and said: 'Clive, drop by for a moment, when you've finished with Caroline?'

'I already have,' said Clive, standing up.

*   *   *

Nigel de la Mere treated him to an extended recap of the meeting with Strang, complete with reinforcing statements as regards his own distance from everything that had happened, whether known or unknown, and everything that might subsequently occur, along with many non-committal hints that if Clive confirmed Nigel's general absence from the loop then, in return, he would do what he could to smooth things over with Sir Iain.

'I'll trust you on that, shall I, Nigel,' said Clive, 'on the basis that you always stand shoulder-to-shoulder with colleagues under fire?' Now that the pressure of Strang's presence was gone, he was feeling mulish and ill-treated. 'Why has Anemone been iced?'

'Why was it ever given life?'

'You're the project sponsor – you're supposed to be supportive,' said Clive.

'And you're the project manager. If Anemone hadn't been quarantined, Sir Iain would have killed it off anyway. Because, frankly, we'd have got better results if we'd sent a carrier pigeon over North Africa with a camera up its bum.'

'It's an innovative methodology. It was always going to take time.'

Nigel de la Mere gave him the raised eyebrow and Clive turned away in exasperation.

'Listen, Clive, read the bloody runes for once. Anemone was set up under pressure from the Treasury to trial some cost-cutting proposals that were doing the rounds – remember?'

'It was only a think piece. And I didn't leak it – I've told you that a hundred times.'

'You wrote it, though. *Resourcing in the Age of the Specialist* – do you have any idea how much trouble it caused? Every time Sir Iain went off to the Treasury to scrap for our budget, he found them tittering over your wretched paper. They had whole chunks off by heart. *The proposed cuts in funding can act as a catalyst for beneficial change* – that was their favourite bit.'

'What was I supposed to do, claim everything was perfect?'

'Exactly. Instead, you made Sir Iain look a fool. He once told me he was using your paper to wipe his arse, and I'm not even sure he was joking.'

Clive felt cowed by this evidence of the disgust he aroused in the MI6 chief. 'Everyone else uses private sector specialists,' he said weakly, 'why shouldn't we?'

'Have you ever asked yourself why you've spent eighteen months in exile at Grosvenor?'

'So that's it? No one ever believed in Anemone? It was just a sop to keep the Treasury off our backs?'

'I didn't say that. We've all put our best foot forward, myself included. But Anemone has been badly compromised by this business with the IPD400 – and if you want to know whether Sir Iain is devastated, I can tell you that he isn't.'

De la Mere's words filled him with gloom. Operation Anemone was supposed to get his career back on track after Kosovo – now it was just another ineradicable entry in Caroline Hampshire's personnel file.

'You really think I helped Zender and Palatine get hold of the IPD400? Sir Iain thinks that?'

'We need to confirm that you didn't, that's all.' He paused. 'Look, it's bad luck that Anemone's got snared up in this, but now that we have a solid lead on the IPD400, Sir Iain will find a way of getting it back. Just keep your head down, you'll get a chance to redeem yourself.'

'I haven't done anything wrong.'

'No? Well, neither had Jesus. I've seen this sort of thing before, Clive. Once it's all been tidied up, the mood will be more forgiving. Until then, you'll survive.'

Chapter Eleven

James was laying out his belongings on the mattress. About half a pound of meat salvaged from the food he'd been given over the last week, soused in the diazepam prescribed by the doctor, then dried. A pocketful of dates and half a dozen flatbreads, hard as plates. Some lumps of fat. Ibuprofen. A dozen plastic-sheathed ethernet cables purloined from Nazli's lab, three of which he had braided into a yard-long plait. A screwdriver and two spoons, hooked at the ends. Strips of canvas torn from the mattress cover. Three lengths of plastic hose. The jeans and T-shirt he had come in. No shoes – they'd taken them away on arrival and he'd been barefoot since.

He'd run through the idea of breaking into Nazli's lab, stealing the IPD400, loading it into one of the compound vehicles and hightailing out before the guards could stop him – run through it countless times without being able to envisage anything other than a disastrous and bloody outcome. He had to go quietly, which meant going on foot. Which meant he couldn't take Little Sister with him.

He drank from the shower, then bound one end of each of the hoses with copper wire from a length of cable, filled them with water and fastened the other ends. There was maybe half a litre in each, which would buy him an extra day in the desert. He secured them round his waist, then put the dried meat in one pocket of his jeans, the rest of his belongings in the other.

That's it.

The muscles of his back were suddenly alive with the smooth, powerful feeling he'd got from popping that youth's shoulder in the Camden park. The feeling that whisked caution away, then sent it back as guilt. He felt his heart punch at his ribs. *You may not need to kill anyone*, he told himself. For all the water he'd drunk, his mouth was sticky and the taste of the cornbread he'd had for supper clogged his throat.

Sam would have no truck with this. *To doubt is to bare your belly to the sword of your enemy.* He went up to the roof, repositioned the cowling, and crept along towards the corner where his two guards slept. He looked over, saw the arm of a white plastic chair, one leg stretched out: Younes, sleeping fitfully. The feet of the chair scratched at the concrete as he shifted position in an irresolute attempt to keep himself awake. He'd be difficult to get at, slumped in his seat like that, with a ridge of plastic protecting the back of his neck. James searched the roof with his fingertips until he found a few chips of stone, then tossed some at Younes's head, a few more at his feet. The bits of gravel skittered across the walkway. Younes came awake, shook his head. He stood up, took a few paces forwards. James padded along the roof behind him.

Younes stopped.

James dropped off the roof, locked his right arm like a hoop of steel round the guard's neck. He wrenched Younes's head round, getting the guard's torso beneath his as they thumped down. The AK47 crunched against the concrete. The warm, knotted body writhed powerfully beneath him. Right arm still clamped around Younes's neck, James gripped the bicep of his left and swung his forearm round behind the guard's head, used the leverage to compress his throat. Younes's struggle became wild and James smelled fear. He was strong and managed to roll James on to his side, get one hand on the forearm crushing his neck. But that was all. James felt euphoria coursing through him, giving terrible strength to his arms. Younes's ribcage pumped in a frantic attempt to suck air down his swollen windpipe, his back twitched as the muscles around his spine began to tear. After a moment, James felt the big body fading beneath him, the vigour seeping away, leaving only a slack, meaty weight. His elation disappeared. Instead, a foretaste of the revulsion that would follow.

He released his arm. Air whooped into Younes's bruised throat and he pressed his hand against the guard's mouth to muffle the noise. As soon as his breathing quietened, James rolled off him, dragged him into the passage that led out of the yard. He crossed to the guardroom door, knelt, listened. The door was ajar – snoring from within. The passage was silent, its walls criss-crossed with shadow from the steel lattice of the exit gate. James turned to watch the door to the room occupied by Mansour. No lights, no movement. He went back to Younes, tied the semi-conscious man's arms and gagged him with a strip of canvas, then ran back for the AK47.

He stepped into the guardroom and waited for his eyes to adjust to the darkness. Salif was sleeping on a mattress in the corner of the room. There was a wooden table and two chairs, and a steel cupboard against the wall by the door. James moved over to Salif's mattress, studied the side of his skull for a moment, then hit him with the butt of the AK47. Salif gave a groan of protest and his head rolled back.

He found the Beretta Tomcat under the mattress, along with the key to the steel cupboard. A row of labelled keys hung from hooks fastened to the underside of the top shelf, above a tatty cardboard box with spare rounds for the AK47 and the Tomcat. He took the keys to the two rooms nearest the guardroom and went and unlocked them, then dragged Younes into the first. He stripped off his sand-coloured fatigues, canvas belt and trainers and put them on, then used a plaited cable to tie Younes's hands behind his back and lash them to the iron bars of the window. He heaved Younes upright, fed another cable through the bars and secured it round his neck.

He went back for Salif and tied him up in the second room. He checked his pockets and found an old bone-handled hunting knife in a makeshift leather scabbard, the grip worn smooth and bound with electrician's tape at the heel. An embroidered wallet with three hundred dirhams, a prayer card in decorative script, and a cracked photo of two little boys of eight or nine dressed up in clean white shirts and with their hair carefully brushed.

He crept to the corner of the yard and checked the number of the room he had seen Mansour enter the previous night: 7. He got the key from the guardroom, then crouched at the door. A muggy, faintly acrid smell. The hackles on his neck stirred. Still no light on, but a leather sole scuffing the floor. Fabric swishing. He rose and stood close to the wooden panel, put one hand on the handle. It started to move down, pushed by a hand on the other side. He released it and waited for the click.

He burst the door open and reached for Mansour's neck. Mansour stepped back and ducked down, shielding his head with his arms. James moved alongside him, used his left foot to sweep the man's legs from beneath him. As he fell, James drove his right palm down into the back of his head and Mansour's nose smacked into the concrete. James straddled him, got the fingers of his left hand under his chin and pulled his throat into a high arc, like a man wrestling an alligator. Mansour was choking noisily, making no attempt to break free. *You're not much without your Taser and your shears*, thought James. He slackened off, rolled him over onto his back, reached under his beard and gripped his throat. It was slippery beneath his fingers, and the beard gave off the sweet, musky perfume that brought back the house in Oran, the barb in his ribs, the sap held high.

'Answer my questions or I'll kill you. Speak quietly. I'll ask you once only. What is your name?'

'Mansour.'

James's fingers mangled the nerves beneath Mansour's collarbone. His heels scrabbled at the floor.

'Mansour Anzarane.'

'Who do you work for?'

'I will answer your questions, I swear it. I work alone.'

James probed the soft tissue at the top of Mansour's left lung. Mansour gasped and blood bubbled from his nose.

'No. You work with Etienne.'

'Please, Etienne has gone now.'

'Where?'

'Home. Oran. Etienne made me cut you, it is he— '

'Who told you to kidnap me?'

No answer. James jammed two fingers up Mansour's nostrils and gouged his sinuses. Panic swirled in the man's eyes.

'Sheikh al Haqim. He ordered this. I am his poor servant.'

The name was such a shock James almost let him go. Ibrahim al Haqim, founder of al Bidayat... He'd been abducted on the say-so of the second most wanted man after Osama bin Laden himself?

So that was why the Playpen was watching this place.

'Where is al Haqim?'

'I do not know... I am not permitted to see him. I did what he said, I made him promise you would not be harmed, you must believe me... '

He was starting to gabble. James looked down into his eyes. *I told you everything*, they said. *Now spare me.* He applied a fatal hold, the shime-waza, to the superior carotid triangle and watched the man's eyes flood with disappointment and loneliness. Ten, nine, eight, seven, six... His face fattened and puced. Mansour passed out at two. His heartbeat stumbled on. Another twenty seconds. Add ten to be on the safe side. And because, James thought, whatever you'll feel about it later, there's a certain sordid pleasure to be had from squeezing the nasty life out of Mansour Anzarane.

* * *

He searched Mansour's room for the key to the gate that led out to the compound. His guards didn't have one, but surely an al Bidayat operative who took orders from Ibrahim al Haqim himself did not have to whistle to be let out. Mansour travelled light: a nylon grip with a change of clothes; a wooden box with a bar of soap, a biro and two Egyptian passports. One was in his own name, Anzarane; the other had the same photo but bore the name Mansour el Shaafi, and had visas for the UK and Germany, and stamps showing Mansour had entered Algeria the day before James had. The only key he found was the one to his room.

He was tempted to hunt down Etienne. But what if he couldn't find him? Younes would be expected to collect food for them at seven – that gave him less than six hours before they set off after him. He went back to the guardroom and found two old prayer mats, which he left by the door. He wiped the firing mechanism of the Beretta Tomcat with a lump of goat fat, loaded the clip and shoved it into the pocket of his trousers, then found the key to a room that was out of view of the guardhouse but close to the hollow where the dogs usually slept.

Once inside the room, he went to the shower and drank again, shocked at how thirsty he was. He pulled the lumps of diazepam-impregnated meat from his pocket and wet them, then went to the barred window and held out the handful of doped meat, squeezing to loosen the high, sweet odour. After a minute, the heavy snout of one of the dogs cocked up, the delicate flaps of its nose quivering. Its movements disturbed its neighbour and the two dogs got up and trotted towards James. The other two woke up and followed. James scattered the meat in a semi-circle round the window, and watched them padding around, snarling sleepily at each other as they went for the same scrap. One of them got his paws up onto the window ledge and licked where drips from the wet meat had fallen, then whined and scratched for more.

He watched them drift back to the fence, circle and settle, then counted out six hundred seconds to give the diazepam time to take grip. The dogs lay still. He collected the prayer mats from the guard-room and tossed them onto the roof near the south-east corner of the guest wing, the opposite end from the guards and the dogs, then climbed up, crawled across the roof and dropped off the other side, his legs absorbing the impact and his feet making no more noise than if they had landed in cotton wool.

He ran to the five-foot-high roll of razor wire and laid the mats in a channel over the coils, then took ten paces back and focused. He'd dived over razor wire before in training. It wasn't any great feat physically, but required precision and a certain bravura. Mistakes were messy. He breathed and prepared for his run. Then he saw the dog.

It was already ten yards in from the corner, coming fast in a flat, low run. Its broad muzzle seemed to enlarge as it raced from the gloom into the ambient light from the barracks, the black, stubbly cheek-skin pulling back from its incurved teeth. James crouched and braced, right arm poised, fingers forming a spearhead like the hood of a python. He stared into the dog's shining amber eyes, waited until its front paws left the ground as it leapt for his throat, then plunged his hand between its open jaws. The dog's momentum and his own arm-speed together drove his fingers deep into the wet tissue of its gullet. He seized the roots of its tongue, using his nails to grip the slippery muscle. For a second the dog stood still, impaled on James's arm, unable to come on or retreat, bite, bark or breathe. James pushed and twisted, grabbing the animal's front paw and flipping it onto its back so it couldn't use its legs to fight free. The dog was trembling, its eyes rolling. He trapped its front paws under his foot and used the side of his fist to hammer a point directly over its heart, already stressed to bursting point by the hand still clenched in its throat. Three heavy blows in quick succession and the dog was dead.

James gingerly withdrew his hand. It was lacerated by the dog's teeth, but not badly hurt. He rolled the body into the razor wire. One more lump of dead evidence in his wake.

He stepped back from the razor wire, took his run-up and hurled himself head-first into the air, felt his shins brush the mats, came down hard into a forward roll. He went back for the mats. A barb snagged his sleeve. The wire bounced and hummed, vibrations coursing through the coils, steel blades plucking at the dirt. He used his free hand to unpick the wire. Clear.

He rolled up the mats and tucked them under his arm, ran hard and low for the cover of the bunker between the guest wing and the barracks. He bound his forearm to stop the flow of blood drawn by the dog's teeth, then checked around him. Not much of a moon, just a shaving of pale bone suspended above the southern horizon. Beyond the wire, a profound darkness lapped at the features of the sand. He couldn't see any of the guards from here, though he knew there'd be some by the warehouse and some by the main gates. No one else about. Then, as he scanned the wall of the barracks a second time, he saw a shadow that didn't look right… A ripple of black – a large bird, maybe, scavenging at the base of one of the two galvanized steel rubbish bins. He watched for five minutes, then the shadow became a crouching figure who stood up slowly and leaned against the bin, turning irresolutely from side to side. The figure stepped unsteadily to the corner, one arm against the wall, feet catching in the rough ground. A tall woman, wearing a headscarf that seemed to stick out on either side... And suddenly in his mind's eye James saw a girl with a halo of frizzed hair stooping to climb into a taxi on Camden Road, her black courier bag catching on the door.

Sarah. A London girl from a good family. It was shocking to see her here, stumbling round in the darkness by the waste bins. She disappeared round the corner of the barracks and James ran to the corner where'd she'd stood. She was slumped against the wall a few yards away, knees drawn up, head down. James moved in quickly beside her, but the moment she felt his hand over her mouth she twisted away from him, legs flailing, arms struggling to push him away. There was a strange floppiness in her movements, and as they grappled in the dirt, James's long, powerful arms suddenly recalled the feeling of Younes's convulsing limbs. Horrified, he relaxed his grip, felt her exhausted body subside into a succession of short, half-suffocated breaths.

'It's me, James Palatine,' he whispered.

He pulled his hand from her mouth and she peered at him in the gloom.

'They're going to kill me. I don't know why. But they are.'

'Speak very quietly,' said James. 'Does anyone know you are out here?'

'No. They don't lock me in.'

'If they meant to kill you, they'd have already done it.' He tried to sound more certain than he felt.

'I don't know why they brought me here. I don't know.' She was trembling, clutching at his arm. 'They killed Hamed. A man called Mansour made me look at his body. I felt sick and then I fainted.'

'They just want to frighten you.'

A feeling of dread uncoiled in his gut. She's a prisoner, he thought. The man she worked with has been executed, and the stream of homophobic invective was no more than a pretext. The real reason is that Hamed knew who was behind my abduction.

'Sarah,' he said, 'do you know who was giving Hamed his orders?'

'No, I didn't know they were going to bring you here. I didn't know about any of this. I swear I didn't. God, I'm so sorry.'

'Then they have no reason to harm you. How did you get here?'

'Hamed said his charity would pay for me to visit a refugee camp. We flew to Oran. I think they drugged me, because I passed out soon after we got to the hotel. When I woke up...'

'Listen, it's going to be OK. I killed Mansour.'

She looked up at him, searching his eyes for signs of hope. She wiped the tears from her cheeks and drew a shuddering breath.

'What will they do to you?'

'Nothing, I'm on my way out.'

'Take me with you. Oh God, please take me with you.' She was crying again, clinging to him. 'Take me. I can't stay here, they'll kill me. The other one will kill me. He wants to hurt me, I can see it in his eyes.'

Go after Etienne, hunt him down... It might take all night to find him. And was Etienne the only person in this place capable of murdering a young English girl? *Then take her with you.* He started to work through the implications. He'd planned for two days in the desert, but with a twenty-year-old English girl at his side...

'Do you have access to food and water?'

For a moment, she didn't respond. Then she looked up at him, and her large eyes were like wind-blown lanterns that could barely hold the darkness at bay. 'You can't take me. I don't even have any shoes.'

'We'll find some.'

'The drugs they gave me… I'm so weak I can't even walk without holding on to something.'

James remembered the feebleness in her limbs as she'd struggled in his arms, then thought of his own grim battle to overcome the doctor's hypodermic cosh.

'How long since you arrived?'

'I don't know. I came round yesterday, I think. Maybe a few times before. I can't eat anything. Christ, I'm scared.'

'I'll come back for you.'

'You won't. Why should you. I did this to you.'

'I will. Trust me. I haven't finished with this place – they have something of mine.'

They sat in silence for a while, then he felt her disengage her arm. She pulled away and curled herself tight like a frightened animal.

'You have to go,' she said faintly. 'Why are they doing this to me?'

'Listen, Sarah, there's a tall man in officer's uniform, older, maybe sixty. Have you seen him?'

'I don't think so.'

'Try to find him and speak to him. He didn't like what happened to Hamed, and he has some kind of authority here. Appeal to him and I think he'll help you.'

'Do you know who he is?'

'No, but the guards respect him. Tomorrow, they'll be too busy looking for me to worry about you.'

He stood up and helped her to her feet.

'How long, do you think?'

'Not long. Don't lose heart.'

He hugged her, watched her shuffle laboriously back to the edge of the building. She looked back and gave a discreet wave, then turned the corner and was gone.

* * *

It seemed a terrible thing to abandon Sarah here. The encounter had affected James deeply – how much courage had it taken to defy her terror, acknowledge she was too weak to escape, release him, curl back into herself? He thought of her on the bench in the open space off Camden Road – how angry it had made him to see the lanky youth lock his arm round her neck and force her head down towards his groin. Then she'd sat opposite him in the pub, pride and embarrassment competing for supremacy in her fine-looking face. She'd played her part to perfection, but they hadn't told her how the drama would end – how she'd find herself imprisoned in the desert, waiting for vicious little Etienne to decide her fate.

He must put Sarah from his mind, focus on getting away from the compound.

He ran on to the perimeter fence, paused to check his sightlines again, then started along towards the warehouse. After a hundred yards he came within range of the two guards on duty by the main doors. No cover now until he was past the north wall of the warehouse, but the glare from the arc lights mounted either side of the hanging doors faded quickly at the periphery and the moon was not bright enough to give him away. He strapped the prayer mats to his back, then wet some dirt and muddied his face and hands. He had seventy or eighty yards to cover, on his belly. Three minutes at most.

He went at it fast, enjoying the vigour and fluency of his motion, the rasp of sand on his arms. The bodies of the guards cast black silhouettes on the ribbed steel wall of the warehouse, and when one of them raised his arm to rub the back of his neck, it looked like the wing of a giant bird. He scrambled on until he reached the lee of the warehouse. He stood and walked to the far end. Just in from the far corner of the building was a safety exit, jammed open with a concrete block.

There was emergency lighting only inside the cavernous hangar, but you don't need much light to recognise an arms cache when you see one. The assault vehicles with their flanks of toughened plate; the stacks of grey steel crates stamped with the coy hieroglyphs by which the arms trade described itself; the damp, grainy smell of oiled steel. If you'd used such weapons in anger yourself, you knew well what they could make of your enemies, of your fellow men, of you. In this box, two severed arteries and a shattered pelvis. That one, half a dozen flayed limbs and a burst aorta. A stockpile of human savagery, lying patiently in wait for young bodies to assault.

He stepped inside and was confronted by the battered flank of an antiquated Russian-made BTR-60P open-topped assault vehicle, and the raised bonnet of an equally venerable Renault flatbed truck, with bits of engine set out on a workbench alongside. There was a long wheelbase armoured Land Rover of the kind that protected you so steadfastly from popgun fire, and a Mitsubishi pickup. A freshly oiled 7.62mm calibre M240 machine gun had been set up by the doors at the far end. Incongruously, a black Citroën DS saloon was parked by the front entrance, so low on its hydraulic suspension that it looked as if its wheels had sunk into the floor. In a far corner of the warehouse there was something hidden under a plastic tarpaulin. James went over and looked underneath: a British-made Light Gun, hitched up to a stout-looking Unimog 404 truck. What was it doing here, this desert arsenal gleaming sulkily in the orange glow of the emergency lights? If it all belonged to al Bidayat, then never mind a few car bombs, Ibrahim al Haqim must be planning a full-scale invasion.

In among the cache of small arms was a low stack of crates stamped with the legend PH-PDW. Parker Hale Personal Defence Weapon – special forces issue, and then only when the budgeteers were feeling flush. He unlatched the top crate and pulled the submachine gun from its foam template, feeling how small and light it was for such a powerful and accurate weapon. He clipped on its strap and put it to one side, along with half a dozen spare clips from a compartment in the base of the crate.

A set of steel steps led to an office on a platform above the main doors and he ran up to take a look, keeping to the edge of the treads to stop the frame from vibrating. The first thing he saw was a two-litre bottle of water on the floor by a filing cabinet. He picked it up – almost full. There was a steel chair with a canvas holdall slung over the back – empty but for a folded square of black cotton. A computer stood on a desk next to a printer and a wire basket of papers. He was about to take a look when he was seized by a feeling of desolation, as if he'd fallen sick. A reaction to the killing he'd done, to Sarah's distress, the endorphins running dry…

How much more trouble do you want?

He ran back down to the warehouse floor, shoved the bottle of water and ammunition in the holdall, slung the Parker Hale on his back, then took a last look round. Spike the vehicles? That would take another hour, and there might be others he hadn't seen.

Salif's the wiry type, what if he's got free?

He left the warehouse by the fire exit and ran over to the perimeter. The looming structure hid him from the rest of the compound, with only one dark corner of the administration block in sight. As good a place as any. He took off Younes's trainers and threw them over the high fence, unrolled the prayer mats and took them in his teeth, then wrapped his hands in canvas and took out his hooked spoons.

The fence was 358 prison grade with a welded 9mm mesh designed to resist cutting or climbing. He reached up with his right arm and felt wetness – fluids leaking from the hole in his side, blood and some kind of watery lymph. He ignored it, reached up with his other arm and hooked the spoons into the steel grid, then hauled himself slowly up the fence. When he could go no higher, he worked the corners of his toenails into the wires to take a little of his body weight, then detached one spoon and inched it upwards. He went at it carefully, deliberately, moving his weight around to keep the distribution even – conscious that the hooked handles of the cheap steel spoons would unbend if he slipped and yanked at them. The fence was topped with a triple line of razor tape strung between brackets, but the brackets were angled outwards, making the final hurdle easier. As soon as he could rest some weight on the topmost wire, he laid the mats across the razor tape, wrapping the last six inches around the outermost line of barbs, then eased himself over and swung down to the ground on the far side.

Western Sahara: desert to the east, ocean to the west. James put the trainers on, crept a hundred yards into the darkness, then turned and looked back at the four buildings of the compound that lay like mismatched pieces of Lego dropped from on high by some irritable infant god. He allowed himself to raise one fist in a gesture of triumph.

How disgusted Sam Hu Li would be to see that. *The future is for children, the past is for old men.* He was still a long way from getting clear of this place – and what was he going to do when he did? Re-group and come back. For Sarah. For Little Sister. Leaving his device in the hands of al Bidayat wasn't an option, and if he didn't take it off them, no one would. The beady eye of MI6 might be roving over their network, but watching from the shadows wasn't what was needed now.

Chapter Twelve

Nat dialled the last number on her list of hospitals and medical centres in Marrakech. After explaining the reason for her call, she was put on hold and forced to listen to a loop of jaunty music. She'd been on the phone for over an hour now, and her reserves of stoicism were all but exhausted. She'd been woken during the night by a horrible dream in which, after climbing interminable flights of stairs, she'd come across Claude Zender sitting in a high-backed chair with a plate of cakes and a flask of oily yellow wine on the table beside him. *My dear Natalya, look what happened to you!* She'd reached up to her face and felt the flesh raw and slick with blood around the hole where her lips had been. *When did this happen?* she'd asked him. *I just went to sleep and then...* The nightmare still twitched at the fringes of her consciousness – along with an image of poor Aisha weeping in the casino loos.

The music stopped and a woman answered, put her on hold again, then came back on the line and told her in an insincerely solicitous voice that no, they had not taken in a Monsieur Kocharian. Was she perhaps the same woman who had called yesterday? Nat admitted that she was and gave a description of Nikolai. The woman became irritable: they did not photograph patients on arrival, of course. Nat hung up, called the Casino des Capricornes and asked for the floor manager. After holding for ten minutes, she crashed down the receiver in a fury and rang the Police Commissariat. The clerk recited the criteria for filing a missing person report, which Nikolai did not meet.

Her brother had been jumped at the casino on Tuesday night – it was now midday on Friday. In the long minutes waiting for lines to connect and receptionists to check their admissions lists, she'd imagined herself sitting by Nikolai's hospital bed and ticking him off for getting himself into trouble while she was away. Now she felt guilty. She'd begged, yes, begged her brother to come to Marrakech and help her, then she'd swanned off to LA while he got beaten up and imprisoned somewhere.

For the first time since she'd dreamed up the IPD400 deal, she found herself wondering whether it might be possible to back out. She thought of Sir Peter Beddoes and Clive Silk, wagging the corporate finger at Grosvenor HQ… Thought of Grey Tony Schliemann, back in Washington by now, sitting in his beautifully appointed office and trying not to choke on his own venom… She'd made an enemy for life there, and fuck all she could do about it.

You're being a wimp, she scolded herself. *Killing off the deal isn't going to bring Nikolai back.*

Was that the voice of greed or the voice of pragmatism she was hearing? She might as well touch base with Grey Tony's man in Rabat, anyway. She fished out the piece of Marriott notepaper on which she'd written the name Grey Tony had given her. Pete Alakhine. He answered on the first ring.

'When can you get to Casablanca?' she asked.

'When I need to.' There was the hint of a sneer in his voice.

'You don't want any notice, then.'

'Notice would be useful. But my instructions are simply to transfer the funds on receipt of the hardware and then to arrange transit to Washington. This is not going to take up a whole lot of my time.'

'You mean transfer the funds, that is, thirty million dollars, *before* receipt.'

'Yeah, that's right,' he said, as if confirming something Nat had failed to grasp. 'So, we have a date?'

'You need to be ready to move quickly when I give the green light,' said Nat, struggling to hold on to the initiative. 'I'll be in touch.'

'Look forward to it.'

Alakhine hung up a fraction before Nat could. His tone had been studiously indifferent, as if Little Sister were no more important than a box of biros. The conversation left her with a renewed sense that her grand deal, which she'd convinced herself was almost foolproof, had unlimited potential for coming unstuck.

* * *

After three hours the pre-dawn light began to bleach the cool darkness from the sky at James's back. It was hard to keep up a steady jog without tripping on the lumps of grey rock strewn across the desert floor, and his feet were bruised, his toes swollen tight against the tatty nylon mesh of Younes's trainers. He stopped and listened for the sound of a diesel engine grumbling in the distance, then scanned the gloom about him. He saw no shape or feature that would offer shelter from the heat or cover from pursuers, nor the slightest indication of what lay in this direction, or that, or any other. It was as if the earth had been vandalised: scraped flat, blasted with sand and rock, then abandoned in disgust. You could measure time here in tens or hundreds or even thousands of years, nothing would change. A thornbush would wither, another would take its place. A colony of ants would mine an oval of baked dirt until it collapsed, leaving a tiny depression behind. A rock would split.

He'd covered fifteen miles – no more, perhaps less. In an hour the sun would be up. In three, the surface of the desert would start to warp in the heat.

It is far too early to lose heart.

He swung the holdall over his shoulder and ran on. The sun pushed up behind him, a slice of dirty ochre in a blank sky. At first it was good to feel the warmth on his back. Then the warmth turned into heat. He remembered the black cotton square in the holdall, and tied it over his head so that it covered his neck. Some time in mid-morning he came across a path. It tracked the contours of the desert and the landscape had folded in around it, vegetation drawing sustenance from the droppings of passing beasts, stones accumulating in little ridges by the wayside. He wondered if he'd crossed others during the night. Paths are for following… But this one didn't look well used. And it ran north–south.

He carried on west. An hour later he saw a vehicle: the Land Rover from the warehouse, a swathe of dust curling up from its tyres, feathering off into the haze. He dropped to the ground and snatched the black bandana from his head, but as soon as he saw it he knew they wouldn't find him. Younes's fatigues were the perfect camouflage; and if you wanted to catch a man on foot, you followed him on foot – lumping around the desert in a 4x4 would get them nothing but sore backs and gritty eyes. He watched the vehicle toil north, leaving an oily stain on the sun-scraped sky.

The guards weren't the danger now. The danger was the sun, exploding slowly in the vastness above his head. The pulsing, swirling heat, contorting the air so you couldn't see what you were looking at. He slackened his pace and drank from the plastic bottle he'd found in the warehouse office. Immediately he felt sweat start to trickle from the pores of his back. *This is nothing*, he told himself. *You can't stop yet.*

He walked on for twenty minutes, then knew it was suicide. He needed to shut himself down, conserve water and energy while the sun boomed on through the midday hours. He found a place where the desert dipped into a shallow bowl, and there was a fallen magaria tree, holding out a pair of twisted limbs. He rolled the black cotton square in the dirt and arranged it over the two branches. So forensic were the sun's rays, you could make out the weave of the cotton in the patch of shade it cast. James crawled into it, drew his knees up to his chin, settled down to bake.

* * *

Nat arrived in the Djemaa el Fna for her dinner at Adela's with Claude Zender. She was ten minutes early, so she climbed a set of stone steps to an upstairs dining room to wait for him. She wore a long black evening dress, gold leather pumps and a gold silk shawl. The outfit was too waspy, she'd decided, inspecting herself in the mirror in her room at the Riad; but the black and gold set off the pale rose of her skin, and anyway, it was the only one she had.

The market below was in full swing, the pleasant hubbub of human commerce rolling lazily through the warm night air. A many-coloured ribbon of heads meandered between the many-coloured stalls. Arms ushered them towards leather barbers' chairs or pans of lentils bubbling on coronets of blue flame. Hands were held out to repel them. A gang of boys tore through the crowd, leaving a litter of shrieks in its wake.

Why had Zender told her that Nikolai had been seized by casino security for starting a fight? He'd seemed so certain about it, too. But her brother had been set up, and that was just the sort of thing Zender would make it his business to know about. She was determined to make Zender explain, but she hadn't worked out how to counter his likely evasions without putting the girl from the casino in danger. Nat hadn't decided how she should treat him, either… Nor whether to tell him about her conversation with Mehmet al Hamra… In fact the whole prospect of the dinner had put her in so many different minds that she had drunk three gin and tonics before setting off from the Riad, and now she felt a little tipsy and not at all ready to get tough with him.

Her attention was caught by a Mercedes drawing up in an area set aside for police vehicles. Two black-suited bodyguards got out from the front seats, and opened the rear doors. An elderly man extracted himself from one, and from the other emerged the ample figure of Claude Zender. The arms dealer shook hands with the elderly man and pointed out a tourist restaurant nearby, then turned and set off alone towards the souk. He seemed to walk without moving his legs, as if he were floating and need only flap his feet a little to propel himself forward. As he reached the arched entrance, Nat called for a boy to escort her across the square and set off down the steps to meet him.

* * *

Needles of sunlight herded James round the magaria tree, nudging his square of shade aside, reaching in to burn his skin. His hand throbbed where the dog's teeth had scraped, but at least the hole in his side had stopped leaking. Twice he heard a diesel engine, fractious and puny on the shimmering air. He didn't bother to hide the black bandana. If chance brings them here to my sleepy hollow, he thought, I'll kill them and drive away in the Land Rover.

The air cooled a little and he roused himself out of his stupor. It was about six o'clock, he guessed. He ate some dates and a flatbread, drank the remaining water in the bottle from the warehouse, then shielded his eyes and looked west. He thought he'd covered twenty-five miles so far, but there was still nothing remotely encouraging to see in the landscape stretched out before him, now striped with shadow as the earth turned its face away from the battering sun. He had to find something, get somewhere. The night ahead was critical. Tomorrow, he'd slow down. Then he'd run out of water. He'd last through the following night, but the following day? Probably not.

He picked his way through the scars and striations in the desert floor, counting his steps to keep the sense of futility at bay. Names lay in wait behind the chain of numbers. *Etienne. Mansour. Al Bidayat. Anemone.* Mansour Anzarane was a terrorist, a member of al Bidayat, Etienne his sidekick. But the compound wasn't a terror camp, it was an arsenal, a warehouse full of military assets, a business enterprise. *Anemone.* What was Anemone? The name lodged itself in his thoughts, irritating and inaccessible as a splinter beneath a fingernail.

Darkness lowered itself around him, and a tide of cold air rose up from the grey sand to meet it. His burnt body shivered and the joints of his legs and arms stiffened so he walked like an old man. Thornbushes hovered like ghosts among the swags of shadow. The dead silence was broken by whistles and croaks and scratching sounds, and he became aware that creatures were moving about him, scuttling unseen from their dens to feed.

* * *

'Dear Natalya, how pleasant to be escorting the most beautiful woman in Marrakech to the best restaurant in Marrakech,' said Claude Zender. 'It would bring joy to the hardest heart – and I, as you know, am soft as a fresh madeleine.'

Nat drew her shawl around her shoulders and took his proffered arm. Its girth made her feel tiny, like a sprite in a fairy tale. She saw that in his free hand he was carrying a folded copy of *Jane's Defence Weekly.*

'Catching up on the trade gossip, Claude? Anything about me?' she asked, as they walked into the souk.

'You have won the Most Beautiful Woman in the Industry Award for the fifth year running. And there's a small ad you might want to follow up… ' He paused in order to suppress a surge of hilarity. 'A special offer on a used IPD400. One careful owner, instruction manual not included!' He bellowed with laughter. 'Oh dear, there's no need to look so solemn, Natalya. I don't mean to mock. We'll have Champagne at Adela's – they'll crucify us on the price, but there is no substitute for lifting the spirits.'

They turned a dark corner and the medley of shouts, yelps and laughter from the Djemaa died away behind them. They were passing through an area given over to butchers' shops, and the smooth, clammy tang of fresh meat lingered from the day's business. Nat heard a scuffle ahead of them and simultaneously felt Zender release her arm and pirouette sideways. A sharp crack punctured the air. She saw Claude's huge frame recoil. She stared into the gloom. A man, down on one knee thirty yards away, arm held out. For a moment she thought he'd been shot and was summoning her to help. Then the darkness was pierced by a spearhead of orange flame and she heard a snap at her feet. Why was she just standing here! A flat boom thumped in her ears. She ran to the edge of the alley and dropped down into the gutter. Claude was sitting opposite, aiming a large silver handgun down the alley.

She saw his finger close on the trigger twice in succession: the heavy blasts walloped off the walls and made her ears sing. The crouching man fired once in reply, the bullet spat off the cobbles between them. Then he turned and ran back round the corner.

'*Merde!*' said Zender. 'I was once a better shot, but in this light… '

Nat pulled herself up and ran over to him.

'Claude, you've been hit.'

'I have, yes.' He shifted his weight and put an exploratory hand to his left side. 'Their incompetence is astonishing,' he muttered.

'What do you mean?'

'They missed. Happily, though there is plenty to aim at, little is of vital importance.' He produced a huge white linen handkerchief and wiped the damp folds of skin at his neck.

Natalya flipped her phone and started to dial. Claude's fist reached out and closed over it. 'No need. The bullet did not lodge.'

'Claude, don't be stupid. You must go to hospital. Please let me. You may be bleeding inside.'

He thought for a moment. 'You can take me to Saint Jerome's, in the Palmerie.'

Zender levered himself up onto one knee, then laced his fingers into the steel lattice of the shutters over the shopfront behind him and heaved himself upright. Natalya pushed at his arm in a futile attempt to help. A first-floor window just down the street had been opened a crack. Someone she could not see was staring at them.

'The gun, Natalya.'

'I must call the police,' she said, looking around at her feet. The gun was propped in the angle of the wall and pavement: a Desert Eagle, a massive gas-operated semi-automatic. She passed it up to Claude, who quickly inspected the safety – leaving it off, Natalya noticed – and stuffed it into his pocket.

'The police,' she said again.

'I should not be carrying a gun.' His breathing was snatched, uneven. 'It would cost me a fortune.'

'Let me look,' she said, and reached tentatively for his jacket. There was a patch of wet crimson just above the waistband of his trousers.

'Leave it. We must get back to the Djemaa.'

The souk suddenly seemed a savage place, its putrid, meaty breath swirling in the grey fluorescent light reaching in from the Djemaa. A small crowd had gathered round the arched entrance, and now peered at them as they made their way back round the corner. Zender walked steadily, but Natalya had never before felt so powerful an urge to run, and for the thirty or forty paces to the square she felt like a bird trapped in a narrow tunnel, her heart flapping in terror. She kept looking back for the kneeling gunman, expecting to hear the crack-snap as he fired at them again.

At last they reached the sanctuary of the square. The crowd drew back to inspect them. Nat looked round for Zender's Mercedes, but it had gone.

'Taxi, taxi, *toute suite*,' she ordered. Fear lapped at her throat and her voice was weak. The boys in the crowd, any number of whom would usually have hared off to find a driver, stared back at her. She saw on their faces the dull-eyed, vindictive look of those to whom the vulnerability of people they are taught to revere has suddenly been revealed.

'Trois cent dirhams pour nous conduire à la Palmerie,' she said, forcing herself to shout. It was an absurd fare for a fifteen-minute drive. After a pause, one of the boys raced off, followed by two others. Claude was breathing badly, head down. She led him over to the taxi rank, and soon a car drew up and the driver hopped out.

'Vous me payez avant que je vous conduis— ' He stopped abruptly when he saw Zender. 'Je m'excuse. Je n'avais pas compris que mon passager... I did not know,' he said, his face quivering with fear. He seemed paralysed by the huge presence of the wounded arms dealer. Nat pulled open the passenger door.

'Push the seat back as far as it will go,' she ordered.

Zender squeezed in, wincing. The thick flesh of his cheeks was ashy and sunken, and sweat trickled from his scalp. An odour of over-ripe melon mingled with the smell of dirty vinyl inside the car. The driver leaned on his horn and sent the Mercedes surging forward. Once clear of the Djemaa, he glanced sideways, clearly horrified at the state of his passenger. They passed through the gates into the Palmerie and soon after drew up in front of Saint Jerome's. The low, off-white building hovered over an oasis of clipped desert grass set with miniature palms and low-set lamps that threw out fans of eerie green light. Nat ran up the path to the main entrance and twin doors whispered open to receive her. Inside, a thin woman in spotless white cotton asked in a self-consciously formal manner whether she had an appointment.

'It's an emergency.'

'I am sorry, Madame, we do not cater for emergencies,' she said, and reached for a photocopied sheet showing the route to the public hospital.

Natalya placed her American Express card on the counter. 'Get four orderlies and a stretcher to the taxi at the front. Have two nurses on standby and call in the best surgeon on your books. I have a very important person in the car and he's been shot. If you turn him away, you may be responsible for his death, and even your lovely white uniform won't save you then. Do you understand?'

The receptionist looked suitably awed and did what she was told. It was twenty minutes before they had manoeuvred their patient into a treatment room and uncovered the wound. Nat stood in the corner and watched. It was an ugly gash four or five inches long, clean enough at the front, where the bullet had started to cut its channel, but where the lead had tumbled out the flesh was mashed and flayed. Was this the opening exchange in the *impending downfall* of Claude Zender, she wondered. *Complicated* was the word al Hamra had used to describe the state of Zender's affairs. Wasn't this just the sort of thing you could expect if you complicated your life by consorting with terrorists?

The doctor was a sour-faced man in late middle age who didn't seem to know who Zender was. He maintained a stubborn silence as he assessed the damage and recorded the details on a form handed to him by one of the nurses. When asked for his name, Zender replied, 'Vianney Malthus', and gave the Riad des Ombres as his address. The doctor stitched him up, while Zender sucked gas and air through a rubber mask. His spirits soon recovered sufficiently for him to demand, between lusty inhalations, that they send for a bottle of Cognac from La Mamounia: he was very specific about the brand.

'Don't let them pretend they haven't any – I drank a glass two nights ago,' he informed the bewildered orderly.

'I am sorry that our evening has come to such a pitiful end,' he said to Natalya when, half an hour later, the doctor had finished. 'But see, the clouds are lifting and the silver lining is revealed: our Cognac has arrived.'

Zender watched eagerly while Nat poured the brandy.

'A generous glass is in order,' said the thirsty patient. 'The bartender who usually serves it is a dreadful miser.'

Nat tasted the brandy and thought back to the scene in the alley – the man kneeling with arm outstretched, the jet of grey-orange flame... But the precise sequence of events was a blur. She couldn't recall when the second bullet had been fired, or which was the one she'd heard striking the cobbles at her feet, or even how many shots there had been.

She put down her glass and stood up.

'Claude, I'm going back to the Riad.'

'Of course, how thoughtless of me.' He extracted his phone from the jacket laid over the back of the chair by his bed and called a taxi. 'Five minutes. We'll go together.'

'We? Claude, don't be ridiculous. You must stay here tonight, so they can look after you.'

'I will not remain in this house of death a moment longer. There is nothing more they can do, besides which, they will be hoovering every dollar of credit from my cards even as I speak. Where is my wallet… Oh, here it is, quite unmolested. Excellent. We will leave without paying, hah!'

'I left my card at reception when we arrived.'

'Florence Nightingale is a hideous old hussy beside you, my dear Natalya. I owe you a deep debt of gratitude, which I propose to repay at an exorbitant rate of interest.'

'I won't hold my breath,' Natalya retorted.

'Nor I, for I am almost out of it.'

The taxi arrived. Zender waved away a disclaimer presented by the woman at reception and they drove back into town. When they reached the Riad, Zender started to clamber out after her. 'I feel rejuvenated by my fortunate escape. Let us see if the Riad can find a bottle to match this *joie de vivre* that has filled me despite everything we have endured. I predict we will yet finish off the evening in style!'

She turned to face him and saw something sorrowful in his eyes, his big, restless eyes in their oyster pouches of baggy skin. She had seen it before, the momentary lapse of his affable façade, to reveal a seam of sadness that she had always found touching in a man so powerful. It lay there in the thick folds of his broad forehead, in the uneven line of follicles with their sparse outcrop of bristly black hairs, in his freak's body, mired in its surfeit of flesh.

'Claude,' Nat said, 'there's a bullet hole in your side. Go home!'

* * *

Clive Silk was in his study, ostensibly to review the day's events and work out how best to save himself from the circling vultures; but so far he'd done nothing but stare out of the window at a misshapen blob of smoke-grey moon lurking behind the horse chestnut tree at the entrance to his driveway. It was 2.30 a.m. A pair of stone-faced men bearing SIS IDs had visited his house early in the afternoon and 'checked' his computer, then insisted on examining Claire's and his daughter's also. He'd arrived home to find the pair of them in a state of indignation that was not much mollified by his protestations about such things being a routine annoyance for MI6 staff.

This was not routine. They were squeezing him, prodding him, trying to trip him up. He'd drunk two glasses of whisky, but rather than making him feel calm and decisive, the alcohol sent a giddy parade of images reeling through his mind: de la Mere kneeling beside him in the lobby outside the MI6 conference room, up to his hips in purple-upholstered foam; Sir Iain Strang gripping the table with his butcher's hands; the large, smooth knees of Caroline Hampshire... How much had Strang enjoyed having a go at him while the others watched. Like being held down and bitten.

Did he want to speak to Claude Zender? He'd been toying with the idea all day. Zender wouldn't tell him anything, but perhaps he could glean something from the obfuscations and denials. He went downstairs, pulled a coat over his pyjamas and put on a pair of trainers he wore for gardening, then went out to the shed and took a pre-paid mobile from a collection he kept in a fertiliser box. He got out the Range Rover and drove for twenty minutes, up into the Surrey Hills, to a parking area where he and Claire sometimes came for a Sunday walk. He took out the phone and dialled Zender's number. To his surprise the arms dealer answered.

'*Mon cher Monsieur Soie*, you are calling me once again. I feel a certain frisson, like a young girl with an attentive beau,' said Claude Zender, who had done honour to the wound in his side with a cocktail of narcotics and was now enjoying a near euphoric sense of his own inviolability.

'What game are you playing with Palatine?'

'Where are you, I wonder? In a remote car park, with your cloak and dagger?'

'Did Palatine pay you to get hold of the IPD400?'

201

'Palatine, Palatine. Remind me… '

'Have you still got it? You said you'd moved it on.'

'You wish to be informed of every little wrinkle in my affairs?'

'This is not a little wrinkle. People here know that Palatine is holed up with his box and running live tests.'

'A fantastic notion. How do they know it?'

'What does it matter? Our networks have some code that alerts the duty officer when it tries to break in.'

'Technology is so flighty, don't you think?'

'Did you pay someone to corrupt the Grosvenor database?'

'What an excitable frame of mind you are in, Clive. I prescribe a milky drink and a good night's rest.'

'I'm up to my neck in it here, Zender. You can't take our money with one hand and piss all over us with the other.'

Zender laughed mightily. 'What a superbly maladroit metaphor, *mon soie*! I do urge you to confine yourself to the argot of the administrative office before some unspeakable embarrassment occurs.' He paused, and when he next spoke, the bantering tone was cut with menace. 'What would His Holiness Sir Iain Strang do if he knew you were making untraceable calls to Marrakech at three in the morning?'

'Sell the thing back to Grosvenor. Natalya Kocharian can make the arrangements. And do it quickly.'

'You wish me to arrange the return of a piece of equipment that inspires such acquisitive hysteria? The shame would haunt me for all eternity.'

'Then get the next flight to Geneva and hide in the fucking lake.'

Chapter Thirteen

James rested for an hour before dawn. As soon as the sky started to lighten, he finished the water in the bottle, ate another brittle disc of bread, and scoured the desert ahead. Something odd: a strip of smooth, muddy yellow between the horizon and the desert floor, as if someone had drawn a line along the foot of the sky with a dirty felt-tipped pen. Five or six miles away, he thought, though distances were hard to judge. It must be a trick of the light. It will go when the sun gets higher.

The sun got higher but the muddy line thickened. Tarmac? *Don't clutch at straws. Not out here.* Hunger was sapping his legs, tiredness lapping at his heels.

An hour later he found vehicle tracks, faint patterns embedded in the flattened dirt. Like the nomad's trail he'd seen the previous day, this track ran north–south. He crossed and went on west, still watching the horizon, fixated in spite of himself.

His foot made sharp contact with a fist-sized rock. He watched it go bouncing away in front of him. The rock hit a ridge and gave a little hop. He traced its gentle arc, saw where it would land…

He got his feet out from underneath him just in time to duck the main force of the blast. Then a splinter of pain seared up his shin and stabbed into his knee. He felt the patter of hot debris on his back, smelled the fierce, gritty reek of explosive. His mouth was full of dirt.

Landmine. He was in a minefield.

No wonder the tracks went north–south.

Smoke and dust drifted over his head. He lay still, trying to gauge how badly his leg was injured. Even through the haze of endorphins, it felt like there was a skewer scratching at the nerves beneath his kneecap. The road was seventy or eighty yards behind him and he could retrace his steps. That would get him to the dirt track. Then what? He spat sand from his mouth and drank from one of the pipes at his waist. How far north to… to anywhere? He lay for ten minutes, fighting the urge to roar at the sky.

* * *

Nat woke up and checked her messages. Nothing from Nikolai. Nothing about Nikolai. No bad news, from the police or the hospitals. No good news, either. A girlfriend back home who didn't even know she was away. Sir Peter Beddoes: *Call urgently.*

She was about to do so when her phone trembled in a dire attempt to render *Nessun Dorma* as a ringtone: Zender.

'I have good news for you,' said the arms broker, 'with caveats. It seems that my clients may be willing to deal.'

'That's a change from the line you spun me last night. Maybe I should arrange to have you shot more often.'

'I beg your pardon?'

'You were wounded, remember?' said Nat, thinking it was unlike Claude to be nonplussed by a joke.

'I recall the event both as indistinctly as can be and yet with quite horrible precision,' he replied. '*Alors*, regarding my client, I was able – most skilfully, should you ask – to turn things to your advantage, an act of chivalry that risks destroying my career, but I remain devoted to your interests, to the point of obsession, one might say—'

'You're such a prima donna. What are the caveats?'

'I am gunned down in the street and you call me a prima donna? The injustice would confound a man unaccustomed to your barbs. In any case, Natalya, it would be invidious of me to give undertakings on your behalf and I have arranged for you and my client to conclude this matter face to face.'

'Suits me,' said Natalya, thinking this was all rather incredible. 'Aren't you afraid we'll cosy up together and do a deal behind your back?'

Claude cleared his throat. 'It is an unhappy truth that even one's most valued associates may be rendered cruelly disloyal by the chance to line their pockets at one's expense. But who can live his life on the basis that friendship and trust mean nothing? I would prefer to die begging for potato peelings in a pauper's jail.'

'I rather see you enjoying a dish of pommes dauphinoise and selling the peelings to the highest bidder.'

'Ha-ha! We'll not quibble. And my client's invitation?'

'Accepted. Where's the meeting?'

'In the Southern Provinces, which the locals like to call the Free Zone. It lies about a hundred kilometres east of Smara.'

Was this the place al Hamra had told her about, Zender's arms cache? What was she walking into? The Moroccan spy's warning about bombs and terrorists now seemed like a dreadful prophecy.

'Claude, do we have to?' she said.

'The owner of the device you seek is most particular. It's a magnificently remote location, and one must fly there, unfortunately, and stay overnight. But you will have a splendid opportunity to admire the Saharan landscape. The epitome of desert, one might say. A camel could not ask for more.'

'If it's good enough for a camel...' The Saharan landscape held no attraction and remoteness was not something she craved at all, but before she could raise further objections, Claude had said he would collect her shortly after two and hung up.

Nat sat down on her bed. She tried to muster some feeling of elation at the prospect of setting in train the series of transactions that would net her the best part of four million dollars, but it was quickly displaced by a sense of apprehension that had been lurking in the shallows of her mind ever since Nikolai had gone missing. Why couldn't the meeting take place in Marrakech? Who was Zender's client? The government suits who'd so obsessively staked out the IPD400 while it was still under embargo in the Grosvenor warehouse would rather be caught engaging in an act of devil worship than doing a deal with Claude Zender: from what she knew, his customers were blinged-up dictators, coup-plotting mercenaries and warlords who liked to pay for their wares with a couple of dump trucks full of kimberlite. If only Nikolai were around to back her up.

She showered, dressed in a sober outfit of dark blue chinos and a cream linen shirt, then rang Sir Peter. It was a relief to be diverted to his answerphone. *I'm not getting anywhere*, she said, the little-girl-lost voice sounding all-too plausible in her ears. *An awful thing happened last night and I don't know what to do.*

* * *

Something had slashed through the side of James's foot, torn a ribbon of flesh from his shin, and lodged under his kneecap. He couldn't see it, but he could feel it all right – every time he bent his knee. A sliver of shrapnel, squatting in a net of bloody sinew like a little steel spider.

He dragged himself back to the dirt road, stopping frequently to look for his footprints. The wound had made him thirsty. He was low on water and the sun knew it. The shrapnel had to come out.

All he had was Nazli's screwdriver, two hooked spoons and Salif's knife. He tested the five-inch blade with his thumb – it was wafer sharp and had the flat blue sheen that comes from years of grinding. He cleaned up the tools as best he could, then laid them out on the holdall in dismal imitation of a tray of surgical instruments. The steel shard would be small and slippery. He studied the spoons. Like fishing for minnows with a meathook. Why had he got out the screwdriver? It didn't look useful now. He bent the knee as far as he could, sluiced a little water over it and dabbed away the blood. There was a ragged cut about an inch wide, but no steel protrusion. He could feel the shrapnel in there, plucking at the ligaments. He grabbed the knife and used the tip to probe for the shard. A nerve twanged, making him gasp and freeze. He shoved a wad of canvas between his teeth, and eased the knife-tip under the skin at one edge of the cut. Blood teemed to the surface. He let out an anticipatory groan and swiftly widened the incision by half an inch. The feel of the sharp blade parting flesh made him suck in his breath. He pressed the skin above and below the wound and pulled the lips apart. He thought he saw the shard, but it was immediately swamped with blood. He had to do the same on the other side or he'd never get a spoon handle in there. The sun was high in the sky now, making the sunken plateau of sand palpate like a drumskin. Hunched down in the desert, diligently probing the underside of his knee with a dirty old knife, he felt faint with insignificance. Why go through this? Why not lie down and be obliterated?

Stop fiddling around. Get on with it.

Sweat was streaming over his face. He took a sip of water, positioned the blade… Bit down on the canvas and sawed through the skin. He flung the knife aside and it skittered against a rock. He swallowed a wave of queasiness and peeled back the skin-flap, but still he couldn't see the steel fragment. He retrieved the knife. The blade curved slightly at its tip, away from the sharp edge. If he could get that curve in the right place, he might be able to pull the shard out far enough to reach it with a spoon. It would mean using the cutting edge of the blade as leverage, but hey, who said this was going to be fun? What would Sam say now, the sanctimonious little prick? *Why you scared like a baby? Baby scared because he don't know what happen next. You know what happen. So why you scared?*

The pain, Sam. I don't like it when the pain scoots up the nerves.

Nerves got to tell you when they cut. They can't speak so they give you a little pain.

Smug little shit!

Why you make it worse with shaking? Why you go so slow?

If you say one more word...

Why you—

The blade scraped on something, but he couldn't see what through the sticky red ooze. He thrust the knife in deeper with a moan of disgust, bent his knee another five degrees, raised the handle to prise open the wound. Panting like a sick old dog. The knee joint pulsed and winced. The sun laid a hissing iron on his neck. There! If he could just get a grip with his forefinger and thumb... No. They slid off in the slops of blood. He reached for a spoon and pushed the hook up into the wound below the knife-blade. Sweat dripped over his hand. He felt the edge of the shard and tried to pinch it between the spoon handle and the knife, but it clicked free. Bellowing without restraint, he widened the wound again, drove the two steel instruments as deep as he dared. This time it held. He drew it out by tiny fractions like some hideous conjuring trick. It wasn't coming easy. He kept tugging, willing his hands not to shake. Blood splashed onto the sand. It was cutting as it came, a live thing, thrashing and lashing its sharp little tail.

When it was done, he held in his hand an inch-wide frill like the paring from a pencil sharpener that twisted off at one end into a ribbon of corkscrewed steel. He flexed his knee gingerly – it felt better, in the grateful way the body does when foreign objects are removed. He finished the water in the second tube. One left. How long would that last? His overalls were sodden with sweat, turning the desert dust to mud that clung to him like pale scabs. He looked down at his leg. It was spattered and streaked with blood from the knee down, and a hank of torn skin flopped from his shinbone. It might be better for him now if the guards caught up and took him back. His face was clammy and his hands shook like a drunk's. A thin, vomit-like odour clung to him. The odour he'd smelled on Younes, and on Mansour. And many times before when death was about.

* * *

Nat made her way to her favourite table in the courtyard of the Riad des Ombres. She was only a few feet away when she looked up and saw that it was already taken. The usurper was lounging in a semi-recumbent posture, one leg stretched out across the kelim-covered banquette, one arm draped across its back. His intention seemed to be to show that he was entirely at ease, but the effect was ungainly. And the grey hair sticking up from his head gave him, she thought, the expression of a startled goat.

'Natalya Kocharian,' he said. 'We've not met.'

'No,' she replied, and turned away to find another table.

'Nigel de la Mere. You've been liaising with our mutual colleague Clive Silk, but I thought we should cut out the middleman, as it were. Please, sit down.'

She knew who he was – Director of the North-West Africa Office at MI6. A profoundly unwelcome visitor. He had not stood, and was looking her up and down from his inelegant roost. The arrogant manner and blatantly lascivious eyes told her that he knew her reputation for sexual generosity and wished to count himself – a man of status and influence – a potential recipient of her favours; and yet he suspected that she would refuse him, and the prospect of that humiliation filled him with latent hostility.

'Is Clive with you?' she asked, then turned in her chair to summon a boy to take her order for breakfast.

'I've already eaten,' said de la Mere. 'But go ahead. I might filch some of your coffee. Then you can tell me how you're getting on with Claude Zender.'

What did he know? That she'd been to Washington to see Grey Tony? If she'd flown from London, he surely would have found out – but from Marrakech? What did he want to know? What should she tell him? Men of de la Mere's type were unpleasant to deal with, but his low opinion of her would be useful. She'd play the ditzy blonde and get away from him as fast as possible.

'I'm glad you came, anyway,' she said. 'I feel a bit out of my depth with all this, and Clive's not much help.'

'There there,' said de la Mere.

The sarcasm was gratuitous, like being taken suddenly by the throat.

'I'm told James Palatine's in town,' he said. 'Has he been in touch with you?'

'Is he? No. I don't know why he would want to.'

'Or with Claude Zender?'

'I've no idea, sorry.'

'When did you last speak to your fat friend?'

'We had dinner last night,' she said, realising it would be risky to lie.

'And?'

'It's hard going, Mr de la Mere. He says he's not interested in handing back the IPD400. In fact, he says he can't.'

'A negotiating position, obviously. He'll do anything for the right price.'

A negotiating position... The exact phrase she'd used when she'd called Clive Silk from Marrakech Airport. The thought made her feel claustrophobic.

'I don't have the right price to offer him,' she said.

'Grosvenor will foot the bill, whatever it is. That I can guarantee. Has he told you who his client is?'

'He wouldn't dream of it.'

'What happened in the souk last night?'

'We were shot at. Poor Claude was injured.'

'Badly?'

'A horrible wound in his side, but he's not in danger.'

'Shame. Does Zender have an idea who the gunman was?'

'I don't think so. He didn't tell me, anyway.'

'He doesn't tell you much, does he. When's your next meeting?'

'I'm waiting to hear,' Nat lied. Flying south with Zender, even if his place was teeming with terror suspects, now seemed like her best and perhaps only means of escape.

'Make it today. Use those well-documented charms of yours. Tell me the time and the place and I think I might join you.'

'Wouldn't it be better if you made the appointment yourself?' said Nat, beginning to feel riled. 'I'm just the salesgirl, after all.'

'For now you are. If you don't co-operate with me on this, you'll be lucky to get a job flogging knickers off a market stall in Kiev.'

Nat was saved from delivering the response this insulting threat deserved by the arrival of her breakfast tray. The boy arranged the dishes before her, his demeanour so graceful and sweet she felt like taking him in her arms. 'Please bring coffee for Monsieur,' she said.

'I'm finding your manner obstructive, Ms Kocharian,' said de la Mere. 'I came here to talk to Zender and I don't intend to be balked by you.'

Al Hamra's warning, she thought. *I'll tell him. Why not?* She could hardly be expected to make serene and rapid progress on restoring the IPD400 to Grosvenor if the Moroccan intelligence service were plotting Claude Zender's imminent downfall. It would buy her time – and keep this foul man off her back.

'There's something I guess I ought to tell you, since you're here.' She made him wait while she spooned a helping of yoghurt into a bowl and decorated it with chopped dates and hazelnuts. 'I was approached by a Moroccan agent called Mehmet al Hamra last night. He said Zender's in trouble – something I didn't really follow, about a man called Mansour Anzarane?'

The supercilious expression left Nigel de la Mere's face so fast it was as if someone had torn it off. Now he looked merely bored, but Nat could see he was struggling not to give more away.

'What about him?'

'They think he was responsible for the Agadir Bombing, and they say he's been hanging out with Zender at his base in the Free Zone. It made no sense to me – what do you think?'

Nat arched one eyebrow and stared at de la Mere, greatly relishing the fact that she'd put him on the back foot.

'Who told you this?' he said, declining to meet her eye.

'Mehmet al Hamra, of the DG something or other. He's a spy, I think. Like you, Mr de la Mere.'

'He approached you where?'

'At the Casino des Capricornes.'

'You were hoping to bump into the owner, but you ended up with the Gnome of Rabat.'

'Is that what you call him? I thought he was from Marrakech.'

'Al Hamra goes where he pleases these days. What else did he say?'

'Nothing. Oh yes, he advised me not to do business with Zender, which makes things tricky. What do you mean, bump into the owner?'

'Claude Zender. He owns the casino – co-owns it, rather.'

Nat's neck flushed hot, adrenalin prickled in her armpits. Aisha had said she'd been paid to set up Nikolai by *Rich men who own the casino*... Could it be true? She stared at de la Mere, her poise completely gone.

'Another thing you didn't know about Zender. The special favours are over-rated, clearly.'

What did he mean by that? The SIS man stood up and positioned himself very close to her chair, so he could look down at her.

'Call me at six this evening, when you have the meeting set up. Don't tell Zender what you just told me, and don't say I'm in town. Clear?'

*　*　*

It was several minutes after Nigel de la Mere had stalked off before Nat succeeded in quelling the panic flapping in her stomach. Zender had set up Nikolai at the casino – *his* casino. She was besieged by spies. James Palatine was in town. In a few hours' time, she was going to climb obediently into a private aeroplane and accompany Zender to a *magnificently remote* location in the Sahara desert.

She ordered a glass of brandy and tried to work through everything that had happened since she'd returned to Marrakech from LA three days ago; but her thoughts kept oscillating queasily between Nikolai's disappearance and the IPD400 deal and refusing to settle or resolve themselves into any kind of order. All she could think of was that Claude Zender had betrayed her. Client, mentor, lover... That Zender was gone, but still her mind kept pawing pathetically over the vacated space. She wanted to call the fat arms dealer and scream at him. But it would not be wise to show her hand too soon: he'd slither away into the shadows, leaving her spinning in stark sunlight. *I must stay close to him*, she thought. Anyway, what else could she do? Go back to London, leaving Nikolai in Marrakech, or wherever Claude's men had taken him, if they had taken him at all – which, she now realised, since the casino had more than one owner, she still couldn't be certain about? Stay here at the Riad answering the questions of spies until the police came to arrest her?

Eventually she calmed down sufficiently to conclude that she was in trouble and needed all the help she could get. Anton and Mikhail… The realisation that she had no one else to turn to was dispiriting. Still, Nikolai trusted them, and he was no fool. Anton's phone was switched off – no doubt he was treating the blonde casino hostess to a festival of lovemaking such as only the star of *Bitches of the East* could provide. She got Mikhail instead and told him to come with Anton to the Riad immediately.

'Where is the ree-add?' he asked stoically.

'Just tell the taxi driver to come to the Riad des Ombres.'

'Ree-add domz.'

'Mikhail, get a pen and write it down.' She spelled it out for him.

'I don't know where is Anton. He's got this girl— '

'Oh for fuck's sake, just find him and bring him here.'

She went down to the courtyard and leafed through a copy of *Le Figaro* without reading a thing. After half an hour, she was rescued by the arrival of one of the Riad's bellhops.

'Gentleman to see you, Miss Kocharian.'

Mikhail was dressed in black tracksuit bottoms and a sky blue T-shirt. He looked as if he had not left his room at the Holiday Inn since arriving, and the thick, rubbery skin of his face was wonderfully pale.

'Sit down – where's Anton?'

'Gonna come soon.'

'Like soon in an hour or soon next week?'

Mikhail shrugged, then took to massaging the muscles in his left shoulder.

'What do you think happened at the casino?'

Mikhail shrugged. 'Got the wrong guy,' he said. 'Nikolai got no enemies here.'

He doesn't, thought Nat miserably. *But I do.* She turned back to her newspaper, leaving Mikhail to sit in docile silence. Eventually Anton turned up, looking every inch the drowsy-eyed lothario.

'You took your time,' said Nat.

'A pleasure to see you too, Ms Kocharian.'

He was wearing a pair of pointy tan loafers and carrying a cream jacket that was obviously fresh from the souk. As he hung it on the back of his chair, his eye was drawn to a smudge on the cuff and he set to brushing it away with the back of his fingers.

'For fuck's sake leave the jacket alone,' said Nat.

'You're a big poof,' said Mikhail.

'Maybe you guys should have followed my example and stayed in bed,' said Anton.

'You been fucking that girl,' observed Mikhail sagaciously.

'What can I say? Love-making puts me in a great mood.'

'You'll have to tear yourself away,' said Nat, 'because you and Mikhail are going to Smara.'

'Where's Smara?'

'A fourteen-hour drive south. I'm meeting someone who may know where Nikolai is,' said Nat. 'I want you two there as backup.'

'Backup for what?'

'Backup in case I need help from a retired gym-bunny and a gigolo?' said Nat. 'How the fuck should I know? If you don't fancy it, Anton, stay here with your casino whore. I'll go alone.'

'I would never let Nikolai down,' said Anton theatrically.

'I'll arrange the transport. Get back here for midday. Bring your passports and be ready for an overnight trip. I'll call you tomorrow in Smara.'

*   *   *

James took a double dose of ibuprofen, bound his knee with canvas and set off north. The sun swooped and swung overhead, beating the air into glassy shapes, filling every iota of sky. He was a blip on its radar. It was following him. His tongue was starting to thicken, his knee throbbed where the shrapnel had twirled, the hole in his side wept. He wasn't drinking the water in the last tube round his waist, though he knew he should take what he needed – knew that in deserts just like this men had preferred to die of thirst than face the despair of finishing their last drop.

The pain kept his mind from circling in on itself, from swaying into darkness. *One step at a time*, he said out loud. *Count them.* Before he'd reached a hundred, the words were back: *al Bidayat. Anemone.* You could walk to their beat, one step per syllable, eight in all. Repeat. Ten times for eighty steps, or eight hundred, or eight thousand. Better than counting. Where are the guards in the Land Rover who will take me back to my yellow-curtained room, to my shower tap and my bloodstained mattress? The sun was moving towards its apex, land and sky so ferociously bright he could barely open his eyes. *Al-Bid-ay-at. An-em-o-ne.* You could do it for ever.

James saw the man some time later. He came out of his trance and watched him, half a mile off, his outline wobbling like poured water. Beware of light-headedness. That's when your thoughts unravel and scamper behind your eyes. He drank from the tube and raised the Parker Hale to his hip. The man started to walk away, a patch of colour drifting over the scorching void. James followed. They walked in tandem for ten minutes. *I'm not gaining on him.* If anything, the gap between them was wider. He realised he wasn't walking, but shuffling. He forced his legs to swing and straighten properly, and watched the man's gait intently, hoping for signs that he was tiring. His eyes ached from squinting. *There's no one*, he thought, *I'm chasing something my own mind put there.* The ghostly howl of the one o'clock sun flattened everything. Another ten minutes and the gap had closed again. Had it? The man broke into a trot. It had. James lengthened his stride. *Stay in touch.* He wondered when to make the decisive move. Whether he was capable of making the decisive move.

Twenty minutes passed. He wasn't gaining any further, but lurching along on empty. The dogged, desperate pursuit was in stalemate. His tongue was gagging him, a wedge of dry gristle in his throat. He sucked from the tube at his waist and felt his mouth fill with plastic-scented air.

He must catch this man now, or the chase would finish him.

Concentrate, the way Sam would demand.

He cleared everything from his mind, everything but the long, fluid movements of his arms and legs, the steady pumping of air in his lungs. The gap closed to five hundred yards. The man noticed, picked up speed. But he was crossing rough, untracked desert, and the harder he ran, the more he stumbled. James closed on him again. His quarry veered towards the smoother surface of the dirt road James was on and the angle he took worked against him. In a few minutes, James could bring the Parker Hale to bear. He quickened again, willing his mind to overcome the heaviness tugging at his bones. His breath was losing its precious rhythm, whooping and rasping in his throat. The pursued man was struggling through a series of dips and ridges, but soon he would reach the road and the race would even up.

The effective range of a Parker Hale was no more than 150 yards, but you could get a bullet to kick up the dirt at twice that distance. The man scrambled up a short rise and on to the road. James came to a standstill and unslung the machine gun, aimed it a couple of yards above the man's head.

'Stop!'

The word disappeared like a scrap of confetti in the turbid layers of superheated air. His quarry did not stop. James fired a burst from the Parker Hale and saw flickers in the sand just short of the man's heels. He aimed up and left, fired again, then sent another burst to his right and sprinted forward. The man was running full pelt, but panic disrupted his steps and he spun to the ground. Now he was in range, and James had the machine gun snarling in triumph, ripping up the sand around his victim's ankles.

The man didn't get up, but turned to face him. It was Salif.

Chapter Fourteen

Nat watched the landscape tilt and flatten as the little Cessna tore into the sky. They banked sharply to the west, and all life seemed to be set out below: the city of Marrakech with its dense, jumbled centre and desiccated outskirts strewn with tiny houses, the lines of tarmac strung with beads of traffic, the patches of cultivation like pieces of a half-finished jigsaw; and beyond them, the crumples and gashes of the pristine desert stretching to the far horizon.

'I confess I don't quite like these aerial antics,' said Zender unhappily. 'I tell the pilot not to veer in so dramatic a fashion, but air traffic control shout at him until he has left the commercial lanes. 'Ouf! Dear me… ' he exclaimed as the little plane hit a thermal and dropped like a brick, the pitch of the engines whizzing up a register as the propeller mashed the lighter air.

Nat had been treating Zender with icy reserve, awaiting the moment to confront him with the fact that as co-owner of the Casino des Capricornes he must at the very least know more about Nikolai's disappearance than he had so far let on. She'd made another connection, too: according to Aisha, the rich men who owned the casino hadn't just told her to set Nikolai up, they'd ordered the disfigurement of her friend. *One girl, they cut her lips…* But Claude could not be capable of such a thing – not knowingly, anyway. Aisha must have got that wrong, Nat concluded – it was something else altogether. But the taint of the story would not quite leave her.

'Every time I fly in this toy,' said Claude Zender, 'I vow never to do so again. This seat was designed for an underfed child.'

'If they made a seat for you, it would be the only one on board.'

It was the kind of jibe she had delivered many times before – but it came out as an insult. The hostility penetrated Zender's funk and he looked at her with curiosity – but if he was composing a reply, it was silenced by another patch of turbulence. Soon, the plane levelled out and skimmed south through calmer air. Claude rearranged himself and pulled a leather-bound flask from the pocket of his jacket. He poured a tot into the glass top and knocked it back gratefully, then took several deep breaths.

'I said we were visiting a client of mine. But perhaps now is the time to explain that I still have possession of the IPD400.'

Natalya turned to face him.

'Fuck the IPD400! What have you done with my brother?'

'Your brother, yes. The Improbable Hulk, as I think of him. You know that as well as marching up and down outside Zizou's and patrolling the casino like a trainee Cheka, he used my name to obtain a free rug worth two thousand dirhams from my friend Mr Choukri in the souk?'

Nat was thrown by this – what had Nikolai been thinking of?

'I thought he was an envoy from my past – I have enemies who would employ men just like him to take their revenge. But I should have guessed, after this extraordinary act of chutzpah, that he must be a Kocharian.'

'Where is he?'

'You will be reunited with him in due course.'

'He has nothing to do with this.'

'Nothing? You did not bring him to Marrakech in the belief that having a small-time Ukrainian gangster at your side might prove useful in your pursuit of the IPD400 and the riches you expect it to bring you?'

Nat lost her temper. She threw herself forward, wrapped her arm round the neck of the pilot and tightened with all her strength. The pilot's hand jerked the joystick and the plane banked and set off into a shallow upward arc.

'Stop, you'll kill us!' Claude bellowed.

'Where is my brother!'

Claude tried to reach out for her arm but his seatbelt held him back and when he released it the angle of the plane's ascent sent him crashing against the exit door. The pilot was grunting for breath, hand clamped on the joystick but unable to push it forward sufficiently to bring down the nose of the aircraft. With his free hand he clawed at Natalya's arm, but her grip was tenacious. The fuselage started to rattle as the engines strained to haul the plane upwards.

'We will stall,' Claude shouted, heaving himself forward in his seat. 'Let the pilot go, I beg of you!'

'I don't care if we die! What've you done with Nikolai?'

The plane was losing momentum as its climb steepened, fast approaching the point of weightlessness when gravity would outweigh the propeller's thrust.

'I swear to release him, I swear it! Let the pilot go!'

Natalya released her grip and slumped back in her seat. The pilot's hand shot forward. The plane gave a shudder and hung in the air like a kite in a dying breeze. For a moment it seemed that there would not be enough power to get the tail up. They must fall back... Then the Cessna tipped sideways. They dropped for several seconds, not flying but tumbling. The plane began to corkscrew. Air roared over the wings. Nat's bag banged against the front windscreen. Claude lurched forwards and clung to the empty co-pilot's seat. Five slow seconds passed. As the pilot fought the joystick, the spin became a broad spiral, and then the spiral opened into a long, breathtaking swoop. The Cessna vibrated with the ferocious velocity, then flattened off at last. Once again, they were shooting through the skies on level wings.

'You still want to play your fucking games with me, Claude Zender? Do you?' Nat shouted, trying to keep her voice from trembling. She hadn't realised how close the pilot had been to losing control of the plane. But Zender was in no state to reply: he was wedging himself back into his seat, clamping his seatbelt shut with trembling hands. His face had the hue of codfish belly, and sweat mixed with blood from a graze on his forehead streamed into the already sodden collar of his shirt.

'Tie her up!' the pilot yelled. 'We're going to land.'

'Shut up and fly,' said Nat.

'Point made, Natalya,' said Zender, when his terrified panting had abated sufficiently to allow him to speak. 'Though it is hard to imagine a more foolish way of doing so.'

'I don't like to be cornered.'

Claude closed his eyes and began to breathe heavily. His mouth dropped open. Then he lifted his head and glared at her. 'If I die in this foul aircraft, they won't know what to do with your brother other than to kill him.'

His monstrous head fell back and he closed his eyes again. Natalya watched the jowls below his jaw quiver every time the plane bumped. A few minutes later, they hit another pocket of turbulence and he jerked upright, looked at her accusingly, drank from his flask, then lay back again. Nat thought she would like to open the door and push him out, watch him plummet until he were no more than a speck in the pale brown landscape below.

* * *

Their transport was an ageing Peugeot 504 estate which their driver, a nervous, dark-eyed old man, had decked out with an array of religious artefacts covering both the Christian and Islamic faiths, Virgin Marys and crucifixes jostling for space with a compass decorated with a picture of the Shrine of Kaaba and a selection of prayer cards. These apparently gave him licence to drive at a relentless pace. As they catapulted past the vans and lorries grinding up the hills south of Marrakech, Anton imagined the Holy Mother's benedictory hand embedding itself in his back teeth. Mikhail, meanwhile, had stretched out on the back seat, arranged a T-shirt over his face, where it was held in position by the bristles on his cheeks, and gone to sleep.

At three o'clock, they stopped and ate houmous and chips off paper towels. Their meal was interrupted by a furious whining overhead. Anton looked up to see a single-engined Cessna whir up into the sky, then flip over into a chaotic dive.

'This country would be a fuck of a lot safer if they still went around on camels,' he observed.

After Agadir, the road straightened and emptied.

'Souss-Massa National Park,' said their driver, jabbing his finger into the west. 'Bald Ibis. Many other birds.'

'I really don't give a fuck,' said Anton.

'Tiznit: two hours. Guelmim, Tan Tan, border – maybe eight hours. I don't know. Maybe many more hours.'

The landscape of ochre hills and black rocks rearing out of the rumpled sand made Anton feel depressed. Where was everyone? He longed for the comforting plumpness of Maria's bottom wriggling on his groin. He was actually fond of the girl. He closed his eyes and pretended to go to sleep. At Tiznit, a town of salmon pink buildings with blue doors, they stopped to drink mint tea and be stared at by a café full of thoughtful Berbers. Three hours later, they arrived in Guelmim.

'Why would anyone build a town here,' said Anton.

'On route to Timbuktu,' said their driver. 'Sahara begin now.'

'And I thought we were about to come out the other side.'

'Sahara is big,' said Mikhail, whose capacity for sleep appeared to have reached its limit.

'Oh thanks a fucking lot for that, Micky, I didn't know we had a tour guide with us. Anything else you can tell me about this fascinating land?'

Mikhail gave a bellow of hilarity. 'I tell you it is *big*. Now I tell you… ' He was barely able to get the words out between wheezes of mirth: 'It is *sandy*.'

'Wow. And it's hot, right?'

'Yes… ' Mikhail gasped, snorting mightily. He could say no more but fell to nodding and mouthing the word *hot* over and over again.

'Ignore him,' Anton said to the driver. 'Which way now, then? Let me guess: straight on?'

The road seemed a tenuous thing, its verges lapped by scurrying eddies of sand. Up ahead, the two lanes narrowed into a thin grey line and vanished at a point unnervingly short of the horizon. Anton pictured them three months hence, arrangements of leathery flesh and parched bone imprinted in the dust.

* * *

Salif glowered at James from beneath one eyebrow. The other was too swollen to move. James tied his hands, then searched him. Salif carried nothing except a canvas bag with two plastic bottles of water. James took one and drank until he felt he could speak without choking on his tongue.

'What are you doing out here in the desert, Salif?'

Salif raised his head and looked at James, but didn't answer. Anger flickered in his eyes, but there was no outright hostility as far as James could see, and he remembered the conciliatory look Salif had given him after his treatment at the hands of Etienne and Mansour. Just then, he heard the drone of a light aircraft overhead – a twin-engined Cessna, dropping low over the desert to the east and apparently intending to land not far from the compound.

'Let's go,' James said.

'Have dirhams?' Salif asked, a censorious frown creasing his forehead.

'Yes, I've got your money.'

They set off north along the dirt road, James limping a few paces behind with the Parker Hale levelled at the small of Salif's back. His prisoner hadn't yet explained what he was up to, so James tried again.

'Why did you leave the compound?'

'Look for you,' said Salif.

'The big man in the black cap sent you?'

'No. Not work for him. I come alone. I am Polisario soldier. Good for fight Moroccans.'

'Are all the guards Polisario?'

'Guards not Polisario men.' He turned round to waggle a bony finger and glare at James, as if the suggestion were an insult. 'I am Polisario soldier. Younes Polisario soldier. Report to Colonel Sulamani.'

'Sulamani was the officer who shot Hamed, the one they tried to execute?'

'Yes. Colonel Sulamani is Polisario officer. I work for him many years. My people always work for Sulamani people.'

'Won't he be angry that you left the compound?'

Salif looked crestfallen. 'I let you run away. Sahrawi men proud. Proud people.'

'So who are the other guards?' James asked, prompting Salif to start walking again.

'Report to Commander Djouhroub.'

So that was the name of the big lump of muscle and bone in the black military cap who'd presided over Mansour's botched execution of Hamed. James had thought at the time that there was something confused about the relationship between the commander of the guards and the dignified old officer who had shot Hamed – that they must operate under different lines of command.

'Then who pays Commander Djouhroub and his guards? Who gives them their orders?'

'Monsieur Zender.'

Zender… The name scythed through James's tangled thoughts. Claude Zender was said to be the kingpin behind every nefarious deal in north-west Africa, so it wasn't exactly unexpected. An arms broker manages an arms depot held at a remote compound on behalf of the Polisario; he hires a suitably brutal sergeant-major type and a cohort of guards to protect it. Why not?

Another question: had al Bidayat hired Claude Zender to arrange his abduction? It was the most plausible explanation he'd thought of yet – which did not necessarily make it true.

'Monsieur Zender is at the compound?' he asked.

'I see him there many times. Big man, fat. Fat like a king.'

'So you are Polisario and report to Colonel Sulamani and the other guards work for Zender. What about Etienne and Mansour?'

'Bad men.' Salif turned and spat. 'Not Polisario.'

'No, al Bidayat men.'

'I not know what is al Bidayat,' said Salif suspiciously.

'Come on, Salif. Mansour and Etienne took orders Ibrahim al Haqim, and al Haqim runs al Bidayat.'

'I not know al Bidayat,' Salif repeated.

They walked on in silence. The words which had dogged him the previous day came back to stump through his head: *al-bid-ay-at... An-em-o-ne...* He should drink, but there wasn't much water left. He looked around for shade, and the movement made his head wallow. Get off the road, then. Rest.

He led Salif a few hundred yards into the desert to the east and lay down behind a thicket of thorns that gave no shelter. Salif squatted down a few yards away and watched him thoughtfully. Balloons of heat billowed off the desert floor. The lowest branch of a thornbush lay across his field of view, a brown zigzag, gnarled and collared at the joints like an old man's finger. He looked up. The sun dangled in a spinning sky. Salif was standing beside him. He slid upright. The desert tilted up and he leaned in towards it. A soft clout. Sand crunching against the thick length of his jaw.

* * *

'Exactly where are we, Claude?'

The Cessna had plonked down on a carpet of warped concrete laid at what seemed to be a random location in several thousand square miles of sand. Then they'd been driven to a hideous military compound that seemed to wobble in the early evening haze, as if it didn't really exist. A large black, red and green flag drooped over the entrance to the main building.

She followed Zender through a pair of double doors into an entrance hall with a tiled floor, a deliciously dim and cool place after the sapping heat outside. A huge chandelier hung from the ceiling, though the wiring was coiled up by a rough hole in the plasterwork above. To left and right, a pair of staircases rose up in three flights to an iron-railed gallery. Ahead of them was a set of doors bearing a lengthy inscription in Arabic, with two stone benches set on either side.

227

'This building? It is, if you can believe it, the future seat of government for an independent state in the Western Sahara,' Zender replied. 'That is their flag above the door, and there's a debating chamber behind those doors. The establishment was built by a wealthy Algerian, though I don't believe the intended occupants like it much. It is ugly, certainly, and they are fond of their tents. For now, it serves as a base for their military wing, the Polisario.'

'We've left Morocco, then?' said Nat, suddenly feeling nervous.

Zender didn't reply, but set off towards a passage under the right-hand staircase. 'The United Nations, in their clever way, have designated this a Non-Self-Governing Territory,' he said, 'and this particular stretch of vacancy they call the Free Zone. Certainly it is free of any kind of regulation, which makes it an excellent place to do business.'

He ushered Nat into a large, square room with two windows facing west.

'My office – which I have endeavoured to make at least passably inviting.'

The room was decorated in a sickly shade of bleached apricot, with glazed floor tiles to match. The focal point was a Chinese rug with a pattern of birds and butterflies in flight through a fantasia of coiled tendrils and extravagant blooms. A pair of plum-coloured sofas was arranged either side. Between the windows was an Art Deco desk with an olive green leather top, and a reclining chair, its black leather upholstery discoloured with use. Bottles of Badoit, red wine, whisky and vermouth stood on a sideboard next to the door.

It wasn't even passably inviting, Nat thought. It was unutterably dingy, like a hotel lounge in a no-longer-fashionable spa town. She realised that until now she had only ever seen Claude in hotels and restaurants, and had assumed that his private space would prove fascinating to anyone privileged with an invitation to enter it. This room revealed nothing – or that there was nothing to reveal. Again she felt a sense of foreboding. *You're being ridiculous*, she told herself. *What were you expecting, a Labrador dog and a collection of DVDs?*

'The decor lacks a woman's touch,' said Zender, as if reading her thoughts. 'The furniture is from Damascus – quite fine, if that sort of thing appeals.'

'It doesn't. And don't blame the absence of women for your poor taste. Where is Nikolai?'

'You'll have to give me the benefit of your advice, Natalya, I'm sure I am lost without it.' He was looking for something in the drawer of his desk. 'I apologise. I am somewhat distracted. The business of running this place would draw blasphemy from a saint. You would like to wash, I expect.'

'What I would like is to see my brother.'

'And you shall, if you would just allow me to…'

He didn't finish. It was exasperating but, now that she'd had time to think through what Zender had said to her on the plane, her righteous fury had lost some of its force. He'd discovered that Nikolai was following him and taken steps to defend himself… Unnecessarily violent steps, but then Zender would have violent enemies. At least Nikolai was safe. Besides, she was entirely at the arms dealer's mercy now; and she felt too worn out to scream at him again. So when a boy in a white shirt came to escort her to her bedroom, she satisfied herself by saying as she left: 'Five minutes, Claude. Or else I'll go and find Nikolai myself.'

Her room had a large but meagrely upholstered bed and a rank of fitted cupboards with no rails or shelves. The wall of mirrored tiles in the bathroom had been unevenly laid and made her look as if she had been dismantled and put back together again in a hurry. But even the most flattering mirror could not have disguised the fact that she was exhausted, absolutely shredded by the events of this horrible day.

She stared out of the window. Ahead of her was an ugly, two-storey edifice that reminded her of an office block in Kiev's decaying industrial belt. To the left was a low building surrounded by razor wire, and up the slope to the right, a big warehouse. And now that she was too weary to suppress it, the thought which had been festering away in a dark corner of her mind finally erupted: the shooter in the souk had been waiting for her, not Claude. Grey Tony wasn't pinned beneath her heel at all: he was sitting in his office in Washington, arranging for her to be killed.

She replayed her phone call with Pete Alakhine to see if she could wring some cause for optimism from their desultory conversation, but all she could manage was that he hadn't actually refused to speak to her. Then she remembered Magda. She must call her, warn her that Grey Tony was fighting back. She found her cellphone: no network. She switched it off and on again, but it hunted in vain. *I misjudged Grey Tony.* She shuddered. Fucking with the NSA procurement chief was the worst mistake she'd ever made. She'd assumed that if you'd spent the last ten years accumulating the demeanour of a superannuated B-lister, you must have gone soft. But Grey Tony was a control freak, everyone knew that – even the waiters at Holworthy's knew that. She thought of him orchestrating their dinner at the awful, stuffy restaurant, like a superstitious old woman arranging bones and beads to ward off evil. Remember the panicked reaction when she'd run her naked foot over his calf? The horror on his face when she'd told him he had to buy the IPD400 or face ruin and disgrace? She'd goaded him beyond endurance.

Misjudged Schliemann, is that what she'd done? Or had the rush to make herself a few million dollars richer made it essential that she blind herself to the obvious risk that Grey Tony would not behave how she wanted him to? She hadn't made an error of judgement, she'd made no judgement at all – and not because she was stupid, but because she was greedy. In the space of a single day, her entire plan – and she now saw with horrible clarity what a naïve and impetuous plan it was – had disintegrated. Why had she thought she could blackmail Grey Tony and play Zender for a fool? She wasn't a criminal mastermind but a sales director who traded on her looks. And they were powerful, ruthless men, in a different league from her.

The room faced east – so much for enjoying the Saharan sunset. The scrub bushes scattered across the surface of the desert looked like dead flies. She remembered the conversation she'd had with Sir Peter and slimy Silk, two weeks that seemed like two years ago. She should have told them what they could do with their job and walked away. But she hadn't and now she was here.

* * *

Something sharp was pressing against his Adam's apple.

'You not know desert.'

The point of Salif's knife at his throat.

'You hit me, take dirhams. Maybe I kill you.'

James didn't move. The Parker Hale was slung over Salif's back.

'I could have killed you, and Younes. But I didn't. I killed Mansour.'

'Mansour killed?' Salif looked pleased. 'Take water,' he ordered.

James reached for the bottle and drank deep, felt his muscular function and mental acuity restoring itself. He was suffering from early-stage heat exhaustion, he realised, and had momentarily lost consciousness.

'Why they take you at compound?'

'I was your prisoner, Salif. And you're Polisario. So you tell me?'

'No. Not Polisario prisoner. Colonel Sulamani is good man. Not let them do this thing.' He gestured at James's ribs, where the shears had cut. 'Not Polisario prisoner,' he confirmed with a vigorous shake of the head.

'Move the knife and I'll tell you what I know.'

Salif took the knife from James's throat and held it between them, lightly poised. He's an experienced knife-fighter, James realised, who knows that a tight grip only slows you down. But in any case, his manner was not so much threatening as triumphant: he'd turned the tables, but James didn't think he had any intention of killing him. He explained what had happened. It was hard to know how much Salif understood, but James was careful to lay the blame squarely at the feet of Claude Zender – mention of whom provoked much spitting and tongue-clicking on Salif's part.

'You said I was not a prisoner of the Polisario, Salif. So you do not have to take me back to the compound.'

Salif frowned and rasped the blade of his knife across the pad of his thumb.

'If you take me back there, Etienne will kill me.'

'Bad man,' said Salif again. 'Not Polisario.'

'Commander Djouhroub's guards insulted you. They flapped their arms and made noises like a chicken. They do not respect the Polisario. They are mercenaries who are interested only in money.'

Salif gazed off into the desert and muttered to himself. *Move on him, now*, James thought. But something in Salif's demeanour held James back, told him it wasn't necessary. After a further moment of contemplation, the Polisario soldier stood up, unhitched the Parker Hale and dropped it in the sand. Sahrawi honour had been served by James's re-capture, and it seemed that was enough.

'You make fool of me,' said Salif. 'I think: this man afraid like old woman.'

'You never really thought that,' said James, taking the gun and dusting sand from the breech. 'Remember when I was naked on the bed with my dick out – you looked like this!'

James pulled an expression of exaggerated disgust and Salif's face broke into a smile like a battered old treasure unwrapped from a dirty cloth. He laughed, an unruly cackle that made his eyes water.

'Younes want go back and fuck you. He say you like it.'

'It's a good thing you stopped him.'

'Wah wah wah! Ow! Don't hurt me,' he mimicked, twirling the knife in his fingers and sheathing it. James felt a surge of warmth towards this man who had once been his guard and now seemed set to be his saviour.

'What now?' he asked.

'Walk two, three hours,' said Salif. 'Moroccan army post. Wait for night. Six soldiers there – they take money. Cross Wall of Shame.'

'Wall of Shame?'

Salif seemed disappointed by the question, as if James had revealed a depth of ignorance that was nothing short of disgraceful.

'Moroccans build wall,' he said.

It was coming back to him now – a *berm*, in military terminology, studded with forts and command posts like something set out on a wargames table by a pair of elderly generals whose marbles had long since rolled under the skirting board. A military folly on a spectacular scale, probably visible from space. This was the blurred line he'd seen on the western horizon and taken for a trick of the light.

Salif pointed north, then swung his arm south. 'Mauritanie, Algérie, Maroc – twenty-five hundred kilometres. Maroc army hide behind wall. Hide like rats.'

'The Moroccan soldiers will let us through, if we pay them?'

'They don't care. Ten years, no fighting, nothing for them.'

'Isn't it dangerous for you in Morocco?'

'Not Maroc.' Salif spat. 'Is my country, my people.'

They walked on in equable silence. The sun began to withdraw from the edges of the sky. The desert was changing, the leached, ashen white giving way to a warm gold. Shadows appeared alongside them, leaning into the east. 'Wah, wah, wah, don't hurt me!' Salif said occasionally, the invariable prelude to a burst of merriment. After an hour, Salif stopped suddenly and turned, raising his hand to shield his eyes.

'Djouhroub guards. They come now.'

James followed his gaze and saw a cone of dust drifting up from a point on the dirt road several miles to the south. They ran east a few hundred yards until they found a hollow, then scraped together a ridge of rock and stone along its rim. If it wasn't enough to hide them, they'd have to fight – and the Land Rover was a tempting prize. But Djouhroub's men weren't mugs and it wasn't worth the risk, if they could avoid it. Fortunately, the sand-coloured uniforms he and Salif wore – Polisario uniforms as he knew now – were perfectly suited to hiding in the desert. He couldn't see the vehicle, only the dust in its wake. After a few minutes it bounced into view, sunlight flashing off its windscreen, field glasses blinking from the passenger window. The quivering fan of dust rolled level, then past, the particles thinning out in the motionless air, merging with the ribbon of muddy sky at the horizon.

They waited until it was some miles past, then moved on, watching the horizon for any sign that the vehicle was turning back. But James didn't think the guards would find them now – their noisy, dust-trailing vehicles were too conspicuous, and Salif's eyes and ears seemed perfectly attuned to the desert. In an hour or so it would be dark, and they'd be forced to drive back to the compound empty-handed.

A few miles further on, the Polisario soldier stopped and looked towards the Wall of Shame to the west, then paced up and down the road, studying the terrain from different angles.

'Track here, no mines. Wait for night. Walk to fort.'

'I blew myself up once already,' said James, looking in vain for the safe channel through the minefield. 'Reckon I'll use the jetpack this time.'

Chapter Fifteen

The five minutes she'd given Zender to reunite her with her brother was up. Nat opened the door to her bedroom and beckoned to the boy in the black trousers and white shirt who was waiting in the passage.

'What is your name?'

'Adel.' He placed the palm of his hand over his heart and bowed.

'Adel, could you bring me a bin or a plastic bag? I need to dispose of something – you know, a ladies' something.'

Adel went scarlet and shot away. Nat made her way along the passage and down the staircase. As she approached Zender's room, she heard voices. She stood close to the door and listened.

'Your scruples do you credit, Colonel Sulamani,' Claude Zender was saying, 'but you are like a man covered in mud who frets over the state of his fingernails. I do urge that you leave me to my business, as I leave you to yours.'

'The staging of executions is no part of your business here,' replied a deep voice, resonant with suppressed anger. 'I am required to explain to my superiors why a man was brought here to be killed, and to provide the identity of the executioner, whom you call Mansour el Shaafi.'

'This man Hamed was a danger to all of us.'

'A danger to you, Zender. He is no concern of the Polisario.'

'He had to be disposed of – I assure you I did not specify that it be done in such flamboyant style.'

'You employ those brutes el Shaafi and Etienne to do your dirty work and yet you expect them to behave with decency? They take no part in guarding the compound, and I told you a week ago that they must leave.'

'Etienne has gone and Mansour is dead, so really, the matter need not detain us.'

'Yes, killed by the Englishman you held prisoner here. After a week examining your computers, this man has disappeared and is probably now discussing what he knows with Mehmet al Hamra.'

'We are taking all necessary steps to find him, and I doubt he will get twenty miles without stepping on a mine. Nor was he abducted, but was found poking around inside one of our offices in Oran.'

'You found a spy in your office, so you brought him here?'

'There's nothing to suggest he is a spy,' said Zender testily.

'It is a characteristic of intelligence agents that they hide what they do.'

There was a moment's silence. Nat was about to move away when the man called Sulamani continued:

'I understand from Salif that you had him tortured.'

'An absurd suggestion, which I note he is not here to repeat. I dare say you are upset that he has deserted you— '

'This has nothing to do with Salif,' his interlocutor cut in icily. 'It is intolerable that you should expose us to such uncertainties. What is to stop your Englishman from reporting that he witnessed a Taliban-style execution on Polisario soil? In speeches to the UN, the Western Sahara is routinely referred to as the new Afghanistan.'

'Nobody listens to the Moroccans on this subject. The chamber empties the moment it is their turn to speak.'

'It is not just the Moroccans. The Security Council will not allow another cradle for Islamic fascism to emerge in the Western Sahara, however weak the evidence. Let King Mohammed have his bit of desert, they will say. These shameful activities of yours, which you still decline to explain, hand the Moroccans a far more potent weapon than all their tanks and guns.'

Nat heard footsteps in the entrance hall, coming her way... She retreated into the doorway of the room opposite. Under the sinister influence of the conversation she had overheard, she felt a strong impulse to conceal herself. She tried the door behind her. It opened and she stepped into the room. The shutters were closed and thick drapes hung over the window – all she could see was the greenish glow from a monitor with a pattern of Microsoft logos chasing around its screen. It smelled peculiar, plastic and antiseptic mingled with a sweet, chemical whiff that tightened her throat. She pulled the door shut and listened.

A knock on Zender's door.

'Entrez,' said Zender.

She heard the door open and a woman's voice, too quiet for her to make out what was said. Then the door clicked shut.

A slow, crackling exhalation of breath behind her. Nat spun round and peered into the gloom. A luminescent face with no eyes or mouth shone from the far corner, bobbing and nodding like a balloon suspended in a draught. A whimper issued from her throat. She swallowed, tasted in her mouth the sickly odour that haunted the air. *There must be a light switch.* The hand she moved towards the wall beside the door was heavy with dread. Her fingers scrabbled over the square of plastic, found the switch.

The buzz and flicker of a striplight. A body laid out on a wheeled hospital gurney. The plump white bag of a medical drip hanging from a steel frame.

My God, Niko!

Nat ran to her brother's side. He was unconscious, naked but for a towel folded over his groin, his face sunken and grey. She laid her hand on his chest. His skin was hot and yielded like putty to the pressure of her palm. His heartbeat was sluggish and lumpy. She looked away for a moment, tears stinging her eyes, then saw the yellowy pink flesh of his leg puckered around an eight-inch gash cut on one side of his knee, the skin and muscle peeled back to the bone like an anatomical model.

'My darling Niko, what have they done to you?' she whispered. 'My poor angel, don't worry. It's me, Natalya. I'll take care of you.'

She smoothed a few dank crinkles of hair from the furrowed skin of his forehead. His breathing was shallow, interspersed with sudden gasps and long, laboured exhalations such as the one she had heard earlier. She cast about for some way to bring him relief – a damp cloth to wipe his face and chest. Then she noticed that his wrists and ankles were strapped to the frame of the gurney. Quickly she unfastened the buckles and brought his arms up to rest on his chest. Like that, he looked as if he had been laid out for burial. She felt herself begin to sob, tried to check herself, then brought his hand up to her cheek and allowed the tears to come.

'A morbid infection. I think now we see improvement.'

Natalya swung round, releasing Nikolai's arm, which fell down beside the gurney, tugging the dripline and causing the bag of solution to swing on its steel hook.

'Be careful!'

A small, white-coated woman had appeared in the room as if from nowhere. She had a square face, a thin, taut mouth, and protruding eyes beneath neatly plucked eyebrows. Her mouse-brown hair was cut off abruptly beneath the ears and a straight fringe ran high across her forehead. Her face was expressionless and her eyes as empty as a snake's.

'What have you done to him?'

'I have treated him for his wound and the infection. It was so bad. I had to cut it open to let the air in. He has taken half our supply of antibiotics. You are his sister, I think.'

Nat didn't reply. The little doctor moved to the gurney, replaced Nikolai's arm, checked the needle taped to the back of his hand and the flow control half way up the dripline. Moving to the desk, she pulled latex gloves from a pack beside the monitor, snapped them on, and returned to the gurney, hands held up stiffly in front of her. Then she bent over Nikolai's leg and prodded the skin around his knee.

'The wound has dried and the swelling has receded.' She brought a gloved finger up to her nose and sniffed. 'The smell has almost gone – it was so bad! I will suture tomorrow. First the muscle, then wait to be sure the infection does not return. After, the skin. The knee is forever damaged, I think. But he is on the mend.'

The chirpy English colloquialism sounded creepy as a lullaby on the lips of a paedophile, and Nat thought this woman would just as soon cut her brother's throat as stitch his wound. Now, she was re-fastening the buckle at Nikolai's ankle.

'Leave that off,' said Nat sharply.

The doctor ignored her. Nat came round to the end of the bed and faced her.

'You will not tie up my brother.'

'It is for his own good,' the woman said angrily.

'Fuck that.'

Natalya reached over, seized the doctor's wrist and pulled her away from the gurney. It seemed to take no effort at all to move her, but suddenly she was only inches away and bringing her knee up fast into Nat's midriff. The blow doubled her up, but she didn't release the woman's wrist and they hit the floor side by side. Nat felt wild with fury. She grabbed the doctor by the hair, swung her head up and banged it back down to the floor, then clawed at her face with her free hand, fingernails gouging her cheek. A vicious pain lashed Nat's forearm and blood spattered onto the floor. She drew back sharply and saw the curved blade of a scalpel protruding from the doctor's fist. The fist arced up and Nat jerked her head back just as the sliver of steel whirred past her nose. She rolled away, but the doctor was already up on her feet and moving in. Nat looked up and saw in her eyes an absolute and unequivocal desire to cut her again. She scrambled across the floor to the desk, blood from her forearm smearing the grey tiles, then reached up and hurled the chair in the direction of the white-coated figure now almost upon her, eyes bright with impatience.

The door burst open and a tall man in army officer's uniform ran into the room. He came up behind the doctor, seized her by the wrist and forced her down to the floor, where he anchored her with a large boot in the armpit. One by one, he unclamped her fingers from the scalpel. She cursed and spat. Natalya sat on the floor, legs stretched out before her, trying to staunch the flow of blood from her forearm by clamping it against her T-shirt.

Claude hurried in. 'My dear Natalya… ' He brushed past the officer and the prone doctor and knelt at her side. 'Are you hurt?'

'I am fucking hurt, yes. That bitch… My brother… '

The pain made her gasp. Her T-shirt was sopping with blood.

The tall officer wrapped the scalpel in his handkerchief and dropped it into the pocket of his shirt. 'What would you like me to do with her?'

'Lock her in the conference room, Sulamani, if you wouldn't mind.'

'What the fuck's going on?' Natalya screamed into the thick flesh of the face bowed over her. 'My brother's half dead on a stretcher and I'm cut to shreds by this… ' Nausea swam in her throat and her voice dropped to a whisper. 'What are you doing to me?'

'Be calm, I beg of you, Natalya. This should not have been allowed to occur. I will find something for the cut.'

He fetched hydrogen peroxide, a roll of bandage, swab packs and dressings from a steel cupboard by the door and started to tear them open with clumsy fingers.

'You may as well use gloves,' said Nat weakly.

'Of course.'

He pulled on a pair of latex gloves and continued. When Nat pulled her arm away from her shirt, blood cascaded out. Claude tipped the bottle of peroxide and Nat yelped as the stinging fluid sluiced the long cut. She held a dressing in place while Claude wound the bandage over and over. *You're not good at this*, thought Natalya. As he bent forwards, she saw him stiffen and noticed the bulge of the dressing over the wound in his side – the wound from the bullet that she now thought had been intended for her. His face looked more discomposed than she had ever seen it before, and he seemed grateful for the need to concentrate on this unfamiliar task, exchanging only the necessary words. *How is it that I still feel compassion for this man?* she asked herself, disgusted at the confused emotions that were tumbling inside her.

Zender swept the debris into a pedal bin and stood helplessly surveying the blood-splodged floor.

'Never mind that,' said Natalya. 'Get the boy to bring my bag. And tea and water, and a mattress or cushions – something to sleep on.'

'Surely it would be better if I were to help you to your room. It is unpleasant in here.'

'Fucking unpleasant, but I'm not leaving Nikolai with Madame Mengele on the loose.'

'Oh yes, very good – I'm delighted to see that your sense of humour was not damaged in this deplorable attack.'

'Ha fucking ha. Are there painkillers in that cupboard?'

'We needed a doctor here, it was not easy to find someone— '

'Another time, Claude.'

He found codeine and gave her the bottle, then hurried out. Nat lay back against the wall. Nikolai. Still alive. Just. What had she got them into? What had she overheard? Zender had ordered an execution. *I did not specify that it be done in such flamboyant style.* An Englishman had been tortured. A spy… *I'm too exhausted to think,* she decided. Zender returned, with Adel carrying the things she had asked for. She arranged a makeshift bed and sat on it, sipping the hot, sweet tea and contemplating the glass of wine he had poured for her.

'A Lezongars, 2002 – not a great wine in the classic sense, but— '

'Give me the key and get out.'

He detached it from a ring and put it in her hand, then left, looking chastened. Natalya crawled over and locked the door, leaving the key sideways in the lock so another could not be inserted from the other side. She crawled back to her makeshift nest, took four codeine, knocked back the glass of wine, lay down, arranged her aching forearm, and passed out.

*   *   *

At dusk the sky turned swollen and purple, the sand a muddled grey. The sun lowered itself slowly down behind the Wall of Shame, its face, so blindingly ferocious by day, now filtered by a screen of fine dust that rose up from the desert floor. The wall meandered away into the darkness to north and south, while directly ahead of them the Moroccan fort stood silhouetted in the distance like an upraised thumb. They shared the remaining water, then James buried the Parker Hale in a depression on the other side of the road.

'You, go there,' said Salif, indicating that James should walk behind him as they entered the litter of shapes and shadows that lay between them and the Moroccan fort. James's knee was no longer a joint but a throbbing tube of swollen tissue, and he was feeble and clumsy with hunger. His memory had helpfully presented him with the army slang for an anti-personnel mine: *toe-popper*. He limped along in Salif's footsteps, trying not to stagger off course when his feet met uneven ground.

They didn't talk. When they were less than half a mile from the Wall of Shame, a searchlight flicked on and an oval disc of brilliant light raced over the sand towards them. James shielded his eyes. They heard the percussive hiss of a loud hailer and a voice that sounded shockingly close:

'Face down, donkey-fuckers!'

They obeyed. After a minute, the oval of light swept off into the desert. The air had cooled but the sand beneath his chest was soft and warm as the pelt of a snoozing beast. James felt an unexpected sensation of lassitude. A few hundred yards away was something akin to safety. The desert has kindly moods, he decided, and one might as well enjoy them.

He could see the Wall of Shame properly at last: a thick ridge of bulldozed rock and sand, ten or twelve feet high, that looked to be in a state of constant decay – at several points the crest of the ridge had collapsed and cascaded down to the base, and there was evidence of numerous repairs. It was hard to believe that a structure so crude and transient could extend to more than two and a half thousand kilometres – perhaps they'd forgotten to tell the men building it when to stop. The fort, built directly behind the wall, was a single-storey concrete building, no more than twenty feet across, with no doors or windows on this side. From the centre rose a five-metre, flat-roofed tower, on top of which were mounted the searchlight and a heavy machine gun. There were three men up there, their heads intermittently suffused with amber as they passed round a cigarette.

'They look for other men,' Salif hissed. 'Then come for us.'

They lay there for ten minutes before the soldiers grew bored. The narrow column of light angled down on their prone bodies.

'Stay down!' said the loud hailer.

They heard a scuffling on the wall to the left of the fort and the top rungs of a wide wooden ladder appeared. A soldier clambered into view, hauled up a second ladder, and lowered it on their side. Two more soldiers crossed the wall by the ladders and the three of them ran over to where James and Salif lay.

'We have run from a gang of thieves,' said Salif in Arabic. 'We need to get into Morocco, where it is safe.'

The soldiers did not reply. One of them gave James a speculative kick in the stomach. A reaction seemed to be required, so James groaned. The soldier knelt on James's back and searched him, then attended to Salif, pulling the Beretta, the knife and roll of banknotes from various pockets of his overalls.

'Up!'

They were taken up and over the wall, then led across an arc-lit concrete apron to a steel door at the base of the fort. A generator chuntered in the background. The apron was fortified by mounds of earth and rock on either side, ending in a gap that gave on to a track leading west. An ancient 4x4 and a small bulldozer were parked up on the far side. The soldiers hustled them in through the steel door.

The room inside was a bare shell crammed with narrow bunks – enough for maybe thirty men, though it was obvious that only a few were in use. There was a cooking stove, a wooden table and steel chairs slung with canvas, and a set of shelves with a dismal collection of cooking pots, catering-sized cans and jars, tin cups and plates. The smell could not have been more fetid if there'd been a dead dog in there with them. Two men lay on their bunks, a third sat at the table – a sergeant, judging by the chevrons on his shirtsleeves. One of the soldiers who had brought them in – he was younger than the others, couldn't have been more than seventeen – put the cash and Salif's knife and gun on the table. The other two went and lay on their bunks to watch.

'*Bienvenue*, Polisarios,' said the sergeant at the table, leaning back in his chair.

'We're not Polisario,' said James in French, feeling that the words might choke in Salif's throat.

'No?' The sergeant laughed sharply and looked at his men, who obliged with an assortment of derisive grunts. 'On this side, Moroccans. On that side, filthy donkey-fucking Sahrawi.' He stared at Salif.

'We just want to get to Smara,' said James placidly.

'Français, English?'

'Je suis Anglais,' said James.

'Why are you in the Free Zone?' he asked, switching to Arabic and staring at James, obviously assuming that he would not understand. He was wrong, but James thought it prudent not to enlighten him and looked blankly at Salif. The Moroccan sergeant was a scrawny, pale-skinned man with a shaved head and close-set eyes. His voice was thin and wheedling, as if he were used to making excuses. If he wasn't running this little outfit, jail would be a good place to keep him, James thought.

'We have money,' said Salif.

The sergeant unfolded the notes and counted them, then tucked them into his breast pocket. 'You want to buy your way to Smara with this? Maybe I'll kill you and keep the money anyway.'

He picked up the Beretta and pointed it at Salif. 'And this. Who gives a fuck? *Je vais vous tuer!*' he said for James's benefit.

The soldiers stared at James. Salif looked down at his hands. The uniformed men suddenly seemed very close. James turned round, but saw no hostility in their eyes. They've seen this all before, he told himself again, it's a little power-play, a rite of passage.

'If you kill us, who knows what will happen next?' he said in French, keeping his voice calm. 'Could be nothing. Could be trouble? Who knows?'

The sergeant swung the gun round and pointed it at James.

'Look what I found lying in the desert, a big Englishman and his donkey-fucking friend. They'll make me a captain and give me a fancy hat.'

'They'll ask me why I came here to cross the wall,' James said. 'I could cross anywhere, so why here? What will I tell them?'

'This gun is shit,' said the pale man bitterly.

James shrugged. 'You have anything to eat?'

'You think this is a café?' He put his feet up onto the table, the soles of his boots pointedly facing Salif. James wondered how many more insults his companion would endure.

'I've been out in the desert all day,' said James. 'I could eat a horse.'

'We got a horse?' he asked his fellow men, reverting to Arabic. They laughed. 'No horse.' He stood up. 'The Englishman can fuck off. This Polisario with a face like a goat's arse, I'm giving him to the police. They like to play with Sahrawi. They put wires on their dicks and make them dance.'

James folded his arms. 'I'll stay with him.'

'You like each other, huh. He gets tired of donkeys, he fucks you instead?'

There was a rumble of amusement from the watching troops.

'Any rice, beans maybe?'

'Any rice?' the sergeant mimicked. 'Any nice white rice for the nice white Englishman?'

Salif raised his head and addressed the soldiers in solemn Arabic. 'The trouble with donkeys is, their cunts have bristles. It's like fucking a bag of straw. Trust me, you're better off with a nice soft piece of English arse.'

The timing was perfect and it brought the house down. The soldiers on their bunks roared. The boy-soldier blushed. The sergeant looked on with a condescending smile fixed to his mouth. He was not entirely pleased that Salif had swung the mood in their favour.

'What did you say to them?' James asked Salif with a show of indignation.

Salif grinned. 'I said you had the arse of a lamb, milky white and soft as a dumpling,' he replied, still in Arabic.

'Let's stick to French,' said James, with a show of indignation. 'Oh yes, I like French very much,' said Salif in Arabic, beaming. The soldiers bellowed their approval.

'OK, ramzis, I'm going to let you go. Tell your Sahrawi friends it costs fifteen hundred dirhams to cross here.' He waved an arm at the boy-soldier. 'Get them chickpeas and water. See how nice I treat you?' he said to James and Salif, as the boy pushed open the steel door.

'I take the knife,' said Salif, reaching for it. 'The Englishman's like a bitch on heat when he gets excited.'

The sergeant's hand closed over the scabbard, then spun it across the table. 'Take the knife and fuck off.'

The soldiers fell silent, the mood of hilarity gone. The boy-soldier returned with a can of chickpeas and two plastic bottles of water. James took them and moved quickly to the door.

'Remember what I said about donkeys,' Salif said, but the blokey tone had gone and the soldiers merely stared.

'We don't fuck donkeys, we fuck Polisario,' said the pale-faced sergeant, his voice sour.

James pulled Salif out of the stinking guardroom before he could speak again. They set off across the steely light of the concrete apron and heard the door slam behind them.

'You, me, we kill stupid *Marocains*.'

'We got out, OK?'

'He call me Polisario donkey-fucker,' Salif seethed.

'You were smart in there, Salif, let's not throw it away.'

'You give me idea. Wah wah wah, don't hurt me!'

'Yeah, OK Salif, the joke's over.'

'Wah wah wah!'

*   *   *

James and Salif walked for five minutes, then opened the chickpeas and ate, scooping handfuls into their mouths and taking turns to drain the viscous, salty syrup from the can. Invigorated by the food in their stomachs, they walked as fast as James's knee would allow. It felt like a reprieve to be out here with Salif, after a day that should have seen him dead. The track dipped down to follow a dry riverbed across a wide, shallow depression, where the sand lay in billows like a painted sea. After an hour they saw a signpost set in a concrete block lolling by the side of the track. It was decorated with a Moroccan flag and read: *Poste Militaire 309, Provinces Maroc du Sud*. Beyond it the tarmac road gleamed beneath a swirling skein of windblown sand.

Salif spat at the foot of the signpost and pointed south. 'Smara.'

After twenty minutes, Salif took him by the arm and pointed: a vehicle approaching from the south. They retreated from the road and lay in a hollow while a white Toyota Land Cruiser passed by. It bore the logo of MINURSO, the United Nations Mission for the Referendum in Western Sahara, and had little flags flapping self-importantly from either wing. The referendum was supposed to have taken place at least fifteen years ago, as far as James could recall, but had been successfully obstructed by the Moroccan government. The vehicle blasted past in a furious crescendo of noise and was gone, leaving a diesel-scented vacuum in its wake.

'Off to do not very much and write a long report about it,' James said. 'How far, do you think?'

'We get a ride. Be in Smara soon.'

They walked on through the immense night, little breathing things traversing the earth's circumference, footsteps tapping at the silence. No border here would ever be more than the fantasy of a bureaucrat with pencil, ruler and map. And yet they had marked it with two and a half thousand kilometres of rubble wall, garrisoned it with soldiers marooned in their little forts, surrounded it with secret gardens sewn with mines that burst up to pop your toes. And the people for whom this unearthly land was home had been herded into a place called the Free Zone and told to wait while the world twiddled its thumbs.

James's reverie was interrupted by Salif, who had taken him by the elbow again.

'Car.'

They stepped away from the road and turned to watch. It was still perhaps three miles off. Compared to the MINURSO Land Cruiser, its headlights were feeble, a smudge of yellow on the arrow-straight road. It came on slowly, its progress still utterly silent to James's ears until, when it was about a mile off, he caught the faint chirring of its engine.

'Not army,' announced Salif. 'Peugeot 504.'

He stepped into the road and stood blocking the way. James thought it would be prudent to stay just where he was. The headlights tunnelled the darkness. Then the left-hand beam caught

Salif's dusty fatigues and the vehicle slowed to a halt. The driver got out and uncurled himself stiffly. Salif walked up and the two men stood in the road and conversed. Salif pointed up the road; the driver nodded and indicated his car. They seemed to have reached an agreement, so James stepped forward from the roadside, hand outstretched, a large smile on his face. The Peugeot's horn sounded behind them, its interjection harsh and offensive. A second man pushed open the passenger door and stood up.

'Get the fuck back in the car or we'll drive to Smara without you,' he said: a tall, thin European, speaking in an odd Scottish accent, wearing a Bermuda shirt that managed to look loud even in the dim light from the interior of the Peugeot.

'Hi,' said James, walking briskly towards him. 'What a piece of luck to bump into you guys. We thought we might have to walk to Smara.'

'You do have to walk to Smara,' said the man, ignoring James's proffered hand. 'There's not enough room in the car.'

'You can get ten people in one of these if you pack it right,' said James. 'I've seen it in Dar es Salaam.'

'We can't take you,' the man insisted.

James disliked him on sight, with his ridiculous shirt and shifty eyes, and wondered whether to just dump him by the side of the road. The driver had already taken Salif round to the rear of the Peugeot and opened the boot so he could clamber in.

'You can keep the front seat,' said James, opening the rear door. He climbed in and found himself being eyed up by a squat, powerful man with arms that would have been folded if their girth had not made that impossible. His expression was formidable, but it was hard to know what he thought of this incursion into his rear-seat space. At least he didn't seem inclined to side with his companion, who remained fuming by the roadside as the driver slammed the boot shut and returned to his seat.

James wound down the window and looked up at him. 'You coming?'

'Fuck this fucking place,' said the man in the Bermuda shirt, yanking open the passenger door. 'And fuck you all.'

The five men set off south to Smara. The vehicle was now so low on its springs that its exhaust scraped the tarmac at the slightest undulation in the road.

'James Palatine,' said James above the din.

'Mikhail,' said the man beside him. They shook hands.

'And you are?' said James into the ear that presented itself over the back of the seat in front of him.

'What the fuck's it to you? You're paying for this ride, I hope you know.'

'He is Anton,' said Mikhail. 'Pissed about something.'

'Why're you making friends with these dickheads?' said Anton. 'If they try to rob us, they are fucking ant-food.'

'You boys have business in the Western Sahara?' James asked.

'No,' said Anton, 'we're on holiday.'

'Found the sand OK,' said Mikhail. 'Still look for the beach!'

*   *   *

An hour later, the line of Smara's rooftops appeared – like a zigzag of cream silk thread lain out across the inky sky. They drove through an outer fringe of corrugated iron shacks and low breeze-block huts strung with electricity cables, then turned into a larger thoroughfare. A scattering of streetlights cast a wan orange-sodium glow over a parade of stone-built buildings. At the end of the street was a square with a ruined fortress occupying one side.

'Zawiy Maalainin,' said Salif. 'Spanish blow up everything, not Zawiy. Zawiy not fall.'

The evidence suggested otherwise, but no one disagreed. To the left of the fortress was a modern municipal building; the other sides were lined with houses and shuttered shopfronts. Three diminutive pickups were parked outside a café in one corner. Their driver left them in a smaller street just off the square, opposite a three-storey concrete building with a narrow glazed door. Someone with a bucket of yellow paint and a brush but not much in the way of sign-writing skills had painted HOTEL vertically down the façade. You wouldn't have known, otherwise.

Chapter Sixteen

Nat woke up feeling awfully sick. A faint smudge of colour still played over the walls in rhythm with the screensaver, and for a moment she tried to identify the sequence, find the point of repetition that would make its motion predictable. The skin of her forearm felt sore and scratchy but she couldn't remember why. Then the memory of the fight with the little square-faced, snake-eyed doctor came back to her and she sat upright and stared at the door. Still locked. Blood had seeped through the bandage on her arm. The cut was deep and ought to be stitched, or she'd have an ugly, clotted scar.

It was 7.15 in the morning – she'd been asleep for twelve hours. She got to her feet and checked her brother. His breathing seemed easier and he looked as if he might be asleep, rather than out cold. She glanced at his leg, laid out like something in a butcher's shop. The drip bag was empty and he was going to need the doctor soon. But for the time being, he could sleep. There was a clipboard at the foot of his bed with a diagram of his wounds drawn on a pre-printed human figure; temperature, pulse and blood pressure charts; and a list of medications with dosages and a schedule. Nat read off the drugs: penicillin, midazolam, methadone – no wonder he was out of it. She searched the steel cupboard and packed supplies of each into her bag, adding syringes and field dressings. Just as she was closing it, there came a knock on the door.

'Monsieur asks if you are awake.' It was the boy, Adel.

'Get me some food.'

'Mam'selle wishes to go to her room now?'

'No. Bring it here.'

After a few minutes, Monsieur himself came knocking. 'Natalya? I trust you had a good night's rest. May I extend an invitation to join me for breakfast?'

She didn't reply. It was gratifying to have the all-powerful arms dealer reduced to talking to her through a solid oak door.

'You are upset by this episode, *bouleversée* as we say. It is to be expected, and indeed is testament to your loyal and affectionate nature. But I believe that on reflection you will acquit me of anything worse than a desire to protect myself from the violence that pursues me, of which the channel cut by the bullet that passed inches from my liver is a painful reminder.'

Nat thought that if he didn't leave her alone she would shortly pursue him with a violent kick in the shin.

'The pilot you throttled on the flight down has refused to return,' he said through the door. 'A prudent decision on his part, I feel. It will take a day or so to organise a replacement.'

She heard Zender walk away. Ten minutes later, Adel returned with tea, bread, a dish of bean mash and two oranges. When she had eaten, she took her bag and went to her bedroom. Adel trotted along behind, informing her that Monsieur was waiting for her and if she would please now follow him? She showered awkwardly, keeping her bandaged forearm clear of the scant trickle of water.

Back downstairs, she went over to Nikolai's side. He was squinting against the harsh light. A pool of watery vomit had settled in the hollow where his shoulder compressed the plastic mattress.

'Nikolai?'

He tried to pull himself upright.

'Don't, Niko.' She put a hand on his damp chest.

He turned his head to one side and retched painfully, then lay back, eyes clamped shut.

'It's good to see you, Niko, how're you feeling?'

His good eye opened and he stared up at her.

'It's me, Natalya.'

'Natalya.'

'Yes.'

He stared up at her. 'Natalya. Where am I? What's going on?'

*   *   *

James woke up in his room in the Hotel Maghrib, Smara, and stared at the ceiling for an hour. The rickety wooden frame and lumpy mattress were everything you could possibly ask for in a bed, he thought. Heat was stirring the white nylon curtains, but it wasn't yet uncomfortable. He heard voices from the street below, the sound of a man cajoling his companion, then shouts and footsteps running. He smelled coffee and imagined a pot rattling on the stove. A small engine ripped bossily down the street.

You carry too much garbage in your head, Sam Hu Li had told him once. *I give you black plastic bag, you put garbage in, you throw it away!* OK, James had responded meekly. Upon which Sam had produced a black plastic bag from a trouser pocket, thrust it at James and given way to the gale of laughter that he'd clearly been promising himself since the moment he'd first devised this tremendous jest. *I got plenty more if you need them, charity student!*

He could have done with one of Sam's bags last night – a night full of scraps and leftovers from his flight from the compound, the sighs and twitches of men choking in his arms, the bone-hammering blast of the landmine, homosexual charades in the barrack room of the Moroccan army outpost, and finally the surreal appearance of two East Europeans in a Peugeot, gliding along the empty desert road at night.

Really, he should go back to London now, get the Playpen to sort it all out. But their grubby fingers were in this pie and James trusted them even less now than he had three weeks ago when he'd set off for Oran. He'd spend a month traipsing from dank SIS back-room to musty GCHQ antechamber and back again, justifying himself to an unspeakable procession of debriefers who'd convinced themselves they were looking after the nation's interests and there-fore ought to be rather superior and inscrutable – though none of them would have recognised the nation's interests if they'd formed a choir and sung Rule Britannia in the Foreign Office lobby. How long, anyway, before his captors moved Little Sister somewhere else, before they dealt with Sarah the way they had dealt with Hamed? Not long enough for the Playpen to flounce into action, anyway.

He sat up and found that his knee had seized up – in fact it had disappeared altogether under a fat sheath of tight red skin. He limped downstairs and persuaded the hotel manager to part with an ancient first-aid box and a razor. Back in his room, he opened it and found a small hypodermic still sealed in its wrapper. He eased the needle in under the kneecap and drew off a quantity of murky pink fluid. The barrel was so small he had to repeat the procedure half a dozen times, but the relief was palpable. He hobbled into the shower and stood under the dribble of warm water, then laboriously scraped off three weeks of beard. His old face reappeared in the mirror, and he looked into the deep-set eyes that always seemed to make women want to ask him what he was thinking.

Well, what are you thinking?

That over the last twelve hours he'd seen all the vehicles and weapons he would need to get him back to the compound.

He dressed in the now filthy and tattered fatigues he'd taken from Younes. They rather spoiled the new-day, new-dawn feeling, but he had nothing else to wear. In fact, he thought, searching his pockets and finding only the black cotton square and a handful of pills, you have nothing else full stop. He stared at himself again. Death-junkie. Blood-addict. Were you always like that? Or is that what they made of you, when they got you to take a commission in Army Intelligence and sent you to Kosovo? The only honourable employment for someone with your unique talents, they'd flattered.

Kosovo. That little episode had employed his unique talents all right. He'd run away from that *honourable employment*, run away from the sickness that had lodged in his soul. Yet here he was dressed in gore-stiffened army fatigues, one dead body already on his mind and god knows how many more in his sights.

*   *   *

He joined Salif in the dining room, and they ate eggs, bread and dates in copious quantities. World Cup football replays were showing on a tiny television mounted high up on the back wall, and the feverish drama of the commentary made conversation difficult. James went over and turned off the sound.

'Salif, can you take me back to the compound?'

Salif, who was dipping a hard-boiled egg into a dish of some gritty red spice, looked up at James and then back over his shoulder, as if to check whether there were any witnesses to this new evidence of the addling effect of Saharan sunlight on the European brain. He shook his head quickly and went back to his egg.

'No. I go compound. You stay Smara.'

'There's an English girl there, I have to help her. And I need to get back the computer I was working on with Rakesh Nazli. I can go alone, but I don't know the desert like you do.'

It was evidently mystifying to Salif that this man he had led to safety now seemed determined to put his head back on the block.

'Take me as far as the compound, then,' James said. 'I'll talk to Colonel Sulamani. He can decide what to do.'

At the prospect of taking orders from his Colonel, the wariness and confusion cleared from Salif's face.

'OK, I take you,' he said. 'You crazy man. Get killed.'

They ate in silence for several minutes, then Anton and Mikhail entered the dining room. James stood up and made a show of welcoming them, clearing space at their table while Salif went to the doorway and shouted for more food. Mikhail took a chair opposite James and immediately started chewing on a flatbread. Anton looked around disdainfully and at length, flexing his shoulders inside his cream jacket and muttering some imprecation at Mikhail before eventually deigning to sit down.

Salif beckoned to James from the door. 'I hide now. Not safe for me.'

'Meet me at six,' said James. 'One kilometre outside Smara, on the road north.'

Salif nodded and James went back to the others. Anton was scowling at a basket of dates in the middle of the table.

'You know what? Where I come from, something that looks like shit and tastes like shit, we generally don't eat.'

'You sleep OK?' said James. 'Planning a day at the beach, I guess.'

He grinned at Mikhail, feeling that there must be more to these two than met the eye and wondering how they could be useful to him. Mikhail gave a polite nod in acknowledgement of James's poor attempt to resurrect his joke. Anton pulled out a cellphone and started to fiddle with it.

'I guess Vodafone won't have seamless integration with Smara Telecom,' said James. Anton looked at him sourly and tucked the phone back into his pocket.

'Let me explain how I got here,' said James, thinking that his own story might loosen their tongues. 'I was tricked into going to Oran, then abducted and taken to a compound out there in the desert...' Already his audience looked sceptical. 'They got hold of a computer intercept device I built—'

'This is bullshit,' said Anton.

'I escaped, obviously.'

'And here you are having breakfast with us in sunny Smara. Amen.'

'I still don't know who's behind it,' James ploughed on, 'but Salif told me that an arms dealer called Claude Zender is involved.'

Anton's eyes steadied. Mikhail stopped eating.

'You know him?' James said.

'No,' said Anton. But the lie was sabotaged by Mikhail's eager face.

'You came down here to find Zender?'

Mikhail addressed Anton in Russian. James didn't speak the language, but there was a throaty roll to his voice that sounded exactly like the man who'd been locked up in the cell opposite him at the compound.

'There's another man being held at the compound. Heavily built – like you, only bigger,' James said, nodding at Mikhail. 'I heard him shouting in Russian. Someone's given him a beating.'

'You see Nikolai?' said Mikhail.

Anton hissed at him.

'He's there all right. Salif said he'd been caught spying on Zender.'

The two men conversed in Russian again.

'Fuck you,' said Anton eventually.

'Salif and I are going back to the compound. You should come, get your friend out of there. The longer he stays... Well, having spent a week there myself, I don't fancy his chances.'

'He know where is Nikolai. We don't,' Mikhail observed.

'So he claims,' said Anton. 'And if he's lying? We follow him into the big sandy desert and what, have a frigging picnic?'

'Why would I lie?'

'How the fuck do I know? First you hijack my taxi. Then you claim to be mixed up with spies. Now you say you know where Nikolai is. I've heard better lines from a pissed-up beggar in a cardboard box.'

'He's not drunk,' said Mikhail.

'I'm going to the café in the square,' James said. 'You can find me there. You got a few dirhams I could borrow?'

'What did I tell you, Micky,' said Anton. 'The guy's a shyster.'

Mikhail pulled a note from his wallet and handed it over.

They're in, thought James.

*   *   *

The café in Smara's main square smelled of coffee and sweetened tobacco, and was full of old men in spotless white shirts and black trousers, or *bishts* the colour of oatmeal with embroidered collars. They fell silent as James entered through the bead curtain over the door and picked his way through the thicket of chairs that filled every square inch of the brown-painted concrete floor. There was a computer set up on a rickety steel table in the corner. James paid for half an hour's internet access and bought a cup of sweet, grainy coffee to drink while he browsed.

The connection was slow, and every image download choked it. In any case, nothing he needed to find out was going to be readily available on the web. How about a Google search: *British computer scientist abducted by al Bidayat in cahoots with arms dealer Claude Zender while MI6 watches...* He looked for al Bidayat: their site had been taken down – within the last twenty-four hours, it seemed, because there was a link to it in a blog posted the day before – but there were plenty of news reports. The organisation had been started by an elderly Professor of Islamic Jurisprudence who had disappeared from his post at Cairo University in early 2005. Its goal was predictable enough – 'to overthrow the tyrannical hegemony of the western imperialists' – but its modus operandi was unique: al Bidayat would not commit acts of terrorism itself, but supply backup and support services – funding, training, equipment and logistics – to anyone who could 'demonstrate a commitment to driving the imperialist crusaders from the cradles of Islam in Africa and the Middle East'. Its record in this endeavour was opaque – there didn't seem to be firm evidence that it had done anything at all – but the intelligence community clearly believed it was successfully plying its trade behind the scenes. They'd even given it a nickname: the Terror Consultancy.

If Ibrahim al Haqim was al Bidayat's elder statesman, then Mansour Anzarane – a former student of his – was its poster boy. He paraded his terrorist credentials like an obnoxious ten-year-old with a row of gold stars, and majored in long, repetitive calls to arms, bloody and righteous in equal measure. But it all seemed a little flimsy. His calling card was that he claimed to be the executioner in a video depicting the beheading of a Saudi intelligence agent. James found a copy and watched. Unless his swordsmanship had since deserted him entirely, the man who whisked the Saudi agent's head from his body in the video was not the same man who had butchered Hamed at the compound. A cruel and dangerous narcissist, yes, but the right-hand man to a terrorist mastermind? Etienne was the more likely candidate, but there was no record of anyone by that name being associated with al Bidayat.

What else? Anemone… Not much point searching for that. He created a webmail account and keyed Clive Silk's home email into the address box. He remembered the message he'd found in the Centuries Deep log on the compound network, the one with the header that had led him to the gates of MI6, and wrote:

REF ANEMONE, NO SIGNIFICANT ACTIVITY TO REPORT.

As he pressed send, there was a chinking sound from the door. The bead curtain was being held open by a small, chubby man of about thirty in a light brown suit with a wine-red shirt. An old white Mercedes thrummed in the square behind him. The man looked quickly round the room. The café's customers lowered their heads to avoid meeting his eyes. They were nasty eyes: pale and unblinking in his round, childish face. He saw James and grinned. It was a nasty grin, too, mirthless and triumphant. He approached James's table.

'Come with me, mister,' he said in rough French. He had a high pitched, expressionless voice, and you could imagine that he only used a dozen phrases, all of them much like this one.

'You want to talk, sit down,' said James equably. 'Otherwise, go and tell Monsieur Zender that I'm looking for him.'

The other men in the café were leaving, quietly and fast. He didn't have much time. The man in front of him had his right hand up by the lapel of his jacket, ready to pull the gun lodged in his left armpit. He was keeping his other hand out of view.

James stood up.

'OK, let's go.'

He threw a rabbit punch at the man's throat. The man swayed neatly to his right and James's fist glanced harmlessly off his neck. There was a snarl on the man's face and excitement in his eyes. He'd done this before, he enjoyed it. He feinted for his gun. A stiletto blade arced towards James's groin. He was really quick, frighteningly quick. James threw himself backwards, came down on his right shoulder, and grabbed for a chair. The gleeful, child's face loomed over him. James kicked hard and caught him in the gut, but the man rolled back easily, almost disdainfully, and with keen precision drove the point of his knife into James's calf. He gasped with the shock of the intruding steel, jerked back his leg as the cut nerves shrieked. Pleasure flared in the man's pale eyes. James swung the chair up at the babyish face, using the momentum to roll him back to his feet. Again the man was quick enough to dodge the blow, again the blade darted forward. But the legs of the chair hampered him and the point of the blade stopped six inches short of James's face. With James on his feet, the chair was the better weapon and the man knew it. He stepped back, ducked and reached for his gun. James followed through with the chair. The blunt wooden legs snared his neck and the little man's neat evasion turned into a fall. He flipped sideways and the side of his head banged against the edge of a bench. James pressed on, concentrating all his weight into the foremost leg of the chair and spearing it into the man's unprotected chest as he hit the floor. He felt springy resistance, then the give as his ribcage cracked. The man wheezed noisily, coughed. A shard of rib must have punctured his lung. Should keep him quiet.

There was a click behind him. A man in the doorway, gun levelled, waiting to get a clear shot. James dived through the maze of chairs and a bullet smacked into the wall above his head. He scrambled for the narrow corridor that led out back, flinging chairs aside. Another shot and the top of a chair to his left disintegrated into a bouquet of splinters.

James drove on, gained the mouth of the corridor. It was dark and harboured the harsh, salty stench of old urine. There was a door at the far end and he made for it, keeping low. He was three feet away when the door swung open. A big man stood silhouetted in the doorway, peering in, fist clamped round the butt of a handgun. There was a stairway to James's right. He took it.

He ran up four flights of stairs, then a set of steep, narrow steps that led to the roof. Shots cracked and spat in the stairwell behind him. The door to the roof was unlocked and he stepped out. Adjoining roofs led all the way to a taller building at the corner of the square. He ducked under a line of washing and jumped a low wall on to the next roof, then hid behind a chicken coop and some old paint tubs planted with red peppers. He heard his pursuer kicking open the door. The alley to his left was about eight feet across, but the building on the other side was just a two-storey concrete shell – leaving him with a ten-foot vertical drop as well. He judged the run-up to the parapet, then set off with short, vigorous strides. Just as he was about to jump, two things happened.

He heard a shout from his left. And he realised that because of the stab wound to his right calf he was about to launch off his left foot. The one connected to the buggered knee he'd so successfully forgotten about.

In mid-air he stretched his arms out and got ready to land belly-first against the opposite edge. He took it as best as he could, but that wasn't well. The ridge of concrete ripped into the muscle of his stomach and slammed every last pocket of air from his lungs. Then he was slipping down the wall, fingers scratching across the gritty surface. His chin crunched down onto the edge, halting his slide for a second. But there was nothing to grip, nothing to dig his fingers into… Then his feet weren't bumping against the wall but kicking into the empty space that would one day be a window. Just before his fingernails ran out of concrete to scrape, his toes found the ledge below and he stopped.

Precarious, but not lying in a bloody heap in the alley. He worked his toes to the very outside of the ledge, bent his knees inward and slid down as quickly as he dared, conscious that if he lost his balance he'd dive backwards onto the baked dirt twenty feet below. He got one arm under the top of the window opening, reached for the inside face of the wall and pulled his head inside the building. Stepped gratefully off the ledge, and fell.

*   *   *

REF ANEMONE, NO SIGNIFICANT ACTIVITY TO REPORT.

Clive Silk re-read the email and a bubble of panic swelled inside him. He looked reflexively over his shoulder, even though he was in his office at home and no one could be standing there watching – or at least, no one who was at all interested in anything he did. The return address was friendoftheplaypen@hotmail.com. Fucking Palatine. What did it mean? That he did know about Anemone. That he hadn't been abducted. That he was poking around where he didn't belong, sniffing out things that would allow him to keep the expression of contempt on his face for another few years.

Super-saintly, super-heroic Dr Palatine. And Strang really believed I might be colluding with him over the IPD400. Me, help Palatine, who treats me like something that crawled out from beneath a filing cabinet? Clive wondered if, having deleted the email, he could shut down his webmail account and pretend it had never existed. He searched through pages of settings and discovered that you couldn't – there was simply no option to close it. The message would sit there on the webmail servers like a telltale stain, and they'd send smug little Julian Twomey-Smith in to find it.

He had to report this to Strang and de la Mere. The thought of their gleeful expressions, incompletely hidden behind a mask of inquisitorial gravity, made him feel weak with anxiety. They'd find a way of making it his fault that Palatine was goading him over the email. *Can you explain, Clive, why Dr Palatine chose to contact you?* He'd called Claude Zender, too, the night before last. *Can you explain, Clive...*

He couldn't explain, no. He'd done nothing wrong, but they were going to bully him. Sir Iain Strang, Nigel de la Mere, Zender, Palatine. All of them, taking it in turns to have a good kick, because he was a nonentity and they would drive him away like a dog that's farted under the dining room table.

*   *   *

Mikhail heard gunshots. He leaned out of the window of his hotel room and saw a man run onto the roof of the row of buildings to the north of the square. Now he was looking round for a place to jump across the alley below. It was James, Mikhail saw, running from a man who was just now emerging onto the roof, gun in hand. He heard a door banging in the alley and looked down to see another man, also armed, run out and turn his head up to look at the rooftops above. The man on the roof couldn't see James, but the man in the alley would, when he jumped.

Mikhail watched carefully, and as soon as he saw James start his run-up, he yelled:

'Hey!'

The man in the alley turned. James jumped. Mikhail ducked back into the room.

'Someone is shooting at James.'

'Good luck to them.'

'We gotta help him.'

'We do not have to help him, Micky. If he wants to travel to the arse end of the universe and start a fight, that's his business. Anyway, he can handle himself.'

'You coming or do I go on my own?'

'Fuck you, why?'

'This stuff is what we do,' said Mikhail.

'In Kiev. This is someone else's patch.'

'Yeah, and someone else got Nikolai.'

'I get shot, I'm blaming you.'

Mikhail grinned. 'I'm blaming God.'

'Yeah, but God is not going to say, *Sorry Anton*, and bring me beer and cake every day until I'm better. But you are, right?'

They left by the back entrance to the hotel. The man Mikhail had shouted at was patrolling the street behind the café, so they circled round and entered an alley that seemed to run parallel. The air was making a thin humming noise, like a trapped insect. The alley took them left, then meandered back on itself, narrowing all the while. A harsh banging up ahead... They turned a corner and found a man of about thirty, naked other than a torn T-shirt, squatting in the dust and hammering on a wooden door with a lump of rock. He was shouting some words over and over again. A dismembered chicken lay by his side. He saw them and swivelled on his heels, rock in hand. His face was filthy and heavily bearded, his elongated scrotum trailed in the dust.

'Where to, tour guide?' Anton whispered.

Mikhail moved forwards purposefully. The man turned and stared, then dropped his rock and pinned himself back against the wall. Mikhail walked by, Anton at his heels. They ran along the alley for twenty yards before taking a right turn into a tiny yard occupied by a plastic hopper shedding mangled bags full of refuse. They crouched in a patch of shade and heard footsteps behind them. There was an angry shout, then the man yelled out his repetitive phrase and smashed the door with his rock. Then they heard a cry and a thud. It sounded like he'd been hit. Then another thud. Silence.

'Why we hiding?' Mikhail asked.

'I thought we were being followed.' Anton suddenly felt how ridiculous it was to be crouching among the filth and flies in a Smara alley. 'Why the fuck did I follow you into this shithole,' he hissed.

'James must be round here,' said Mikhail.

'We're lost. Let's go back.'

Round the bend, they found the crazy, half-naked man uri-nating over the figure of a man lying face down in the dirt. The hot fluid splashed over a purplish lump that was forming on the back of the prone man's neck. It looked like the one who'd fired at James from the roof. The triumphant stream of urine was improb-ably copious. There was something about this grotesque ritual that seemed to demand of Anton and Mikhail that they watch until it was complete.

The half-naked man leaned back against the wall. Blood from a cut on his cheekbone was dripping into his T-shirt. The man on the ground was still breathing. Anton's eye was drawn to the gun in his hand. The half-naked man was now stroking his penis, not in search of arousal but as one might a household pet that has done some-thing useful. Anton bent down and disengaged the unconscious man's fingers from the revolver, then patted the pockets of his jacket and extracted a couple of spare clips.

'Nice work, friend,' he told the half-naked man. 'Take my advice and hide before he wakes up.'

They hurried on, but without paying attention to their route, and within five minutes were standing arguing at the junction of two alleys and a yard being used to store building materials. Heat was gathering between the densely packed buildings. They crossed the yard, and found themselves inside a dark, cavernous concrete shell. The air had the caustic smell of wet cement. To their left was a mixer next to a pyramid of sand, a stack of cement bags, two concrete-encrusted shovels and an oil drum full of water. Anton went over, cupped his hands and dashed water over his face, taking some of it surreptitiously into the corner of his mouth. Mikhail joined him.

'I wouldn't drink that,' said James.

* * *

The tall army officer turned up with the little doctor in tow. She showed not the slightest hint of remorse, but stamped around the room – *her* room, from which she had been unjustly ejected – deliberately treading on Nat's makeshift bed. Reviewing the contents of her cupboard, she scowled and cursed in her cramped English. When Nat ordered her to stitch the wound up fully, she refused, insisting that this would bring on gangrene in an instant. Neither Nat nor Nikolai knew how to assess this warning, but the army officer stepped forward and confirmed that it was indeed sound practice to stitch up a wound in stages, so they let her get on with it. She told Nikolai with ill-disguised pleasure that she did not have local anaesthetic and it would be *uncomfortable.*

'I've been stitched up before,' Nikolai told her, 'and I know exactly how much it hurts.'

Nat turned to the tall, angular figure who had taken up station by the door. 'I should thank you for saving my life last night,' she said.

The doctor sniffed contemptuously.

'We were never introduced. I am Nat Kocharian.'

'Colonel Nejib Sulamani, of the Army of the Sahrawi Arab Democratic Republic. You know us, perhaps, as the Polisario.'

Colonel Sulamani gave a small bow, and as their eyes met, his grave, drawn face reddened just a tinge under its sun-battered exterior. *Perfect*, Nat thought, *he fancies me.* She looked at him with the interest she naturally felt in men who might fall into her bed: late fifties, six foot three or four tall, but slightly stooped, with wide, curved shoulders that stretched the cotton of his sand-coloured shirt. His expression was guarded and his manner formal, lugubrious even; but these traits were belied by the compelling richness of his voice and the desire swirling in his eyes.

'Can you help us get out of here?' said Nikolai. He saw perfectly well what was going on; and while he didn't begrudge Natalya her pleasures and rated her sexual manipulativeness highly, he had no inclination to witness the ground being laid.

'The situation is complicated,' said Sulamani, without taking his eyes from Nat's. 'Monsieur Zender will make the arrangements for your return to Marrakech.'

'And here was I about to pack my bags and head for the bus stop,' said Nat. 'Do you have a satphone I could use, Colonel?'

'Monsieur Zender— '

'Zender and I are engaged on a complicated business deal, and I'm afraid I don't trust him not to listen in. But I'm sure he wouldn't dare tap your phone.'

'We would not allow it, no.'

They agreed to meet at five, when Nat could make her calls from Sulamani's office. The doctor had finished and was inspecting her work with evident satisfaction. 'I do not have the equipment or the skills to deal with the damaged ligaments,' she said, 'but I have saved the leg.'

'Halle-fucking-lujah,' said Nat. 'Out you go.'

The woman's pinched face glared up at her, then she turned and marched through the door, with Sulamani at her back.

'I feel like a corpse, lying here,' said Nikolai when they had gone. 'Help me onto that chair. You going to fuck the old boy?'

'None of your business.'

Nat lowered the gurney, then manoeuvred him into the wooden chair by the doctor's desk. She arranged his bad leg on another chair, trying not to look at the flesh that was puckered like a blanched aubergine and the livid puncture marks left by the doctor's needlework.

'It is good to have this pain,' Nikolai said stoically. 'My leg is mine again, you know?'

'Not really, my hero.'

They told each other what had happened since they'd parted at the airport a week before.

'I thought I'd been taken to hospital,' said Nikolai. 'I fucked this up for you, that's for sure.'

'It was me who got you into it,' said his sister. 'I wish I hadn't.'

'Kocharians are tough,' Nikolai replied. 'We'll come through, huh?'

Natalya agreed and they hugged and pledged their toughness to each other. She then had to wheel her brother off to find a lavatory, a task they accomplished while engulfing the building with the noise made by Ukrainians enjoying a bout of vulgar humour.

'I need to eat – I'm weak as a baby,' said Nikolai when they returned. 'And get me Zender, I have things to say to him.'

'Remember what Sulamani said: we can't get out of here without Zender's help. Anyway, you don't look very threatening on one leg.'

'Get to work on lover boy, then,' said Nikolai crossly.

'Fuck's sake, Nikolai, I don't like being here any more than you do.'

'Yes you do, you like the food and you like the heat. That's two things you like that I don't.'

'You're so childish,' she said, opening the door to look for the boy Adel, who was usually to be found fidgeting somewhere nearby.

* * *

'What happened to you?' Anton enquired, looking James up and down as he might a teenage recruit in downtown Kiev who had got himself into an unnecessary scrape.

'Zender's Smara office found me.'

James noticed the butt of a handgun in the waistband of Anton's trousers. It looked like a Firestar, a Spanish-made 9mm semi-automatic. The light crack of the charge in its chamber would sound very much like the gun that had been shot at him on the roof – and here it was tucked into Anton's trousers. James was impressed. I was right about these two, James thought. Clowns, but only up to a point.

He'd lost track of the men who'd set on him in the café, but now he detected a sliver of daylight winking at the edge of one of the boarded-up windows: there, then gone, then back again. He was about to warn the others when a diesel engine revved hard in the alley. The clunk of a gear engaging, then a corrugated iron sheet cartwheeled from the doorway with a clang like a bathtub dropped into a skip. The bonnet of the white Mercedes lunged towards them. Before he jumped, James saw in the driver's seat the man who'd knifed him in the calf, his smooth, round face contorted with malice. No one beside him, which meant—

A bullet spat across the skin of his shoulder as he dived – would have torn his heart in two if he'd moved a split-second later. The big man from the alley stood in the opening where the corrugated iron had been, a heavy calibre semi-automatic levelled in both hands. James pancaked to the ground and three shots slammed into the dirt behind him. A stinging plume of cement dust erupted in his eyes. He rubbed them with his thumb and forefinger and the film of grit cleared enough for him to see the chrome fender of the Mercedes less than ten feet from his nose.

He rolled, felt the heat off the engine as the wheel arch blasted past his ear. The nearside wheel rumbled over his hand. The big Merc slammed sideways against the far wall. His head swam with diesel fumes. He heard the car's rear wing screech against the wall and the rattle of flying grit as the rear wheels gouged the dirt, then gripped and sent the oily steel chassis bucking towards him again. He scrambled sideways, feet skidding in the dirt. The Mercedes rocked back on its springs, its back end snagged on a stack of steel joists.

He spun towards the big gunman, but he wasn't silhouetted in the doorway any more. James ran for the pile of sand, heard a bullet ricochet off the steel belly of the cement mixer as he hurled his body into the lee of the mound. *Bad place to hide.* Already his mind was rehearsing the moment of shock that would come when the bullet struck.

Shots – but high-pitched, sharp, not the boom of the big semi-automatic. Anton was beside him, stretched out with his elbows embedded in the sand and the Firestar pointing into the corner beyond the doorway.

'He's down. Not dead,' Anton shouted over the roar of the Mercedes' engine.

The driver had floored the throttle, trying to drag the car free of the joist that had snared it. With a series of heavy, jarring clanks, the Mercedes bounced clear and the black mesh of the radiator grille swung round towards the sandpile.

'Move!' James shouted.

Mikhail ran in from his left, straight towards the rearing white snout of the Merc. Anton loosed off one, two shots into the corner. Mikhail kept on, then just as the Mercedes emblem was accelerating into his pelvis, gave a graceful skip-hop and launched himself head first through the windscreen. The glass shattered with a pop and his head and shoulders disappeared inside the car, his barrel-shaped torso jolting with the impact. The Mercedes heeled round towards the open doorway. The revs died and the car slowed. It clipped the wall by the door and ground its way ponderously into the corner, emitting a final shriek as it came to rest just about where Anton had put down the big gunman.

'He loves to do that,' said Anton. 'It's his party piece.'

'I got him,' said the former weightlifter, extracting himself from the Mercedes' windscreen.

They went over to join him. Anton stooped over the big gunman, while Mikhail, whose face sported innumerable abrasions from the shattered glass, tested his massive neck for damage by rotating it and massaging the tendons and muscle. Satisfied, he dragged the baby-faced man from the car. His head no longer aligned with his shoulders, but lolled.

'That's disgusting,' said Anton. 'Here.'

He passed Mikhail the big man's weapon, along with three spare clips.

'Makarov. Nice.'

Mikhail found a place for it in his tracksuit trousers. James pulled another Firestar from the holster in the driver's armpit.

'Let's get the fuck out of here,' said Anton.

'Agreed,' said James. 'We'll take the Merc.'

Chapter Seventeen

Mikhail manoeuvred the Mercedes out of the yard while James stood in the alley and tried to work out which way was north. The sun was moving up overhead, bearing down on Smara town as if in fulfilment of a dreadful curse. They rumbled along the alley, throbs from the engine reverberating through the open windows. The blank walls of the buildings on either side were inches from the car's flanks. If they hit the slightest bend, they'd be wedged in tight, unable even to climb out and run.

Eventually the alley released them into a wider street. There was a shop on the corner with a sign saying *All Good Things* above the door, and James went in to buy flagons of water. It felt dangerously hot inside the Mercedes, so the three of them stood in a narrow strip of shade, like insects hiding from the beak of a hungry bird.

'Every time we step outside,' said Anton, splashing water over his head, 'we start to die.'

'You're wasting it,' said Mikhail.

The silence was broken only by a sonorous barking up ahead, and the occasional snort from a diesel engine changing gear somewhere along the main road out of Smara. They got back into the car and navigated towards the outskirts of town, then drove for a kilometre along the road north. Another of the white MINURSO vehicles came past, heading into Smara. James glanced at Anton's watch: 3.20 p.m. A few minutes later, they pulled off and lurched across the rocky sand until they came to a hut made of lumps of rock stacked in a rough square with a blue plastic tarpaulin doing service for a roof. Mikhail parked up behind it. The hut was occupied by a goat with three kids no more than a week old. The goat looked up and gave a token bleat of protest, but the kids were suckling and she was too weary to move. They clambered in and sat down. The goat examined them one by one, swallowing nervously.

'It's close, but I think I preferred the hotel,' said Anton. 'Will someone tell me what the fuck we are doing here?'

'Going to get Nikolai,' Mikhail declared, as if this were exactly the way he'd expected the mission to commence.

'You still don't get it, do you?' said Anton in Russian. 'This mad fuck just wants us to help him get his spy thing back.'

'He gets the spy thing, we get Nikolai. S'what we came for, right?'

'Fuck off, Micky. We have no idea what we're getting into.'

'Never know what's around the next corner,' said Mikhail amiably.

'Oh well, that's settled then.'

One of the kids had decided to investigate its new companions. Mikhail was charmed. He stroked its belly and pointed out to Anton how astonishingly soft the fur was.

'Will you leave that fucking thing alone and talk to me?'

The kid nibbled on Mikhail's finger, then settled against his thigh and fell asleep.

'Talk about what?'

'You are a lump of cow crud,' said Anton. 'When did we ever talk about anything anyway? You just do what you have to and I come along.' He watched Mikhail tickle the kid's chin. 'It thinks you're daddy,' he said. 'You're not, are you?'

'We've only been here one night,' said Mikhail.

Observing that their pow-wow seemed to have petered out, James asked: 'So, who is your friend Nikolai? And how did he get on the wrong side of Claude Zender?'

Anton gave Mikhail a reproachful look, to which the latter responded by folding his arms. By this means, they evidently decided that the time for being cagey was past. Anton gave him a curt explanation, and the connection became clear: Grosvenor had dispatched Natalya Kocharian, their legendary head of sales, to retrieve a computer device which had gone missing; she'd enlisted her brother Nikolai's help, and they'd both ended up as 'guests' at Zender's desert motel. James remembered Nat Kocharian from a Grosvenor conference he'd been paid to attend: petite, red-gold hair, and a fuck-me-or-die-trying look in her green eyes – sexy, if that was the sort of look you went for.

'So, you guys coming with us?'

'Yes,' said Mikhail.

Anton looked back at the town of Smara, so wan and friable it seemed it might disintegrate in the heat. Within lay the maze of alleys where the sun scratched and shutters banged, where sad-eyed men assaulted passers-by and pissed on them; beyond, untold miles of hot, sandy desert. They'd already killed two men, and somewhere, no doubt, was a hot cell and a sadistic police chief.

'Shit,' he said.

* * *

Having seen her brother restored to consciousness, Nat was beginning to believe that her plan to sell the IPD400 to Grey Tony might also be raised from the dead – and in this, Colonel Nejib Sulamani would make an ideal ally. It was him she had overheard arguing with Zender the previous night: Nat had never heard anyone force Zender to explain himself the way the Polisario officer had.

Sulamani arrived at five o'clock sharp and escorted Nat to another grand, high-ceilinged room along the corridor from Zender's. A black leather briefcase sat open on a trestle table, next to a laptop, a satphone and an empty wire tray. Against the left-hand wall was a narrow canvas camp bed heaped with clothes. When they entered the room, Sulamani hurried over, scooped up the clothes, couldn't see where to put them, and finally made a feeble attempt to hide them behind the briefcase.

'Please don't do that on my account,' said Nat. She stretched over the table to retrieve the clothes, taking a little longer than was strictly necessary, then folded them one by one and stacked them in the wire tray.

'There,' she said, 'I've come over all wifely. Whatever next?'

Sulamani looked aghast, as if this were a question that required a considered answer. Nat recognised the faintly idiotic look that had come over his face as a sure sign that soldierly reserve was losing a one-sided battle to raw lust.

'It's such a comfort to find you here, Colonel,' she said, dropping her voice until it caught in her throat.

'It is nothing… You dial seven, six, seven, eight to get a line,' said Colonel Sulamani, indicating the satphone. 'Then your number, including the international code. It can be slow to connect.'

He gave a smart bow and left. Nat watched him go and wondered what he'd be like. Rather shy and eager, she guessed, like a schoolboy who can't believe his luck. Rough lips, a taste of warm earth and cigars. Something to look forward to… She sat at the desk and called the hotel in Smara. None of them were there. She tried Anton's mobile, but it didn't connect. Nor did Mikhail's. She knew she ought to make contact with Grosvenor, but she hadn't worked out what she was going to tell them. She called Pete Alakhine instead. Grey Tony's man in Rabat. It sounded as if he were sitting in a cave full of wasps.

'Terrible line,' he said. 'Where are you?'

'I have a date for our transaction to complete,' she said. 'Tomorrow week, that is, Thursday the third of November. Ten a.m. at the Clement-Dufour warehouse on the Boulevard Moulay Slimane.'

'Let me check my diary.'

'No need. The date isn't negotiable,' said Nat, even though she'd only just made it up. 'I take it the financial arrangements are in place?'

'Sure. You have the goods in hand?'

'You mean, am I carrying it round in my handbag? Anything else you'd like to ask?'

'I have your number, anyway.'

'See you next Thursday,' said Nat, and hung up.

She allowed herself a moment to imagine Grey Tony's reaction when he discovered that Natalya Kocharian was not just alive and kicking, but also required him to complete on the IPD400 deal. At some point, she thought blithely, he'll work out that handing me $30 million is a much more sensible way of suppressing Magda's dossier than trying to have me killed.

Magda. She checked the time: 5.45 p.m., 9.45 a.m. in LA. She dialled her friend's office. It rang for a long time, which was unusual – Magda was a stickler for office etiquette. Eventually a woman answered and said that Magda was unavailable. A chill of apprehension crept into Nat's stomach.

'When will she be back?'

'Magda's been taken to hospital. I can't say any more.'

'What happened? Which hospital is she in?'

'I've been advised not to release that information.'

'But, she's alive?'

'The hospital will only talk to her family,' said the woman self-importantly.

Nat took a moment to still the tremor in her throat, then asked: 'What law firm do you use?'

'Keslake and Swift. Julie Swift is our attorney. I don't think they'll tell you anything, either.'

Nat got the number from her, dialled and asked for Julie Swift.

'Did Magda Podolski leave some papers for me?'

'Who am I talking to, please?'

'Nat Kocharian.'

'Oh, right. Ms Kocharian. I'm glad you called in. Ms Podolski left a question for me to ask to verify your identity. Please hold.' Nat heard her tapping at a keyboard. 'OK, what restaurant did you and Ms Podolski eat at when you first met?'

'The Opera Café in Frankfurt.'

'Thank you. Ms Podolski left a sealed dossier for you. Do you wish to come in and collect it?'

'Is Magda OK?'

'She was badly hurt – I believe they are keeping her unconscious because of a head injury. This dossier she left for you – could it have anything to do with the break-in? The police are asking for information about her cases.'

'Did you tell them about the dossier?'

'May I give them your co-ordinates, Ms Kocharian?'

'No… Later perhaps.'

'May I ask why not?'

Nat didn't reply.

'It does sound as if I should release these papers to the police immediately. May I do that?'

'No.'

Nat hung up and went and lay down on Sulamani's narrow canvas bed. She felt dazed. Magda, unconscious in a hospital bed? Tears welled in her eyes and she wiped them away furiously. *Another person half-killed because of you.* She'd known from the start Magda would not refuse to help her. Magda loved her, and Nat had used her affection to secure the information she needed to make herself rich. Big, sweet-natured Magda with her brassy talk and sisterly smile. Magda, who'd faced seven shades of shit in her life and come out swinging. Magda, who'd made a pass at her and blushed.

Fuck this, she thought, *I'm turning Grey Tony in. I'm taking him down.*

That would mean nixing the deal, once and for all. *Quitting*, Magda would call it. She'd hate that. As long as the dossier was safe, the deal was on. Grey Tony had shown that he'd do anything to suppress it. She knew exactly where she stood with him now – and if the stakes were high, well, that suited her fine. I can still put Grey Tony away, she thought. And I'll double Magda's cut. We can start a charity: the Podolski Fund for Gay Polish Women: Fighting Prejudice on Three Fronts…

She called Alakhine again.

'One more thing, Pete. Tell your boss that the dossier we discussed is ready for release.'

'I can do that,' said Alakhine. 'What does it mean?'

She hung up. If Grey Tony could organise a break-in at Magda's, she realised, he could have a crack at Keslake and Swift, too. She got Julie Swift again and instructed her to send copies of the dossier to half a dozen addresses, a task which the lawyer felt entitled her to extract $1,200 from Nat's credit card.

'If you haven't heard from me within a month, hand the dossier to the *Washington Post*. I'll be dead,' Nat said, feeling that if she wasn't, she certainly deserved to be.

* * *

Claude Zender had been knocking on and off for two hours before Nat finally opened the door to him.

'I see the patient is much recovered,' he said, looking over her shoulder. 'Good evening, Mr Kocharian.'

'Is that the fat fuck who had me beaten up?' Mr Kocharian shouted from his gurney. 'I'll rip your balls off and string them from your ears!'

Nat ushered Zender back into the corridor.

'He seems in good spirits,' Zender said.

'Just keep out of his way.'

'Will you dine with me, Natalya? I hate to think of you shut in here like a caged bird.'

'Why ever would I feel like that?'

She consented to join him at the table in his office. They helped themselves to lamb and couscous from a charred tagine. The sweet aroma of cardamom filled the air and made the room seem less inhospitable. Nat ate hungrily. She was in no hurry to strike up a conversation.

'How is your poor arm?' Zender asked.

'My arm is sore, where your doctor cut me. And the fingers of this hand feel fat and clumsy. I'd be dead if Sulamani hadn't come in, don't you think?'

'Dronika is unpredictable. But she is not entirely murderous, I suppose.'

'Claude, I'm leaking blood like a sponge because of that woman. As far as I'm concerned, she came straight from hell and I hope she goes back there.'

'You are perceptive, Natalya. Hell *is* where she came from. She's an Albanian, captured by Serb militia in Kalinovik in I think '98. They discovered she had medical training, and she was forced to remove organs from her fellow prisoners. There was a brisk trade in kidneys at the time. Most distasteful. When the Serbs retreated towards the end of the war, she wreaked a certain amount of revenge which I imagine was of a rather extreme nature. Then she opened a practice in Sarajevo, which is where I came across her. I do not think things were going well, and she came within the week when I asked her. We needed a doctor here and the desert is not to everyone's liking.'

'A doctor to look after people like my brother, who you had beaten up in your casino,' Nat said hotly, her resolve to maintain a strategic calm deserting her completely. 'Which you told me you knew nothing about?'

'I have explained, Natalya, that it was a case of mistaken identity.'

'Why didn't you talk to him at the casino? You would have found out in a minute who he was.'

'He was unconscious and injured. I thought it best to bring him here, where he could be properly treated.'

'There are plenty of hospitals in Marrakech. I took you to one, remember?'

'I wonder why you insist on interrogating me like some street thief whose fictions will unravel at the drop of a hat,' said Zender, casting his large face into a caricature of the wronged innocent.

Several reasons came to mind, but Nat said nothing.

'Let's not quarrel,' he went on, 'for I intend a happy outcome to this affair. Though I trust you are not expecting anything by way of an eleventh-hour cavalry charge from those two buffoons you dispatched to Smara in a taxi yesterday. It will be a miracle if they arrive at all, and if they do, they will find themselves separated from the Kocharians by the largest army in North Africa.'

Nat felt disappointed, and realised that in some part of her mind set aside for improbable fantasies, she'd been hoping her brother's sidekicks would perform a dashing rescue.

'I still have Dr Palatine's box, as I told you,' said Claude Zender after a pause, 'though I would gladly swap it for Pandora's. As you predicted, it does not work.'

'Was Palatine the Englishman you held prisoner here?'

'An Englishman, here? Your brother is imagining things, Natalya.'

He looked at her steadily, and the guileless expression on his face was all the more repellent to her because she might once have been taken in by it. He didn't know, of course, that she had overheard him discussing the Englishman with Colonel Sulamani the previous night.

'Pay me enough, and I'll take the IPD400 off your hands,' she said.

They negotiated – Zender seemed uncharacteristically indifferent, she thought. He quickly agreed to accept a mark-up of $1 million over the price his client had paid to Grosvenor. When they flew back to Marrakech, they'd take the IPD400 with them and the transaction could be completed.

'Well, that was easy,' Natalya said. 'You must be getting old.'

'You routinely credit me with the cunning of Machiavelli, whereas if that man could have witnessed our discussions over the years he would testify that I have always been putty in your hands.'

Nat knocked back her glass of Lezongars. Was her deal to buy back the IPD400 and sell it on to Grey Tony for a $4 million profit really almost done? Nearer $5 million, in fact, now that Zender had rolled over so easily. The events of the last few days seemed to have battered her natural optimism into submission, and it was hard to savour this almost surreal triumph. All she knew for sure was that so long as they were marooned in this grim compound, they were at Zender's mercy.

She pushed back her chair. 'I'll sleep next door again.'

'Your devotion does you credit, but really, it isn't necessary. Dronika is locked in the conference room, where she will stay until you say otherwise.'

'I won't risk it. She can probably walk through walls.'

'All day I have been observing how fury and indignation brings the tone of your cheeks to perfection and lends an uncommon brilliance to your eyes. Even weariness becomes you. I believe we might soothe away our tribulations in the time-honoured way?'

'No.'

'You are very beautiful, Natalya.'

She stood up to leave. Zender laboured to his feet. *He's exhausted, distracted and carrying a bullet wound, yet still he makes a pass at me!* But his eloquence had lost its charm. *It has nothing to do with me,* she thought, *it's like turning on a tap.* His bulk was not impressive but gross. And his expression, which she'd thought so full of devotion, was merely dogged now.

* * *

The flow of traffic picked up towards six o'clock. James was stretched out in the shadow of the goat shed, watching the road, while the two Ukrainian men dozed inside. One of the white MINURSO Land Cruisers passed by, heading south into Smara. James checked the time: 6.20 p.m., exactly three hours after the one they'd seen as they'd fled town. At 6.40 p.m., another turned up, this one going north. A regular patrol, thought James, in and out of Smara every three hours.

Salif arrived, bringing with him a tall, bony boy in his late teens with a length of cotton wrapped round his head and dressed in an extensively holed blue T-shirt and a pair of dusty canvas trousers which were wide enough for two of him.

'Brother's boy,' said Salif, throwing an arm around his companion's hunched shoulders. 'Benoit. Ready to fight for Polisario!'

Benoit looked far from ready. He was thrusting out his jaw and surveying the scene with a show of manly indifference, but his large eyes had the look of a startled fawn. James shook him by the hand, then told Salif what had happened that morning. When he came to the fight in the café, Salif sucked his teeth and asked James to describe the man who had stabbed him.

'In jail for kill his friend. Many like him in Smara. Flies on shit. Other men, they come with us?'

'Anton and Mikhail?' James indicated the shed. 'In there, with the goat.'

As if on cue, the goat trotted out, kids bleating in her wake. A look of glee spread over Salif's face. 'Princes from Europe,' he said, 'they find love in Sahrawi goat shed!' He crumpled with laughter, wheezing and cackling until the tears streamed from his eyes. 'Now she walk out on them!'

He straightened up and gave his nephew a thump in the chest. The princes from Europe now emerged, and the expression on Benoit's face changed to one of astonishment. Seeing them through the boy's eyes, James was filled with misgiving.

'Everyone still up for this?' he asked, wondering if his visions of driving out of the compound with Zender and Little Sister in the back seat were about to evaporate.

Salif grinned. Mikhail pressed a hairy fist into his solar plexus.

'Just about,' said Anton. 'You have a plan?'

'Sure,' said James. 'It goes like this.'

Part III

Chapter Eighteen

I had an email from Palatine. He knows about Anemone.

The words played compulsively in Clive Silk's head, but he found he could not speak them. He'd asked for a meeting with Sir Iain Strang and Nigel de la Mere so he could report that James Palatine had made contact. Now, seated in Strang's office, he was trying to suppress the panic caused by the unsuppressable thought that Strang already knew about the message and would regard it as incontrovertible evidence that he'd been colluding with Palatine. Or perhaps they'd recorded his phone call to Zender from the car park in the Surrey Hills. *He's an intelligence chief, not a soothsayer,* Clive told himself. *But GCHQ hear everything…* He couldn't even remember quite what he'd said.

'We still don't know anything concrete about our psycho-geek's role in this?' Strang was saying. 'Or even where he is?'

De la Mere shrugged.

'I'll take that as a no-fucking-clue, shall I?'

'I had an email from Palatine. He knows about Anemone.'

The two men turned and stared hungrily at Clive. He felt himself redden. 'I thought you should know.' He took a printout from his jacket pocket and handed it to de la Mere. Strang's butcher's hand shot out and snatched it.

'What a bilious little missive,' said de la Mere, reading it over his boss's shoulder. 'No wonder you're a bit jumpy. The wording is identical to the secure messages we get from Zender. He must have seen them.'

'Did you reply?' asked Strang.

'No. I— '

'Don't. I won't be goaded by Palatine.'

'The return address is friendoftheplaypen@hotmail.com,' said de la Mere. 'Droll. We could try and establish a location for the IP used to open the account.'

'Get Julian on to it.'

While de la Mere called through to Twomey-Smith, Clive pretended to look through a file he'd brought with him for just this purpose. He could feel the MI6 chief inspecting him – it was like being sized up by a bored cat.

'Maybe we should tell the Moroccans about Anemone,' Clive said when de la Mere rejoined them. He was still under investigation, as per the diktats of Caroline Hampshire's book of Service protocols; but having secured a temporary readmission to the inner circle, he was eager to make a contribution. 'We should be able to guarantee— '

'Tell them what exactly?' said Strang viciously. 'It's a bit fucking late for the truth.'

'Of course, yes. I was just thinking… ' Clive mumbled, unable to complete the sentence because what he was now thinking was that he wished he hadn't spoken at all.

'Attempting to discuss Anemone with me is a breach of quarantine procedure. Go away. Let Lisa know where to find you.'

* * *

'I was visited by a detachment of Foreign Office groupies this morning,' said Sir Iain Strang when Clive had left. 'It seems the Moroccan contingent at the UN have spent all morning lobbying the Security Council to let them launch a lightning raid on the Zender-Polisario compound.'

'They're after Mansour Anzarane,' said Nigel de la Mere. 'Their supposed Agadir Bomber.'

'He's at the Polisario compound in the Free Zone, they say, chuckling over photos of dead American holidaymakers. Remind me what the Gnome of Rabat said to the Kocharian girl in Marrakech.'

'Al Hamra told her Zender's been hobnobbing with Mansour in the Free Zone and she ought to give him a wide berth.'

'And this was on Friday night.'

'Correct.'

'But he said nothing to you?'

'We had a pointless little joust over brandies and soda.'

'You were never much good at that sort of thing.'

'Let me understand this,' said Nigel de la Mere. 'The *UN* Security Council are going to authorise a raid in a *UN*-protected territory?'

'Don't be dense, Nigel, they won't authorise anything. The Moroccans will be given to understand that Washington will look after them if they get caught. The worst they can expect is a motion of censure – along with a chorus of briefings about the right of sovereign nations to defend themselves from acts of terror.'

'Can't the FO dig their heels in, say it's not UK policy to support such adventures, threaten to go public and so forth?'

'Why would they? They're standing shoulder to shoulder, where they belong. Thirty-eight US citizens died in Agadir, don't forget – no one in London or Washington is going to risk being accused of obstructing efforts to bring the bomber to justice. The Moroccans are also saying that the arms cache at the compound is in violation of UN resolutions.'

'They've been on about it for years,' said de la Mere. 'The Polisario say it belongs to Zender and Zender says it belongs to clients who shall remain anonymous.'

'No one cares, anyway. The hawks at the Pentagon are demanding something be done to stop the region becoming the new Afghanistan – and here are the Moroccans trotting round with proof on a platter that it's already started. They expected al Qaeda in the Maghreb to kick off first, but anything that starts with *al* will do. The chatter says they've already been told to get the raid over and done with before anyone notices.'

Strang reached into a drawer of his desk and took out a small leather case, from which he extracted a rubber mouthpiece. He thrust it between his lips and started to chew. His eyes blanked over, wads of muscle fattened over the hinges of his jaw, and a sequence of rhythmic squelches issued from his mouth. The ritual was familiar to de la Mere, and he knew not to comment. Strang had the habit of grinding his teeth, and his dentist had advised that he'd wear them down to the roots if he didn't use the mouthpiece periodically through the day, particularly at moments of stress. The MI6 chief had even once produced the revolting thing at a meeting attended by a posse of officials from the Ministry of Defence.

'Al Hamra and co don't have a shred of evidence against Anzarane,' de la Mere said after a moment. 'If they do catch up with him, they're in for a disappointment.'

Strang extracted the horseshoe of wet silicone and brandished it at his colleague. 'The only kind of evidence al Hamra needs is proof that Anzarane's been a guest at the Polisario compound in the Free Zone. If he has that, al Hamra will finger him for Agadir even if he finds out he was on a yoga retreat in Tipperary. The face fits and it's an unmissable opportunity to implicate the Polisario in an act of terrorism.'

'So, he gets to raid a Polisario stronghold and then sling some very toxic mud in their outraged faces.'

'Of all the preening holy warriors on offer, al Hamra had to choose Mansour-fucking-Anzarane.'

'It's awkward, certainly. Why did al Hamra give Ms Kocharian a heads-up on this two days before they got to work at the Security Council? I specifically instructed her not to tell Zender, by the way.'

'She disobeyed – you're not the alpha male of old, Nigel. Anyway, she told you, which was what al Hamra intended. He knew we'd have to sever our ties with Zender. Now, the obese one no longer feels safe in Marrakech – though he's quite happy shacked up at the compound with his bit of Grosvenor fluff. What he can't know is that his bolthole is about to be overrun by Moroccan Special Forces.'

'You think al Hamra will join the raiding party, trump up a bit of fresh evidence that Mansour was hatching terrorist plots at the compound?'

'I'm sure he will. Plans of the basement of a certain hotel in Agadir, good-luck emails from his al Bidayat brothers. Just the kind of work the Gnome enjoys.'

'It's a neat play, you have to admit – and kudos to you for unravelling it, Iain. I wonder if the shooting in the souk was al Hamra's doing.'

'Not his style. Scheming little shit.'

'He's got a tad too close for comfort, that's for sure.'

'So close that the rancid stink of Operation Anemone is seeping into his nostrils?'

'I feel in my waters that the answer is no.'

'Let's keep your dodgy prostate out of this. In any case, if the raid goes ahead, the IPD400 will likely fall into Moroccan hands.

Then Palatine and al Hamra will have a cosy chat and we can book ourselves a couple of suites at Ford open prison.'

'Why assume Palatine will expose Anemone?'

'Because he's taunting Clive.'

'We do that all the time. He's very tauntable.'

'Palatine's a natural-born whistleblower. Hoping he'll keep his mouth shut is like giving a teenage boy a blowjob and expecting him not to come.'

'Speculation. What's his motive?'

'You have the imagination of a fig roll, Nigel,' said his boss. 'Think of the sequence: within days of the IPD400's carefully plotted sale to Claude Zender, Palatine flies to Oran. Next, he's set up his box of tricks on Zender's network and is trying to hack our servers. Then Silk creeps in and tells us he's getting sarcastic emails about Anemone. There are plenty of unanswered questions, but I've seen enough to guess where this is heading. Palatine's still nursing a grudge over what happened in Kosovo and he's decided it's payback time.'

'You think he's having a rootle in the Service file system – looking for something to exonerate himself and expose wrongdoing on our part?'

'We don't do wrongdoing, Nigel, just things that are complicated to explain.'

'Why not do his rootling when he had the IPD400 set up at Imperial?'

'A festering resentment, eating away at him. There's no set timetable for acts of revenge – I should know, I have long-term plans for several myself.'

'Something to look forward to.'

'And don't forget that Palatine's suffered a bad attack of the civil liberties over the IPD400 – he's been wanting to kill it off ever since he delivered it to Grosvenor. This lets him press the self-destruct button without having to admit that he's deliberately nixed Sir Peter Beddoes' prize investment.'

'In the meantime, he digs up Anemone and realises it could be complicated to explain, as we say in the Service.'

'You're a supercilious cunt, Nigel, did you know that?'

'He hasn't launched any more raids on the service network.'

'So Julian says, but d'you think he'd know about it? Whenever he mentions Palatine, his hair stands on end. One day we'll find him in the basement chanting prayers and sprinkling the servers with holy water.'

'What if we make a full confession and appeal to Palatine's notoriously honourable nature?' said de la Mere. 'Grovel, plead, flatter – that sort of thing. Al Hamra will play ball, as long as we let him keep Mansour.'

'How very old school. And once that's done, we can all walk away from this smelling of grateful fanny.'

'That'd keep the wife on her toes,' said de la Mere.

'She knows what it smells like, does she? Don't answer that. There isn't time for the touchy-feely stuff. We're in an absolute shitstorm of coincidence. First the IPD400 goes AWOL, then Palatine finds out about Operation Anemone, now we're embroiled in al Hamra's plan to smear the Polisario and rid himself of Claude Zender.'

'It was a mistake to dirty our hands with that man in the first place.'

'You may as well be wise after the event.'

Nigel de la Mere appeared on the point of objecting to this slur, but Strang spoke first. 'At least Zender's one of us. A secrets man, understands that the strongest hand is the one you never have to show. He's not trustworthy, but he's predictable. It's the unexploded Palatine I'm worried about. I don't fancy tuning in to al Jazeera one morning to find him explaining to a forest of mics just what he's unearthed over the last few weeks. Anemone's every nook and fanny exposed to public view, *Guardian* types drooling in the background. He'll be St James the Impeccable and we'll be off to hell in a pair of gimp suits.'

'Plus ça change,' said de la Mere.

'You're thinking what I'm thinking, right?'

'Probably not, Iain. I've never been as devious as you.'

'Fuck off. There's only one solution here and it's as obvious as a dick on a pole-dancer.'

'If you say so – you're the Big Chief.'

'I want to know if you've thought of it, Nigel,' said Strang, leaning back in his chair with a condescending expression that even his imperturbable colleague found odious.

'If I say it first, it goes down as my idea, is that it?'

'It's not going down at all. Not if I can help it.'

'You want to go nuclear. You want to tip off the Polisario that al Hamra's planning to raid their base in the Free Zone.'

'I can't see any way round it.'

'We're going to start a war in the Western Sahara.'

'There's already a war in the Western Sahara. We're doing what we're paid for, which is to look after the national interest.'

'Not to mention our careers.'

'My professional analysis is that no good is served by MI6 suffering public humiliation. If you can think of another military force with a licence to operate in the Free Zone, we'll ask them.'

'I know: the UN?'

'Ha fucking ha. You've got a line in to the Polisario, haven't you?'

'I'm not going. Christ, Iain, I'm retiring in six months' time.'

'Clive's going. What's the man's name?'

'Manni Hasnaoui – studied IR with me at Balliol.'

'Good old boys, eh? I'll find out when the raid is scheduled, you tell this Hasnaoui to get their compound reinforced.'

'Tell Clive to tell him, you mean.'

'Face to face. Nothing on record.'

'Surely the Polisario will just complain to the Security Council, get the raid called off?'

'It's a risk. Make sure the timing's right – they mustn't have a moment to waggle their beards at each other. Anyway, you think they'll throw up an opportunity to catch the Moroccans with their dicks out in a UN ceasefire zone?'

'Probably not.'

'Whatever, we need the disruption. It's a chance to hose off the telltale filth under cover of a meaningless little skirmish in which we've played no obvious part. We may even get the bloody IPD400 back.'

'What about Zender?'

'Fuck Zender. Hand him over to Beelzebub.'

Sir Iain Strang went over and lay on his sofa beneath the window overlooking the Thames, chewing violently on his silicone mouthpiece. His lean, thickset body made the sofa look flimsy. After a moment, he swung himself upright.

'We can't pussyfoot around with Palatine any more. It's one thing to be an awkward customer, but he's crossed the line. There's going to be a fight out there. Back end of beyond, no one watching.'

'Jesus Christ, Iain.'

The two men exchanged a look so dark that neither could hold the other's eye.

'I've lost control of this,' said Strang. 'I want it back.'

'We still don't know for certain that Palatine's in the Free Zone with Zender.'

'See if Julian's found a location for the friendoftheplaypen email yet.'

While Nigel de la Mere made the call, Strang looked out at the Thames and combed his shiny black hair.

De la Mere hung up and said: 'It's going to take thirty-six hours. Seems Palatine might have scrambled the IPs. And getting things out of Microsoft— '

'Fuck Microsoft. He's there. Ask your waters.'

'Suppose Hasnaoui won't play ball?'

'He needs to believe Palatine has seen Mansour Anzarane at their compound and is ready to confirm the Moroccan claim that Mansour is the Agadir Bomber. The Polisario can't let that happen, or it'll be several decades before they get another sniff at independence. If Hasnaoui doesn't buy it, what have we lost?'

'If he does, we've lost the best computer scientist of his generation.'

'Palatine's coming after us, Nigel, and he's armed and dangerous. I won't have it. Anyway, people say he's peaked.'

De la Mere shifted in his chair, then started scratching the back of his neck. 'You really want to do this?'

'I don't want to, no. Clive does. So make sure he knows it. Anemone is his fucking mess and it's all over my shoes.'

Chapter Nineteen

The old Mercedes had reacted badly to its brief excursion off-road: sections of undercarriage kept scraping the tarmac as they drove north. Thirty kilometres out of Smara, they pulled over and hid until the southbound MINURSO vehicle had passed by.

'Twenty minutes,' said James.

Salif drove the Mercedes into a gully on the outside of a jink in the road, then they rolled it onto its side. Salif got to his knees and rehearsed the demeanour of a car-crash victim, which he pulled off with no little finesse. Benoit hid behind the Mercedes, while James, Anton and Mikhail lay beside the road twenty yards back from the bend.

'Ten minutes.'

A delivery truck clattered along and slowed to offer help. Salif pulled his knife and made a run at the driver's door. The truck swerved and accelerated away, honking indignantly.

'It looks like a trap,' Anton said. 'Only a moron would walk into it.'

James tied the square of black cotton round his face and settled down to wait. The northbound MINURSO Land Cruiser arrived at 9.45. The Mercedes' undercarriage loomed in its headlights. The vehicle braked hard, then continued at walking pace, tyres crackling on the road. Three men: driver, officer next to him, another in the back. It rolled past, shuddering on its chassis. Salif sat in the road ahead, cradling his face in his hands, then levered himself stiffly up on one knee. He beckoned, then fell onto his side and groaned. The Land Cruiser came to a halt. Mikhail crawled out onto the road, stuffed his T-shirt into the Land Cruiser's tailpipe and held it there. The engine coughed, then stopped. Silence bloomed in the emptied air. James ran up and rapped on the passenger's window with the muzzle of the Firestar.

'Hands up where I can see them! Now!'

The face that looked out at James was pasty white in the Land Cruiser's cabin lights. He saw the man raise his hands, then heard him saying something. The driver's hands shot up. The man in the rear hadn't moved.

'You want a new hole in your ugly face?' Anton shouted at him. 'Ditch the fucking gun.'

Mikhail came round from behind the car and aimed the giant Makarov through the driver's window.

'Drop the gun you stupid shit,' the driver shouted.

'He talking to me?' said Mikhail, steadying himself for a shot.

'He's talking to the fuckwit in the back,' said Anton. He banged the glass hard with his handgun and finally they saw the man's hands come up.

'Open the door. Step out,' James ordered the officer.

A tall, fair-haired young man, shivering with fear. James looked at the insignia on his uniform: Finnish Army. Smart idea, that, sending to the Sahara Desert a man who's been trained to fight in a forest, on skis. James had him lie face down, then disarmed him. Mikhail marched the driver round and threw him down beside the Finnish officer. James heard a thud from the far side of the vehicle and ran round to find that the man in the back seat had got hold of

Anton's gun hand and was banging it against the side of the Land Cruiser. This one was the size of a small bear and was overpowering Anton easily. But just as James was about to drive the point of his elbow into the soldier's temple, he went down, retching like he'd just had a thistle shoved down his throat.

'The bigger the man, the easier his balls come to hand,' said Anton, dropping knee-first into the MINURSO soldier's midriff.

James signalled to Salif and Benoit to roll the Mercedes back onto the road. He found zipties in the back of the Land Cruiser and they tied the hands of the three MINURSO men. James took the Finnish officer and his driver over to the Mercedes and bundled them into the rear seat.

'Do what I say, or you will be killed,' he said. 'Understand?'

They nodded emphatically. It was much easier to listen to the tall Englishman than to look at the Arab in the front seat, who was rasping the blade of a hunting knife across the pad of his thumb and examining them from above his shemagh with amusement in his eyes. James slammed the rear door shut and the MINURSO Land Cruiser drew up alongside. He climbed into the back seat next to the bear-like soldier. This one was Finnish, too, and his eyes were cast down. Well, thought James, for a man who can probably uproot a twenty-foot fir tree, it's humiliating to be reduced to a gagging wreck by a skinny Ukrainian in a garish Bermuda shirt.

*   *   *

With the MINURSO Land Cruiser up front and the Mercedes rattling along behind, they drove until they reached the sign that read *Poste Militaire 309, Provinces Maroc du Sud*; then they turned off the road, doused their headlights and continued until they were about a mile from the fort. They got the MINURSO men out of their uniforms and handed them round: Mikhail was wider in the girth than the driver and couldn't do up his trousers, but Anton looked almost dashing in the captain's uniform, and James reckoned he would pass muster. The two Finnish soldiers had been carrying PIST 2003s, a variant of the Walther P99. James strapped one on – Anton already had the other. There wasn't a lot of ammunition to go round, but if they got into a spray-and-pray, James figured they may as well shoot themselves and have done with it.

Salif made the three MINURSO soldiers lie face down in the sand.

'Benoit has to stay and guard them,' said James.

Salif nodded and summoned his nephew. James handed over Firestar, then blindfolded their captives – he didn't want them to know they were leaving a gangly teenager in charge. Benoit checked over the Firestar, evidently keen to demonstrate that he was perfectly familiar with a handgun. James walked back to the MINURSO Land Cruiser.

'You think Benny-boy can hold them?' said Anton.

'Of course. We'll be in position by ten-thirty.' He drew a diagram of where he wanted them. 'Stay well to the right of the barrack room door, so they can't see you from inside.'

In the glove compartment of the Land Cruiser was a thick sheaf of paperwork: standing instructions, letters of authority to border personnel, complete with official stamps in violet ink, permits from the Moroccan military allowing them to cross restricted zones, and even a letter from the future president of the Sahrawi Republic ordering that the bearers be given safe passage through the Free Zone.

'Make the sergeant look at these,' said James. 'Keep him busy.'

He and Salif set off at a jog.

The fort came into view, stark and luminous in its dome of arc light. They circled round to the southern end and crouched down to wait. The men inside were arguing, and James heard a bang.

The door was kicked open and a soldier came out, stripped to the waist, boots unlaced. He spat and muttered something. There was a shout from inside and he made an obscene gesture, then stomped along the wall of the building – a big man with a spreading waist and shoulders covered with thick black hair. He came to a door and unlocked it with a key from a set attached to a loop of twisted wire cable. He went in and they heard the sound of boxes being heaved around.

The MINURSO Land Cruiser swept onto the concrete apron and into a broad right-hand sweep that ended thirty yards from the barrack room door. The vehicle rocked to a standstill and Anton stepped out with all the swagger of a tinpot dictator arriving at his birthday parade. Mikhail stayed put and kept the engine running. Anton slapped the MINURSO paperwork down on the bonnet of the Land Cruiser, then looked over at the fort. The soldier came out of the storeroom with a crate in his hands. Anton turned his back and started to leaf through the documents.

The tall, shaven-headed sergeant emerged, buckling on a holster. The soldier with the crate stood by the door to watch. Anton turned to face the sergeant and saluted briskly. The sergeant gave a sloppy imitation in response – the insolence calculated to remain just within the bounds of what could be ignored without loss of face. Anton stared into his close-set eyes, then indicated the papers laid out on the bonnet of the Land Cruiser.

'Check these documents, Sergeant.'

The sergeant stepped forward, his face sour with contempt. The other soldier still stood in the doorway. So long as he stayed there, James and Salif were pinned down.

Anton flipped impatiently through the papers beneath the sergeant's nose, pointed to a random paragraph of legalese, then looked up and summoned the soldier by the door with a gesture full of peremptory authority. Just then, someone yelled from within the barrack room. The soldier carried the crate inside, then re-emerged and started across the concrete apron towards Anton. He'd pulled on a shirt and was trying to button it as he walked.

Anton stared at the soldier coming towards him, thrusting his head forward, making him feel the force of his superior rank. James signed to Salif: *Stay here, wait.* Mikhail revved the Land Cruiser's engine, then threw open his door and hopped out. The sergeant looked up.

'Read!' Anton barked, and rapped the bonnet with his fist.

The sergeant turned quickly back to the documents. Mikhail strolled round behind him. The approaching soldier was fifteen yards away. Anton shouted at him to hurry up. The soldier didn't hear James move up from the corner, coming fast and low.

James hooked one arm round the soldier's neck and squeezed, trapping the shout in his throat. The sergeant spun round. Too late. Mikhail's powerful hands clamped his windpipe.

James seized the soldier's wrist and drove it up between his shoulder blades. There was brute strength in him, and for a second or two his free arm battered at James's stomach. But he didn't really want to fight. James hustled him behind the Land Cruiser, worked him off balance and threw him down against the front wheel. He clubbed him unconscious and tied him up. Anton and Mikhail had the sergeant down and disarmed beside him.

The door to the barrack room slammed shut.

'They've seen us,' said James.

He beckoned to Salif, then got the sergeant to his feet and held the P99 to his head.

'Salif here wants to cut your liver out,' he said in French. 'He wants you to watch him eat it. So do what I tell you, OK?'

James marched him over to the barrack room door, one arm hooked round his neck, the other pressing the P99 into his side. There was silence from within and they'd turned out the lights. It was a fair bet they'd armed themselves and taken cover. The door was steel plate with shielded hinges. It was, after all, a fort.

'Tell them to turn on the light.'

The sergeant shouted in Arabic.

'You OK, sir?' came the response.

'Turn on the light, donkey dick! You want to get me killed?'

James thought that question was a mistake, and he drove the barrel of the P99 into the sergeant's armpit. He yelped in alarm. A few seconds later the light came on.

'Tell them to put their weapons on the table and lie on the floor.'

The sergeant did so. There was silence. Salif stepped in close, pulled up the man's lip and tapped his front tooth with the tip of his knife. The man's eyes swivelled down. Salif jabbed his gum and a trickle of blood ran down over his teeth.

'I don't think they heard you,' said James.

The sergeant screamed at his men. The panic in his voice must have impressed them. They heard movement behind the steel door.

'Order one of them to open up,' James said. 'Use his name. Say you'll be coming in first.'

The sergeant nominated a man called Walid for the task. There were protests from within. Salif twirled his knife in the vicinity of the sergeant's left eye and the protests were answered with an explosion of curses. They heard bolts being pulled back. Mikhail grabbed the handle and pulled it open. James hustled the sergeant up to the door and fired three rounds into the ceiling.

'Stay down!'

Four M16s on the table, the soldiers lying on the floor. James bundled the sergeant inside. Anton and Mikhail moved in behind him and stood over the prone men, guns drawn.

Salif brushed past James, then turned and drove his fist into the sergeant's ribcage. The man stiffened in his arms. Salif was leaning in, whispering something into the sergeant's ear. James felt the slight body being forced up, then Salif pulled his fist away and he saw the knife, slimed with blood. The sergeant coughed and exhaled. James released him and he slid down to the floor.

'No speak insults to Sahrawi man,' said Salif, wiping his knife on the dead sergeant's shirt.

'I'll certainly bear that in mind,' said Anton, surveying the foetid room. 'This looks like the point of no return.'

'Go with Salif and tie them up outside the storeroom,' said James. 'Mikhail, get Benoit and the MINURSO boys.'

The soldiers stared slack-jawed. Nothing in their numbingly tedious lives had prepared them for the sight of their boss being knifed in the arms of a MINURSO officer. On Salif's orders, they picked up their boss's dead body and filed meekly out of the barrack room.

* * *

The storeroom yielded a French-made TDA 81mm mortar and an RPG-7 launcher with a collection of boosters and warheads. There were two cases of old Russian-made RGD-5 hand grenades, and a stack of M16 rounds to go with the soldiers' rifles. They started to load up the Land Cruiser, then Benoit arrived and James asked him to prepare food for them. Looking faintly aggrieved at being assigned such a menial role, he picked tins from the storeroom shelves and carried them to the barrack room stove.

'Mikhail, reckon you can put that bulldozer through the wall?'

It took Mikhail forty minutes to get the machine fuelled up and running, but the fortification did not look capable of withstanding the ensuing assault for long. Anton lounged against the wall of the fort, listening to the din of the labouring engine and the crunch of rubble on the steel scoop of the bulldozer as it pounded away at the wall. The uniform had put him in a good mood, and he found that he rather liked being out here on the fringes of the world, under the desert sky. He lit a cigarette and blew ragged swirls of tobacco smoke up towards the stars. Unlike Mikhail, whose loyalty rendered all other considerations irrelevant, Anton remained sensitive to the absurdity of their situation: somehow, he had placed himself entirely at the disposal of this stunningly arrogant Englishman who they'd found hitch-hiking at the side of the road and had now declared war on the Moroccan Army. Those clean blue eyes of his that look so trustworthy, Anton thought, are actually the eyes of a lunatic. Still, the payback for fighting his war for him – while rescuing Nikolai, of course, though it was a mystery how those two had become one and the same thing – was the story he would have to tell when he got back to Kiev. He could think of at least three very lovely girls who would find it irresistible.

The bulldozer's engine died, its final cough echoing away across the vast silence. Mikhail came trudging over, a six-feet-wide gap in the wall behind him. The sight of his friend knocked Anton out of his reverie. He threw away his cigarette, ashamed that Mikhail might guess he was indulging in a heroic fantasy with sex as its happy conclusion. Micky might not say much, but that didn't make him stupid.

'You look like a fucking movie star,' said Mikhail pleasantly, wiping a layer of dust-caked sweat from his face.

'I am a fucking movie star,' said Anton. 'Quite literally.'

They set off to the fort, where they found James dozing on a bunk while Benoit boiled rice and heated a can of mutton ragout.

'It's just like home,' said Anton. 'What's on TV?'

*   *   *

James forced open a steel cabinet and found the money taken from them the night before, along with a map that purported to show the location of the mined areas in the vicinity of the fort. The map looked as if it had been drawn by someone who knew he was never going to have to use it, and incorporated vaguely defined areas of cross-hatching and a number of hand-drawn skulls. He decided it would be safer to use the bulldozer as an ad hoc minesweeper. Mikhail would drive – because he insisted and because Anton said that dodging landmines was the sort of thing Micky did for fun. Salif would ride beside him and keep him on course. While experimenting with the operation of the bulldozer, the two of them had struck up a comradely relationship based on a liberal exchange of instructions and advice that neither could understand.

They locked their prisoners in the storeroom, then lined up their vehicles on the far side of the wall. Mikhail engaged gear and the bulldozer jolted forward. The Mercedes followed, with Benoit driving. James and Anton brought up the rear in the Land Cruiser.

They ran without lights for a few hundred yards – a pointless precaution, as it turned out, because the noise of the scoop rumbling over the desert floor could have been heard in Timbuktu. The cacophony was unbearable to listen to, like someone shouting in a crumbling mineshaft. We should carry on in the cars, James decided. Salif knows the way and this business with the bulldozer is absurd. He'd just thought the word *absurd* when a violent clang sheered off into the darkness ahead. A stone cracked against their radiator grille. Lumps of earth and rock rattled down onto the roof. James got out and walked the few yards to the bulldozer. The explosion had poked a bell-shaped dent in the left-hand side of the scoop.

'Think we should change course?'

Salif was peering into the night. 'You follow me and Micky,' he said, as if James needed to be discouraged from haring off across the minefield in a Land Cruiser packed with explosives.

The convoy ground ponderously east. Hitting a mine meant they must be off track. It would be hard to regain the safe corridor now, even if they knew where it was. Ten minutes, maybe five miles an hour, not yet half way. James felt sure they'd hit another bomb soon, and every jolt made the muscles in his groin contract. *If I were a soldier*, he thought, *I'd be sitting on my helmet.*

The bulldozer blundered on. The scoop screeched over a patch of rock, and the front of the vehicle reared up like a toy in a sand-pit. Mikhail had to reverse the left-hand track to swing it back on course. Behind the bulldozer, the Mercedes hit a rampart of loose shale and started sliding sideways.

They saw the scoop of the bulldozer flip upwards a split-second before the second blast. Something heavy thumped against their windscreen and they both ducked. Rocks pummelled the roof, then silence, broken only by the tinny clatter of the vehicles' engines. This time, Mikhail didn't bother to stop. The bulldozer picked up speed and lumbered along behind the dim, yellowish beams of its headlights. At last they saw it trundle up a short slope and tip forward onto the road. The Mercedes laboured after it, then stopped half way up, wheels skidding in the sand. James brought the Land Cruiser's bull bars to bear and shunted it to safety.

He got out and went over to the Mercedes. 'Good work, Benoit.'

The boy swallowed hard, but he looked elated.

'Micky here is worried about his bulldozer,' said Anton. 'I think he'd like to take it home.'

'Get it back off the road,' said James. 'Salif, can you find the Parker Hale?'

They watched Mikhail park the bulldozer. He put the ignition key in the breast pocket of his shirt, then started back to the road.

'Follow the tracks, for fuck's sake!' Anton shouted.

Mikhail stopped. 'It's just a few steps.'

'A few steps *in a minefield.*'

'Fuck it,' said Mikhail, and carried on. They watched as he marched stolidly over the booby-trapped sand. Salif came back with the Parker Hale and handed it to James. He was thrilled by the display of bravado: 'Micky no care!' he announced proudly.

Mikhail stepped back on to the road.

'Boom,' he said, and gave a jump.

'That's what passes for a joke in Bulgaria,' said Anton.

* * *

They'd been toiling along the dirt road for just over three hours when Salif told Benoit to slow down so he could study the way ahead. Twice he got out and walked a short way into the desert. At the third stop, he beckoned to James and pointed to a broad track marked by a line of rocks.

'Road to Polisario compound.'

'OK, let's get the artillery in position.'

They drove on for ten minutes until Salif found a second, rougher track. Benoit guided the Mercedes gingerly off the main road, and they lurched east for half a mile until they came to a depression barely concealed by a line of wizened bushes. They were close to the compound now – a corona of light half a mile to the east. There was a two-way radio in the Land Cruiser and James gave one of the handsets to Salif.

'I'll get Colonel Sulamani to call you. If you haven't seen or heard from us by midday, you're on your own.'

Salif nodded.

'How can I prove to Colonel Sulamani that you're with us?'

Salif thought for a moment. 'He save my life at Nouakchott. Hurt in leg, here.' He tapped his left thigh. 'Colonel Sulamani carry me back.'

They slung the RPG launcher under the Land Cruiser – it was not a weapon usually associated with UN peacekeeping missions – and stowed the grenades in the spare tyre compartment. The Parker

Hale and M16s went into a steel locker in the rear. They checked the IDs they'd taken from the MINURSO men – they would do, so long as no one inspected them closely.

'If we can get in and out without a shot being fired, we will,' said James. 'This is not a revenge mission. We get my device and your friend Nikolai and his sister, that's it, we're happy.' He didn't mention Sarah, since they didn't know anything about her.

'So the little arsenal we've brought along with us, that's just in case?' said Anton, the scepticism adding a sing-song quality to his deadpan Scottish burr.

Chapter Twenty

The MINURSO Land Cruiser was two hundred yards from the main gates, and the three guards on duty had heard them coming. By the time they'd picked up their rifles and elected one of their number to go and address the MINURSO officer scowling at them from the passenger seat, the Land Cruiser's bull bars were two inches from the barrier, its wing-mounted mini-flags shuddering to the tune of the idling diesel.

The officer's uniformed arm, replete with captain's stripes and insignia of both MINURSO and the Finnish Army, rested on the window frame. He did not look over when the blue-overalled guard reached his window, but passed out a wad of documents and said:

'Captain Jay Laakso, MINURSO. I have urgent business with Colonel Nejib Sulamani of the SADR Army. Which you may know as the Polisario.'

The guard took hold of the papers reluctantly. He wanted to look as if he knew just what to do with such items, where to check for names and stamps and signatures, but he did not. He started to unfold the one on top, but he hadn't slung his rifle properly and when he moved his free hand it fell from his shoulder, the strap jogged his arm and he dropped the papers on the ground. Now the

MINURSO officer did look at him, lips pursed. The guard knelt to gather up the papers, but one of them was caught by a dusty breeze and tumbled off down the track, and he was forced to scurry after it.

Anton sighed heavily and beckoned at the guard. He took the documents back, then held them up one by one.

'Identities. One, two, three. Letters of authority from the UN, the Moroccan Interior Ministry and the SADR government. MINURSO mission statement for distribution to anyone who wishes to read it. When I said urgent business, I meant that I did not wish to sit around explaining protocol to the grunt at the gate. Understand?'

The guard did not understand. He looked over his shoulder. His fellow guards were sniggering at the sight of their comrade dropping his weapon in front of a MINURSO officer. Mikhail was playing his trick with the engine, increasing the revs by imperceptible degrees so that the big diesel clattered impatiently and released a smell of hot oil.

Anton jabbed his finger at the large building ahead of them. 'Colonel Sulamani, now!'

The guard was too browbeaten to think of doing anything other than follow the MINURSO officer's order. He gestured angrily at the other guards to raise the barrier. The Land Cruiser accelerated into the compound.

'We seem to have ended up in an industrial estate,' said Anton, as they drove towards the large building ahead. They passed James's guest wing behind its coil of razor wire and rounded the north-west corner.

'Pull up to the main doors.'

James leapt out, ran up and stood to one side, while Anton followed at a leisurely pace. They marched into the entrance hall, and Anton shouted:

'Captain Jay Laakso of MINURSO, to see Colonel Sulamani!'

* * *

Claude Zender heard the shout.

MINURSO, here? Why? Laakso was one of the Finnish contingent – Zender's contact at the MINURSO base in Laayoune had reported that Laakso was unimaginative, by which he meant unlikely to take a bribe. He opened the shutter a crack and saw their vehicle. For MINURSO to turn up unannounced was unprecedented. He should have paid closer attention to the bleatings from London. And the whispers round Marrakech: al Hamra was unusually active, apparently, and had met with, among other people, Nigel de la Mere of MI6. Things were moving faster than he'd anticipated.

He snapped his briefcase shut and stepped out of his office, turned left, walked down to the end of the passage and entered a cloakroom. There was a door in the left-hand wall, which he opened just far enough to see out. When he was sure there were no MINURSO soldiers about, he walked quickly across the concrete yard to the barracks, found Commander Djouhroub's room, knocked and entered.

'Good morning, Commander.'

Djouhroub sat up in his bed and stared. He had the weight and girth of a bullock. And the smell, thought Claude Zender.

'A delegation from MINURSO has arrived. I'm going to Marrakech to find out what they're up to. Farouk will drive me. You must keep them in the compound until you hear from me.'

Djouhroub looked befuddled, whether by sleep or because he hadn't followed the instructions it was hard to tell.

'If they try to leave?'

'Use all necessary force to stop them. You can say they fired on you first – which MINURSO may not do, so you suspected a trick.'

316

Djouhroub nodded. He was an ex Foreign Legionnaire, a formidable soldier, constitutionally incapable of disobeying an order, and with not the slightest semblance of intelligence about him. Which is just as well, thought Zender, for only an idiot would follow an order such as that.

'The contents of the warehouse are your responsibility,' he told Djouhroub as he left. 'Carry out my orders in full, and you'll get a bonus of ten thousand dirhams.'

These MINURSO officers had come to arrest him, Zender assumed, hurrying up the stairs to the first floor. He did not care to be chased across the Free Zone like some brigand on the run from the local jail. Nor could the IPD400 be permitted to fall into MINURSO hands – the financial loss would be intolerable, and he had his reputation to consider. No, Djouhroub would hold them here and Sulamani could deal with the consequences – make himself useful for once. It was a shame to leave Natalya Kocharian behind with her improbable hulk of a brother, but it couldn't be helped.

The tidiest possible outcome to a most unpromising sequence of events, Zender concluded, entering Farouk's room and rousing him from sleep. His driver was about forty, all bone and gristle, with a sombre face and eyes that followed you like those of a dog or a thief. They went to Nazli's lab and Zender unlocked the door, thinking that if the computer scientist was there he would have Farouk wring his neck. The man had been worse than useless. But the room was deserted. Zender disconnected the IPD400 and packed it in its case.

'Bring that.'

They went out into the yard, and set off for the warehouse. Djouhroub and four guards were running across the paved square to the double doors beneath the Polisario flag.

* * *

There was no answer to his shout, so Anton repeated it.

'Captain Jay Laakso of MINURSO, to see Colonel Sulamani!'

James was investigating a pair of doors at the back of the entrance hall when he heard footsteps hurrying along the passage. He stood just out of sight and watched as Colonel Sulamani strode into the hall.

Anton saluted with a wildly exaggerated snap that made James wince. Sulamani saluted in return and eyed him suspiciously.

'It is a surprise and an honour, Captain Laakso, to find a MINURSO officer east of the Wall of Shame. May I ask what brings you to the Free Zone?'

'I have important business to discuss with yourself and Mr Zender.'

'What business?' Sulamani asked.

'Please tell Mr Zender we are here,' said Anton.

'Your papers, please.'

'In my vehicle.'

Sulamani went over to the window and looked out. It was preposterous that MINURSO should be here and there was something very un-military about its representative. But there were rumblings – some scheme being hatched by the Moroccans. Expect the unexpected, his commanding officer had unhelpfully told him.

'It is just you and your driver?'

Anton's unease was palpable. 'We must see Zender immediately,' he repeated, avoiding the Polisario officer's gaze.

'Please wait here while I put on my uniform,' said Sulamani.

As soon as he was gone, James stepped out of the shadows.

'He's not going for it,' said Anton.

'Take him to the vehicle. Show him the paperwork but not the IDs,' said James. He was still hoping to get to Zender before their ruse was exposed. 'Refuse to say anything else without Zender present.'

'He does not believe I am Jay fucking Laakso.'

'Stay with it, Anton, just a while longer.'

James returned to his hiding place and soon afterwards, Sulamani reappeared. He opened the front door for Anton, then followed him out. James slipped down the corridor he had come from. It smelled peculiar, antiseptic and musty. He walked along until he came to a door on his left. He put his ear up against it. Nothing. He tried the door handle and it turned. A man's office – bleak, oddly furnished. It felt as if someone had been here only moments before. On the desk was a computer with the side panel unscrewed. Someone had extracted the hard drive. He went to the window, pulled open the shutter a crack and looked out to see Anton shrugging as the Polisario colonel inspected the MINURSO documentation.

Something was happening.

He crossed the corridor and, without troubling to keep silent, tried the door on the other side. It was locked.

'Who is that?'

A woman's voice, frightened, trying not to show it.

'James Palatine.'

The lock clicked and the door was thrown open. A woman in her mid-twenties was looking up at him from deep green eyes. Natalya Kocharian. Her upper lip, a little swollen from sleep, had risen up over her small white teeth. She was wearing a pale blue T-shirt which she was untucking from a pair of jeans. One forearm was swathed in a stained bandage. Her short, honeycomb-coloured hair was awry and there was a faint crease in the pink-flushed skin of her cheek.

'Please excuse me,' James found himself saying. His voice had gone slightly hoarse.

'Excused. Aren't you the IPD400 man? I thought you'd escaped?'

'I came back. Do you know if Zender— '

There was a pile of bedding behind her. And her brother Nikolai, asleep on a hospital gurney. James felt Nat inspecting him, eyebrows curved upwards as she waited for him to finish his question. He broke himself free from her gaze, ran to the window and pulled open the shutters. The big man with the black military baseball cap he had seen at the execution was hurrying over from the barracks with four armed men at his heels. Djouhroub, commander of the guards. He needed to get to Sulamani before they turned up. As he turned from the window, something caught his eye: two men, walking towards the warehouse. One of them was fat. The other was lugging an aluminium case.

Little Sister.

James sprinted across the room and back down the passage to the entrance hall. Colonel Sulamani and Anton were standing beneath the gallery to his left. 'I insist that you tell me who you are and what you are doing here,' Sulamani was saying. James ran over, turned his back to the door and faced the Polisario officer.

'There's no time to explain, Colonel Sulamani,' he said. 'Djouhroub will be here in a few seconds and it's important you send him away. I am the man who was held prisoner here. I came back with your man Salif. He says you saved his life when he was wounded in the leg at Nouakchott.'

James watched the old officer's eyes soften at the mention of Salif's name. Behind him, the door banged open. He heard the tramp of boots on the stone floor. James kept his back turned and pretended to be looking for something in his pockets. Sulamani was looking at James with intense curiosity. Then the Polisario officer held up his hand and marched over to the contingent of guards.

'Thank you for coming so quickly, Commander Djouhroub,' he said. 'These officers from MINURSO are here for a meeting – it has been arranged for some time. My apologies, I should have told you.'

Djouhroub looked confused. The men behind him were still.

'I will send one of the guards if I need to consult you,' said Sulamani. 'Good morning, Commander Djouhroub.'

He saluted and re-joined James and Anton.

'This way, gentlemen.'

He ushered them towards the rear of the entrance hall.

'I am delighted to find MINURSO taking an interest in Polisario affairs,' Sulamani went on in a loud voice. 'We feel as if we have been forgotten.'

Djouhroub and his men did not follow, and as soon as they were out of sight, Sulamani stopped.

'You are the Englishman Zender brought here?' he said. 'Why are you dressed as a MINURSO officer?'

'I'll explain, but first we must stop Zender leaving. I saw him heading for the warehouse. Can you go after him? I'd be recognised.'

'How is that you and Salif are working together?'

'When I escaped, Salif came after me. We talked and he agreed to help me – I came back because I have unfinished business with Claude Zender. Salif told me the Polisario had nothing to do with my abduction.'

James watched for a reaction to suggest this wasn't true, but Sulamani looked him square in the eye and James saw only anger brooding beneath the layers of reticence and formality.

'Zender is getting away even as we speak,' James said. 'Will you try and stop him?'

'The MINURSO Land Cruiser would be useful.'

James and Colonel Sulamani left Anton in the corridor and ran back to the entrance hall.

*   *   *

Nat was still in the doctor's room with Nikolai, watching the barracks opposite and wondering about the unexpected arrival of James Palatine. She'd seen blue-overalled men running across the yard, then heard voices from the entrance hall. Now she went to the door, cautiously pulled it open, and found Anton observing her from the entrance to Zender's study. He was sporting a smile of such breadth that it had driven the habitually insouciant expression from his face entirely. The sight was so astonishing that Nat's mind went blank.

'Good morning, Ms Kocharian,' said Anton. 'We thought we should come and set you and Nikolai free.'

'Un-fucking-real,' said Nat. 'You're wearing a uniform.'

'Steady now, I'm on duty,' he said with a wink.

'I guess that proves it really is you.'

Anton crossed the corridor and looked in. 'Morning, Boss.'

'Anton!' said Nikolai. 'What took you so long? Micky with you?'

'Waiting by the limo.'

'You boys – awesome, really fucking awesome. Natalya, didn't I tell you they'd be good to have around? How'd you find us?'

'We hijacked a UN Land Cruiser, captured a fort from the Moroccan Army, bulldozed a hole in their wall, drove through a minefield, crossed a hundred kilometres of desert and bluffed our way here,' said Anton. 'Seeing your happy faces makes it all worthwhile.'

Nat found herself wondering if there might be more to Anton than the hotel-lounge creep she'd taken him for.

'Nice work,' said Nikolai. 'When do we leave?'

'We can decide what to do when Palatine gets back,' said Nat.

'I'll tell you this for nothing,' said Anton. 'I wouldn't want to be around if that guy ever stops taking his medication.'

* * *

Farouk loaded the IPD400 into the boot of the black Citroën DS, locked it, then fired the ignition. The starter turned over and the engine caught, emitting a steady, nasal whine that belied its power and hardiness. The servos that built pressure in the hydraulics clicked and whirred, and after twenty seconds the car lifted itself smoothly up off its chassis and settled into its characteristic pose of a shark idly contemplating a light meal.

Zender came down the steps from the warehouse office to find Sulamani standing in front of the idling DS and the MINURSO Land Cruiser blocking the exit.

'Where are you going, Zender?'

'Sulamani, I see you have called in the cavalry.'

'I would like you to remain here until the matter of these MINURSO officers is resolved.'

'I'm sure you'll manage very well on your own. There's not much a fat old fraud like me can do. Commander Djouhroub will help you.'

'Djouhroub and his men take orders only from you, as you have often insisted. If MINURSO require you to answer for their actions— '

'I shall refuse. Shall we move these vehicles, before we're all poisoned by exhaust fumes?'

'You have been in my office, deleting all evidence that you ever existed,' said Sulamani, looking at him fiercely.

'There's no need to be paranoid. Ah, here is Djouhroub to help clarify things.'

The Polisario colonel turned to see the big man jogging up the track with a cohort of guards in tow.

'Commander Djouhroub, you join us just in time. Colonel Sulamani wishes to prevent me leaving the compound. I don't know why, though I'm sure he has his reasons,' said Zender, giving

Djouhroub a conspiratorial look that did not pass the Polisario colonel by.

Djouhroub seemed pleased at the prospect of a confrontation. 'The Colonel cannot stop you,' he said, folding his arms at Sulamani.

'Quite,' said Zender. 'If you could help him move the MINURSO vehicle he has commandeered, which seems to be obstructing the exit?'

Zender manoeuvred himself into the rear of the DS and motioned Farouk to drive. Sulamani was locked in a stare with Djouhroub, one he knew he could not win.

'Get your little pig to shift his minibus,' Djouhroub said. 'Or I'll do it for him.'

Sulamani held the man's eyes for a moment longer, then turned and signalled to Mikhail. As soon as the way was clear, the Citroën DS hopped elegantly over the ridge at the entrance and slid off down the track. Zender, reclining in the back seat, favoured Sulamani with a presidential wave.

'I don't know what lies Zender has told you, Commander,' said Sulamani, looking dispassionately at Djouhroub, 'but you'd better start planning what to do if he never comes back.'

'Monsieur Zender will find out what's going on, then we'll see,' Djouhroub replied. He puffed out his chest, and started to chivvy his men back down towards the barracks.

Sulamani stepped into the Land Cruiser and told Mikhail to go after the Citroën. By the time they reached the main gates, the Citroën had already left the compound. The barrier had been lowered and three guards were lined up in front. Two of them raised their rifles and aimed them directly through the windscreen. Sulamani sighed heavily.

'Turn back,' he said to Mikhail. 'They will shoot if we try to leave.'

*   *   *

James had taken the RPG launcher up to the roof and primed it for a shot. Sand had got into the slides and catches and by the time he had cleared it and loaded the grenade and booster, Zender was driving out through the gates. He raised the weapon to his shoulder, got the Citroën in his sights. The swirling skirt of dust made it look as if the car were hovering and might at any moment ascend into the skies. In the corner of his vision, he saw a line of guards with rifles raised, the MINURSO Land Cruiser reversing away from the barrier.

His target was diminishing fast, heading beyond the weapon's effective range. He switched the grenade to self-detonate: it would explode exactly 4.5 seconds after launch. The missile would cover eight hundred to a thousand yards, depending on environmental factors. From this elevation, maybe eleven hundred. A highly technical shot, much favoured by training field instructors. The DS sailed on. He triangulated everything he knew, estimated the distance and started to count: nine-twenty, nine-forty, nine-sixty, nine-eighty... Exhale. Pause. Fire.

The warhead erupted into his field of vision and he felt the backblast of scorched air balloon out from the rear of the tube, filling his nostrils with hot, powdery smoke. The projectile swerved after the Citroën, streaking the air in its wake. It was true enough, curving slightly right, but losing height...

The explosion blew the boot open and hurled the DS forward like a pebble kicked along the pavement. The car slewed sideways, then skidded to a halt. James saw Little Sister glinting in the boot. He grabbed another booster and re-loaded. As he brought the weapon up, the car started moving again. The first explosion had already propelled it to the limits of the launcher's range and in another 4.5 seconds... Wasted shot.

325

James fired anyway, giving it as much height as he could without losing distance. He saw the air wobble and fill with a rosette of smoke and debris, then heard the explosion. The car veered. Probably just the driver reacting to the noise. It didn't stop. From the corner of his eye, he saw movement at the door to the barracks: Commander Djouhroub and two guards, raising rifles to their shoulders. He dropped to his knees and ducked down beneath the parapet. The bullets whined in and a section of parapet shattered, sending chips of concrete rattling across the roof. The firing stopped as abruptly as it had started. He lifted his head and saw Commander Djouhroub staring up at him, eyes shaded by the peak of his black cap, rifle perched on his hip. The big man raised a finger of admonishment and wagged it slowly from side to side.

Chapter Twenty-One

On arrival in Algiers shortly after midday, Clive Silk was driven to a private house near the port for his meeting with Manni Hasnaoui. Hasnaoui was a long-standing Polisario elder whose official title was Ministre d'Etat, Affaires étrangères in the government of the Sahrawi Arab Democratic Republic – government-in-waiting that should have been, for at present they presided over nothing.

Nigel de la Mere had set up the meeting, and briefed Clive over lunch at a gloomy Italian restaurant in Charing Cross – the sort of place that could have been chosen only for its anonymity.

'I've been talking to Sir Iain about you, Clive – there's no need to look sullen. You've been exonerated, as of course we expected, so we think it might be time to take a step up in the Service. Become one of us, so to speak.'

Clive felt a flutter of gratitude, then realised there was going to be a price to pay for his absolution.

'Some things can't be shown on one of Caroline Hampshire's org charts, you understand? There's a network of trust, a network of influence that… Well, put it this way, it's not going to appear in your job description.'

'But I'm not a member.'

'You haven't always made yourself popular with the executive.'

'I've only ever done what was asked.'

Nigel had dismissed this impatiently, then proceeded to lecture him on the delicate conundrums faced by those obliged to defend the national interest in a world where moral principles were a luxury one simply had, on occasion, to forego. But for all the years he had spent composing circumlocutions and half-truths on behalf of his employer, the art of subtlety had eluded Nigel de la Mere; and long before his speech plodded to a halt, Clive understood that he was going to be asked to do something *black*, as intelligence jargon would have it. Something deniable. Something wrong.

When de la Mere finally got round to telling him that he was to fly to Algiers to tip off the Polisario about the impending Moroccan raid on the Polisario base in the Free Zone, Clive felt unmoved. What was it to him if there was a skirmish between old enemies in the Western Sahara? If this was the means by which they got themselves off the hook, then better get on with it.

'So we keep Palatine and the IPD400 out of Moroccan hands. Suppose they're not actually there?' he said.

'The evidence says they are. In any case, we can't take the risk. Sir Iain is quite clear on that score.'

'And the Polisario hand them back to us – in return for the favour we've done them?'

'They might also like to know that the UK government is inclined to lend weight to their claim on the Western Sahara, given the right circumstances.'

'Suppose they don't go for it.'

'You'd better make sure they do. I surely don't need to remind you of the consequences if Anemone unravels any further.'

No, thought Clive, *you don't.*

'For you more than anyone.' Nigel de la Mere helped himself to a mouthful of breaded veal, then said: 'To be frank with you, Clive,

I don't think anyone would be sorry if the good doctor were to get caught in the crossfire. Now that the wretch Anzarane has been put up for Agadir… '

'We could breathe a bit easier.'

'My thinking precisely,' said de la Mere. 'And Sir Iain's,' he added pointedly, when Clive didn't reply. 'If the service could be saved from public disgrace by a stray Polisario bullet – well, you might think that was a price worth paying, taking a strategic view of it.'

'A Moroccan bullet, you mean.'

'Oh well, bullets don't have flags on them,' said de la Mere impatiently. 'I suppose that if the Polisario knew Palatine had seen the notorious terrorist and purported Agadir Bomber Mansour Anzarane lounging around at their compound, the idea of him flying back to London and holding a press conference on the subject would make them fret.'

'So, to be clear about this: I'm going to tell the Polisario that they'd better eliminate Palatine, or he'll destroy their dreams of independence?'

Nigel de la Mere gave a theatrical wince. 'As I've always said, Palatine is a natural-born whistleblower – that's an insight the Polisario might think quite consequential.' He paused. 'And perhaps it would do no harm to make them aware that we too can corroborate the Moroccan claim that Anzarane was a resident at the compound – not that we would, of course, given a good reason to keep it under our hats.'

'Even though we can't.'

De la Mere gave him a look that seemed to suggest his membership of the trust-and-influence club was on hold. But what Clive had come to appreciate as he travelled to Algiers was that, should the unmentionable objectives of his mission ever be made public, then Strang and de la Mere would say he had been sent merely to ascertain whether Palatine and the IPD400 had ended up somewhere in the Free Zone. Alerting the Polisario to the forthcoming raid had been Clive Silk's idea and his alone, they would insist – an outrageous and irresponsible idea, which had not and would never have been sanctioned by the senior men, whose personal integrity, deep understanding of Service protocol and years of high-level experience would have rendered such sanction inconceivable.

As to the notion that the head of the North-West Africa Office had discreetly proposed that if Palatine should show his head during the course of the war they had not started, it should promptly be shot from his shoulders… They would shrug in astonishment at the extraordinary lengths to which a man like Clive Silk could be driven by a desire to save his skin.

Exposing himself to this horrible risk was his passport to preferment, apparently, though Clive was beginning to wonder whether he would actually get to join the trust-and-influence club, how he would know if he had, and whether in fact it existed at all. As these thoughts coalesced in his mind like clots forming in soured milk, Clive would very much have liked to turn round and fly straight back to London. But he was trapped – not only by the straitjacket into which his employers had buckled him, but also by the knowledge that if the IPD400 was to be retrieved and Anemone spared from a very public disaster, the Moroccan raid really did have to be stopped, and that Strang and de la Mere had worked out the only way of doing it.

Things would go badly for him if Palatine went blabbing to Mehmet al Hamra – or indeed to anyone – about Anemone. And would it not be sweet relief to have the supercilious computer scientist off his back forever? Sitting on a sparsely upholstered bench in a sparsely furnished first-floor meeting room overlooking the port of Algiers while he waited for his audience with Manni Hasnaoui, Clive felt strangely calm. The endgame was set out and all he need do was play the final moves. He would step beyond the pale, utter certain words that would never be set down or repeated, and there the matter would end.

*   *   *

'Commander Djouhroub is under orders to stop us leaving the compound,' said Colonel Sulamani, frowning angrily at the RPG launcher slung from James's shoulder. 'I had hopes of persuading him to change his mind, but now he has seen a man posing as a MINURSO officer firing an RPG at his paymaster, I think that will be impossible.'

They had gathered in the doctor's room. From the window overlooking the paved yard, James had seen Djouhroub direct-ing his guards to various positions around the compound. Now, four of them were practice-firing their rifles at a corrugated iron sheet propped up against the perimeter fence beyond the barracks. Another pointed warning, to add to the finger Djouhroub had wagged at him after he'd launched the grenades at Zender's car.

'He had Little Sister,' said James morosely. 'I had to do some-thing. Do you know where Sarah is being held?'

'Who is Sarah?' Nat asked. They all looked at James.

'An English girl. She's being held prisoner here.'

'She left with Zender's man Etienne,' said Sulamani. 'The day after you escaped.'

'With Etienne...' James felt numb. *He wants to hurt me*, Sarah had said. *I can see it in his eyes.* Why had he not taken her with him that night? He had failed her, run away across the desert and left her for Etienne to deal with as he pleased.

'She asked for my help and I told Zender we would not tolerate any further executions at the compound,' Sulamani was saying. 'For once he seems to have listened. She was involved in your abduction, I believe?'

'She had no idea what she was doing,' James said. 'Do you know where she was taken?'

Sulamani shook his head. Nat was watching James closely. He lowered his head, then turned to look at her, his deep-set eyes almost black in the gloom of the shuttered office. *He wants to be a hero*, she thought. Who was this girl he was so determined to rescue? She felt, absurdly, a little spurt of jealousy.

'Where will Zender go?' she asked, to cover the silence – though it hardly seemed to matter, since there was no chance of pursuing him.

'He will have to cross the Free Zone,' Sulamani said. 'I can ask for him to be detained, though my superiors may decide not to do so. After that… Well, who knows where Monsieur Zender will turn up next?'

No one spoke. Nat was observing the gloomy faces around her and thinking that she had as much right as anyone to feel angry. Zender had run off and left her, as if she were of no more account than a stray cat that had taken to feeding off scraps from his table. Deserted her, and taken Little Sister with him – which was probably what he'd always intended.

'Zender's guards will hold us here for as long as it takes him to get wherever he's going,' she said, 'and there's fuck all we can do about it.'

'I will speak to my commanding officer,' said Sulamani, 'inform him of Zender's departure and request my orders.'

'When can you do that?' asked Nat.

Sulamani seemed vexed by the question, and James guessed that he dreaded the prospect of calling his CO to report trouble at the compound. The arrangement with Zender was his responsibility and, as things stood, seemed likely to end in humiliation.

'I will contact them now, but we cannot expect an immediate response. It is not an emergency.'

'Let me know when the emergency starts,' said Nat, her face bright with fury, 'and I'll put on a nice dress.'

Sulamani looked at her nervously. 'Dr Palatine, we must keep close watch on Commander Djouhroub and his guards. I can think of no reason why they should attack us, but Djouhroub is a fool, and you have already provoked him. You seem to have some military training – can I ask you to set lookouts while I speak to my superiors?'

James nodded.

'Where is Salif?' Sulamani asked.

'I left him half a mile south of the perimeter fence. He awaits your orders.'

James handed him the two-way radio.

'Salif must stay there – Djouhroub's men may open fire if he approaches the gates.' He paused. 'Can I speak with you in private?'

They stepped out into the passage.

'I wish to apologise,' said Colonel Sulamani. 'You were held prisoner at our compound – I should not have let that happen.'

'Accepted,' said James, 'though I did wonder why two men of yours, Salif and Younes, were guarding me. Why not Djouhroub's men?'

'I believe Zender intended to implicate the Polisario in your capture – he is a man who stores up untruths like a dog burying bones. Salif tried to object, but I did not listen. I have allowed Monsieur Zender to turn the compound into his personal headquarters. It is a great failing on my part.' He looked earnestly at James. 'You must understand how much the Polisario rely on Monsieur Zender: we could not carry on our struggle against the Moroccans without the arms he supplies. I am sorry for your treatment at the hands of those rats. It brings us great dishonour… ' He tailed off unhappily. 'Can you please explain why Zender had you brought here?'

*   *   *

There was nothing to do but wait for Sulamani to summon help. Midday came and went. Heat poured into the building, flexing its dried out seams till they creaked like burning husks. Blades of sunlight sliced through the gaps in the shutters. Even breathing seemed dangerous, as if the air might scorch your throat.

It's like knowing the place has been soaked in petrol and hoping no one strikes a match, thought Nat. She was standing at the first-floor window where James had stationed her to keep an eye on the guards at the western end of the compound. She'd been there an hour when James came visiting.

'All the others are armed to the teeth,' he said. 'So I brought you this.'

He handed her a rifle.

'M4 – a lightweight variant of the M16.'

She knew exactly what it was, and how to fire it. But James didn't have to know that.

'Oooh,' she said, 'a lady's gun. Show me how to use it.'

He did so. She felt his hands on her shoulders and smelled the sweat on his skin as his big, powerful body moved courteously around her.

'It's loaded, and there's no safety catch,' he said.

'Do you think I should put it down before I powder my nose?'

She was teasing him – but watchfully, James saw, in case he took offence. He was touched.

'I'm fussing,' he said sombrely. 'Sorry. Being trapped in this place is putting me on edge.'

'Me too.'

'I'm worried about Sarah.'

'Sulamani said she helped get you abducted. I guess she wasn't worried about you. Any news from the Colonel?'

James shook his head. 'Sulamani's right, what happens to us is of no great concern to the Polisario. We just have to sit it out.'

'Sitting things out is not my forte,' said Nat.

James smiled. He'd dismissed Natalya Kocharian as a bit of decorative corporate skirt, but he couldn't have been more wrong. She had an extraordinary grace about her: when he'd shown her how to use the awkward steel gun, their bodies had pressed against each other and it felt to James as if she'd known him for years. Their eyes met briefly, and hers were full of warmth and optimism. And yet she seemed vulnerable. It was astonishing that she'd pursued Little Sister all the way to this terrible place.

'James, you're looking bashful,' she said. 'Why?'

'Sorry... I mean, I don't know. I guess I was hoping we'd come here, confront Zender, and drive off into the sunset. Instead, we're stuck in this stand-off with a bunch of over-armed guards and their brainless ogre-in-chief.'

'Cheer up,' said Nat. 'Hey, I reckon the female warrior look suits me pretty damn well.' She hitched the rifle to her hip and made a fierce face. 'What do you think?'

'Frightening,' said James. 'I'd surrender immediately.'

She was actually beautiful. He remembered how he'd come upon her earlier, tousled and glowing from sleep. He wanted to reach out and touch her, but she was walking back to the window.

'On duty,' she said. 'Come back and see me soon.'

* * *

At last the Polisario colonel reappeared. He took James to his office and shut the door.

'I have been briefed by my CO,' he said. 'We are ordered to take control of the compound immediately.'

He spoke in little more than a whisper, thrusting his hands into his pockets to conceal the fact that they were shaking.

'I cannot hold it otherwise. Even then… '

'Hold it?'

'The Moroccans plan to raid the compound tonight. I must defend it at all costs.'

'Are you sure? Wouldn't that be a breach of the ceasefire?'

Sulamani gave him a searching look. 'The source is reliable, I am assured.'

'What do you stand to lose if we pull out?'

'Materiel – more than we should – I have always said we keep too much here. If they destroy the compound, we will suffer loss of face.'

Nejib Sulamani lowered his head. It looked as if the suffering had already started.

'Do you know the identity of the man you killed here three nights ago?' he asked.

'Mansour Anzarane. He told me he worked for al Bidayat – or at least, that he took orders from the terrorist leader Ibrahim al Haqim.'

'Yes, Mansour Anzarane. What I have just heard is that the Moroccans are trying to implicate us in the Agadir Bombing. They say it was organised by al Bidayat and carried out by Anzarane, and that we gave him shelter and support. Well, it is true that he was here. Zender said his name was Mansour el Shaafi. I never questioned it. Right here, on Polisario soil, while I stood by and watched… ' For a moment, he was too distraught to continue.

'Do you know what business Zender has with al Bidayat?'

'He is a man of many schemes and no scruples. If they paid him enough… '

'And was Mansour responsible for the Agadir Bombing?'

'I am quite sure he was not. But the Moroccans have persuaded the world that al Bidayat is second only to al Qaeda in the hierarchy of evil. I will be indebted to you, Dr Palatine, if you deny having seen Mansour here at our base.'

'Of course,' said James quietly.

'If this raid succeeds, the Moroccans will claim they have entered the Free Zone and destroyed a terrorist HQ. A great victory in the War on Terror, they will say – a victory that exposes the true character of the Polisario.'

'Won't Djouhroub and his men help defend the compound?'

'I think not.' Sulamani rubbed his eyes with the heel of his hands. He took them away and blinked, and James saw an old man, worn and sad. 'If he had any sense, he would recognise that our situation is desperate: the Moroccans know what to expect and will bring a force large enough to overwhelm us. The guards are fit and healthy, but they are not battle-hardened like you and I.' He gave James a rueful look. 'No, it is much more likely that Djouhroub will think this is a scheme to get him out of the compound and seize Zender's materiel.'

'I thought it was yours?'

'Much of it is, but for political reasons we say it is all Zender's. Djouhroub believes the compound is just a staging post for his arms business. It will be a matter of pride for him to refuse to leave, and with the guards here we cannot prepare any kind of defence.'

'When can you expect Polisario reinforcements?'

'Dawn. At the earliest.'

Neither of them spoke. *Special Forces*, James was thinking, *set loose in a place like this...*

'Is there another exit from the compound,' he asked, 'apart from the main gates?'

'Yes. To the south, beyond the warehouse.'

'Djouhroub doesn't know about Salif and Benoit, or the mortar we brought along,' said James. 'Let's say we shell the compound and fire on the guards at the main gate, maybe get off a few rounds from the RPG as well. We create as much noise and confusion as we can, then we pause. You beg Djouhroub to let you leave. Then we start the bombardment again.'

'And fool him into running off,' said Sulamani.

The colonel paced to the window and looked out. The desert had turned a ghostly white in the annihilating glare of the overhead sun. After a minute of contemplating this emptiness, he walked over to James, straightened up, smiled and held out his hand.

'Thank you, James. This plan appeals to me. It is a guerrilla tactic, and guerrilla tactics bring out the best in we Polisario.'

They shook hands.

'You don't think it's crazy?' asked James.

'Yes, perfectly crazy. Get ready to join Salif, while I prepare a speech for Commander Djouhroub.'

*　*　*

James found Nat and told her what had happened.

'Christ, James, this is it. We've got caught up in a war. The guards will let us leave now, surely?'

'Sulamani says not. But we have a plan to get them out.' He explained. 'Can you go over to the guards at the main gates and divert their attention, so I can get over the fence? Maybe just chat to them a bit, or… '

'James, are you advising me how to distract a group of bored young men?'

He found himself studying the surfeit of freckles on her nose, the way her upper lip had again come adrift from the lower.

'That would be a silly thing to do.'

'Just say when,' she said, enjoying the effect she was having on him. It was exciting. She reached out to touch his arm.

'Be careful, James.'

He went and briefed Nikolai: he, Anton and Mikhail would create a diversion at the south end of the administration block. At two o'clock, Colonel Sulamani marched out into the paved area between the two buildings.

'Commander Djouhroub,' he shouted. 'We must talk.'

Djouhroub emerged from the barracks a minute later. Three armed guards knelt beside him and made a show of preparing their rifles. Djouhroub beckoned to Sulamani, then stood with arms folded across his chest while the Polisario colonel approached.

'I am obliged to pass on to you some urgent intelligence I have received from Polisario HQ,' said Sulamani.

'What intelligence?' Djouhroub rolled on the balls of his feet and stared aggressively into Sulamani's eyes.

'Moroccan Special Forces will attack this compound later today. I do not have an exact time. Monsieur Zender knew about the raid – that is why he departed in such haste this morning. I advise you to follow him immediately. You know how Special Forces operate: they will not take prisoners.'

Commander Djouhroub rearranged his arms. 'Is this what your MINURSO friends came to tell you?'

'The raid is connected to the presence of Mansour here at the compound. He is accused of being the Agadir Bomber.'

The commander broke his stare and looked behind him for a moment, then turned back and emitted a laugh like rubble rattling in a steel chute. 'It's a lie, Sulamani. A lie to get us out of here. The Moroccans have not entered the Free Zone for... ' It seemed he did not know how long. 'They are not allowed to. Under international law,' he said finally.

'No, but who will stop them? MINURSO? We have a Polisario force on the way, but they cannot get here today.'

'It's a lie,' Djouhroub repeated. 'We will stay here at the compound, Colonel Sulamani. And so will you.'

*   *   *

James left the administration block by a door at the rear and scanned the open ground between him and the perimeter. A long bank of earth had been piled up to the north, and he could reach the far end without any danger of being seen. He jogged over and squatted down: less than a hundred yards from here to the fence. He saw Nat at the main gates, four men arranged in a rapt semi-circle around her. Nikolai, Anton and Mikhail were hurling abuse at the guards from a ground-floor window. Now was the time. He ran hard to the fence, checked his sightlines. No shouts, no one running after him. He climbed fast, using a pair of hooks fashioned from the clips of a rifle strap. A scrap of the thick rug from Zender's office protected him from the lines of razor wire. He dropped down the other side and crawled off towards the thicket of bushes where they'd left Salif and Benoit before driving into the compound.

He found them ten minutes later, squatting in the shelter of the Mercedes. James explained what had happened and passed on Sulamani's orders.

'Work your way round until you find a good position to fire on the main gates.'

'Where you go?' asked Salif.

'I'll be here, with the mortar. Don't be seen and don't move up until it's time to open fire.'

James unslung the Parker Hale and passed it over to Salif, along with a canvas bag containing spare magazines. 'That'll give you plenty of firepower. They'll shoot back, so keep the range at around a hundred and fifty metres. You don't need to kill anyone, just scare the shit out of them.'

'Guards not Polisario men,' said Salif, running his hands over the machine gun. 'No leave Polisario compound, we kill them.' He didn't look in the mood to be contradicted on this point.

'In forty-five minutes, you'll hear the mortar bombs,' James said. 'Then there'll be a break of fifteen minutes. When the mortar starts up again, start shooting.'

*　*　*

James bedded in the base-plate of the mortar, levelled it off, checked the firing mechanisms and arranged the shells. Twenty in all: eight for the first barrage, the rest for the second. The TDA 81mm LC, which stood for *Léger court*, was a fine weapon, robust and reliable, but this piece wasn't fitted with sighting optics, so he'd have to set the range and direction by calculation. He'd worked out the distance to the barracks as accurately as he could and now set the tube to the correct angle of elevation. It was a risky shot, with Nat and the others sheltering inside the administration block, and he allowed a high margin for error.

When he was satisfied, he called Sulamani on the radio. The Polisario Colonel was stationed on the roof so he could help James sight the mortar.

'Ready here.'

'Salif?'

'In position by now.'

'Wait for my order.'

*　*　*

Having made ardent admirers of all four guards at the main gate, Nat joined the others in a passage off the entrance hall – away from windows and close to the core of the building, as Nikolai had advised.

'You all ready?' he said. 'We move after the sixth round.'

'I'd be a lot more ready if I didn't think the first round was going to blow us into an early grave,' said Anton.

'You're a big pussy,' said Mikhail.

'Yeah, a big pussy with more brains than the entire population of Bulgaria.'

'Anyone ask you to squabble like a couple of schoolgirls,' said Nikolai gruffly. 'Get yourselves together or fuck off and hide under the bed.'

Ever since they'd been asked to lay down their rifles and leave the manly tasks of combat and leadership to the others, the three men had been sulking, and Nat was fed up with them.

'If we don't get on with it,' she said, 'I'm going to gnaw my arm off.'

* * *

James got the OK from Sulamani. He wrapped his ears, then balanced the first shell over the mouth of the mortar. He dropped it and ducked away, heard the rasp as it slid down the tube, the clunk of the firing pin, the whump as the propellant ignited. The bomb sailed into the sky, a collar of burnt gas blooming around the streak of exhaust in its wake. He watched the missile turn through the top of its parabola then hurtle down, felt the heavy thump as it landed. A patch of dirty smoke drifted across the façade of the administration block.

The radio handset was winking and he realised he couldn't hear its buzz. Sulamani: *You hit the perimeter fence, on your side. Direction is good. Add one-fifty to your range.*

'Increase range by one-fifty. Confirm.'

Confirmed.

Now he could aim with more confidence. He rolled the elevation wheel to lower the tube and give him the extra distance. This one was going to plunge straight through the roof of the barracks. He located the bomb, released and spun away from the blast of scorched fuel, then turned and saw it drop from the sky like a falcon stooping on its prey.

Smoke boiled up from the north end of the administration block. James froze with horror. How had he got that so badly wrong? He checked the base-plate and found it had shifted after the first shot. Nikolai had said they'd take cover in the centre of the building. They'd be safe there. But he couldn't afford another mistake.

* * *

The first explosion sounded so harmless and polite, so exactly as an explosion should sound when it isn't going to hurt you, that Nat found herself grinning with relief. She looked at Nikolai. His expression was thoughtful. No one spoke.

The second blast punctured the silence like a shriek in a church hushed for prayer. The building trembled, dust puffed from its joints. A rumble from the far end, and a wave of pulverised masonry rolled down the passage. She hunched in close to her brother, shrinking inside her skin.

'What did I tell you,' said Anton. 'He's got the whole fucking compound to aim at, but he drops one on us.'

The third bomb crashed down somewhere outside the building, but still Nat was grinding her teeth at the brutal impact. Two more followed at thirty-second intervals. After the next, they were going to step out into the open… She gripped her brother's forearm. The sixth explosion seemed nearer again – she felt it in her bones. They ran to the entrance hall. The huge chandelier swung slowly from side to side. Anton and Mikhail carried Nikolai to the doctor's room. They set him up on a table with the loaded RPG cradled in his arms, then ran back to join Nat and Sulamani. They were climbing into the MINURSO Land Cruiser when the seventh blast thundered out from the far end of the barracks.

One more, Nat told herself.

Mikhail drove. The north end of the barracks had been torn open. Dust streamed from its cratered walls, and a dazed guard was picking his way over the chunks of breezeblock that lay round the entrance. Two more were dragging an injured man through a ground-floor window. One of the galvanised steel rubbish bins had been flung into the coils of razor wire around the guest wing, and the dogs were shying and barking as if only their frenzy could keep it at bay. Mikhail accelerated up towards the warehouse as the eighth explosion reverberated somewhere behind them.

'Not too fast,' said Colonel Sulamani. 'We need Djouhroub to see us.'

The commander of the guards was half way to the warehouse, roaring orders at his men. A pump-action shotgun dangled from one fist. He turned as he heard the Land Cruiser behind him, stopped and raised the shotgun to his shoulder. His face was red, his eyes full of savagery. Mikhail braked and Sulamani jumped out.

'They are here,' he shouted. 'We must leave the compound!'

'This is your doing, Sulamani. It is not Moroccan Special Forces but fucking Polisario. Get back!'

Sulamani stopped. 'Why would we bomb our own base, Commander?'

'Get back!' Djouhroub pointed the barrel of his shotgun over Sulamani's head and pulled the trigger. After the crunching weight of the mortar bombs, the report sounded puny in Nat's ears. She saw Djouhroub pump the breech, the spent cartridge tumble to the ground. Three other guards now had their rifles up and aimed at the Land Cruiser.

'This bombardment will be followed by a ground assault from the north,' Sulamani said evenly. 'They may not know about the gates beyond the warehouse. We have minutes to get away.'

'Won't your MINURSO flags protect you, Sulamani?'

The three hunting dogs suddenly bowled past. They gathered round Commander Djouhroub, whining and snuffling at his feet.

'Look at my dogs,' he said. 'They know when we are under attack. They howl for blood. But they are silent. The shelling has stopped. It is just some thieves with a new toy. Clear the MINURSO vehicle, I'm taking it.'

'We are wasting time,' said Sulamani.

'I have orders not to let you leave, so I won't.'

'You must. We can go by the south gates and drive east – the Polisario units will look out for us.'

'If I decide to go, I don't want to get caught with a Polisario officer.'

Djouhroub shouted orders. Four guards ran over to the Land Cruiser and started pulling at the doors. One of them grabbed Nat by the arm, and for form's sake, she spat at him. She was about to follow up with a kick to the shin, when a tall, foppish looking man ran up the track from the barracks.

'It's over!' he screamed at Djouhroub, sweeping a hank of sweat-soaked black hair from his eyes. 'Zender has run for it. He knew the Moroccans were coming. We must get out!'

Djouhroub backhanded him across the cheek. The tall man staggered back, and his legs gave way beneath him.

'You and you, take Nazli up to the warehouse,' Djouhroub ordered.

The guards who had pulled Nat and the others out of the Land Cruiser started to edge towards the warehouse too. The foppish man's hysteria seemed to have unnerved them.

'Sons of bitches, stay where you are!' Djouhroub ordered. He moved among them, slapping at their heads.

'We may go or we may stay. I will decide, not this old man who is pissing himself over a few little bangs. Drive the Land Cruiser up to the warehouse,' he said, manhandling one of the guards into the driver's seat.

As the vehicle set off, one of the dogs backed away from the track, the hackles bristling along its spine. It gave a strange croak deep in its throat, then threw its snout in the air and howled, a long, clean note like the wail of a siren at night. Djouhroub marched over and swung his boot at the dog's ribcage. The other two started to growl, but before they could open their throats, the roof of the administration block erupted and a sheet of flame slashed at the sky. A few seconds later, the shrill clatter of machine-gun fire struck up from the far end of the compound. Right on cue, a grenade from Nikolai's RPG slammed into the wall of the barracks.

The guards didn't wait for Djouhroub to decide their fate. They fled for the warehouse, the sounds of bloody mayhem pounding in their ears. Nat saw their commander open his mouth to shout at the retreating men… Then he thought better of it and strode after them, the dogs skulking at his heels.

* * *

Nat, Anton and Mikhail followed Sulamani along the flank wall of the warehouse until they reached the emergency exit door. He pushed it ajar. The place was in uproar. Djouhroub's men had fired up the big Russian-made BTR-60P assault vehicle and the interior of the building was already obscured by the oily black smoke pumping from its exhausts.

'They are taking my Mitsubishi,' said Sulamani, 'and the two compound Land Rovers. I believe they mean to leave us without transport – but they have forgotten the Unimog.'

'Hallelujah for the Unimog,' said Nat. 'Whatever it is.'

Two men were pulling open the hanging doors at the far end of the warehouse, where Commander Djouhroub stood by the MINURSO Land Cruiser. Another mortar shell thumped down behind them, then the crash of a second grenade. The interval between the blasts was filled with the angry hammering of small-arms fire.

'Mount up!'

The man called Nazli, whom Djouhroub had struck earlier, was being bundled into the rear of the assault vehicle. No time for the cook who fed you, thought Nat, nor for the boys who served you. And what about the guards she'd distracted at the main gate? Little boys in big men's bodies… She stepped further into the warehouse and watched through the open doors as the smaller vehicles bounded across the open ground. After thirty yards, they pulled over to let the assault vehicle past. The driver gunned the throttle and the monstrous, boat-like machine thundered on towards the perimeter fence. Nat didn't see the gates until one of them was sent somersaulting into the air by the vehicle's steel prow. It lumbered down the slope beyond, then its stern tipped up and disappeared from view. The three smaller vehicles swarmed through the broken gates just as a mortar shell detonated on the roof of the barracks, adding another cloud of smoke to the dense pall of burnt explosives drifting over the shattered building.

*   *   *

James made his way round to Salif's position and managed to convince him and his nephew to stop firing. As soon as they did so, two guards emerged, one with his hands up, the other cradling a bloodied forearm. The guardpost had been shredded by the attack: of the two who hadn't surrendered, one was dead and the other had been shot in the stomach and thigh and was grey with shock. The two Sahrawi swaggered over to take possession of their prisoners. They were in high spirits, taking it in turns to praise each other's marksmanship and steadiness under fire, until Benoit caught sight of the dead and injured men and vomited in the sand at his feet. Salif clapped him on the back, then went over to taunt the uninjured man. James intervened, sending them off to fetch a stretcher and bear the wounded man to the doctor's room.

He went over to the barracks. Perhaps Sulamani had been wrong about Sarah. She might still be here, hiding. He clambered over the rubble and entered the building. The air was thick with dust and he coughed and covered his mouth. There were signs of rapid evacuation, T-shirts and trainers spilled on the floor. He searched the bedrooms one by one. His knee ached with every step, and whenever he turned, his ribs creaked and the muscles in his stomach stiffened where they'd crunched into the rooftop parapet in Smara: a rollcall of injuries, clamouring for attention now that there was no fighting to distract him. He found Sarah's room directly below Nazli's lab. In the cupboard was a small vinyl suitcase, a collection of dirty clothes in a Tesco carrier bag, and a book with pencil annotations and a stamp from the library of the University of Leicester. *The Wretched of the Earth* by Frantz Fanon. A book for the compassionate, for a girl touched by the injustice that sent her to a good university while the wretched of the earth lay down to die. Sulamani had said he would not tolerate further executions at the compound, so Etienne had taken her somewhere else. But that didn't necessarily mean...

He packed her things in the suitcase, then couldn't think what to do with it and walked out, leaving it on the bed.

He went back to Zender's room and sat on the green sofa. Djouhroub and the guards had fled, but he felt no sense of triumph. Instead, the familiar grim tension was throbbing in his veins: the Kosovo feeling he'd worked so hard to suppress, now jerked into life by the fight for the compound. Could it ever be sated? Not just by lobbing over a few mortar bombs, anyway. His mind chugged pointlessly through the events of the day, as if it might not be too late to rearrange them by some as yet unrecognised power of endlessly reiterated thought. But no. Zender had cruised off hours ago – perhaps to be detained by the Polisario, more probably to reach the Algerian border with nothing but a little discomfort to complain about. Zender is untouchable, he thought bitterly, there is no part of his fate in which he does not play the decisive role. Unlike you, who go galloping round every bend like a blinkered horse.

His bout of self-recrimination was interrupted by the Polisario colonel, with the uninjured guard from the main gate at his heels.

'James, the others are ready to leave for Bir Lehlou,' Sulamani said. 'We will eat first, but the sooner you leave the better. This man will drive you.'

The guard bowed and Sulamani sent him to wait in the hall.

'I asked that all Polisario units in the Free Zone be told to set up roadblocks and search for your IPD400,' he went on. 'But it seems the order had already been given. I don't know how they knew about it.'

James didn't either, but he could guess: whoever had tipped off the Polisario about the Moroccan raid was also after Little Sister. This had the Playpen written all over it.

'Are they searching for me, too?'

'I told my CO you had escaped, not that you came back,' said Sulamani. 'I thought it best.' He shifted awkwardly, evidently unwilling to explain why he had lied.

After a pause, James said: 'There's a Light Gun in the warehouse.'

Sulamani nodded. 'We captured it five or six years ago.'

'It might be useful tonight.'

'I am not trained to fire it.'

'I am. Let's say the Moroccans attack soon after midnight. Your reinforcements are due around dawn – that's a long time to hold off a Special Forces unit. What if we tow the Light Gun out of the compound and fire on them from several different positions, convince them they're being shelled by a much larger force?'

'They will not retreat,' said Colonel Sulamani. 'Retreat would be disgrace.'

'No, they come after us and we play shoot and run. We play it all night if we have to.'

'We? You wish to fight alongside the Polisario? Why?'

'The Light Gun can make the difference. We'll need the mortar, too – Salif can manage that. Which leaves you and Benoit to deploy, fire and strike an artillery piece that usually has a crew of four trained men.'

'And Younes, too. But this is not your concern.'

'I got you into this. If I hadn't burdened the world with the IPD400, and then allowed myself to be captured because I was too stupid and arrogant... '

James felt himself reddening. He did not want to admit that the events of the day had left him feeling desolate – nor that the promise of a fight was making the blood race in his veins.

'I owe it to you to finish the job.'

'You owe us nothing. These are not good reasons to risk your life.'

'If your people get the IPD400 back off Zender, I'll owe you a lot. In fact, the whole world will owe you a lot.'

*   *   *

The conversation was curtailed by the arrival of the rest of their party. Salif had been out to fetch the Mercedes, and he, Benoit and Mikhail had changed its oil and made running repairs to its battered suspension. Meanwhile, Nat, Anton and Nikolai had been exploring the arms cache in the warehouse. The opportunity to tool up had been irresistible to the Ukrainian men, and some of the arsenal now lay packed into the Mercedes' boot.

'Are we going to eat soon?' said Anton. 'Micky hates to lose too much body mass.'

'We can start with an aperitif, courtesy of Monsieur Zender,' said Nat, indicating the bottles on the sideboard.

Glasses of whisky were passed round. Salif drunk his in one gulp and immediately became garrulous. 'This Polisario base now. All Polisario weapons safe,' he kept saying.

'They were safe when Zender and his guards were here and the Moroccans were hiding behind their wall,' Colonel Sulamani observed.

Undeterred, Salif took Mikhail to one side and started to tell him the story of their assault on the guardpost, illustrating the narrative with vivid enactments of the critical moments in their triumph. Aware that the others were watching, Salif's gesticulations became extravagant, and ended with a noisy imitation of Benoit vomiting beside the bodies of the injured men.

'I see people dead, I feel bad also,' said Mikhail with a conciliatory glance at Benoit. 'Fuck it.'

'Kiev doorman, Saharan tour guide – now he's gone philosophical!' said Anton. '*I see people dead, I feel bad also. Fuck it.* You're a genius, Micky, you know that?'

Nikolai was shaking with laughter. 'Feeling bad? Fuck it!' he shouted. 'Fuck it! It's the secret of happiness!'

'Make a joke about everything,' said Mikhail crossly.

'He has spoken!' said Anton. '*Make a joke about everything.* This stuff is going to change my life.'

'Hey, Micky, tell us some more,' Nikolai demanded.

'Fuck off.'

'*Fuck it. Make a joke. Fuck off.* Life in a nutshell!' Anton raised his glass in toast while Nikolai roared with delight. 'He always makes me laugh, that boy,' he managed to say.

Nat was thinking about the guards at the main gate, puffing out their chests and grinning at her. Now one of them was dead and another badly injured. The moment of hilarity passed her by, and she felt glad when it was brought to an end by a knock on the door: the boy Adel, bearing a tray with two large clay pots. He rushed away and returned with a stack of flatbreads, then arranged the side table so the eight of them could sit round it. Nat observed the three Sahrawi men opposite her: they ate reverently and with great consideration, passing the food to others before helping themselves, taking modest mouthfuls and chewing carefully. Sulamani's expression was bleak. Salif was keeping his head down, while sneaking surreptitious glances in her direction. His nephew was surveying his empty plate as if wondering whether it would be acceptable to lick it. Nat pushed the remains of the stew towards him. *The Moroccans will come expecting twenty-five well-armed men*, she thought, *and they'll find these three.*

'One of the guards they left behind is a local man,' said Sulamani, breaking the silence. 'He will drive you to the Polisario HQ in Bir Lehlou – it is a complicated route, and there are minefields. But it is safer than trying to get to Smara, especially with Moroccan Special Forces about. I hope the Mercedes is strong enough for the journey.'

'It may be,' said Nikolai. 'But with six people inside it, we'll be lucky if it gets to the front gate.'

It seemed absurd to be stymied by such a mundane problem, but after several minutes' discussion, no one had come up with a solution. The meal over, they went up to the warehouse to try it out. With all six of them stuffed inside, the Mercedes bottomed out on the rail across the entrance, which was barely an inch off the ground.

'Maybe unload the boot,' Nat suggested.

Mikhail and Anton unpacked the weapons they had pilfered earlier, taking care to avoid Colonel Sulamani's indignant gaze. It helped, but not enough to make the Mercedes a viable means of escape.

'You'll need water in the back anyway,' James said. 'Try without me.'

He got out and the suspension rose several inches. Mikhail engaged gear and the elderly vehicle sailed forward. He drove them down to the gates and back.

'Amazing,' said Anton. 'Almost twice walking speed and it's still in one piece.'

'James, we're not going to leave you,' said Nat. 'What about the Uni-thingy.'

'The Unimog,' said Colonel Sulamani.

'You need the Unimog to tow the Light Gun,' said James. 'If you can only fire from one position, you'll be lucky to survive an hour, let alone the whole night.'

'It's the Colonel's decision,' said Nat, 'not yours.'

Sulamani looked down at his hands, then over to the horizon, then back at his hands. Finally, he cleared his throat and said:

'My orders are to defend the compound. The Light Gun is our only hope and it is useless without the Unimog to tow it. James, you offered to stay and help us. I accept, with deepest gratitude.'

* * *

Before the Ukrainian contingent set off for Bir Lehlou, Nat led James to Zender's room.

'Why don't I try and persuade Sulamani to give up this place? We can all drive east together. It's a lost cause, isn't it?'

'There's too much at stake for the Polisario. Sulamani would rather die than run.'

Nat was disappointed, and made no attempt to hide it. 'You actually want to fight, don't you? You're kind of addicted to it.'

The truth, so baldly stated, was unsettling, but how could he admit that she was right? Her candour made his reticence seem shabby.

'What about Sarah?' Nat said.

'I don't have any idea where she is. Anyway, I'll be delayed by twelve hours at most. When it's over, Sulamani will let me have the Unimog – it'll be much quicker over the desert than the Mercedes. I'll catch you up before Bir Lehlou.' He paused, reluctant to have their conversation end on this accusatory note, then asked: 'Do you think your brother is up to the journey?'

'Madame Mengele is seeing to his stitches now. Maybe the Mercedes can tow the gun. We could at least try. If not, Anton and Mikhail can walk.'

She was searching his face again, but he could not take her gaze.

'Fine,' she said. 'You get ready for your heroic fun and games with the Polisario and we'll get ready to leave you to it. Please come and kiss me goodbye.'

* * *

They assembled beneath the Polisario flag at the front of the building. The air was silky warm now, soft as fleece on the skin. The desert to the west seemed to ripple and flex as the shadows of evening unfurled. Their elongated silhouettes danced along the wall behind them.

Their driver was called Suli. Relief at being allowed to leave and terror that Sulamani might change his mind had put him in a wretched state of obsequiousness, and he would have fawned over them for several minutes if Sulamani had not ordered him to sit in the driver's seat and keep his mouth shut.

'The limousine,' said Nat, eyeing the Mercedes with fresh misgiving. 'Why do I think we're going to end up pushing it to Algeria?' She'd decided that she owed the men a good-humoured parting, though really she felt overwhelmed by melancholy.

James shuffled awkwardly. He was still smarting from Nat's accusation of bloodthirstiness. Now she was standing in front of him, looking up at him from those impossibly lucid green eyes. He was wondering if she was going to say something challenging, then realised she'd already spoken.

'Sorry, I was miles away.'

'I said, look after yourself tonight. Come after us the moment it's over, right?'

'I will.'

'We'll go nice and slowly, so you can catch up.'

'Why don't you two exchange phone numbers and continue this back in London,' said Nikolai.

'Get in the car,' said Nat, 'and don't forget the leg.'

She put one arm on James's shoulder, pulled herself up on tiptoe and kissed him. He felt a little wetness from the underside of her upper lip, cool and sweet on the parched skin at the corner of his mouth. Her breasts brushed his chest, so light a touch he hardly knew it had happened. He breathed a sigh of desire, quite unbidden, and reached to prolong the moment. But it was over. Nat was shaking hands with Salif and then Sulamani, whom she also kissed.

'Stand at the end of the queue, Micky,' said Nikolai from the back seat of the Mercedes. 'You might get one, too!'

Mikhail bolted round to the other side of the car and climbed in.

'Ouch,' said Nikolai as the Mercedes moved off and immediately jolted over a rock. 'Drive carefully, you little shit. I haven't forgotten that you shot at my friend Salif.'

'Sorry, sir,' said Suli. The car rocked to a standstill.

'The trip of a lifetime,' said Nat to her men, 'and hasn't it started well.'

Chapter Twenty-Two

Darkness fell. James went up to the warehouse to check over the Light Gun. It was old and didn't look well maintained, but the L118 105mm towed howitzer is one of the most successful artillery pieces ever made because, as well as being powerful and compact, it is virtually indestructible. So was the Unimog 404 to which it was hitched – something like a cross between a tractor and a truck and probably made in 1960-something, but it still looked like it could churn its way across the Himalayas. He fitted the gun's A-frame, cleaned the loading chamber and lubricated the transom and running gear. For crossing rough ground you could reverse the barrel of the gun and clamp it to the trail. That done, he loaded the ammunition trailer and hauled the rig out of the warehouse behind the Unimog. At just over 4,000 lbs in weight, the Light Gun's lightness was relative, but the Unimog didn't protest and after a trial run round the compound, James was satisfied. The firing mechanism was battery operated and needed a re-charge, so he plugged it in, then went down to find Sulamani.

The Polisario colonel was standing by a crater left by a mortar bomb which had overshot the barracks. A puddle of orange flame flopped and flared in the charred hollow. Benoit was prodding something with a shovel, releasing a smell of burnt petrol and human flesh. It was as if the fabric of the place had been blown open and here were its twitching entrails.

'Mansour?' asked James.

Sulamani nodded. Salif arrived with a crate of documents and started to feed them into the flames. James took the Polisario colonel to one side.

'Do you have an idea who might be commanding this Moroccan force?'

'Most likely it is Hassan Zaki. He is the nephew of a member of King Mohammed's inner circle. The other Special Forces commanders are pure fighting men, and this mission may be thought too sensitive for them.'

'If he comes under fire, will he seek orders from on high?'

'Yes, certainly.'

'I may be able to knock out the satellite channel they're using.'

'That would make him cautious. Can you do it?'

'As long as Nazli's lab hasn't been damaged.'

'Good. One of the guards they left behind is not badly injured: I will try to recruit him. There is nothing for him here, though all I can offer is a fight in the dark.'

'Tell him it's a sure-fire ticket to paradise,' said James, attempting to lighten the mood.

'You would like me to make fun of his religion? These boys don't have much to believe in.'

The rebuke took James unawares. All he could think to say in reply was, 'I'm not a Christian.'

'Godless, then.'

'I believe there is much we don't understand,' James said, a little more angrily than he'd intended. 'But we should face our ignorance squarely, not sanctify it with mumbo jumbo.'

'Perhaps you are right,' said Sulamani. 'But we in the poor half of the world know very well that you in the West are rich at our expense. If it takes the mantle of Islam to save us from this plunder, then I will wear it gladly, whatever I may privately believe.'

'You think I'm to blame for this?'

'No – and nor were the clever liberals I knew at Cambridge. But still, your children grow fat, while ours are too weak to brush the crust from their eyelids. You send your rock stars to weep over their graves, while your leaders consort with the financiers who ensure that food is kept from their mouths. You lecture us about democracy, while propping up any tyrant who promises to supply your oil. Everyone says they are not to blame. All I know is that the power to change things lies in the hands of the rich – who have no interest in change, and indeed a great fear of it.'

He spoke like a man who has brooded a great deal but lacks an audience for his thoughts, and so, when he finds one, unleashes a tide of well-turned polemic.

'But nothing lasts forever, and the West is already in decline. Speculators tear the value from everything they touch. Your leaders squabble over trivial things. We here must watch that we do not get hurt, for the dying empire will lash out terribly.'

'I'll try and sink with dignity,' said James.

Sulamani looked at him steadily. 'I have offended you. I am sorry. You cannot escape where you come from, but you are a good man, and I lecture you as if you were wicked. Salif says I should trust you – he judges men simply by their actions, and no doubt he is right. And yet I know so little about you, Dr Palatine. You have appeared in our midst at a critical moment in our struggle, and now you offer to help us avert a disaster. Perhaps you are a god!'

Explained in this manner, Sulamani's reservations seemed entirely justified. 'Half the time I don't know why I do things myself,' James confessed. 'The more I think, the more I flounder. But the doing has a way of setting things straight.'

'*Flounder*,' said Sulamani. 'An excellent word. We must hope Colonel Zaki will flounder when his satphone goes dead.'

*   *   *

The Mercedes heaved itself east with as much facility as a slug in a sandpit. There was no speed with which Nikolai was content, and Nat could not persuade him to stop his stream of complaints. Darkness fell, pressing itself in on the cramped interior. Anton declared himself ready to get out and walk, which he said would be quicker and quieter. Mikhail sat between them and snored.

An hour after they'd left the compound, headlights flared behind them and the Mercedes was filled with sliding shadows. A pickup lurched alongside. Rap music grunted from a speaker in its rear. The vehicle swung in front of them and bumped the Mercedes to a standstill. A second pickup pulled up behind. Nat saw long, elegant arms resting on the stocks of automatic rifles, skinny chests girdled with bandoliers, chewing teeth and dirty eyes.

'Suli, are they Polisario?' said Nat.

The boy was trembling. His hands moved over the steering wheel and gearstick as if contemplating some kind of action that his mind could not.

'Suli?'

The car suddenly reeked of fear.

'Not Polisario.' Suli shook his head. 'Bad men.'

'Keep your weapons hidden,' Nat said. 'I'll talk to them.'

'Fuck's sake, Nat,' said Nikolai. 'They don't look like the type to talk.'

She threw open the door and stepped out, calculating that the sudden appearance of a beautiful European woman would stall them. There was a shout from the cab of the lead vehicle and the music stopped, leaving a fluttering silence.

'Bonsoir, messieurs,' she said. 'Nous avons arrangé un rendez-vous avec quelques officiers du Polisario. Vous pouvez sans doute nous diriger vers Bir Lehlou?'

It seemed to Nat that a dozen pairs of eyes were wandering like proxy hands over her face and body.

'Où est le chef? Who's the boss – I want to speak to him.'

Two of the men were peering into the Mercedes, tapping on the window with the muzzles of their guns to make the occupants look round. Then one of them opened the driver's door, caught Suli by the wrist and dragged him out. The man's demeanour was of one unwilling to expend much effort on such a demeaning task.

'Le chef, hein?' said Nat, speaking as loud as she dared.

There was a brief discussion. The men's naked backs glistened, their guns clanked. Nat heard *Zender* and, several times, *Polisario*. Then one of them looked at her and beckoned. 'You, come.'

'Don't do it, Nat,' Nikolai growled. 'We can take them out or die here. I don't want you to go with them.'

Nat ignored him. They were shoving Suli back into the driver's seat and ordering him to follow, pointing at her by way of a threat. Two of the men came round and stood in front of her. If either of them touches me, she thought, I'm going to kick him so fucking hard he'll be gagging on his own balls. Their eyes were empty, khat-numbed, the eyes of disturbed children that you couldn't read any further than to say you wished you hadn't tried. But still, she could see they weren't sure how to treat her.

'Allez-y!' she said briskly, and marched towards the nearest man, forcing him to step aside. The one who had beckoned to her was standing by the open door of the cab, a smile playing around the edges of his mouth. He had an oval face and thick, curly hair. In other circumstances, you might have said his expression was genial, but here it looked cruel. His rifle lay over his shoulders, his hands and wrists dangling either side. The skin was so tight over his ribs it was like looking at someone being crucified.

Nat stared at him with distaste. 'Alors, nous restons ici toute la nuit?'

She climbed up into the cab and slammed the door. The boss swung into the driver's seat and the rest of them mounted up. The music came on, a succession of blundering thumps. The vehicle behind them honked and shunted the Mercedes into the pickup ahead. The men in the back whooped and a burst of automatic rifle fire stammered into the empty night.

*   *   *

James made his way over to Nazli's old lab. A smell of panic still clung to the air. He wished Nazli were there, fidgeting away like a testy child. He checked the cabling to the dish on the roof, then booted up the Sun and hunted for the software that controlled the satellite.

It was dull, fiddly work, and he had to be careful not to terminate his own connection before he was through. Sulamani's words played in the shadows of his mind: envoy from a putrefying civilisation that had brought his people nothing but war and starvation, cloaked in the stench of sanctimony – is that what the Polisario colonel thought of him? *But you are a good man*, he'd said. A polite retraction. Was he? Hadn't he recently abandoned an innocent girl to a horrible fate? The evidence in favour of his goodness seemed thinner with every passing day.

He prepared a sequence of commands that would force the satellite to look for non-existent fields in every data packet that came its way, then wrapped them in a timer and sent them up. The connection went dead, then came back up when the timestamp expired.

When he was sure he could turn it off at will, he left a series of false leads for the operating company's technicians, then set the timer to twenty-four hours and dispatched his final piece of mischief into the good heavens above.

CONNECTION TERMINATED.

Darkness had fallen by the time he left Nazli's lab. The scarred buildings made a desolate spectacle under the cold gaze of the exterior lights – like the corpses of powerful men exposed to public ridicule. He found Sulamani and the others by the kitchen door, along with Adel and two small boys, the cook and a young woman who looked like her daughter. He remembered them from nine days ago, waiting outside his room with a clean mattress, giggling at his nakedness. Standing a short distance away was the man he'd strangled almost to death on the night of his escape: Younes. Catching sight of James, he lowered his eyes and backed towards the shelter of the doorway.

'Follow the road east,' Sulamani was saying to the cook. 'I have told them to look out for you.'

The two boys were crying. Adel and the young woman comforted them, then she ran off and returned with an armful of shemaghs and two pairs of men's trainers. The boys stood in them doubtfully, then practised shuffling forward. It looked as if progress would be slow. Sulamani, Salif and Benoit escorted the bedraggled party to the gates and James was left with only Younes for company. James walked over and held out his hand. Younes shook it nervously. He carried his head stiffly and his neck beneath the sparse beard was mottled with bruising.

'Colonel Sulamani good man. Good!' said Younes eagerly, as if this declaration might somehow dissuade James from launching a new assault.

'You OK?' James asked, slapping him on the shoulder. The feel of the thick flesh under his hand brought back the moment he had nearly killed this man – the absolute power in his arms, the smell released by the guard as his muscles went slack. *Perhaps you are a god*, Sulamani had said.

The Colonel returned, Salif trotting at his side in great agitation. 'Sir, Colonel Sulamani,' he was saying, waving a hand at Younes. 'You must send this donkey away. He is a great fool and will get in our way.'

'No,' said Sulamani, 'he can help us carry shells for the gun. We need dark paint and camouflage nets for the Unimog – go up to the warehouse and find some.'

'Sir, he cannot even carry his own head.'

'He is a Polisario soldier and must be accorded respect. I will not discuss this further. Go. Take Younes with you.'

'The satellite's down,' James said when they had left. 'Zaki's on his own.'

'Thank you,' said Sulamani. 'I spoke to the guard. His arm is only scratched, but I could not persuade him to join us. The doctor also refuses to leave. The other guard is badly hurt and she says he will die if she does not stay and care for him. But perhaps the three of them will be safe here. I am beginning to believe that with your help, James, we have a chance of keeping the Moroccans at bay.'

'And if we do?' James asked.

'They will have to deny there was ever an attack. We can get video of their retreat and announce the expulsion of some Moroccan agitators. Ha! Help us camouflage the Unimog, then we might rest for an hour or two, while Salif keeps watch.'

*   *   *

The headlights picked out a large square tent of stained canvas with slack guy ropes and sagging pitched roof, like the travelling pagoda of a paladin who has fallen from grace. Nat's captor killed the engine, then came round to the passenger door and started to tug her out.

'Let go, dickhead. You think I'm going to run away?'

He pulled her over to the tent. A flag with an elaborate device of swords and rifles against a red and yellow background hung over the entrance. A dying fire glowed dimly ten yards ahead and Nat saw two men lounging on spread blankets, their jaws working on khat leaves, their shot-pink eyes watching her with easy malevolence. The man leading her stood just outside the tent and spoke to someone inside, his hand gripped round her bicep. Nat pulled the flag aside with her free hand.

'Are you going to invite me in, or am I just going to be manhandled by this foul-smelling boy?'

The man shoved her inside the tent. The interior was lined with tattered cotton drapes and lit only by a red glass lantern suspended from the centre pole – at first she couldn't see who she had spoken to. A fug of tobacco smoke laced with the sour smell of dung caught in her throat and made her cough.

'My sincere apologies, Mam'selle,' said a high-pitched voice. 'Please, sit where you like. Kossi, bring tea.'

Nat's eyes searched the gloom. The floor was covered with a filthy camel-hair rug and a collection of lumpy cushions. There – something shifting in the far corner. She edged over to her right, staying close to the entrance. As her eyes grew accustomed to the darkness, she made out a hooked nose and a pair of large black eyes with yellowish whites; then a thin face beneath a helmet of heavily oiled hair that dripped in dressy curls around a sinewy neck. The assemblage lolled sideways, propped on a thin forearm with the wrist bent at right angles under his ear. There was a pile of cigarettes in front of him, and a gold lighter.

'Prince Fara Makhlani al Makhlani,' said the man. His accent was east coast USA, smeared into an effete drawl. 'At your service.'

'Natalya Kocharian.'

She recognised the name as the one Claude liked to put on his end-user certificates. A tribal leader, though there didn't seem to be much of a tribe. She sat down and pulled a cushion towards her, feeling somehow that it would protect her.

'Yes, be comfortable. Why are you here?'

The prince was wearing a Knicks basketball singlet and a pair of baggy shorts in gold satin. He drew his skinny legs towards his chin, as if trying to ease a stomach cramp.

'I didn't come here. Your boys brought me, at gunpoint.'

'I mean, to my lands.'

'Business.'

'Oh, business.' He picked a cigarette from his pile and lit up.

'Why did you bring us here?'

He smoked for a while. 'Would you like one?'

'I don't smoke.'

'You should. It is nice. I am the only businessman here. Do you want to do business with me?' He grinned at her, and she saw that his teeth were brown and shrunken.

'What've you got?' she asked as brightly as could.

He kept grinning. 'Your four men.' He laughed, a succession of disjointed squeaks. 'And you.'

Nat shifted uncomfortably. His eyes when she met them were glittering, thrilled with this statement of his power. She couldn't hold them.

'And this.' He took the corner of a cotton drape that covered a square object behind him, then snatched it away with a flourish to reveal an aluminium case with ribbed sides. 'It is called... ' He unfolded a scrap of paper from the pocket of his shorts and read: 'The IPD400. You know what it is?'

Little Sister. She'd never actually seen it before. Thirty million dollars worth of electronics all packed up in a smart case with a handle on top. It didn't look like much, considering the havoc it had caused.

'No idea,' she said. 'A camera?'

'Wrong. A computer.' He covered it with the drape again. 'Now, what have *you* got?'

He spoke in a sneering parody of her English accent. He was hectoring her, bullying. She needed to take the conversation some place else, but couldn't think what to say.

'Nothing,' said the prince softly.

'You must have spent time in the US, to speak English like that. New York, maybe?'

He stubbed his cigarette on a patch of rug and flicked the butt into the corner behind her.

'You should come to London. I'll show you round. There are plenty of princes in London, though not all of them are real.'

'You think I am a real prince?'

'You have your own flag. I guess you must be.'

'You do business with Monsieur Zender?'

'Yes. You?'

He sat upright and leaned towards her, shoulders hunched beneath his ears, eyes wide open but the irises like little black pellets.

'Zender is always fucking with me.'

'It's just the way he is.'

The flag was pulled aside and one of the men came in with two glasses and a stained silver pot. There was no smell of mint from the steam, only a whiff of wet straw. The prince watched his underling bow out, then said something sarcastic and the man stooped down and slopped tea into the glasses. The prince gestured at Nat to take hers. She did so reluctantly.

'Tell me what Zender's done and I'll try and guess what he's up to.'

The prince sat back, lit another cigarette and blew smoke at her. 'Maybe later.'

He shouted something and a moment later the underling returned with a bundle of khat leaves. The prince sorted through them, grumbling. He started to chew, then stood up. There was a revolver in his right hand.

'Wait here.' He pointed a bony finger at her. 'Get ready.'

He ducked out under his over-illustrated flag. Fear scampered inside her. A car door was slammed, then she heard someone screaming. Suli. There was a grunt and the screams stopped. Another grunt, followed by a series of gulping, panicky breaths. Talking, whimpering.

The gunshot made her jump and she cried out as the filthy tea splashed over her ankles. Footsteps outside the tent. The flag was thrown aside. The prince flounced in like an offended teenager and flung himself onto his cushions. The stuffy tent air was pungent with cordite. Nat tried to stay calm. What had the prince done with his gun? He lit another cigarette and spat out the remains of the khat leaf. The smell of his excitement made her want to retch. *Why did you kill the poor boy?* As if there might be a perfectly reasonable explanation. I'm going to faint, she thought. I can't take the heat, the smell, the smoke. I'm frightened.

The prince was squatting in front of her, his narrow, curved haunches sticking out on either side like a locust's legs.

'Forget business,' he said, tossing the loose bundle of khat into her lap. 'Try this. Better than cigarettes.'

She picked out a leaf, slid it between her teeth. Looked into the prince's empty eyes.

'Zender told me about you. He said you were a good man.'

He shook his head.

'I can see he was right.'

'I should slice you up like a pig,' said the prince. 'But you're a hot bitch. I can do it later.'

'They teach you how to chat up girls in prince school?'

He raised his eyebrows in mock surprise, reached out a clawed hand and took her by the throat. Pushed her down until the back of her head hit the ground, the ground with the filthy rug that stank of old shit. Flakes of khat scratched the back of her throat. If I could just get comfortable, drink some clean water, I could bear this, she thought. He held her down. She saw him looking at her honeycomb-coloured hair and it felt like she was watching him with someone else.

Chapter Twenty-Three

James was woken from tangled sleep by Salif's hand rough upon his shoulder.

'They are here. Come.'

They ran up to the roof. Colonel Sulamani was staring into the north-west. Salif pointed to a slender comb of dust twirling above the moonlit horizon.

'How many, how far?'

Sulamani consulted Salif. 'Seventy or eighty men. Ten, twelve k – maybe an hour away, but now they have halted.'

'They're not doing much to conceal themselves,' said James.

'Perhaps they hope we will be scared and run away. Salif, stay here. Report to me in fifteen minutes.'

Sulamani had drawn maps showing the compound, the northern approach road that would be taken by the Moroccan force, and a sequence of firing positions in a five-mile arc to the south of the perimeter fence, where the ground sloped away and afforded some cover. Each position was numbered, and annotated with the anticipated range and direction of fire. They'd launch five shells, then move on to the next. There'd be long gaps in the bombardment, but over a six-hour period they'd cover six positions and unload all of their stock of thirty shells. At some point, Colonel Zaki would surely dispatch a unit to flush out the gunners.

'I will be happy to see them take a direct hit,' said Sulamani, 'but our first objective is to keep firing through the night. If they come after us, we will hide as best we can. We fight only if we are discovered.'

Salif came down and said the Moroccans were moving again – but slowly, like pregnant goats. James loaded the RPG and a new Parker Hale into the back of the Unimog – Salif had made the other one his own. The rest of them carried M16s, and their pockets bulged with knives, handguns and cartons of ammunition.

The night was clear and the moon tracking low over the horizon as Salif drove them out to their first firing point. They'd knocked all the glass out of the Unimog and, with its peeling grey paintwork and garb of netting decked with flapping shreds of stone-coloured canvas, the vehicle looked as if it had just been driven up from hell. Behind it bounced the Light Gun, barrel cocked at the skies.

'No faster, Salif, we don't want to kick up dust,' said Sulamani. 'See how the compass wanders when we hit a rut. Wait for it to settle or you'll go off course. Remember, you are towing a gun.'

Salif showed how much he needed this advice by changing gear with a deft double de-clutch. They hit the top of the downslope to the south of the compound and the Unimog drifted with the camber. James watched the Light Gun through the rear window, worried that it would detach itself. They reached the first firing point. Salif worked the Unimog to and fro, wrestling the artillery piece into position on an area of level ground. But one wheel was parked on softer sand and promptly sank. They had to start again. Their hands were repeatedly crushed and scraped as they worked the trail on and off the bar, and it was over forty minutes before they had the spade dug in and the gun set up and ready to fire.

'We need to get better at this if we want to do it six times before dawn,' said James.

'Salif, get a fix on their position,' Sulamani ordered.

Salif ran up the slope and disappeared. He radioed ten minutes later.

'I see them. Not much, but I see them.'

They discussed angles and distances. Sulamani amended his map. James ran through the firing routine, used the elevation and traverse controls to set the dial sight, checked the spade, the recuperator assembly, the recoil buffer... Checked bloody everything, then realised he hadn't even remembered to release the transit lock on the barrel, meaning the first round would have sent two tons of hot steel catapulting into the Unimog ten yards behind.

'One minute,' said Sulamani.

He slid an L43 illuminating round inside the breech, then loaded the charge and clanked it shut. If the gun lit up, they'd all be mincemeat.

'Clear,' he ordered. 'Block your ears.'

'Fire when ready.'

James steadied himself, then unleashed the charge. The blast seemed to brush him aside like he was made of paper. The rig hopped into the air and the breech kicked back, writhing in its mount. The shell accelerated up into the night sky, its whiffling noise vibrating on the pummelled air, then burst in a dome of white light. The canister of magnesium flared and spat under its swaying parachute – an unexpected and disturbing sight for the soldiers below.

He slapped open the breech and let the case leap out, felt the burnt charge scorch his nostrils, looked up to see Sulamani with a high explosive round tucked under his arm. He was grinning – they both were. James used the ram to position the shell inside the barrel, then took a fresh charge from Benoit, loaded it and clamped the breech shut.

'Clear!'

The gun hurled the shell from its mouth with a brutal roar, bounced and settled, smoked lazily. Then, in the distance, the soft rumble as it cratered the sand eight kilometres to the north.

Salif came on the radio. 'East, half k. Range good.'

James adjusted the tangent and watched the barrel move fractionally right, then reloaded and fired again. They stood and listened for the explosion.

'Short. Maybe half k.'

This was the problem… They didn't have an accurate location for their target. The illuminating round had run out and the Moroccan force was in darkness again. He fired the fourth shell, ejected the case, noticed how the gun ran smoother now the steel had warmed. They fired the fifth and last immediately, then sat in the reverberating silence until Salif returned.

'They stop. No lights, hard to see.'

'OK, let's strike the gun.'

*   *   *

The prince's hands tugged at her clothes, arranged her like a slab of meat on a butcher's block. Finally, he pushed his crablike thighs between her legs. Nat withdrew into a kernel of herself, felt her body harden against him.

But it seemed that Prince Makhlani al Makhlani wasn't ready after all. He hung over her for a moment, a repulsive, seething greed in his large black eyes. Then he flung himself off her and reached for his bundle of khat. He lay on his back and chewed, then started to masturbate. Nat distracted herself by hunting for his gun, hands inching around under the scratchy cushions but finding only cigarette butts and things that ran over her fingers and stuff that she didn't even want to think about. The prince had aroused himself enough to try again. He kept working away at himself as he crawled on top of her. But again his penis wilted.

This is dangerous, she realised. If he could not actually rape her, what else would he do? She lay absolutely still while he lit a cigarette and played with himself some more. The rasping of his elbow on the cushions made a sound like a panting animal. Time was ticking out. She contemplated killing him with her bare hands. He wasn't very strong. But unless she silenced him instantly, he could shout for help. Anyway, here he was again, clambering over her. This time, she could not prevent herself emitting a sigh of disgust.

He heard her. She tensed in anticipation of a blow. Instead he reached for his Knicks shorts and started to pull them on.

'Now you will have to wait.'

He lay down beneath the red lantern, back arched over a cushion, one knee drawn up, and fell into a kind of black-eyed catatonia. When he hadn't moved for half an hour, Nat crept into a dark corner of the tent, pulled a patch of filthy rug around herself and tried to take what comfort she could from this moment of respite. I'll light a cigarette and stub it out on his dick, she thought. Then I'll die happy. Her tongue felt like a wad of old leather, but she dared not look for something to drink. She found herself thinking back over her life, its dizzy arc from the dismal apartment at the end of the bus line in Kiev, to a seat at the top table in the world of corporate arms sales, to this reeking tent with its khat-wasted 'prince' who was going to slice her up like a pig. The satisfaction she'd got from besting her rivals and dressing every corner of her life in luxury was no consolation now. There weren't many comforting memories to look back on, and she realised that she still saw herself as someone whose life had hardly begun. Her loyal brother Nikolai was locked up in an old Mercedes nearby, and it didn't seem likely that the rest of the night would bring them anything but further degradation and violence.

She heard an explosion. Distant, its percussive quality muffled by several cubic miles of air. A few minutes later, there was another one, sharper and much louder, followed by a third. One of his men came to the entrance and jabbered at the prince. He sat up and extracted his gun from a pocket in the rear wall of the tent – how come she hadn't seen that? – and followed the man out. She lay back in her corner and waited. Two more booms, five in all. Then silence.

Prince Makhlani came back and pulled on a pair of fat-soled trainers that made his shins look like sticks.

'I'm going to see what's going down. I'll leave two men. You'll be safe.'

He gathered up the remaining khat leaves and stuffed them into his pocket, then stood and looked down at her. He pulled out a couple of leaves, dropped them on the rug and walked out, bouncing ostentatiously in his new footwear.

Wow, thought Nat, his compassionate side.

An engine fired up, doors slammed, rap music thumped out. She heard their pickup snarling off to the west. She crawled round the tent looking for her clothes. He'd broken the clasp on her bra and she couldn't wear it. She thought of how Anton would sneak a look at her breasts through her T-shirt. Shame crept over her, settled like a rat in its nest.

* * *

They'd just packed up the Light Gun after its second barrage when Salif hissed at them and got down on hands and knees. He bent his ear to the ground, stroking it inquisitively, cajoling some elusive sound out of the dry earth.

'Diesel, three, four k.' He pointed east.

'Only one?' asked Sulamani.

'Yes.'

'A scouting mission. We'll stay hidden, but if we are discovered, we must destroy their vehicle. James, take the RPG two hundred yards south-east, find a position that will give you a clean shot if they get close to the gun. Fire only if you are sure they have seen us. Younes will cover you. If we see the RPG fire, we will move in. Look out for men on foot. Let's go.'

They unhitched the gun and covered it with camouflage netting, while Salif listened to the approaching diesel. They'd almost finished when he held up his hand.

'Two, west,' he said. 'Three k, drive fast.'

'Not scouting, then,' said Sulamani. 'Attacking.'

He led them to a position five hundred yards further south, where a low ridge afforded some rudimentary cover. A wily old soldier, thought James. A less experienced man would have grouped them round the precious gun, but with three vehicles full of men ranged against them… The term *turkey shoot* came to mind. This way, they could stay hidden and retain the element of surprise. Salif lay on the ground to listen. James loaded the RPG. They waited, hearing each other's breathing, the soft scraping of their clothes against the sand.

It seemed from Salif's stream of muttered updates that the vehicle arriving from the east would cut a line between them and the place where they had left the Light Gun. Then he reported that the two vehicles in the west had killed their engines. A few minutes later, James heard the lone vehicle, and then, following Salif's outstretched arm, saw a pale glow shimmying across the desert towards them. As it drew nearer, they made out the shape of a pickup with men in the back. And what was that sound pulsing on the cool night air?

Rap music.

This was not how elite soldiers went into action. James pulled the RPG to his shoulder and rehearsed his shot. He felt Sulamani's hand on his arm, saw him shake his head.

The pickup passed between them and the gun, slowed, then came to a halt less than four hundred yards away. The rap music stopped mid-beat. A moment later, Salif pointed into the west.

'Engines,' he whispered.

It looked as if the other two vehicles would approach above the brow of the low rise to the north-west of the compound. The pickup cut its lights and started to swing round towards the south.

'Those in the pickup are not Moroccan Special Forces,' Sulamani murmured. 'I believe the other two are.'

As he spoke, there was a roar of engines at full throttle and a cluster of powerful lights bored through the darkness from the west. A 4x4 with a rack of lamps mounted above the cab hurtled down the slope and ran fast on a line that would intercept the pickup if it tried to escape to the south. Behind it, a much larger vehicle careered over the brow of the hill, turned to fix the pickup in its headlights, and thundered down.

The pickup surged forward, zigzagged out of the big vehicle's lights, then slewed east and headed straight for their hiding place. With no headlights, the driver couldn't see the ridge, or the men behind it. Barely twenty yards away, the driver swerved. The pickup skidded violently, its right-hand wheels lifting off the sand, the men in the back flung against its sides. It seemed certain they would roll, but the driver straightened and slowed in time and the vehicle blasted by in a boiling cloud of dust.

The 4x4 now angled in from the south to head off the pickup, lights slashing through the darkness ahead. The big vehicle – James recognised the sinister, snub-nosed oblong of a French-made VAB infantry carrier – rumbled on. It was tracking the dust cloud from the pickup's wheels and would pass within a hundred yards of them, but with luck all eyes would be on their fleeing prey. James saw the outline of the heavy machine gun mounted behind the cab, men crouching and swaying as they rode the bucking chassis. The VAB barrelled past – despite its bulk, it was gaining on the pickup. The smaller vehicle might still escape under cover of dust and darkness... But now the 4x4 turned so that its battery of lamps laid thick columns of light in a wide fan across the path of the pickup. Abruptly, the VAB slewed to a standstill, dust drifting in the beams of its headlights. James watched in fascination. The pickup was trapped between the heavy machine gun behind it and the beams of light the 4x4 had lain across its escape route east: if they ventured into the lights, the machine gunner would have them cold. The driver saw the danger and slowed to a dawdle. The 4x4's searchlights started to rake back towards the idling pickup.

James felt himself willing the driver to make the right move... There! The pickup spun round and accelerated towards a line between the 4x4 and the VAB – they couldn't use the machine gun with their own men directly in the line of fire – then swung through ninety degrees and drove directly at the 4x4. For a few moments it looked as if they might be able to break away to the south and outrun their pursuers. But the 4x4 heeled into a wide semi-circle and from its new position again laid its lights ahead of the pickup. Simultaneously the VAB powered three hundred yards to the south.

They've done this before, thought James, as the pickup slowed again. It was like the endgame of a chess match, powerful pieces meticulously herding the queen to her death.

The shafts of deadly light swept inexorably across the desert floor, found their mark, steadied, tracked their prey as it tried again to accelerate out of trouble. Not this time. The VAB's machine gun hammered into life, raking the offside of the pickup. The tailgate bounced open, shreds of black rubber flipped from the rear wheels, the men in the back went down. Bullets shrieked along its steel sides. The pickup slumped to a halt as the machine gun clattered on. Finally, someone swore at the gunner and he stopped. The 4x4, a Renault Sherpa, James now saw, moved in to mop up and the VAB pulled up behind.

A not very thorough inspection of the rear of the pickup was made, and four shots were fired into whatever was left to fire at. Two men were dragged from the cab and loaded into the VAB. Then the soldiers stood around and smoked. They'd left their engines running, their lights illuminating the remains of the kill. After a minute, the drivers climbed into their cabs and revved their engines. The rest of the soldiers tossed their cigarettes away and mounted up. The Sherpa threw a tight circle round the VAB, then led the bigger vehicle back west. They ground up the slope and disappeared over the brow, leaving only the noise of their engines growling in their wake.

'I do believe they think they've caught us,' said James.

*   *   *

Sulamani decided to delay their next barrage so they could prepare for the likely return of the Moroccan infantry. They drove in close to the perimeter and sent Salif into the compound to keep watch from the roof. Younes went with him to fetch boltcutters from the warehouse. The rest of them set up the Light Gun at the foot of the slope below. The mortar they carried up the incline and positioned close to the mesh fence. They parked the Unimog a hundred yards south of the gun, then dug positions for themselves – deep enough to hide them from a casual sweep of the Sherpa's searchlights. Younes returned with the boltcutters and they cut slits in the fence so they could retreat into the compound if they had to.

'How long do you think before they come after us again?' asked James.

'First, Zaki will seek guidance from his command. You have knocked out the satellite link, so he will not get it. It will make him hesitate. The seeds of doubt are sown and we must help them grow.'

Forty minutes later, Salif reported that two vehicles were headed their way once more.

'I reckon they'll find us this time,' said James.

He thought of the heavy machine gun mounted on the VAB, how it had taken less than twenty seconds to destroy the pickup. Afterwards, they'd fired handguns into the rear. There hadn't been any discussion about that, as far as he'd been able to see. It hadn't required anyone's sanction.

'The Sherpa will find the gun first,' said Sulamani. 'Younes, Benoit and I will shoot out its lights. James, you must deal with the machine gun on the VAB. Salif will man the mortar.'

James didn't think a well-trained and equipped special forces unit was going to acquiesce in this plan – but plans didn't last long in such circumstances anyway. He loaded the RPG and lay it alongside him in one of the two dugouts he'd scraped for himself, placed the box with a spare shell and charge at his feet. The stars were very distinct, winking and shimmering in the gaping, blue-black void. It seemed almost childish to be hiding like this. He closed his eyes. *I want them to find me*, he thought.

Salif gave a croak from his position sixty yards to his left. James's heart gave a jolt. He raised his head above the lip of his hollow and watched. After a few minutes, he made out a ghostly luminescence hovering above the desert floor, then two pairs of headlight beams nodding and swaying through the darkness, feeling their way forward like the antennae of some supernatural beast. The Sherpa crawled past the line of the fence three quarters of a mile away and rolled slowly down the incline. They weren't going to rush anything this time – no doubt Colonel Zaki had been livid that there'd been no Polisario gunners among the men they had brought him so far.

The cab-mounted searchlights flipped on and started to traverse the sand between them. The burnt-oil smell of a fairground ride drifted under James's nose. Now the VAB emerged, a few hundred yards closer to them than the Sherpa. The two vehicles swung round and took up positions two hundred yards apart, then started to move towards them. The Sherpa's searchlight flicked meticulously from point to point, exploring anything that interrupted the monotone spread of sand and rock.

Their position was just over the rim, slightly elevated and with the compound fence behind them. The fans of light weaved closer. On the next sweep, they would touch the sides of the Unimog, then pass directly over his head. James started to count, just to give some dimension to the waiting. The VAB rumbled steadily on, now less than three hundred yards away. For a split second he saw the lower half of the Unimog illuminated in the Sherpa's lights – a length of knotted cord that joined two pieces of netting, a wheel arch thick with paint. The sand silvered ahead of him. He flattened himself into his hole, waiting for the bark from Sulamani's rifle that would set off the skirmish and decide their fate.

Nothing.

The relentless chug of the VAB's engine, the burnt-oil smell. The VAB would be zigzagging back soon. Its headlights would flit over the Unimog from a different angle, forty yards closer. His heartbeat pulsed in his ears. *Don't look until you're sure...*

Again, the VAB's observers seemed to miss the signs. The camouflage wasn't that good... James looked out and saw the big vehicle trundling away from him, searching the empty desert to the south, before swinging back their way. It had broken its routine... This wasn't right. The Sherpa came idly round in a half circle that would bring it towards them at right angles to the VAB.

The formation they used to attack the pickup. They're getting the searchlights in position, then they'll open fire.

Energy crackled through his body, the feeling that obliterated all else, the feeling he'd been craving since they'd driven Djouhroub and his guards from the compound. Time slowed. He knelt and turned to face the VAB, now barely a hundred yards away. He heaved the RPG tube up to his shoulder. Settle, count to three. Aim for the crease between the machine-gun mounting and the body of the VAB. Adjust. Hold.

The hiss of the fuze, then the low howl of the rocket from the tube. James felt the heat on his back, saw the shadowy landscape glow orange as the exhaust gases flared into the sky. He heard the blast, didn't look, grabbed the box with the spare round and charged from his position.

The VAB revved, huge tyres churning as it turned to bring its headlights to bear. The loose sand gave way under his feet, scalpel blades jiggled in his damaged knee. He'd prepared a position sixty yards away to his right, but he wasn't going to make it. A disc of brilliant light was hovering just ahead. He dived down the slope, rolled, the launcher clamped against his side. Rifle fire rattled behind him, bullets snicked at the sand three yards to his left. The steel box banged into his shin. He heaved himself back to his feet and plunged on. A fountain of sand erupted to his right and instinctively he swerved towards it, to confuse the next shot. The pit he'd dug was so bloody well hidden he couldn't see it. Might just as well turn round and loose off the second RPG round. Then he found the row of stones he'd left as a marker and threw himself forward again. A hail of rifle fire from the Polisario men behind him smashed the VAB's searchlight, leaving him in merciful darkness. He scrambled into the hole, dragging the RPG and steel box in behind.

He looked back and saw the VAB grinding towards him, but they couldn't find him without their lights. He assembled the second round. Rocket, motor, grenade. Fingers feeling for pins, grooves and latches while the VAB's engine roared in his ears. *Done!*

He heaved the launcher onto his shoulder and swung round to face his target. The VAB had turned side-on, stopped. He'd blown the machine gun clean off its roof. No point hitting it again – the VAB's flanks were specifically designed to withstand RPG grenades. Bullets from the Polisario men to his left zipped down the slope and clinked against its armour – like shooting peas at a rhino. He saw shadows moving beyond the VAB – they'd be working round to the east to outflank the Polisario position, pick them off one by one while the men in the VAB kept them pinned down. As if in confirmation, three slivers of flame spat in quick succession from gunports in the big vehicle's side.

It was dark and they could still slip the net. But only if they moved now. The Sherpa was turning to follow the men moving to outflank the Polisario position. That would do. A black shadow moving right to left in his sights. A large square bonnet. Angle the round into that and if it sheared off it would take out the cab. Adjust for lateral movement, hold.

The rocket slammed out of the tube, spun down parallel with the gradient and dipped into the base of the windscreen. The explosion blew the Sherpa onto its back end. It teetered for a moment, then its fuel tank ignited and black smoke slashed with orange poured from its side.

The RPG tube was smoking like a power station chimney – as obvious as hoisting a flag over your head. Time to get out. His instincts were screaming that he must disrupt the Moroccan position. He unslung the Parker Hale and ran into the darkness to his right, then started to crawl down parallel with the VAB, watching for the soldiers who would be working their way towards him. Pretty soon, he came across a runnel that might once have been the path of a stream. He dropped into it and crawled along lizard-style. Gunfire snapped and chattered away to the east. Then a shot cracked out so close he thought it must be Younes – the idiot had decided to follow him… He raised his head above the runnel and saw a Moroccan soldier lying in the sand twenty yards away, aiming a rifle at the point where he'd fired the RPG. If there was one, there'd be more. James didn't want to give his position away because it looked as if another few minutes of crawling along the runnel would take him right round the rear of the VAB.

It did and he didn't like what he saw. They were setting up a mortar in the lea of the VAB, a professional little crew of three under the grainy blue halo of a battery-operated fluorescent lamp. Arrogant, to light themselves up like that. Four others were positioned at the corners of the VAB. The rest would be out there on the flanks, waiting in pairs for their assailants to break cover when the first mortar shell hit their position. An exercise straight out of the textbook. Their commander stood next to the mortar crew, four dead or injured men laid out in a row beside him.

The Parker Hale was perfect for laying down suppressive fire. He knelt and aimed at the blue lamp, squeezed the trigger. Nothing. Misfire. He dropped down, checked the weapon as best he could in the darkness, re-fitted the clip. In seconds the mortar would start pounding the Polisario position. He pulled the trigger. Again the Parker Hale refused to shoot. He flung it aside and yanked out the P99, though at this range it wasn't much better than a popgun. Before he could open fire, the mortar tube clunked and spat out a bilious yellow mouthful of flame. The shell spiralled into the sky, absurdly high because of the short range. A sickening wait, then the dull roar as the bomb slammed into the slope opposite, the pattering of rocks and sand falling back to earth…

He emptied the handgun at the mortar crew in their little blue-lit cocoon and heard a shout of surprise as his bullets drummed against the VAB's plating. He dived back into his runnel, started to work his way back to where he'd seen the soldier. He'd kill him and get his rifle, then go back and finish off the mortar crew. He heard men behind him, shouting as they organised the pursuit, rifle rounds scuffing the sand where he'd lain. He crawled till the sand cracked between his teeth and his elbows bled and his knee felt like it might snap. He heard a shout from behind him and stopped.

'Faites gaffe, l'enculé arrive!'

Watch out, asshole's coming your way. Torch beams flicked across the sky. He listened intently, but the basso profondo of the Light Gun had left his ears feeling like they'd been plugged with cotton wool. He thought he saw sand shifting just ahead of him, then a voice rang out, startlingly clear. He slid the commando knife from the sheath at his waist and inched forwards. He got as close as he could get without leaving the runnel. He could sense the hunched shape of the Moroccan soldier above him, his warmth and smell. He raised his head above the edge of the runnel. The man was down on one knee, crouching low, muttering angrily to himself. He'd been spooked by the shouted warning and that made taking him out very difficult. The standard move was a knife-point plunged into the kidney, so acutely painful the victim can't even scream. But that wouldn't be possible. The soldiers who'd come after him were closing.

The mortar fired again, a sound like punching a wad of sodden newspaper. Impact in three seconds. He counted off two and bounded from the ditch. The soldier turned and stared right at him. For a split-second he was transfixed. The mortar shell exploded and he flinched, then swung his rifle up. Too late. James's left arm had already parried the barrel aside. He drove the tip of the knife in under the soldier's chin and shucked open his voicebox, then levered the handle sideways and withdrew, slicing deep across his jugular. Blood gleamed like black treacle on his neck.

James dragged the soldier's shuddering body into the runnel. The firefight had intensified. A long burst of machine-gun fire answered the insistent crack of the M16s, then another mortar shell exploded in a flash of pink-orange light. He turned back to the corpse of the Moroccan soldier, extracted the rifle from his hands and put on his helmet. He set off along the runnel, back to a position where he could take out the Moroccan mortar emplacement. Dark shapes moving towards him, not seventy yards away. He froze. They'd found the runnel and were using it. Take the direct route, then: straight down to the corner of the VAB. He scrambled out of the runnel and crawled fast. He was still thirty yards off when he heard the clunk of another shell hitting the firing pin at the base of the mortar tube. Afterwards, all he could remember thinking was, *That's not where the mortar is...*

Chapter Twenty-Four

A deep absence. Like driftwood on a beach, becoming rock.

The dragging back. Nausea looming. Air whispering through chambers of stiffened tissue. Nerves gnawing themselves.

A sledgehammer banging on an oildrum. You're inside it inside it inside it. Limbs toiling, too thick to lift. Something squeezing your head.

A helmet.

How did that get there? It took minutes to drag it off. His arms were rubbery. The helmet rolled away. Dimpled like an old cooking pot. Blood trickled from his back. It felt like it had been sanded down.

'It *has* been sanded down,' he said out loud.

He couldn't hear himself above the humming and singing in his head. He got up and fell down. *Crawl, then.* Back to the runnel. He rolled in and recoiled as his raw back slumped against the corpse of a soldier.

Silence, filled with noise. Like a fingernail screeching along a guitar string. He watched for flashes, but the firefight seemed to be over. He looked back over his shoulder and saw a faint sepia glow. What was that? He stood up and his head pounded so hard it made him nod. Everything was on a tilt. He dropped to his knees. *Up. Walk.* He shuffled forwards, bent at the waist, legs moving mechanically, as if they'd been wound up, as if they weren't really his. His eyes were playing weird tricks, losing track when he moved his head, shapes forming and vanishing and forming again when he looked away. He stopped and everything went still, as if petrified by the cold moonlight. He meant to carry on, but found himself lying on his side in the sand instead. His head was belting out a rhythm that made his gums throb. Was this why he had lain down? There was a new noise inside his skull, a tuneless whistling. He realised he was confused and that this was dangerous. He had no idea where he was.

He stood up and walked on. He was coming back to something like consciousness, not liking it too much. A stench of charred rubber drifted on the air. He changed his grip on the rifle to stop it slipping from his hand. Shreds of cotton stuck to the flesh of his back, then snatched away as his arms swung. The ground gave way and he stumbled a few steep paces downhill. Then uphill. His left foot snagged against something soft and heavy, like a sodden branch. He peered down. A roll of camouflage fabric, it looked like.

He straightened up and found himself staring at a looming black shape, its outline fringed with flickering orange light. The VAB. Some part of it or something behind it was burning. He'd walked straight into the Moroccan position, but there didn't seem to be anyone here. He stepped back. His heel caught on a sharp edge and he fell. The sky rolled and yawed above his head. He waited for his vision to settle, then levered himself up and studied the thing he had tripped on. Part of a steel frame, a mounting of some kind. There'd been a mortar here, set up in a circle of blue light. Where were they? The whistling was back, but now it sounded like a high-pitched, crackly voice. He lay on his side again, unable to think what else to do. His fingertips brushed against a mat of sticky hair. He prodded his fingers into the tangle. It was human. He pulled himself closer. The soldier was face down. It took James a moment to understand why he could only make out one side of the dead body. The soldier had taken a spray of somersaulting shrapnel and it had torn him in half.

He rolled away, a column of vomit swelling in his throat. His mangled back crunched over the rock-strewn sand. What happened? He got back to his feet and tried to listen, but the zings and roars and hums inside his head shut out everything except the whiny voice. He moved on a few paces, trying not to look down because out of the corner of his eye he'd seen a boot with a bit of splintered shinbone sticking out. He came up against the VAB. It was hot to the touch and listing like a stricken tanker. Then he saw where the whiny voice was coming from: a radio handset someone had dropped in the sand, nagging for an answer.

Movement. To his left. A big man, leaning against the rear of the VAB. The moon was behind him and James couldn't make out his face. He brought his rifle up and aimed it, but the man didn't react. James walked towards him, picking his way through the debris of the explosion. The man just stood there, motionless. The contours of his shoulders were familiar.

'Younes? You OK?'

Perhaps he had only whispered, because Younes made no response. All James could hear was a gurgling that seemed to be coming from Younes's chest. He looked down and saw three white ribs gleaming from a fringe of tattered cotton. Below them, where the next rib should have been, a glistening pulp like a huge wet raspberry. Another rib stuck out from his body. The angle of it made James want to snap it off, as if it offended some macabre sense of propriety. He looked up from Younes's shrapnel-clawed chest and saw that his jaw was moving up and down in a parody of speech. He pointed at his broken ribcage and tears rolled from his eyes.

'Steady, Younes. Let's get you comfortable, huh?'

James helped him to lie down, then cradled the man's head in his lap. Younes looked up, eyes still and unblinking in his big, doughy face.

'You did well tonight, Younes. You can be proud.'

He opened his mouth but James shook his head.

'Don't say anything. We blew these Moroccans away – just the five of us. A big day for the Polisario. You understand?'

He stared up into James's eyes, tried to nod.

'They'll know you fought like a hero. I'll tell them.'

He couldn't think of anything more to say, though Younes still looked up into his eyes, hungry for the consolation of these soldierly rites.

Several minutes passed and James became uneasy. There had been twenty or thirty Moroccan soldiers. They couldn't all have been killed in the blast which had caused such carnage here. He ought to look for Sulamani and the others. He shifted position and Younes's eyes snapped open. The hunger and resignation had gone: now all James saw was terror. Younes tried to inhale, but the breath caught and he coughed a spray of blood, then snorted and sucked as his lungs filled with fluid.

'OK, Younes. Take it easy.'

There was no stilling his panic. He struggled to raise himself, and the effort drew another thick, juddering cough, then a frenzied attempt to expel the coagulating blood from his lungs. His neck jerked up from James's lap, tendons like steel cords. The lobe of his lung ballooned through the gap in his ribs. His body went into spasm.

He held Younes while he died, then sat on the ground beside the remains of his one-time guard. *You chose to stay and fight. You*

knew what it would be like. He had to get away. He made his way
to the corner of the VAB. Sooty flames were lapping round its front
wheel arch. Ahead was a hundred yards or so of level sand, then
the incline. He could just see the outline of the Light Gun against
the sky to the east. He reached the foot of the slope and started
to labour uphill. 'You're getting close,' he told himself. The sand
sucked at his ankles. He stopped and looked back at the mess of
shattered vehicles below, then up at the sky. The stars were dim.
Dawn was not far off. A gust arrived from the west and he shivered
as it brushed the torn skin of his back. Salif had set up the mortar
twenty yards from the compound fence. That would be the easiest
thing to find.

He climbed to the top and set off along the gleaming curtain
of steel. The serried ranks of wire-mesh diamonds seemed to open
out as he passed, giving a fuzzy view of the compound buildings
beyond. The effect was hypnotic, and he didn't notice the mortar
until it was a few yards away. Salif lay beside it, his body wrapped
around a box of shells, the Parker Hale in his hand. He looked small,
like a boy. James knelt down and lifted his head, hoping to sense
some animation but feeling only its weight in death. The sights and
controls on the mortar were dark with blood. Even when wounded,
Salif had carried on firing. They'd been through plenty together in
a few short weeks, and the sight of him guarding the mortar even
after death affected James powerfully. This is the end Salif would
have chosen, he thought. Destroying his enemies in defence of the
cause he loved.

He laid out Salif's body and as he did so, found the Sahrawi
man's knife in its worn leather scabbard. He unsheathed the knife
and wrapped Salif's hands around the hilt, with the blade pointing
down. That looks good, he thought. He looks proud. He looks like
a warrior. He knelt down beside him and wept.

When he'd recovered, James started to zigzag east. Ten minutes later, he found Benoit curled up in a hollow. The boy's lips were moving haltingly around the words of a prayer. The incantation drifted up into the sky, like smoke from a guttering candle. Every ten seconds or so, he shivered, as if his life were being sucked away by a fever.

'Benoit?'

The boy stared up but seemed not to recognise him.

'C'est moi, James.'

The boy nodded, still staring.

'J'ai tout manqué,' James said, continuing in French and hoping the boy would understand. 'I got stunned by a shell. What happened?'

'My uncle is dead.'

'I'm sorry, Benoit. Are you hurt?'

'Colonel Sulamani is dead.'

'Sulamani too… And Younes. I wish they had lived… ' James was too overwhelmed by sadness to continue.

'They were waiting in the darkness, all around us. Uncle Salif fired the mortar. We heard him cry out.'

'But he went on firing.'

'Colonel Sulamani kept them away. I heard him shouting. There was a big explosion.'

James thought of the scene behind the VAB. Salif must have aimed for the halo of blue light and dropped one plumb on their little arsenal.

'Your uncle was a brave man.'

'I hid my head. I am a coward. I did not fire and now they are dead.'

'No, Benoit,' James said quickly. 'You couldn't have saved them. That was an evil fight, as bad as it gets. Dark, no position, outnumbered, outgunned. We were lucky, you and I. Salif hit their position just in time to save us. He did that so we could fire at the Moroccans a few more times. So let's find the mortar and the Light Gun and do it, Benoit. For Salif, for Colonel Sulamani, for the Polisario.'

Benoit nodded and wiped his eyes on his T-shirt. James helped him up, put an arm round his shoulders. They started back towards the place where he had found Salif's body.

'I've gone deaf,' said James. 'You hear or see anything, dive.'

*   *   *

Colonel Sulamani's body had rolled to the foot of the slope about thirty yards from where James had found Benoit. He'd taken bullets to the legs and chest and his uniform was torn and bloody; but his face was unmarked, his features grave and dignified as they had been in life.

They laid out his body and drove a rifle into the sand above his head. Benoit said a prayer, then they walked on. When they found Salif's body, James left him to grieve while he dragged the last of the shells over to the mortar. He set the weapon to maximum range, then he and Benoit wrapped cloth around their ears and sent over twelve rounds in quick succession. It felt like a pointless thing to do, blindly lobbing explosives into the middle of nowhere. But it was noise. The Moroccan commander would be wondering why his men had not returned, and calculating what kind of Polisario force could get the better of a fully manned infantry assault vehicle.

They worked for what seemed like hours to get the Light Gun hitched. If there'd been any Moroccans left within cursing range, thought James as they swung slowly east in the Unimog, they would have released us from that torture. He planned to launch their last shells from the eastern corner of the compound. They might be able to see the explosions and adjust their range. More importantly, it was on the way out. They found a good site and set up the gun for the final time.

'You want to fire?'

James loaded an illuminating round, then walked round and showed the boy where to stand, what to avoid, and how to operate the firing mechanism. He stood clear and gave the signal. Benoit fired and the weapon thundered, pranced, settled in a pall of grainy smoke. The shell soared into the north and hung in the sky above the Moroccan encampment. James let his eyes adjust, then searched the dome of cold light. There… A gleam in the sand, a square silhouette that might be another VAB. He adjusted the range and bearing, checked the dial sight, reloaded and gave Benoit the thumbs up.

'For Salif!' James shouted. 'For Sulamani!'

They fired twenty shells in two salvos, fifteen minutes to rest in between. It was cathartic to unleash the Light Gun's violence, its warlike stench of hot steel and gunpowder smoke, its bone-shuddering noise. They fell into its rhythms, giving it the complete attention it demanded. Even so, Benoit left his hand the wrong side of the trail and snapped a finger from its socket, while James allowed a hot casing to brush his forearm, leaving a blackened welt to remind him of his carelessness.

Just as the last shell had flared in the distance, the sky brightened suddenly to reveal the huge vista of pale, rock-flecked desert stretching away on all sides. They looked east and saw a pale stain smudging the face of the rising sun. They climbed onto the roof of the Unimog for a better view, and saw plumes of powdery brown dancing along the horizon.

Dust.

A column of dust – kicked up by wheels, whirled by gusts and eddies into the clear morning air. You could see it for miles around. You couldn't miss it. Especially not if you were the politically astute commander of a Moroccan Special Forces unit on a mission in a UN-designated ceasefire zone. You really couldn't miss that.

'Benoit,' said James, gunning the Unimog into the east. 'I believe the night is ours.'

* * *

Ten minutes later, the unit of Moroccan Special Forces was putting up a dust-cloud of its own, hurtling west as the brightening sun revealed the size of the Polisario force pursuing them across the desert. Riding in the back of Colonel Zaki's 4x4 was Mehmet al Hamra of the Marrakech office of the DGST.

It was a disappointing end to a weary night – he had been greatly looking forward to a morning of light forensics inside the compound. Colonel Zaki's indecisiveness when the satellite link went down had been painful to see. It could not be helped. The Polisario would come through this unscathed, but his other target had been hit: if that grand vizier of thievery and fraud known as Monsieur Claude Zender ever dared show his face in Marrakech again, then he, Mehmet al Hamra, would take great pleasure in throwing him in jail.

Chapter Twenty-Five

A dry gust made the canvas slap and Nat woke. The lantern had gone out and the drapes that lined the tent were smeared with grey light. *That must be dawn*, she thought. It didn't feel like she'd slept at all. The night had been punctuated by sporadic bursts of gunfire: the Moroccans attacking the compound. James and the Polisario men would all have been killed.

Her head ached, her mouth was parched. She saw the silver pot the tea had come in and reached for it. It was still half full, and though it tasted of dredged mud she drank from the spout until there was none left. She drew up her knees and listened to the wind. The air in the tent had cleared, but it still smelled of groin-sweat, ash and shit. She found the two leaves of khat he'd dropped at her feet and started to chew. She remembered she had some painkillers in her handbag, took a double dose and wished she had saved some of the tea to wash them down. She took out her phone and switched it on. According to the clock, it was just after six-thirty. It started to bleat: low battery, missed appointment… She watched it blink through its litany of demands. A current of wind sent a skein of sand whipping under the flag over the entrance and over her naked feet. She felt cold.

The prince had been gone all night – leaving two men behind, he'd said. Nat didn't feel like trying to escape. She didn't even feel like leaving the tent. The khat had numbed her, put her into automatic. But after a while, she found the canvas pumps she'd been wearing, pulled them on, stood up and dusted herself down. Then she drew back the flag over the entrance a few inches and looked out.

The fire had died, leaving a circle of blackened rocks. A cooking pot lay on its side. A few paces from the firepit was a bush with a pink and white striped plastic bag snared in its branches. She made her way to the back of the tent and lifted the bottom of the canvas up far enough to see out. The Mercedes and one of the pickups were thirty yards away. She'd hoped Nikolai would be looking out for her, but there was no sign of him – or any of them. She guessed they were asleep. Two men wrapped in brown blankets squatted between her and the vehicles. One of them was talking to the other, wagging his finger. An older man, with close-cropped white hair, an automatic rifle between his knees. The other was small and bony, hunched like a vulture, a black scarf stretched tight over his scalp and knotted behind.

The contents of their Mercedes had been unloaded – she saw the water bottles stacked over by the pickup. Nat watched for a few minutes. A wash of cold light had spilled into the sky above the eastern horizon. The desert looked bleak, impassable. That they were here at all seemed beyond comprehension. Then she heard one of those pounding explosions roll in from the west. The men stopped talking and turned to look – Nat dropped the canvas and prayed they hadn't seen her. A minute later, there was another explosion. Then another. Was the fight for the compound still not over? She counted the blasts: ten, then a fifteen-minute pause, then another ten.

She leaned against one of the prince's cushions, gripped by the knowledge that now was surely the time to act but paralysed by the idea of doing anything. It seemed unforgivable that Nikolai was asleep. She spent long minutes pondering the misery and injustice of her plight, until her reverie was broken by a mucous-laden snore from inside the Mercedes. Well, that was just great. She stood up in a fury and ran from the tent.

'Nikolai, fucking wake up!'

She went on screaming, not bothering with words when she ran out of them. The two men threw off their blankets and turned to face her. Then the older man looked back at the Mercedes.

'Stay in car!' he shouted.

He looked stiff in the legs and his back wouldn't straighten up, but the rifle was at his shoulder in an instant. He aimed at the passenger window. Nat saw Anton's head slip down out of sight.

'Stay! I shoot!'

The boy with the black headscarf was staring at her. Nat leaned forward and yelled at him. 'Don't fucking look at me!'

'Get the whore in the tent,' the older man shouted. The boy – he was barely older than sixteen – didn't move.

Nikolai sat up in his seat and wound down the dust-filmed window.

'I wasn't asleep,' he said in Russian. 'Micky's got his door unlocked – the snore was to cover the noise.'

'In tent!' the old man shouted again. He kicked out at the boy, who ran up and grabbed her arm.

'Nat, do what he says,' said Nikolai. He turned to the older man. 'Boss not here. You're in charge. Let me out of the car, I need a piss.'

'The fuck I will,' said Nat, and kicked the boy violently in the shin. He yelped and started to swing the butt of his rifle at her, but before he'd even got close Nat hooked the fingernails of one hand into his eyes, seized the knot of black cotton at the back of his head, and lashed her foot into his groin. He went down, retching. She tore the rifle from his hand and flung it at the Mercedes, where it clattered against the tailgate. Nat turned back to the boy and stamped on his stomach.

The older man pointed his rifle at Nat. 'Back, back,' he shouted. 'In tent!' He glanced over to where the rifle had landed, not far from the rear of the Mercedes.

'Boss won't be pleased if you shoot her,' said Nikolai.

The man's eyes swivelled from the rifle, back to Nat and the boy still doubled up on the ground. He started over to the rear of the Mercedes. Every few yards he paused to look back at Nat, as if he were playing grandmother's footsteps. He got close enough to pick up the rifle, looked again at Nat, then stooped.

Mikhail catapulted out from behind the rear wing of the Mercedes, driving his shoulder into the old man's midriff just as he straightened up. They hit the ground together and Mikhail swung his fist into the man's ear. He didn't need much space to generate a powerful blow, and the man's eyes rolled back. Anton threw open the front door of the Mercedes and ran to collect the rifles. He handed one to Nikolai.

'Nice move, Micky,' said Nikolai. 'Look for his blade.'

There was a knife strapped to the man's calf, barely hidden by the frayed cuffs of his tracksuit bottoms. Nat looked down at the youth. One of his eyes was bulging and laced with red. Anton came and checked him for weapons, then tied him up and locked him in the pickup.

'I thought we'd had it,' he said finally, pulling a bottle of water from the pack. 'I thought I'd spent my last night on earth listening to Micky's nose-music.'

Nat walked over towards the Mercedes. Her head swayed from side to side with each step. She felt hollowed out. Her bones were heavy, the muscles in her legs like soggy string. She slumped down by the stack of water bottles, but couldn't muster the strength to open it. Anton twisted off the cap and passed it down.

'Tie up the old guy, Mikhail, for fuck's sake,' said Nikolai.

Mikhail went and cut a length of rope from the prince's tent. Two of its sides caved slowly inwards. He bound the man's hands behind his back, then his feet, then joined hands to feet and drew the rope tight. The man came round and started a frantic gabble. Mikhail lifted him easily, waddled over to the half-collapsed tent and flung him inside.

'Can we get the fuck out of here?' said Nat.

'What about the kid?' asked Anton.

'Leave him in the pickup. He won't come after us,' said Nikolai.

'Shoot him,' said Mikhail. 'Better for everyone.'

'He's just a kid,' Nikolai said.

'Aren't we going to take the pickup?' said Anton.

'I'll tell you what,' said Nat. 'I'm tired. I've been assaulted. I want to get the fuck out of here. Does that help you make up your minds?'

None of the men could look her in the eye.

'If he comes back, I'll tear his fucking throat out,' Nikolai grunted.

'I won't be around to see it,' said Nat. She walked over and climbed into the driver's seat of the Mercedes. 'You coming?'

'Sweet Jesus, Nat, I'm sorry,' said Nikolai. He reached forward to touch her on the shoulder but she leaned away. 'Mikhail, load the water. And see if there's any diesel around. Anton, find our weapons.'

'The guns have been a big fucking help so far,' said Nat. 'Get the aluminium box that's in the tent. We're taking it with us.'

The IPD400, finally in her possession. Its presence seemed almost offensive, given the suffering it had caused. For a moment she was tempted to leave it here in the desert, see how it took to a colony of ants and a coating of baked dust. Instead, she went and pulled down the flag from over the entrance to the prince's tent. It seemed like the perfect souvenir.

*   *   *

It was late morning when the Unimog, with James at the wheel and Benoit asleep beside him, finally caught up with the Mercedes. Nat threw her arms around James and hugged him, then smiled at Benoit and kissed him on the top of his head. She led James to the rear of the car and opened the boot. The IPD400 was lying on its side in a nest of oily rags.

'We found it in the tent of a... ' She didn't want to refer to him as a prince. 'Some gang of thieves. They must have stolen it from Zender.'

'How did you get it back?'

'Let's not talk about it now,' said Nat. 'Later, maybe.'

James sensed that Nat wanted him to be pleased, but instead he felt deflated. Why was she so subdued? What new horror had the pursuit of his invention caused? He felt he ought to give this moment his full attention, but his mind was grappling with an exhaustion so profound it seemed too much effort even to narrow his eyes against the sunlight flashing off the Mercedes' chromework.

'Thank you, Nat,' was all he could say.

'I didn't think you'd make it, James, when I heard the guns. But you survived. Nikolai is safe... '

Sarah isn't, he thought. Their eyes met, and in a moment of shocking lucidity he saw how much Nat was suffering – that despite her recital of their successes, she was nearly done for. He reached out a hand to comfort her. She brushed her fingertips against his, then shrugged and turned away. She desperately wanted to be somewhere cool and peaceful where they could talk, but instead they were parked up in a gully carved between two low crests of crumbling rock. She shielded her eyes and looked around. You couldn't even see the horizon through the hazy brown air.

'Suli got killed and we're lost,' she said. 'I don't suppose Benoit knows the way?'

It seemed that he did. They travelled on in convoy. Anton joined them in the Unimog and told them about their night with the Mauritanian prince and his savage court, though he did not say what had happened to Nat. After four hours they came to a village with a Polisario outpost. The man in charge handed them dates, a bowl of corn and some pieces of roast chicken in a pink-striped plastic bag, then refuelled the Mercedes and told Benoit how to get to the next outpost. They village-hopped east, and the road got worse. Even the scrub bushes had given up. One of the rear springs on the Mercedes snapped and the vehicle dragged itself along like a wounded dog for a few miles before the other one went and they had to abandon it and cram themselves into the Unimog.

They reached Bir Lehlou in the late afternoon. A detachment of Polisario had set up a roadblock on the outskirts of town. An elderly officer drew out a pair of dilapidated spectacles and treated the letters Sulamani had given them to a ceremonious inspection. Satisfied, he transferred his new guests to a pair of ancient black Chrysler saloons, their creased and dimpled bodywork so highly polished it was hard to look at them in the late afternoon sun. They were driven into town at high speed, arriving at the gates to a mud-walled compound with a Polisario flag out front. The Chryslers drew up to a low, square building with narrow windows and a heavy wooden door. In the corner of the yard they saw the MINURSO Land Cruiser. No doubt Commander Djouhroub would be sitting in a state of stony-faced confusion somewhere in the building. There was no sign of the vehicles in which the other guards had travelled.

They were led off to makeshift bedrooms and shown plastic basins of warm, rust-tinted water in which they might wash. An assortment of clean clothes had been laid out for them. An older woman with a deal of authority about her bustled in and indicated that she had come to see to James's back. James redirected her to Benoit's dislocated finger. She examined it closely and prodded the area round the swelling, then gave him a sweet smile, said something soothing, and tucked his forearm under her powerful armpit. She grasped the finger and rotated it, then levered it back into its socket with a powerful driving twist. Benoit gulped. She patted him on the arm, then wagged a finger at James. He started to unbutton his shirt.

Later the Polisario officer, accompanied by three uniformed boys, led them to a room off the hall where they sat round a trestle table and ate stewed goat and cornmeal. A few minutes into the meal, Rakesh Nazli turned up, looking very clean and very anxious.

'You made it,' James observed. 'I guess you had some talking to do.'

Nazli gave a nervous laugh. 'Dr Palatine,' he said, 'I hope you understand that my role in all this was purely technical. I had no idea... well, how it would all turn out.'

'I'm sure you didn't,' said James. 'Still, the money was good.'

'I haven't even been paid,' said Nazli, the familiar whine returning to his voice. 'When you leave here, do you think I could come with you?'

'No,' said James. 'Stay here and keep talking.'

The diners fell silent. After a few minutes, Nat started to question the elderly officer. It seemed that they were in a building occupied by the Polisario high command – most of whom had gone west to drive off the Moroccan invaders. There was outrage that the enemy had dared to enter the Free Zone, and absolute certainty that they would have their comeuppance. When James told him that he'd seen the Special Forces unit fleeing back to the Wall of Shame, the elderly officer was so overcome with emotion that he could not speak but only shook his fist in triumph.

The three teenage boys, meanwhile, were staring at the foreign arrivals as if they had fallen from the sky.

'It's like being in a zoo,' said Nikolai. 'Hey, boys, know any songs?'

The three boys quailed.

'I don't think anyone's in a party mood,' said Nat.

'Give me a beer, I'll sing,' said Mikhail.

'No,' said Anton, 'you'll make a noise that will have everyone wondering how the pig got into the room.'

*   *   *

The next day, Manni Hasnaoui, to whom Colonel Sulamani had addressed one of his letters, came to see them. He was a fierce-looking man, bent to such a degree that he had to twist his neck sideways in order to direct one eye at James's face. Having observed the effort needed to inspect him, James felt it would be churlish to look away, and so found himself transfixed for the few moments it took Hasnaoui to size him up. His demeanour was gruff, but when James told him that Sulamani had died he wept openly, waiting for the tears to finish before he wiped them away. Then he clamped his bony hand around James's wrist and said:

'You will be driven to Tindouf early tomorrow. From there, I will arrange a flight to Algiers. It will be an Algerian military transport. No movies, no air hostesses!' He laughed and shook James's wrist. 'You will be uncomfortable, and bored!' he declared gleefully.

They spent the day in the sanctuary of the Polisario HQ, its plain, square rooms like boxes into which you could climb when the world asked too much. The nurse came and tended his injuries with good-humoured mercilessness – he was sure she kept a scrubbing brush somewhere about her person and was using it to clean the grit from his back. When food was served, he ate urgently; otherwise, he slept. The longer he slept, the more he wanted to sleep. He dreamed of Younes's ballooning lung, of Sarah's drug-enfeebled limbs. He got up, and the sheet on which he'd lain was imprinted with a map of his wounds. He lay down again and dreamed that Nat was watching him with her beautiful eyes. He wanted to wake up and talk to her but could not.

* * *

Before they left for their flight to Algiers, Manni Hasnaoui arrived again and asked to speak to James in private.

'The device you brought here with you, the IPD400. What is it – a computer, they say?'

James explained, then said: 'MI6 want it back – I believe that's why they tipped you off about the Moroccan raid.'

'Did they?' The eye of Hasnaoui peered up at him. 'I think I'll keep it. What do you say to that, Dr Palatine?'

'Will you keep me, too?'

'Why?'

'I saw Mansour Anzarane at the compound. Now that the man himself is dead and you have Commander Djouhroub and the rest of Zender's guards safely locked away, I'm the only credible witness that the suspected Agadir Bomber was based in the Free Zone.'

'No one in fact suspects him of Agadir,' said Hasnaoui sharply. 'He is a pawn in a smear tactic devised by a pit of snakes in Rabat.'

'I'm just the man they need to make the tactic work.'

'You have become a hero of our young nation, Dr Palatine. Now you talk of betraying us. Will you?'

'I'm not your enemy, Mr Hasnaoui. Let me take the IPD400 away, and I'll deny seeing Anzarane at the compound.'

'Excellent. Nejib Sulamani trusted you and so shall I. He was a perceptive man as well as a fine soldier. When we spoke to him, to warn him about the Moroccan attack, we gave orders that you should be arrested and brought here. Sulamani said you had escaped and no one knew where you were. Do you understand why he did that? He meant to protect you.'

'What would you have done with me?'

'I prefer not to speculate,' said Hasnaoui briskly. 'Nejib ignored his orders and took the matter out of our hands. Well, we Sahrawis have never been an obedient people. Since then, you have helped save us from calamity, so I am pleased that we have reached this understanding. Please tell me why you killed Anzarane?'

'He was in the way. Who told you about the Moroccan raid?'

Manni Hasnaoui remained silent for a minute, and when he spoke again, the brisk tone had gone from his voice.

'We were amazed to receive this intelligence about what the Moroccans were planning – from a new source which had never before shown an interest in our struggle. What was the motive? The return of the IPD400, they said.'

'Why should they prefer the IPD400 to fall into your hands rather than the Moroccans'?'

'This is what we asked ourselves.'

'And?'

'It is said that when a sick man goes to see a doctor, it is not the first problem he describes that troubles him, but the second, the one he mentions as he leaves. The IPD400 was the first problem. You, Dr Palatine, were the afterthought. It seems we are not the only people with a powerful interest in keeping you silent.'

Hasnaoui's head swivelled up and he examined James with an expression such as he might usually reserve for an errant son.

'In Europe they like to say we Arabs hold life cheap. But still, in that regard I think we have much to learn from our new source.'

Shock spread through him, a cold, paralysing poison. 'MI6 want me dead?' He stared at Hasnaoui. 'Why do they care that Anzarane was at your compound?'

Hasnaoui shrugged.

'They're hiding something,' James said. 'Something dirty. Something black. They think I discovered it while I was at the compound. Now they're terrified I'll come home and tell the world what they've been up to.'

Along with the precious tip-off to the Polisario HQ, the Playpen had offered a sly hint that the price of this information was the death of James Palatine... Even with everything he knew about the Playpen – the chronic disingenuousness, the cocoon of self-importance that absolved them from all considerations of honour or principle – even so, he was stunned that Strang and co would stoop to this.

'I don't even know what they've been up to,' he said.

'You should make it your business to find out. As for the Polisario, we deny all knowledge of you,' said Hasnaoui, the brisk tone returning to his voice. 'Dr Palatine? We have never heard of this man. The IPD400? What is that? As far as the SADR government is concerned, these things do not exist.'

He slapped his hand down on the table and shouted for a boy.

'The sooner your computer leaves the Free Zone, the better. It is cursed. There is... How would you say it, there is blood on its keyboard. That is good – my English is still quite colloquial. Blood on its keyboard,' he repeated, emitting a raucous chuckle as the boy arrived to help him to his feet. 'My new friend Clive would be pleased with me.'

Clive Silk. The Playpen's messenger boy. James watched the old man crabbing his way to the door. The masters of the Playpen would not have contented themselves with merely requesting that he be killed – there'd have been threats, too, veiled and unveiled. What a risk Hasnaoui had taken by telling him this.

* * *

They gathered in the hallway, where Hasnaoui made a speech. 'I hope you will return one day and find us enjoying the freedom we have fought for side by side. You will always have an honoured place in our hearts and in the story of our nation.'

'Thank you, Mr Hasnaoui,' said Nat. 'I hope it goes well for you.'

'If you want my advice,' said Anton to Benoit, who was standing respectfully to one side, 'I'd go to Marrakech. I haven't seen many women since we got here— '

Seeing Manni Hasnaoui start to bristle and swivel his head towards the blasphemer at his side, James quickly took the old man by the hand and shook it. 'Please get in touch, if you ever visit London.'

'What is there in London for us, the people of the Western Sahara?' Hasnaoui snapped. 'Turned backs and empty pockets, that's what!'

They were driven across the border into Algeria, then on for thirty miles until they arrived at an airstrip laid out between two hangars. An hour later, a military transport rumbled down out of the sky, refuelled, and carried them north. It seemed to James miraculous that a plane could go so slowly and yet remain airborne. He slept, and Hasnaoui's words wandered through his dreams. *We are not prepared to go to the lengths they demand of us...* He woke, and could not believe that only an hour had passed and they were still slogging on to Algiers. He slept again. *There is blood on its keyboard...* They landed. Papers were inspected, taken away, re-inspected, passed along, inspected again, stamped, queried and handed back.

'Hotel el-Djazaïr,' said Nat to the taxi driver at the head of the queue outside the terminal. 'How much, including tips, parking, petrol, tolls and your daughter's wedding fund?'

Half an hour later, a bellhop was pulling open the doors of the taxi and gazing in astonishment at what emerged.

'Oh yes,' said Anton. 'My kind of place.'

'It's not a whorehouse,' said Nat, 'it's a hotel.'

'All one to me,' Anton retorted, straightening his miraculously well-preserved cream jacket. 'Which way to the bar?'

Chapter Twenty-Six

Next day, Nat and James met Nikolai, Anton and Mikhail in the lobby before they set off to catch the three o'clock flight to Paris. The three Ukrainian men had been drinking all night, with the zeal of men for whom alcohol deprivation is a form of spiritual exile. Nikolai's face, still sporting the bruises he had suffered at the hands of the casino guards, looked like a bowl of rotten fruit, and in the rubbery pallor of Mikhail's features it was possible to see what he would look like in twenty years' time. Only Anton seemed to have survived the festivities unscathed.

'Let's do this again – soon, right Ms Kocharian?' he said.

'I'm going to say no, Anton. I'd never be able to face the women of Kiev if I got you killed.'

They smiled at each other – a recognition that, if nothing else, they were now capable of bantering on roughly the same wavelength.

'Thanks for helping us out,' said James. 'We'd never have got Little Sister back without you.'

'Which little sister do you mean?' said Anton. 'The one which sits quiet in its box, or— '

'Yes, that one,' Nat interrupted. 'Because the other one rescued *you*, remember?' She turned to her brother. 'Get that knee seen to by a proper doctor, Niko, not just some drunk who owes you a favour.'

'Taxi is here,' said Mikhail.

*　　*　　*

Left alone with Nat in the lobby, James felt awkward.

'We should talk,' he said.

'Tomorrow. Today, I refuse to talk about anything that's happened or anything that might happen next. Let's go and explore. You have any money?'

He went to the office of the hotel cashier and organised a transfer of funds from his London account, then they stepped out into the gentle hubbub of an October afternoon in Algiers. Nat had got the hotel to launder her jeans and T-shirt, but James had only the white shirt and ill-fitting black cotton trousers he'd been given by the women at the Polisario HQ. She took him to a menswear store and made him buy a dark grey suit with an indigo shirt, and black leather woven-topped slip-ons that she said made him look like a software salesman.

'I've worked with software salesmen,' he said. 'None of them wore shoes like this.'

'Don't be difficult. All the men in Algiers wear them – you want to blend in, don't you?'

They wandered into the old kasbah, a maze of whitewashed squares and steep, narrow lanes with steps of bowed cobbles. Rooms supported on fissured timber buttresses jutted from the upper storeys of the houses they passed. There were carved stone doorways and patches of plaster splashed with graffiti, walls strung with electric cables and alleys decked with zigzags of bunting that, on close inspection, turned out to be hundreds of children's T-shirts drying in the placid air.

After lunch by the harbour, James bought two pre-paid mobiles from a kiosk. He loaded their numbers in the speed-dial settings and handed one to Nat. He didn't want to tell her that the Playpen wanted him dead, not yet.

'Do you think we're safe here?' Nat asked uneasily. She was thinking of the gunman in the souk in Marrakech, of Grey Tony Schliemann. Soon she would have to tell James what she had done.

'There was a man watching us in the hotel lobby,' James said. 'Thick black hair and steel-rimmed glasses. DRS, Algerian intelligence, I guess.'

'Surely they've worked out that you're on their side, after what you've done to the Moroccan army over the last week.'

'His sort trust people on their side even less than they trust the enemy.'

'You're one of them, really, aren't you?' she said. 'Well, I always wanted to be a Bond girl.'

They walked through an area of ragged tenements where they collected a gaggle of children who looked up into their faces with comically winsome eyes and asked for money. A knot of young men stared lasciviously at Nat and passed remarks among themselves. James stared back, and something they saw in his face made them turn away. Soon they came across a cable-car station. They climbed into the dented cabin and swayed up over the city, serenaded by the grinding and screeching of the truck above their heads. Three old women nodded approvingly at them from the opposite corner.

'I'm more scared now than I was when you blew a hole in the roof over my head,' she said, taking James's arm and smiling at the crones. 'At least then I thought I had some chance of surviving.'

A series of tremendous clanks signalled their arrival at the upper station, high above the centre of Algiers. They emerged opposite the basilica Notre Dame d'Afrique, sat on a bench and looked out over the city arranged beneath them, the mosaic of boats in the harbour, the rumpled sea beyond.

'Hard to believe it's the Med. We're half way home,' she said.

'Just two hundred and fifty miles north there are people drinking buckets of Sangria and throwing up their lunchtime cheeseburger.'

'You're very puritanical.'

'People are always telling me I don't know how to enjoy myself,' said James, wondering what it was about Nat that made him want to reveal such things.

'I'll teach you. We'll start with dinner at the best restaurant in Algiers.'

They got no further than a café on the next corner. A woman sat in the window, slapping dough into shape and baking flatbreads inside a blackened clay oven. Her husband presided over a charcoal barbecue. A collection of CRB Belcourt football club memorabilia, thickly furred with dust, hung on the fat-stained wall behind his head.

'This is in fact the best restaurant in Algiers, but it hasn't been discovered yet,' said Nat. 'Next year it'll be wall-to-wall celebrity chefs and travel writers.'

'All the ingredients are locally sourced,' said James. 'For example, the chicken we are eating used to live under the bed.'

Nat laughed and had to put her hand in front of her mouth to stop the food flying out.

They made their way back to the hotel. Nat went to her room to find out if her friend Magda Podolski had recovered, while James took the lift up to the roof terrace. He sat and looked south over the town. The houses scattered across the hills looked like thousands of multicoloured tealights set out in meandering tiers behind a tissue-paper screen.

Nat joined him. 'She's OK. I spoke to her. Said she had a terrible headache and an even more terrible thirst for revenge.'

'Good,' said James. 'What actually happened?'

'I'll tell you tomorrow… Maybe.'

James shifted heavily in his chair, making the wickerwork creak. 'Every time I sit down for more than a minute, I seize up.' He kicked off his new shoes. 'And these things are ridiculously uncomfortable.'

'I thought you were indestructible. Man up.'

James smiled and massaged his toes. 'So where do you reckon Zender is now?'

'God knows. Somewhere not far from a skilled pastry chef.'

'You think he might have gone back to Switzerland?'

'He's not wanted almost everywhere. But he's rich… and well connected.'

Nat yawned, touching her upper lip with the tips of her fingers. The snorting of traffic in the street below rose up and dwindled into silence under the canopy of stars. James watched her lips form round the O of her yawn and thought of the kiss she'd given him before leaving for Bir Lehlou in the Mercedes. She leaned back and gazed up at the tawny sky, but seemed to grow instantly bored of that celestial vista and fell to examining him instead. Their eyes met. An unchaste image appeared in his mind, causing him to cross his legs. A boy padded over, bowed and took their order.

'I guess we have to get Little Sister back to Grosvenor,' James said.

'I'd rather give it to al Qaeda. You English are so correct. You have a word for it, something like *punctual*.'

'Punctilious,' said James. 'My form tutor used to say I was *too* correct. He said I was a computer which had taken the form of an adolescent boy.'

'He was wrong. Your mind wanders all over the place.'

'Oh?'

'Yes, I can tell. For instance, a minute ago, you asked me about Zender and I yawned, and you thought something wicked.'

'I— '

'Don't say you didn't.'

He looked into her forthright green eyes.

'All right, I won't.'

'What was it?'

'I don't have to tell you that.'

'You don't *have* to tell me, no. But please do – I promise not to be shocked.'

'It's private.'

'It must be very bad. Whisper it in my ear.'

'You'll have to come over here, I'm too stiff— '

She giggled, a sound so pleasurable it made the boy waiting at his station in the shadows of the terrace crane his neck round the fronds of a potted tree fern to see what was going on. The beautiful woman with the red-gold hair moved over and sat on the arm of the tall Englishman's chair, the Englishman who looked like he'd been in a terrible fight. She rested her hand on his shoulder and leaned in towards him until her cheek touched his. He moved his lips close to her ear and whispered something. She shut her eyes and leaned in closer. The boy saw that she was smiling.

* * *

She woke before dawn and found she was clinging to him, forehead bowed against the warm knuckles of his neck. Vile dreams were skulking in the corners of the room, waiting for her to go back to sleep. The thermostat clicked and cold air rushed from the air conditioning vent above the bed. She watched the louvred flaps play slowly back and forth and imagined gas spilling into the room, her enemies counting down the seconds until the toxins took hold.

When the sun came up she turned the air conditioning off and went to open the window, hoping to feel a little heat from the new day. But it was still cool outside and the influx of air made her shiver. She ran back to bed and he woke and folded her in his arms. Then she rolled away, because the nest of pleasure and forgetfulness they had woven for themselves the previous day had come apart and she couldn't pretend that it hadn't.

'We'd better talk now.'

She told him her story. When she'd first decided to buy back the IPD400 and sell it on to Grey Tony, it had seemed exactly the sort of scheme a brilliant and ambitious young arms dealer should devise in response to the opportunity that fate had placed in her path. Now, explaining it all to James, it sounded not just absurd but unhinged. Was the naïve and avaricious woman she was telling him about really her, Natalya Kocharian? She ploughed on as quickly as she could, blaming herself, Grey Tony Schliemann, Claude Zender, in that order. Certain things, such as that she had been Zender's lover, she left out as irrelevant.

When she came to her assault at the hands of the Mauritanian prince, Nat didn't know what to say. The bare fact was that she'd escaped being raped, and that was good. It was a kind of reprieve. And yet the hours she'd spent alone in the prince's tent, at the mercy of his prying hands, his foul indifference to her cries, and even to her contempt... And then again, though she was disgusted with herself for even allowing the thought to enter her head, she felt shamed by his impotence, and did not want to tell James what had happened. And so she said nothing, but a chill passed over her skin, as if Makhlani's bony fingers had reached for her through the open window.

James listened hard and tried not to miss anything – his ears were still so beaten up it sounded as if she were speaking from another room. Nat's face was full of apprehension. Her eyes kept searching his to see how he would take what she was telling him, and when she smiled, her smile faded quickly, as if she feared he might misconstrue. He could see that she expected him to react badly to the story of her wildly audacious scheme to waylay Little Sister, but instead he was touched by her candour. It was such an unexpected quality to find in someone hoping to deceive the likes of Zender and Schliemann.

'So, now you know what the evil arms dealer has been up to,' she said. 'I'm sorry, James.'

'It wasn't you who got the IPD400 out of the Grosvenor warehouse. And you didn't invent the damn thing, either. They taught you to play a rotten game and you played it, that's all.'

'And lost. I've been behaving exactly like a trainee Claude Zender. Only I'm no good at it, and I don't even want to be any more.'

'I'm sorry I didn't come with you when you left the compound that night.'

'You'd probably have got us all killed.'

They fell silent, neither of them wishing to over-extend this moment of quiet apology. Eventually, James said:

'You realise Clive Silk works for MI6?'

'I heard rumours. And he has that smug, I-know-a-secret look.'

'When I was in the Intelligence Corps, I was sent to Kosovo with an SAS unit. Silk was my liaison. He's a prick.'

'So, you've heard my side of it. Now it's your turn.'

'I was walking home to my flat in Camden a few weeks ago, and I noticed this girl was following me.'

He told his story, then said: 'Nat, this isn't over. MI6 started a war in the Western Sahara and suggested I get caught in the crossfire. I need to work out why before they find another way of keeping my mouth shut. Tony Schliemann wants you dead, and judging by what happened to your friend in LA, he's not about to pick up the phone and tell you he's only kidding. And we still don't know who paid Zender to get hold of the IPD400.'

'Do we want to know? Do we actually care? Let's stay in Algiers and set up a kebab shop.'

'I keep thinking about Sarah.'

'Well don't,' said Nat. 'She wasn't thinking about you when she helped lure you to that house in Wembley. What she thought was, how rebellious and saintly I am! Anyway, you did what you could to save her.'

'Did I, though?'

'If you want to be gallant, James, there's always me.'

She wrapped herself tight around him and they lay there for a while, enjoying the perfect warmth of each other's skin. But James's thoughts would not leave him alone and he grew restless.

'Those files I told you about, the ones I downloaded to my cache in Mexico City, I need to get into them.'

So this was how her new lover planned to spend the day. She watched him dress in his indigo shirt, grey suit and uncomfortable woven-topped slip-ons.

'I'll be in my room,' he said. 'I'll call.'

He bent over the bed and kissed her. She thought of pulling him to her, but he looked in the mood to resist and then one of them would have to give way and a little ugliness would come between them. She watched him go, and before the door had clicked shut behind him, wanted him back.

*   *   *

She went to the bathroom to shower. At least James hadn't walked out in a rage because of what she'd done. Dr dazed-and-limping Palatine. She thought of him standing shamefaced in Zender's office at the compound, unable to admit that he actually wanted to stay and fight the Moroccans, the desolate clarity in his slate-blue eyes. He knew it was wrong but couldn't help himself. A man trying to be good, but failing – was that how he saw himself? Did that apply to her, too? No, because the Natalya Kocharian in the story she'd told James had never even tried. How had she got this way, the girl from the ninth-floor apartment on Pyrochova Street with a copy of *Vogue* under her bed? What had she been dreaming of, really? She'd devoted herself to escaping the groggy grey suburbs of Kiev, but then? It felt as if she'd got so used to going round with her claws out and a come-and-get-me smile on her face that she'd overshot the mark and lost her way.

Palatine and Kocharian: what a pair.

She lay on her bed and listened to the early morning noises from the street, the doorman shouting for taxis, the rattle and scrape of crates being stacked on the pavement. Some trick of the light was casting reflections from the roofs of the vehicles below onto the ceiling of her room. It was peaceful to watch the succession of pale coloured oblongs slide out of the gloom to the right of the window, parade along the curtain rail, then slide back into shadow.

*   *   *

Her phone rang and she woke. James, asking her to come over and look through his secret files. It was midday – she'd been asleep for hours.

'If the network here is half way decent, they should start to download straight away,' he said, ushering her into his room. 'Then we can get cracking.'

'Hallelujah for that.'

'They've been careless, or ignorant, or both. What we have here should tell us plenty.'

'I'm ravenous,' she said, opening the room service menu. 'Do you want something?'

'Sure. You choose.'

She rang through her order, then watched him pulling the plastic bags and blocks of polystyrene from around the computer he'd acquired, packing them carefully away in the cardboard box before arranging the hardware on the desk. He's not a bad man, he's a nerd, she told herself. A killer nerd. A killer nerd with a beautiful bum. She laughed and he turned and smiled at her. He's really quite lovely when he does that, she thought.

'James, just get on with it. For every ten minutes you take from now on, you have to take off a piece of clothing.'

Half an hour later he was sitting naked at the computer, scrolling through the first of the downloaded files. She watched his lacerated back rippling gently as his hands moved over the keyboard.

'Come and look at this. I'm reading the instructions for my abduction – sent two weeks before Little Sister left Grosvenor.'

'You already know what happened – you were there.'

'The stuff I read on the computer in Wembley made it sound like I was being pursued by Islamic terrorists. When I found out al Bidayat was involved, it all seemed to tie up.'

'It's not al Bidayat, James, it's Claude Zender. He knew everything about you. He knew you'd be able to trace that girl's phone number and follow it to Wembley. He knew you'd go to Oran and try and get Little Sister back on your own, rather than calling the police or MI6.'

'I took every piece of bait they laid out for me. Even that stalled reformat… I thought I was one step ahead when in fact I was two steps behind. But what if I hadn't?'

'He'd have thought of something else.'

'So why pretend it was an Islamic plot?'

'Too weird for a government or a corporate – a little house in Wembley, a gay Arab and an odd English girl? Anyway, you fell for it.'

'What a fool I was.'

'It was clever, James. Zender used your strengths against you.'

'What about Mansour Anzarane? Mansour *is* al Bidayat. He made no secret of it – and it's all over the web.'

'All Mansour and that other guy did was Taser you in Oran, escort you to the compound and cut you when you didn't do what they wanted,' she said. 'On Zender's orders, right?'

'So you tell me: is Claude Zender a terrorist, the brains behind al Bidayat?'

'No chance. He likes the world just the way it is.'

'No sacred principles searing his soul?'

'He doesn't have a soul.'

'But he has a terrorist on the payroll.'

'Maybe Mansour needed a day job.'

'Al Bidayat is behind this. It must be. They paid Zender to get hold of Little Sister. That's why Mansour was on the team that abducted me.'

'And this explains why Sir Iain Strang tried to have you killed?'

'No, but— '

'You look quite silly sitting there with no clothes on and that confused expression on your face,' said Nat, pulling her T-shirt over her head.

*   *   *

A steady flow of dishes was delivered to his room: coffee, eggs, fruit, skewered lamb with rice and stewed aubergine, yoghurt with honey and pistachio. Coconut cakes soused in Moscatel. Caramelised orange slices. Rice pudding, figs. Sweet, sour, salty, tart: their appetites could not be satisfied.

*   *   *

He said he had to put in a few hours' proper work with the files, so she went back to her room and lay down. The S-shape of his body was still creased in the sheet beside her, like a swirl of silt in the bed of a dried-up stream. The room was dark and her mood swung again and she was frightened. Of Grey Tony, who'd been too timid to make a pass at her, but hadn't balked at hiring a man to shoot her thousands of miles away in Marrakech. Of the Mauritanian prince and his skinny, dead-eyed men. Frightened that she would always remember how suddenly things could get worse. How much worse they could get.

She dressed quickly and went out, leaving the *Do not Disturb* sign on the door handle so the chambermaid would not erase the traces of James that lingered in her room. She went down in the lift, tying a dark green silk scarf around her head, then took a taxi to Rue Didouche Mourad. She bought a long gentian blue satin dress, a matching shawl embroidered with gold thread, and a small leather evening bag. The dress was a fine piece of couture, artfully cut around the waist and thighs. It would go perfectly with James's indigo shirt. Tonight they'd dine somewhere splendid and James would make her feel beautiful again.

The entrance to the street on which the hotel stood was blocked by a delivery van, so she got out of her taxi at the corner. As she approached the entrance, the door to a black Jeep Cherokee was thrown open and a small man with close-cropped hair stepped out and blocked the narrow pavement.

'Please, Mam'selle, we offer you the services of our driver.'

Nat shook her head and turned sideways to get past him. The man threw out an arm and shoved her towards the open door of the car. Big hands reached from within, seized her wrist, coiled round her waist. She thought she could brace herself against the body of the car, but the man behind pressed down on her shoulders and she went sprawling head first inside. The door slammed against her feet and the Jeep surged away from the kerb before she could even start to scream.

* * *

James turned to the square of illuminated plastic before him. His brain checked into the familiar state and set off like clockwork: analyse the data set, parse away the dross, look for the little flags that point to buried treasure. He wished Nat had not gone back to her room, even though he'd pretty much asked her to. The exchanges dealing with Zender's arms business had a peculiar language of their own – *low-visibility channels*, *premium inventory*, *stamp collectors* and *silent transfers* – and were heavily salted with acronyms, some of which James recognised or guessed – GSP for Grosvenor Systems plc, T1RI for Tier 1 Restricted Item, DUI for Dual-Use Item – most of which he didn't. He searched for *anemone*, the word which had appeared in the messages being copied from the compound network to MI6, but got zero results. That was wrong. The download had stalled – he had to identify the missing files and go back for them. That done, he launched a set of scripts that would yield lists of unusual words positioned in proximity to each other. Somewhere in the files, he'd find the malevolent hand of al Bidayat. The hourglass twirled on the screen and he was thinking of Nat, the feel of her limbs as she wrapped herself around him, the scent of her neck and armpits, the sweet taste of her mouth…

Anemone was back. There were dozens of instances, all identical to the one he'd already seen: REF ANEMONE, NO SIGNIFICANT ACTIVITY TO REPORT.

He double-checked the headers: all the messages were going to the Playpen's servers. Little Sister blinked appealingly from the floor beside his desk. The accursed device with its blood-drenched keyboard. What was the secret so dangerous that Strang thought it justified persuading the Polisario that they'd be better off if he were dead? What was Anemone? Little Sister could tell him – might be the only worthwhile thing it would ever do. He swung the case onto the desk and started the configuration routine. The SIS network was impregnable to an IPD400 hack – in anyone else's hands. But he'd installed a trapdoor for himself. It was second nature in his line of work. Artfully concealed inside a standard operating system routine that checked the integrity of archived data – run the routine with certain parameters, and it temporarily disabled the IPD400 alert and allowed him to slip inside the server array like a puff of smoke through a wire mesh screen.

He checked the IP routing to London, then sent a sequence of data trailblazers down the wires to see how the land lay. Within twenty minutes, he had the path mapped out: no obvious bottle-necks, low incidence of disruptive traffic. Like closing a motorway lane for a visiting president. He keyed in the IP data for an off-site server that was used for emergency backup, watched the data pack-ets being identified, pried open, inspected, shut. It took just over four minutes to break into MI6.

UNLOCK COMPLETE.

*   *   *

Nat unleashed everything on the man who had hold of her wrists, and the pain and humiliation and betrayal she had suffered gave such wild strength to her limbs that for a moment she broke free. She drove her fingers into the skin beneath his jaw and reached for the door handle, but he rolled her and pinned her face down to the seat.

'Ligotes ses mains, Etienne.'

The man with close-cropped hair leaned over from the passenger seat and tied her wrists with a length of cord and she couldn't stop him. They pulled her upright and she spat in the face of the man beside her. He made as if to slap her but the one called Etienne said something and he stopped and grimaced.

'You fuckers!'

She hurled abuse at them for a few minutes but they ignored her. They were driving up into the hills, along an avenue of French colonial mansions with steep roofs and tall, shuttered windows. She looked desperately for a street name but there was none, nor any numbers to identify the houses. The Jeep pulled up outside one of the largest, set back from the road behind an espaliered fig tree with leaves like huge, flapping hands. They hustled her across a stone-paved courtyard and up to a set of double doors, which opened immediately, as if he'd been standing behind it.

'*Ma chère Mam'selle*, to grace my house at such short notice – I am touched beyond words.'

'Fuck you, Claude Zender.'

Behind him was a sombre hallway with a green and white tiled floor and a grand, red-carpeted staircase. The men escorted her into a high-ceilinged room, lit by an undersized chandelier and two brass standard lamps with pink hessian shades. They lowered her onto a rose-coloured sofa and untied her hands.

'I must apologise for the less than decorous invitation,' Zender said. 'Time is rather short and I thought it prudent to pre-empt any resistance you might feel to spending an evening in my company.'

'Why the fuck would I feel that?' She stood up. 'I refuse your invitation. Have these dickheads take me back to the hotel.'

He was searching her handbag, extracting her cellphone and handing it to one of his men, whose neck was livid where she'd scratched it.

'Of course. But first we have business to do, then we will dine together. I have the services of a very fine chef here in Algiers, a man for whom one's taste buds are akin to the keys of a musical instrument, which I do assure you he plays like a maestro.'

'Why are you talking to me as if nothing has happened?'

Zender dismissed the two men. Nat started to follow them out, but Zender locked the door.

'My dear Natalya, I implore you not to make difficulties. I intend a satisfactory outcome to this affair, but you must allow me to make the arrangements.'

'No.'

There were French doors to the garden on the other side of the room. She ran over and tried them.

'There is no way out,' he said. 'All the doors and windows are securely locked. Sit down, please, and allow me to present you with a glass of Champagne – acquired in its infancy in 1996 and I swear it has not moved one millimetre since.'

She was trapped, then, with Claude Zender, in this dreadful house with no address in a suburb of a city where she knew no one – except James, who was back at the hotel and didn't even know what had happened to her. She looked around at the olive green walls and lumpen mahogany furniture. The room bore a depressing similarity to Zender's office at the compound, except that here there was a fireplace of veined marble that jutted into the room like the butchered ribs of a giant bull.

'Please excuse the absence of domestic cheer,' said Zender. 'I do not spend as much time here as I would like. Sit by the fire, such as it is.'

A log fire had been lit in a pitifully small grate, its waxy flickers sporadically illuminating the chimney's yawning interior. She went back to the sofa, seeing no alternative. He had extracted the blue satin dress from its carrier bag, the bottom-hugging blue satin dress she had bought to wear for James, and was holding it up.

'You might put this on for dinner.'

She watched him fingering the material, and saw the sadness in his big, restless eyes, the sadness she'd always taken for a touching intimation of his essential humanity. It was nothing of the kind – merely regret that he could not have absolutely everything he wanted. The request that she wear the dress filled her with revulsion. What he was after was not her, Natalya Kocharian, but a pleasing accessory to the dinner he'd planned. The sofa was so deep that her feet would not touch the floor and she had to tuck them beneath her, though it would look as if she were getting cosy when she meant to appear implacable. She had never felt so crushed. He brought her a flute of Champagne and bowed.

'And so, my dear Natalya— '

'Don't say anything. I'm too upset to speak to you.'

'C'est bien compris.'

He bowed his head and they sat in silence.

'I heard what occurred in the tent of that devil Makhlani. I am so— '

'No! How could you know, Claude, how the fuck could you know that?'

'Two of his men survived— '

'What, did you arrange it? Was I part of the deal? He said he did business with you, before he stuffed his fingers inside me.'

'Don't, Natalya, please. You must know that I would never do such a thing, it is beyond imagining. Makhlani and I have had dealings in the past, but this time the scoundrel simply robbed me. He then killed my driver, obliging me to navigate to the border without him!'

Nat was too distraught to reply. Sobs crowded her throat as if there were a whole queue of them struggling to escape.

'My poor Natalya.'

Zender pulled out a white linen handkerchief and passed it to her. She took it, and her mind suddenly replayed the scene outside Adela's, on the evening he'd been shot. He'd mopped his neck with a white linen handkerchief while she'd pulled aside his jacket to reveal an oval of blood-soaked shirt. What had happened next? Her memories of everything before the night in the tent with Prince Makhlani al Makhlani were mangled like old cars in a scrapheap. At last she managed to compose herself. She drank her Champagne and Claude Zender flew from his chair to refill her glass.

'Why did you run away from the compound?' she asked.

'One develops a nose for a bad ending. The whiff began with a panic-stricken phone call from your colleague Clive Silk informing me that the IPD400 had reported its presence to London, and became quite unsavoury when I became aware that my old adversary Mehmet al Hamra was plotting the demise of my clients the Polisario. In the circumstances, the sudden arrival of a troupe of MINURSO officials seemed ominous. I was not to know they were in fact your family and friends in disguise.'

'Why do you live this horrible life?' she said. 'Why do you surround yourself with people like Djouhroub and the doctor who almost cut my arm off? What do you have to show for it?'

He looked at her as if she were a child being deliberately obtuse.

'You may pour scorn on my head, but I operate at the rough end of a dirty trade and must perforce play rough myself. Djouhroub and his men are guards and enforcers, Dronika is a doctor. The wheels of commerce turn and make their particular demands, which I contrive to meet. *Eh bien?*'

'You don't understand.'

'But perhaps I do. You wish to hear some soul-searching of Augustinian rigour, followed by a bout of self-castigation and a confession fit to impress the sniffiest deity. I offer none of these things.'

'You don't regret any of it.'

'A foolish emotion. Certainly I wish I could have found a more felicitous way to conclude this business of ours – I wish it as devoutly as an impious man could – but regret? *Non.*'

'Let's finish it, then.'

'For that, we need the IPD400. I always knew you to be a remarkable woman, Natalya, but to steal the thing back from Makhlani – really, it is your finest hour. But now I believe it is in the possession of the amorous Dr Palatine?'

'Amorous? Fuck you for a filthy snoop, Claude Zender. I suppose you had a spy outside my hotel room door, did you? Taking notes to sell to the big man for a wad of used dirhams?'

'Forgive me, Natalya, the adjective was ill-advised. But I cannot easily forget the pleasures we have shared, you and I, and I confess that the shadow which has fallen between us distresses me greatly. Perhaps I have no right to feel jealous— '

'What distresses you is not having the IPD400, and James will never hand it over, not to you, never in a million years.'

'I believe I may count on that chivalrous gentleman to return my property in exchange for the honour of escorting you back to London.'

He studied her fondly, enjoying the effect on *my dear Natalya* of this carefully composed denouement. He was like a fat spider scuttling round and round her, spinning the thread that bound her into his web, tighter and tighter with every turn, with every word he spoke, swaddling her up like a treat he'd been promising himself ever since the day they had met.

Chapter Twenty-Seven

Seven-thirty. James had been so absorbed in hacking the Playpen's closely guarded data repositories that he hadn't noticed how late it was. Still, Little Sister had done the job – the only real task it would ever perform, if James had his way. He packed it in the computer box and called DHL. When the courier arrived, he gave the address of Grosvenor's warehouse in Essex, put the value as less than €45, and ticked the box that said *Overland*.

'Very slowly service,' said the DHL man. 'Many, many weeks.'

'Perfect,' said James.

The DHL man wheeled the trolley out of the door. *Bye-bye, Little Sister*, said James. The sense of relief was so enjoyable it seemed wasteful not to extend it, so he went out into the corridor to watch the DHL man manoeuvre the box into the service lift. Then he sat on the bed and ran through the events of the last three weeks, tallying them with what Little Sister had ferreted out of MI6's servers. The jigsaw puzzle was almost complete. He picked up his cellphone and called Sir Peter Beddoes.

'Yes,' said the chairman of Grosvenor Systems, in the brusque voice of a man accustomed to receiving phone calls from inferiors.

'Palatine.'

'Palatine?' Now he sounded horrified. 'Hold on a moment.' James heard him hissing instructions, then a door banging.

'Sorry about that, James. Now we can talk.'

'This isn't a social call. Thanks to Natalya Kocharian, the IPD400 is on its way back to your warehouse. It'll arrive by sea from Algiers – good value, I thought.'

'That's marvellous news, James. Has it already left? I can get our shippers onto it?'

'No need. Regarding Ms Kocharian, whom you sacked a few weeks ago— '

'We didn't, in fact— '

'Compensation of half a million pounds would be appropriate, given what she has suffered on your behalf. Unless the money is showing in her account by lunchtime on Monday, I'll release full details of the farcical circumstances surrounding your sale of the IPD400 to Claude Zender. Then I'll issue a statement saying that my relationship with Grosvenor is at an end and I will never allow commercial exploitation of the technologies I developed. I think the reaction of the markets will make settlement of an unfair dismissal case look rather judicious.'

'James, can't we sort this out properly? I understand you're angry, but these threats really make no sense— '

'You think not? She'll check her bank account on Monday. You won't be able to contact me in the meantime. Goodbye.'

Beddoes was a toady, a ship-steadier. The money would be there. He picked up the notepad on which he'd written the number allocated for contacting the MI6 Director-General in a crisis: it had taken some quite imaginative work with Little Sister to prise it out of the day's security log. Sir Iain Strang answered on the third ring.

'Palatine,' said James. 'Calling from the grave. No, seriously, Strang, I thought I should tell you that I know all about Operation Anemone. That is, *everything*. I want you, de la Mere and Silk here in

Algiers tonight. There's a flight at nine-fifteen – you'll catch it if you leave now. Of course, Silk may still be here, after his little errand.'

There was a moment's silence. James fancied he could hear Strang's blood starting to simmer. 'We need to get off this line,' he said eventually. 'Come back to London, Dr Palatine. Take some recovery time, yes? Let the dust settle.'

'I've deposited what we may as well call the Anemone Files with law firms in three different jurisdictions. Hotel el-Djazaïr – 1 a.m.'

He hung up and called Nat from the hotel phone. She didn't answer so he went to her door, saw the Do Not Disturb sign. He left the hotel and walked in circles for half an hour. Swallows dashed across the darkening skies. He stopped to drink coffee and observe the antics of the man from the hotel lobby who was creeping round after him. He shook him off and returned to the Hotel el-Djazaïr by the back entrance. He rode the service elevator to Nat's floor. The Do Not Disturb sign was still in place. He knocked. No answer.

Approaching the door to his room, he saw that the architrave had been neatly cut to give access to the lock. An electric tool had been used, and there were rub marks where a strip of plastic had been eased in to spring the mortise. He put his key in his pocket and stood close to the door, listening. Silence. A baby started to wail from a room down the corridor. Then the latch clicked and the door opened.

The man almost walked straight into him – he had a cellphone out and was dabbing at the keypad. James punched him hard in the solar plexus, and the man staggered back into the room. He was winded and sucking for breath, but managed to lower his shoulder and try to charge past. James side-stepped, seized his arm as he careered past, leaned back and swung him face-first into the edge of the half-open door. The man dropped to his knees and cradled his head. He was wearing dark green overalls with a maintenance company logo. Maybe forty, with thinning hair and a horsey face.

James dragged him to the corner by the TV. The door banged shut behind him. The cellphone had fallen from the man's hand. James picked it up. He'd been sending a text.

Chambre examiné – rien trouvé. Room searched – nothing found. One of Zender's men, after Little Sister.

James pressed send, then yanked the power cord from the TV set and used it to tie the man's hands. He searched him and found the battery-powered cutting tool he'd used to get access to the door lock, and an old .32 calibre French-made MAB C handgun in a holster strapped to his calf. He got a glass of water from the bathroom, threw it in the man's face, and waited for him to come round.

*   *   *

Claude Zender consulted his watch. 'Dinner will be served in a few minutes' time, and the first course is a soufflé for which it is advisable to be comfortably settled, appetite primed and cutlery in hand. May I escort you to the *salle à manger?*'

They sat at one end of a mahogany dining table intended for twelve, in a room with fog-green wallpaper decorated with a pattern of ivory ribbons, excessively flounced. A stout, nervous woman in her fifties came in and lit a brass candelabra set with a dozen cheap candles that would not stand straight. The candles stank of paraffin, and when she came back with the soufflé, Zender told her to take them away. To his irritation, she blew them out first, filling the room with smoke.

'To eat a delicacy such as this in a cloud of paraffin smut... See how the papery golden skin of the soufflé shrinks from the insult. She comes with the chef, her husband, otherwise I would serve the food myself.'

The soufflé was followed by a translucent fillet of white fish in a saffron velouté. Claude prattled on, extolling the virtues of the bone-dry white Burgundy he had found – which he had judged (correctly, as it turned out) would provide the perfect backdrop for the aromatic palette of the fish. When Nat could stand the flow of gourmandese no longer, she said:

'Why didn't you let Nikolai go, when you found out who he was?'

'By then, Tony Schliemann was demanding that something be done about you. I thought to reunite you with your brother and take you out of harm's way.'

'You knew all along that he tried to have me killed in the souk?'

'My dear Natalya, he asked me to do it. Me! I refused. I make it a point of principle not to kill on anyone else's account. But it is simply superb, my dear Natalya, that you blackmailed Tony Schliemann. They will have to invent a new word, for *chutzpah* doesn't do it justice. Kocharianesque, we will say.'

'I misjudged Grey Tony. I thought he was just a man with a pen.'

'He is just a man with a pen, and it is men with pens who rule the world. Yet you treated him as something akin to a stubborn cow at a country fair.'

'I thought he had no choice.'

'Schliemann doesn't think like that. What do I want, he will have asked himself, and how do I use the power I have accumulated over three decades in the NSA to get it? The response, in this order I suggest: one, the evidence you used to blackmail him; two, your head on a plate; three, the IPD400. It seems he is already working on the first and I doubt there is a lawyer's office in the world where it is safe. As for your head, one might say that it has been closely contemplating the pattern on the platter intended to bear it.'

'And the IPD400?'

'That was my assignment.'

She could not prevent a gasp escaping her lips.

'Schliemann? Grey Tony is your buyer, too?'

The moment the question was asked, the full extent of her stupidity came into horrible focus. Her plan to buy back the IPD400 from Zender and sell it to the NSA had been doomed before she'd even thought of it, and every one of her conversations on the subject, with Grey Tony and with Zender, had been a sham.

'All this starts with the NSA's insatiable lust for your Dr Palatine's magic box,' Zender was saying smugly. 'Nothing can be allowed to frustrate them – not Grosvenor, nor their friends in London, nor Dr Palatine, nor you, nor me. It isn't just what they can do with it, but what they can prevent others doing to them. Secrecy is a very pernicious and seductive narcotic, and the prospect of having it withdrawn simply terrifies them.'

'You kidnapped an English computer scientist on Grey Tony's say-so?'

'Dear me no.' Zender gave a brisk laugh, as if to dispel a jinx Nat had conjured into being with her inappropriately bald question. 'My commission was to secure an operational IPD400. The details were not discussed, but I imagine Tony thought I would buy Palatine's co-operation. That seemed improbable, given what I discovered about his character. But I got him to the compound and teamed him up with a technician I hired at ridiculous expense, a thoroughly feeble man called Rakesh Nazli. At one stage it looked as if we might succeed, but the nerd-in-chief was more troublesome than expected – which is an understatement of Homeric proportion.'

The chef's wife came in bearing two plates hidden beneath tarnished silver cloches, which wobbled and clanked as she lowered them to the table. When they were in situ, she reached for the handles and lifted them up, then clashed them together like a pair of cymbals as she drew them out between the two diners.

'A gruelling performance,' said Zender, 'I hope it will not spoil the dish for you. Gigot, lightly spiced, with a purée of aubergines and tamarind. You will not find it in any restaurant since Maurice and I worked it out together. To accompany, a Pauillac 2000 from a little-known chateau I patronise, whose wines put the Petruses of this world to shame.'

Nat felt nauseous. The lamb looked almost raw and the purée was the colour of wet china clay.

'I need the bathroom,' she said.

'I do urge you to try the lamb first, Maurice is most particular about the temperature— '

The look on Nat's face cut him short. Zender directed her to a suite off the entrance hall consisting of a washroom with cracked enamel sink and a closet with a cistern mounted six feet in the air. As she unbuttoned her jeans, she discovered the pre-pay mobile James had bought for her stuffed in the hip pocket – the silly precaution she'd teased him about and then completely forgotten. At any moment he might call and the phone would chirp and give her away. She pulled up her jeans and listened. Was that him breathing just the other side of the door? She threw it open to confront him, but he wasn't there.

* * *

The pre-pay phone buzzed in James's pocket.

'Nat, where are you?'

'At Zender's.' She spoke very softly.

'Leave. Leave now.'

'I can't. I'm locked in.'

'I'll come. What's the address?'

'I was snatched outside the hotel. It's up in the hills behind town. I tried to look for street signs but there weren't any.'

'I'll find you.'

'How will you find me, James?' She sounded close to tears.

'Tell him I know you are with him. Tell him if anything happens to you I will hunt him down and kill him.'

'Don't, though. I should never have done what I did.'

'I found one of Zender's men searching my room. He'll tell me the address.'

'Zender doesn't tell anyone where he lives – I've known him for years and I don't have any idea.'

'Describe the men who took you.'

'The one in charge is small, close-cropped hair and nasty eyes. I heard them call him Etienne. The car is a black Jeep Cherokee.'

The man who had held the pliers while Mansour cut him. James hadn't told Nat his name. Hearing it on her lips was like a hammer-blow to the heart.

'I'll find him.'

'I have to turn the phone off now. It was Grey Tony who paid Zender to take the IPD400 and have you abducted. Be careful, James. He'll do anything to get it back.'

She cut the call. The horse-faced man blinked up at him from the floor. Tony Schliemann, of the National Security Agency – the final piece, and what grotesque sense it made. James felt hatred flare and spit inside him – hatred for the man at his feet, for Zender and Schliemann, for Silk, Strang and de la Mere, and all the rest of them who felt entitled to make the world dance to their ugly tune. He pulled another cable from the back of the TV and dragged the horse-faced man into the bathroom. He stretched him out on the floor, pulled his shoes and socks off, and bound his feet to the chrome pipe that ran up the tiled wall to the shower head. The man tried to pull his legs away, but he was still groggy and his movements had no strength. When James gagged him with a hand towel, he started to struggle in earnest, but it was too late. James went and turned the clock radio on loud, then returned with the marble lamp from the bedside table.

'I'm going to hurt you until you tell me what I want to know.'

The lamp was heavy, with a square base and sharp corners. He smashed it into the middle toe of the horse-faced man's left foot. He howled through his gag. Chips of tile fell from the wall. James started to swing again, then realised he hadn't even asked the man anything yet. He was just venting his bile like any old jailhouse sadist. But what did the state of his soul matter now? He had to find Nat.

He pulled the gag aside and the man started to plead. James slapped him until he shut up.

'Zender's address.'

'Non, non monsieur. Je ne connais pas ce monsieur. Je vous jure que je ne le connais pas.'

James re-fastened the gag and swung the lamp base.

'Zender's address.'

He released the gag and the man started to gabble. He gagged him, pulverised another toe. He held his fingers to his lips – *Ssshhh!* – and lowered the gag again.

'Zender's address.'

The horse-faced man stared into James's eyes and shook his head. 'Je ne sais pas, monsieur,' he said sadly. 'Laissez moi, je vous en prie, je vous en prie.'

He looked down at the man's bloodied eye, his face red and lopsided from his collision with the door. *Zender doesn't tell anyone where he lives*, Nat had said. He went back into the bedroom and saw the horse-faced man's cellphone on the bedside table. He picked it up and looked at the message again. Who was he sending it to? He checked the message details.

Etienne.

He went back into the bathroom.

'Take me to Etienne's place. Then I'll let you go.'

'Oui, Monsieur, d'accord.'

James pulled out the MAB handgun and checked it over, then untied the man's hands and feet and stuffed the cables into his pockets.

'Put your shoes on.'

His broken toes had already swollen to twice their original size and he winced as he packed them into his trainers.

'I know what Etienne looks like, so don't try to trick me. Stand up. Do you have a car?'

'Oui, Monsieur.'

'Take me. Do not try to run or I will kill you.'

*   *   *

'Why didn't Grey Tony tell me to take a hike when I tried to sell him the IPD400?' Nat said, pushing away the plate of untouched food.

'Because you offered to destroy his career. Are you sure you will not try this exquisite dish?'

Nat folded her arms. Zender studied her plate.

'And because your offer made him suspect that I would not be able to deliver unto him what he and his people craved. Tony doesn't trust anyone, least of all me,' Zender went on, pulling her plate towards him and spearing a piece of raw lamb with his fork. 'You presented him with a plan B. He spoke to me after you made your pitch, demanding results in the most irate terms – this, you will recall, was shortly after that enchanting afternoon at the Riad when you favoured me with a procession of unforgettable delights, then asked me to get the IPD400 back.'

Nat did not like to be reminded of the occasion and her voice was tight with anger.

'You were never going to sell it back to me. You just played me along.'

'How much did you persuade him to pay, I wonder?'

'Why should I tell you that?'

'In any event, it simply remains for Dr Palatine to trot along with the miraculous device tucked under his arm, and the deal can be concluded. To that end, Tony is flying in tonight. I expect him imminently.'

'Grey Tony... Here?'

'Yes. I thought it for the best.'

'He wants to kill me, you said so yourself.'

'I dare say he can be pacified, once we have put this blackmail plot of yours to rest.'

As he spoke, they heard a long, fretful whine from the buzzer in the hall.

'Go upstairs,' said Zender. 'Find my bedroom. I will let you know when to make your entrance.'

She took off her shoes and ran into the hallway, up the red-carpeted stairs to a large landing. She stepped away from the banisters, heard the clack of the door lock, then the bland west coast accent, the voice that always sounded as if it needed to unburden itself of a minor gripe:

'It's over an hour since we left the airport. Seems we've been followed by every fucking birdwatcher in Algiers.'

'Etienne looked after you, I am sure.'

'Did he? It would've been simpler to meet in town.'

'Now that you are here, we can be confident that our meeting will remain private. Come in and have some Champagne.'

'Is this where you live? It's like an old people's home.'

She heard leather-soled shoes striking the tiled floor.

'You haven't retired, have you, Zender? Maybe you should.'

* * *

James would never find her – how could he? Nat thought of trying to sweet-talk the chef and his wife into letting her out of the house;

but no one who worked for Zender would ever disobey him. They would alert their boss and then she would be forced into an encounter with Grey Tony. She dreaded an encounter with Grey Tony. The thought of it set ripples of fear lapping at her heart.

She did not care to wait in Zender's bedroom. The next room down the corridor had the numb, disinfectant-tinged air of a place that has not been touched since someone died there. She went and sat down on an ottoman on the landing instead, then got up and opened the door to the room opposite, so she could run there if someone came. Grey Tony won't stay the night, she thought, he'd die without his twenty-five square metres of Hilton, his power shower and sachets of branded body wash.

After a few minutes, she started to feel sleepy. That was all the wine she had drunk. The vintage Champagne, the perfect white Burgundy and impeccable claret. Zender's palatable poisons. She lay back on the ottoman and drew her knees up. It was uncomfortable, but strangely peaceful. If this is all I am, she thought, a woman resting on an ottoman in someone else's house in Algiers, that's fine. I'm not the woman I thought I was anyway. Not the woman I was three weeks ago, when I sold arms for Grosvenor Systems and fucked over anyone who got in my way. Not the woman I was before I got Magda attacked and Nikolai beaten up, before I got mauled by a Mauritanian prince. I'll doze here until Grey Tony leaves, then I'll stroll out into the night. I'll wait tables in a smart café and one day James will be sitting there, reading a newspaper. I lean down and kiss him, his lips are warm and I taste salt on his skin. His fingers tremble with wanting to touch me.

*   *   *

The horse-faced man's car was an old Renault saloon parked in a sidestreet two blocks from the hotel. He drove carefully, while James kept up a flow of threats and instructions to stop him thinking about possible means of escape. They entered the district just off the harbour front where Nat had been stared at by the gang of youths, and pulled up in front of one of a row of tatty apartment blocks.

The horse-faced man pointed at the entrance to a stairwell. 'Etienne. Apartment there. Number forty-one.'

'Where is Etienne's car?'

'Garage.' He pointed down the street.

'Drive there. What sort of car is it?'

'Jeep Cherokee.'

'Colour?'

'Black.'

They turned down a sidestreet and arrived at a row of three lock-ups.

'Drive on.'

When they were thirty yards past, James had him turn the car round and draw up behind a parked van. He checked the time: 9.35.

'Call Etienne,' he said, handing back the horse-faced man's phone. 'Tell him to go to Zender's. Tell him he has to pick up the woman he drove there earlier. Tell him Zender is busy and will not take any calls.'

The horse-faced man looked appalled. 'I not tell Etienne these things,' he said. 'I cheat him, put knife in.' He pointed to his stomach.

James aimed the gun at the same place. 'I'll put a bullet in if you don't. Say Zender is angry and you're only doing what he told you to.'

The man looked at him and started to protest. James got out of the car, then reached in and pulled his captive into the passenger seat and shut the door. He walked round to the driver's side, watching the horse-faced man in case he decided to make a run for it. Not that he could run very well, with his damaged toes. There didn't seem to be much fight left in him anyway. James got behind the wheel and took the cutting tool out of his pocket, switched it on and tested it on the glove compartment door. A wedge of mangled plastic landed in the horse-faced man's lap. James held the whirring grinder up to his prisoner's nose.

'Call him.'

The horse-faced man drew his head back sharply and banged it against the window. 'No. Please. I call him. I call him.'

James switched the tool off. The horse-faced man fumbled at the keypad, unable to get his shaking hands to dial. Eventually he put the phone to his ear.

'Etienne? Djamel... '

Even without the phone next to his ear, James could hear the viciousness in Etienne's voice. He pressed the revolver into Djamel's bruised cheek to stiffen his resolve. Djamel spun the line James had given him. Etienne stopped shouting and listened, then shouted some more and hung up. James took the phone back.

'He not believing me,' said Djamel. 'He pick up man at Marrakech airport, take him to house. Now he have to go back. Why?'

'What man?'

'American man. I not know.'

He took out the MAB handgun and slugged Djamel on the temple. The man slumped sideways against the passenger window. James lowered the seat-back until Djamel was lying flat, then tied his hands and feet with the cables from his hotel room. He turned the ignition and the engine fired readily enough. He turned it off again, got low in his seat and watched the lock-ups. Three minutes later, Etienne walked up to one of them, swung up the door and disappeared inside. Headlights lit up the shopfront opposite and a big Jeep Cherokee bounced out. As soon as it had cleared the end of the street, James threw the Renault into a tight half-circle and went after it.

Etienne drove fast through streets that were familiar to him, and James had to keep his distance or risk Zender's driver noticing that he was being followed by Djamel's Renault. Then he lost him. Etienne had zigzagged up a series of backstreets and was gone. James kept pointing the Renault uphill through the series of bends, driving as fast as he dared. Just as he was turning the last corner at the top of the hill, he caught the high rear lights of the Jeep as it joined a main road and accelerated away towards the outskirts of town. A minute later, he was back on Etienne's trail, following the Jeep up a long, unlit avenue on a steep incline, higher and higher into the darkness stretched out above the southern hills.

The Jeep's brake lights blinked and it heeled abruptly right, then stopped outside a tall, shuttered house screened by a fig tree. James took a left and started looking for a house that might be empty. He found one with no cars and no lights, and drove the Renault up a short drive to the garage. Djamel was still out cold. He'd work the cables off his ankles and wrists eventually, but it might take him all night. Good enough. He got out of the car and locked the doors, then ran back towards Zender's house. When he got to the corner diagonally opposite, he hunched down low and watched. Etienne was standing in the light from the porch, being harangued by someone inside the house. After a minute, the front door slammed and Etienne walked back to the Jeep. He unlocked the door, then checked up and down the street, hand hovering over the lapel of his jacket. Watching Etienne stand there, spiky hair fringed with red from the interior lights of the Jeep, James was jolted by a powerful compulsion to kill him there and then.

Not now, he ordered himself. *You can't risk a gunfight. Anyway, you know where he lives.*

* * *

Nat woke to a shout of laughter from the salon downstairs. The mood of languid fatalism that had stolen over was gone. She sat up and checked her watch: she'd been dozing for twenty minutes. She listened with increasing irritation to the voices below: Zender humorous and affable, Grey Tony businesslike and urbane. The faces they showed to each other, and to the world – sophisticated fronts, carefully wrought and practised over many years. But what were they really like? Different in most ways, but at heart the same: cold, greedy men. *Whatever they're plotting now, I'm not going to be part of it,* she thought angrily. *I won't let Grey Tony satisfy his insatiable lust* for the IPD400 at James's expense, or mine. *And how dare Zender lock me up in his hideous house!* She ran downstairs and threw open the door to the salon.

'Natalya,' said Zender. 'We were just talking about you.'

He was seated in a library chair by the fireplace. Grey Tony was on the sofa, with his back turned. The NSA procurement chief stood and faced her, an expression of schoolmasterly reprimand on his not-quite-handsome face.

'Claude thinks I'm being too hard on you,' he said. 'He's a persuasive fellow, but I'm not convinced.'

'So shoot me,' Nat shouted at him. 'Do it yourself, you spineless dickhead. Not got a gun?'

She ran to Zender's desk, yanked open the drawer and upended it. Amid the torrent of pens, notepads and paperclips, a Remington automatic clunked onto the desktop. She pulled the clip, saw it was loaded. Grey Tony was edging towards the door. She flung the gun at his head. He dodged and the gun crashed into the mirror above the fireplace, sending shards of glass cascading onto the marble hearth.

'Shoot me,' Nat screamed at him. 'You can't, can you. You want to shoot me and you want to fuck me, but you can't do either because you haven't got the balls. You dress up in your fancy suits and flash your NSA badge and run your clever little scheme to make yourself rich, but underneath it all, Grey Tony, you're just a dreary fucking faceless wimp.'

'Dear me,' said Zender, greatly enjoying himself. 'That is harsh.'

'You had my friend Magda beaten half to death,' Nat croaked, unable to shout any more but still shaking with rage.

'She deserved it. I won't be blackmailed.'

'Well you've fucked yourself over big time. I'm giving everything Magda found out to Internal Affairs. Unless you kill me first.' She held out her arms and glared.

This threat goaded Grey Tony into action. He stooped and picked the Remington out of the broken glass strewn across the hearth.

'You're a stupid little whore, Natalya Kocharian,' he said. 'And stupid little whores have to be slapped down, I'm afraid.'

'I would urge against, Tony,' said Zender. 'A glass of Champagne to soothe the nerves, then I'm sure we can find a more propitious way to settle our differences.'

'She's overstepped the mark,' said Grey Tony, pointing the gun at Nat. 'There's nothing to discuss.'

Despite these resolute words, Grey Tony was staring at the gun gripped tightly in his hand as if it had nothing to do with him. Sweat beaded his temples and his jaw bulged. At that moment, the door flew open and James stepped into the room. He aimed the MAB at Zender, then swung it round to the man pointing a gun at Nat.

'Dr Palatine,' said Zender. 'How timely. May I introduce Tony Schliemann of the NSA. A fanatical admirer of your work, whom I don't believe you've met.'

'No,' said James.

He studied the tall, well-groomed man standing in front of the shattered mirror, noted how awkwardly the gun was perched in his hand, and laced three bullets in a diagonal across his heart.

The NSA man stretched out one arm to steady himself, closed his hand over nothing, swayed for a few seconds, then rocked back. His skull cracked against the hearth, and across his ashen face, framed by the florid marble fireplace, there spread a grimace as horrified as you might expect from a man who thought he was untouchable but finds himself nearly dead.

'I'm glad I introduced you,' said Zender, 'for that is something I have often been tempted to do.'

As he finished speaking, Zender threw himself forward and reached over the corpse of Grey Tony for the gun which had fallen from his hand. He moved with surprising speed, but Nat was quicker. She kicked the Remington away, picked it up and joined James by the door.

'A charming sight,' said Zender, regaining his chair and smiling at them as if nothing had happened. 'You were made for each other, I dare say. But Dr Palatine's sangfroid is alarming even for an ex-soldier. I would be very wary of him, Natalya.'

'Hold your hands out in front of you. Don't move.'

'You have dispensed with the master,' Zender said, doing as James had ordered, 'as was your right, and even your obligation, given his murderous intentions towards Ms Kocharian. But why trouble your conscience with the hired hand?'

'You had me abducted and tortured. And when you set your dogs on me in Smara, it wasn't to take me back to the compound.'

'It was. But it is hard to find reliable staff in that infested place.'

'I'd like to kill him, too,' said James to Nat. 'With your permission.'

Nat leaned against his shoulder. 'Don't. I don't want you to.' She felt nothing for Grey Tony, and not much for Zender any more. But she was terribly afraid for James.

'You mustn't fall out on my account,' said Zender, affecting the manner of a thoroughly genial fellow waiting for his after-dinner coffee to be served.

'Let's get out of here,' said Nat.

'I would be happy to assist,' said Zender. 'The border officials know how to make themselves awkward, but there are routes that offer a discreet and even passably comfortable exit.'

'Nat doesn't want you shot but I do. Stand up, take your jacket off and throw it over here.'

Zender did so, with an exaggerated sigh.

'Turn round. Put your hands against the wall.'

Men of Zender's bulk were usually very strong and James wasn't going to take any chances. He searched him at arm's length, taking his time and keeping the gun out of the way. He took Zender's keys and cellphone. Nat found the phone he had taken from her earlier in the pocket of his jacket.

'Stand here, in the middle of the room,' James said. 'Where is Sarah?'

'Sarah? I'm not at all sure I know— '

James crouched, braced himself, and rammed the heel of his foot into the side of Zender's knee. The huge man gave a roar of pain as the joint buckled inwards.

'One for Nikolai.'

Zender succeeded in keeping himself upright for a few seconds, then gave up and crashed to the floor. He tried to heave himself into a sitting position, but managed only to raise himself on one elbow.

'A heinous act of cruelty on a defenceless man,' he panted. 'I should have expected it. Your liking for violence is well known.'

'Sarah,' said James, pointing the MAB at Zender's other knee.

'Etienne is taking care of her – or rather, his wife is. A most gentle creature.' He grunted and, looking reproachfully at James, covered his knee with a large hand.

James led Nat out into the hall and held her in his arms for as long as he dared.

'Will you search the house for phones and computers – any way he can call for help? I want to isolate him here while we get away from Algiers.'

'OK,' said Nat. She was reluctant to leave his side. 'I said not to kill him, remember?'

James went back into the salon. The kick had done its job – the stricken arms dealer hadn't moved an inch.

'What are you doing, Palatine?' he asked querulously from the floor.

James pulled the rose-coloured sofa onto its back and knocked over the side table next to Zender's chair. Zender probably numbered some of his most obligated friends among the Algiers police, and James had no intention of calling them. But it made sense, anyway, to arrange the place so that it looked as if Zender and Tony Schliemann had fought and the NSA man had ended up dead. He checked the room again: no landline, the windows shuttered and padlocked. He found a clasp knife among the things Nat had emptied onto the desk and pocketed it. He searched the side drawers of the desk and found another set of keys, one of which locked the salon door. Then he looked over at the corpse of Grey Tony and realised there'd be a phone in one of his pockets. He found it and brandished it at Zender.

'Almost forgot.'

Zender scowled horribly. Nat called from the hallway.

'I found this in his bedroom.'

She showed James an ornate wooden box that contained half a dozen sets of keys, carefully labelled: *Algiers, Oran, Marrakech, Geneva…*

'There's a computer in that room there.'

She pointed to a door to the left of the main entrance – a bare office with dirty white walls and steel shelves stacked with trade journals and boxes of accounts. James went under the desk, disabled the network card and cut the phone line.

'D'you still have the Remington?'

'Upstairs, in the cupboard where I found the keys.'

'Clean?'

She nodded.

'We need to wipe our prints off everything before we go.'

They went over the house together. Nat collected her bag and the gentian blue dress, then waited in the hall while James went back to the salon. He emptied the remaining bullets from the MAB, cleaned it off and dropped it on the floor by Zender's elbow.

'Wouldn't want you to shoot yourself,' he said.

The great arms dealer didn't reply. He had folded himself into the foetal position, one hand still laid protectively over his knee, the other held up to his mouth. James inspected him for a moment, unable to quite believe what he was seeing. He left the salon, locking the door behind him.

'Zender is sucking his thumb.'

'He does that sometimes,' said Nat. 'Creepy, isn't it.'

'No kidding. Do you think he'll set the police on us?'

'He spends a fortune keeping them out of his life – this doesn't look like a great moment to invite them in.'

Nat followed James into the kitchen, then down into a large cellar. By the far wall was a set of wooden steps leading up to a hatch.

'Is this how you got in?' asked Nat.

'The cook and his wife use it. They keep a key tucked into a crack in the wall.'

He climbed the steps and reached down to help her. Nat looked up and saw his head silhouetted against a sky bright with stars. She took his hand and felt herself lifted up. It was lovely that he was thinking of her, that he could make her feel so agile and light. She reached for his waist and pulled him close so they could kiss.

Zender's Citroën DS stood in front of them. Someone had cleaned it up and secured the damaged boot lid with a length of nylon cord. James padlocked the hatch, then opened the passenger door and bowed.

'Mam'selle?'

'*Enchantée*. Won't someone notice it's missing?'

'I just think we have to drive out of here in a black Citroën DS.'

'Hey, you're learning.'

She tucked herself into the capacious leather seat. He shut the door and went round to the driver's side, pulled the ignition key from behind the sun visor.

'How did you find that? Oh, never mind. Where now?'

'Etienne's. We have unfinished business.'

*   *   *

They drove down the hill into town and parked round the corner from the apartment block where Etienne lived.

'Will you wait here, Nat? Don't come after me, even if… Please?'

She didn't want him to go, knew he would anyway.

James went to the door of Etienne's building. It opened onto a concrete stairwell that stank of urine. It was airless and almost dark, lit only by the feeble orange glow from a bulkhead light above the door. He climbed to the first floor and checked the apartment numbers: 11, 12. Two on each floor. Number 41 would be on the fourth floor, at the top. He carried on up. Each floor seemed narrower and more foetid than the last. On the fourth floor, the dim bulkhead lamp had been replaced with a naked fluorescent bulb that gave off a stark grey light. Number 41 was straight ahead. There were two extra locks on the door, and a spyhole. He stood aside so he couldn't be seen. A bicycle was propped up outside 42, no front wheel and the chain lying broken on the floor. He picked up the chain and coiled it into his pocket.

To his left was a flight of steps that must lead to the roof. He tried the door at the top, found it unlocked, and stepped out onto a square of rumpled bitumen no more than twenty feet across, surrounded by a drainage gully and a low parapet. In the far corner was a huge, rust-streaked water tank. He padded softly over to it – Etienne's flat was directly below. He tapped the tank at several places – it was nearly full. There was a thick iron pipe at the base, tightly wrapped in a tarred rag with a jubilee clip holding it in place. He worked the clip aside and unravelled the sticky rag. You could see why it was needed: the pipe was intact, but the area round the joint was almost rusted through.

The gully carried rainwater out to a drainage spout overhanging the street. James took off his jacket and blocked it, then found a ridge of cracked bitumen that he thought would be directly above Etienne's front room. He unfolded the clasp knife and sliced through the ridge, exposing the chipboard below. The bitumen was soft from the heat of the day and yielded easily. Working as quietly as he could, he scooped out an inch-wide hole in the chipboard. That should do it. He went back to the water tank, put his feet either side of the pipe and wrapped both hands round it, close to the joint. He bent his knees, braced, pulled the pipe upwards with all his strength.

The tank tipped back and he heard water swilling around inside. Again. Water dribbled over his fingers. Once more. The dribble became a stream and he braced for a final heave. That did it. A jagged disc of rusty steel ripped clear and water gushed out. He watched it course into the gully, slop against his folded jacket and spread out across the roof. The flood found its way to the slit he'd cut in the bitumen and started to drain slowly down the hole into the ceiling below.

He stood by the door to the stairwell and wrapped one end of the bicycle chain twice around his fist. A woman screamed. A thump, then a shout – a man's voice, tight and irritable. The man went on hectoring for a moment then, above the sound of gurgling water, came the scrape-click of a door being unlocked. Footsteps on the landing.

James heard a hollow pop and the bar of light beneath the stairwell door went out. Another scream from the woman.

'Tais-toi, salope!'

He was coming up the steps, shoes crunching on the gritty concrete. James crouched. The door banged open.

James swung the chain through a full arc and the steel links lashed the jaw of the man stepping out onto the roof, the tail end snaking round the back of his skull. The man gasped and stumbled forward, knees splashing into the water. Etienne. James moved up behind him and brought the chain down again. It flailed over the top of his head and whipped into his face. James reached down to haul him up, but Etienne wasn't done. He rolled, a knife glinting in his hand, slashing at James's outstretched arm. James drew back sharply, but the roof was slippery now and he lost his footing. Etienne pounced, the knife darting for James's throat. James threw his hand out and the point of the knife snagged in a link of the chain. The blade slewed sideways and sliced into the pad of his thumb. Etienne kicked out at James's groin but misjudged and his foot glanced off James's thigh. James grabbed his ankle and pushed sharply up. Etienne tipped backwards. The momentum of his fall helped pull James upright. He jabbed his heel into Etienne's solar plexus, heard a grunt as his lungs emptied of air. James wound the loose end of the chain round his fist and drove the clump of oily links into Etienne's eye.

'Lost your Taser, Etienne?'

Etienne's face had been ripped open by the lashing chain, but he was tough as a street rat should be and still wasn't out. James punched him again, same place, same eye. He unpicked the knife from Etienne's hand and tossed it over to the adjoining roof. Etienne was too groggy to stop him. Blood from James's cut hand was dribbling into the water at his feet. He ignored it, took Etienne by the throat and heaved him upright.

'Where's Sarah?' he said. 'The English girl.'

The eye James had punched looked like a burst plum. Etienne glared at him with the other one and spat a mouthful of blood.

'Where is she?'

He drove Etienne back until he crashed into the doorframe, then swung his chain-wrapped fist into the man's kidneys. Etienne doubled over and coughed. He was only upright now because James was holding him.

'Where is Sarah?'

'Fuck you. She's dead.'

'No. She's not dead.' Rage and desperation flared inside him. He drove his fist into Etienne's midriff again.

'What shall I do to you, Etienne? Cut holes in your skin? Tear your hand apart to the wrist, the way you showed me?'

'Fucking girl is dead,' Etienne panted. 'You can't— '

James stopped him with another hammer-blow to the kidneys. Etienne dropped to all fours, a strand of bloody drool dangling from his chin. James kicked him in the stomach, and Etienne lay prone. Water from the broken tank streamed over his flayed cheek. A trickle entered his mouth and he spluttered, lifted his head, but couldn't hold it up. James dragged him by the ankles over to the corner of the roof. The gleaming water parted round his torso and slapped gently together at the top of his head, making his spiky hair weave from side to side like seaweed in a tide. James pushed Etienne's face down into the gully, where the water was deepest, and stood on his neck. Etienne tried to twist his face clear of the water, but didn't have the strength. His limbs flailed, shuddered, finally went still. Bubbles formed around his ears. In less than a minute, he had drowned.

* * *

Nat had been sitting in the Citroën, watching the apartment block and thinking James shouldn't have gone in alone, that he was pushing his luck. When all the lights in the apartments went out, she ran from the car and over to the stairwell door, convinced that James was lying somewhere being repeatedly stabbed by Etienne or some other grinning henchmen of Zender's. Dying, alone, without anyone to comfort him.

There was still some emergency light in the rank stairwell. She ran on up. An old man watched her from the doorway of number 22. He shouted something she didn't catch, then gave a sour laugh. Not Etienne. When she reached the fourth, she knew this was it. Number 41. Two extra locks and a spyhole. The door was half an inch ajar. She pushed it open and peered in. A short corridor, ending in a room that seemed to flicker with pale blue light. She stepped inside.

The blue light came from a gas stove with a pot of something simmering on top. A sharp smell of spices and hot fat. Water was dripping from the ceiling light and drumming softly onto the rug in the centre of the floor. A tasselled drape hung over the window, beneath it, a small steel-legged table and a padded bench. There was a door set in the wall opposite her.

She tiptoed over and listened. Muffled breathing. Something else... A whimper, perhaps, or the squeak of a bedspring. She was startled by a bang from the roof above her head, and without thinking she pressed the handle and opened the door.

A woman in full burqa was sitting on a bed, lit from the side by a row of tealights set on the window ledge. She was clasping a long-bladed kitchen knife in both hands. A figure lay stretched out on the bed behind her, hands and feet bound with duct tape. All Nat could see of the woman with the knife was her eyes, shining from the narrow slit in her veil. Nat looked into them and they flicked away, then back to face her. Not anger, Nat realised, nor ferocity, nor zeal. Fear. She said the first thing that came to her.

'Ma pauvre.'

Poor thing. The figure lying on the bed twisted round. She too was veiled, the black cloth bound tight round her mouth with swathes of tape.

'Lâchez le couteau, je vous en prie. Personne ne vous fait mal.'

No one will hurt you.

The woman's eyes brimmed with tears. She spoke, but the words came so fast and indistinct Nat could not hear them.

'Lâchez le couteau,' Nat said again.

'Eh-i-enne,' the woman whimpered. 'Il e-ait-al.'

A thought so awful Nat could hardly bear to let it enter her head...

'Je suis amie d'Aisha. Vous souvenez? Aisha, qui travaille chez le Casino des Capricornes?'

'Oui, Aisha,' said the woman.

The tears were welling from her eyes. Nat crossed the room, reached over to touch the woman's hands, still grasping the handle of the knife. Nat pressed her palm gently over the woman's hands for a moment. They were small, delicate hands, shivering like a trapped bird. She patted the woman on the shoulder and slowly released the knife from her fingers, placed it on the window ledge next to the candles.

'Is that Sarah?' Nat asked. 'I'll help you in a moment. You OK?'

456

The figure on the bed rolled awkwardly to the side, sat upright and nodded. Nat wrapped her arms round the woman beside her.

'Ma pauvre,' she said again.

She pulled away and gestured to the woman's face-veil.

'Montrez-moi, s'il vous plaît.'

The woman looked down, then slowly unhooked the square of black cotton that covered her face. She raised her head and looked Nat square in the eye. Her mouth was a lipless oval, the teeth and gums obscenely prominent. The flesh where her lips had been was etched with bone-white scars.

'Etienne did that? Because you spied on Claude Zender?'

She nodded.

This was the woman Aisha had told her about at the casino. Etienne had disfigured her, then made her his own. At Zender's behest. Zender... Had she ever really seen him for what he was? Nat hugged the woman again, and while they embraced, James rushed into the room. He seemed impossibly huge in the dim, cramped space. One hand was wrapped in a sodden rag and his deep-set eyes were so dark and wild that for a moment she felt afraid of him.

'Etienne?' she asked.

'Dead,' said James. 'On the roof. Is that... Sarah?'

He stepped over to the bed and started to strip off the tape wrapped round her mouth. The woman was hurrying to fix her veil back in place.

'You're safe,' said Nat to the woman. 'Come and see.'

She led the woman from the room. James had Sarah's veil off and the girl fell into his arms.

'Oh Jesus Christ, you came. You came. I thought you'd given up, I thought I was here forever.'

She lapsed into hysterical sobs. James cut her hands free, stood her up and half-carried her into the living room.

'Your passport,' he said. 'Where did he keep it?'

'There, I think.' She pointed to a drawer beneath the TV. James sorted through a pile of documents, found the passport and handed it to Sarah. He put his arm round her shoulders and they left the apartment. Nat came down from the roof.

'I left her up there.' Nat wiped her eyes and hugged herself. 'Etienne was a devil, but she says he was her husband and there are things she must do.'

'Let's get away from here,' said James.

They ran down to the DS, ignoring the astonished looks of the residents who had gathered on the street. James drove in a daze, flooded with relief and euphoria. Nat sat in the back, soothing Sarah, arranging her frizzy hair and telling her everything was going to be fine. James's hand started to bleed through the rag, so they stopped and Nat bandaged it with strips torn from the gentian blue dress she had never worn.

'I can't believe you came back for me,' Sarah kept saying. 'I can't believe it. Thank you.'

They drove to the airport and bought her a ticket for the next flight to London.

'Go airside straight away,' said James, 'and stay there.'

She nodded. 'Will I see you again?'

'We could have a drink at the Lamb and Flag,' said James.

'The place where we met?' She smiled ruefully. 'Guess I deserve to be reminded.'

She thanked them again and they watched her join the queue for security.

'So, is this over now?' asked Nat.

'Not quite,' said James. 'Time to get back to the hotel. We have visitors.'

* * *

They watched the three MI6 men arrive in the lobby of the Hotel el-Djazaïr, trailing overnight bags and with expressions on their faces that suggested their journey to Algiers had not been accompanied by much in the way of good-natured badinage.

Sir Iain Strang saw them first and marched over, mouth fixed in a grin so determined it looked capable of causing physical injury.

'Dr James Palatine,' he said. 'Thanks for setting this up at such short notice.' He reached out to shake James's hand, then saw the blood-caked blue cloth and withdrew. 'You're hurt. Anything I can do?'

Without waiting for a reply, he turned to Nat.

'And you must be— '

'Natalya Kocharian,' she said.

'A pleasure to meet you, Ms Kocharian. Clive Silk you both know – but Dr Palatine, you haven't met Nigel de la Mere, who is about to retire from our North-West Africa Office.'

De la Mere gave the merest possible nod of acknowledgement.

'I'll see if the hotel can find us somewhere private, yes?'

'No,' said James. 'We'll talk here.'

'The meeting gets off to a frosty start,' said Strang. 'I suppose I shouldn't be surprised, after what you've been through.'

'Quite a bit of which seems to have been arranged by you,' said James, sitting down next to Nat on a sofa with its back to the window. The MI6 men took chairs in a semi-circle opposite.

'Are you OK, Clive?' asked Nat. 'There's a bathroom just beyond reception, if you need to be sick.'

Clive Silk gave her a poisonous look.

'You needn't worry about the IPD400, anyway,' she went on. 'It's on its way back to Grosvenor.'

'We heard from Sir Peter. Great news,' said Strang. He leaned towards James, weapons-grade smile still primed and cocked. 'Dr Palatine, why don't you tell me what's been going on out there in the Western Sahara? The intel is so confused it's given Nigel early onset dementia.'

'The Moroccans and the Polisario have been scrapping again,' said James. 'Now, my turn. What do you think the public reaction would be to information proving that the terrorist organisation known as al Bidayat was created, funded and operated by MI6?'

Sir Iain Strang smoothed with one hand hair that did not need smoothing. The smile had gone.

'Disbelief? Laughter?'

'One of yours, is it, Nigel?' said James.

Nigel de la Mere had sunk so low in his chair that it looked as if he'd elected to let his large, misshapen knees represent his interests while the rest of him hid. None of them spoke.

'I know al Bidayat is an MI6 op and I have the evidence to prove it,' said James.

'We're terrorists now, are we?' said de la Mere. 'A jihadi cell at the heart of SIS. Never knew I had it in me.'

'Al Bidayat isn't a terrorist organisation, Nigel, it's a fake. The wannabe terrorist goes to the al Bidayat website, watches a couple of inspiring videos courtesy of Sheikh Ibrahim al Haqim, sees the offers of finance and support and gets in touch. Only the man he gets in touch with isn't al Haqim, it's Claude Zender, and he passes the sucker over to you. You get to monitor a bagful of fledgling bin Ladens and Zender gets his fat fee. You called it Operation Anemone.'

'A bit far-fetched,' mumbled Clive Silk.

'Far-fetched doesn't begin to describe it,' said James. 'But I expect you persuaded yourself it was brilliantly innovative – a cyber-Trojan, wheeled into the mother-node of the terrorist network. Anemone, the world's first wholly virtual entrapment op.' He gave an abrupt laugh. 'Of course, this is the sort of hokum Clive specialises in. Nigel's far too old school. Anemone is Clive's brainchild, if you can call it that. Bravo, Clive Silk.'

Silk declined to acknowledge the congratulations.

'Was it you who nicknamed al Bidayat the Terror Consultancy?' James asked. 'Nice touch. Wasn't reeling them in, though, was it? Ref Anemone, no significant activity to report.'

'This is highly classified information,' said Silk weakly. 'We shouldn't be discussing it here.'

'Of course, you had to be able to deny everything when the need arose,' James went on, 'so you hired Zender to run Anemone for you.'

'That was a mistake,' said Nat.

'Wasn't it,' said Strang, staring aggressively at Silk. 'One of many.'

'I imagine you thought that a rock-strewn no-man's-land with no formal government was the perfect location,' said James. 'I don't know how Zender persuaded Professor Ibrahim al Haqim out of Cairo University to be the front man. Blackmail, I would guess.'

'So what's your point, Dr Palatine?' said Strang. 'We're in the intelligence business and we gain intelligence via Claude Zender's operation in the Western Sahara.'

James was pleased to hear the acid in his voice.

'Mansour Anzarane,' said James, 'the second man Zender hired for Operation Anemone. You must have thought him the perfect recruiting agent: a noisy fantasist, tenuously connected to any number of atrocities, as well as being a devoted former student of Ibrahim al Haqim. And if one of his targets should discover that al Bidayat was a trap, he was entirely dispensable.'

The hangdog look on Clive Silk's face told James that this was the truth, or very near to it.

'Your intention was that he should confine himself to gaudy speeches on the al Bidayat website. But as far as Zender was concerned, he was just another employee – quite a useful one, since he seemed happy to see a bit of blood on his hands.'

'Takes one to know one,' said Nigel de la Mere.

'Unless you have anything useful to contribute, Nigel, you'd better say nothing at all,' said Strang. 'James, I apologise. You were telling us about Mansour?'

James stared at de la Mere until the MI6 man looked away.

'Zender put Mansour on the team that abducted me,' James went on. 'The irony of using an al Bidayat hireling paid for by MI6 to help steal the IPD400 would have appealed to him. Mansour thought he was taking instructions from al Haqim and working in al Bidayat's holy cause – but the orders were actually coming from Zender. He had Anzarane execute a man called Hamed, who helped lure me to Oran.'

'We had nothing to do with your abduction,' said Strang, 'as I'm sure you know.'

'It's telling that you feel the need to deny it,' said James. 'But it wasn't concern for me or the IPD400 that was getting you out of bed in the morning, was it?'

'On the contrary, we were always— '

'The real crisis hit when you heard that your very own Mansour Anzarane had been named by the Moroccans as prime suspect in the Agadir Bombing.'

'Nobody believes that,' Clive Silk said. 'Pure politics.'

He seemed about to say more, when Strang subjected him to a look of such ferocity that Silk instinctively raised his hands in submission.

'I believe it,' James lied. 'I had a chat with Mansour Anzarane while I was a guest at Zender's pleasure. He swore blind he *was* the Agadir Bomber. Quite certain on that point.'

The three men stared at him. Even Strang had been silenced. It was de la Mere who recovered first.

'Anzarane specialises in exactly that sort of preening self-aggrandisement. I can guarantee he'll give a different answer next time he's asked.'

'There won't be a next time,' said James. 'He's dead.'

'Since when?'

'Since I killed him. His last words were, "I am the Agadir Bomber." The Moroccans will be delighted. What will the papers say, do you think? *British scientist confirms that Mansour Anzarane of MI6-funded terrorist group al Bidayat murdered sixty-seven holiday-makers in Agadir.*'

'You know full well that isn't true,' said Strang.

'The Moroccans think he did it. I can back them up. What will you tell them, Strang? That it can't be al Bidayat because al Bidayat was dreamed up by Clive Silk one night after a bad curry? Too late for that: if you force the Moroccans to admit they were wrong about Mansour, they lose their chance of implicating the Polisario in Agadir. Much better for them to tell you that you accidentally had a real terrorist on the payroll and had better keep quiet about it.'

Nigel de la Mere emitted a laugh like a seal choking on a fish bone. 'Sounds to me like the old bits and bytes have been leading you up the garden path, Palatine,' he said.

'What a bind you were in! Your virtual terrorist outfit suddenly brought to life by the pesky Moroccans. They say Mansour Anzarane is the Agadir Bomber; I know that the very same man is paid for out of MI6 funding for Operation Anemone. What will happen if that gets out? Service disgraced. Careers in ruins. Next thing you know, the Moroccans are planning to march into the Free Zone and turn the compound upside down in the hunt for evidence that Anzarane was consorting with the Polisario. You can't let that happen or the IPD400 will fall into their hands. Worse still, you think I'm there and you think I'll talk – or if not, they'll find out some other way that Anzarane is on the Anemone payroll. It's knowledge you can't let them have. So you decide to tip off the Polisario and hope they can stop the raid in its tracks.'

'I wondered when the conspiracy theory would pop up and say hello,' said Strang. 'Perhaps the Royal Family are behind it.'

James ignored him. 'That must have taken some nerve – you nearly started a war out there. Not the sort of behaviour expected of a permanent member of the UN Security Council. But you knew the Polisario had as much interest as you in removing any trace of Mansour and al Bidayat from the compound, so you made the call and tried to pretend you were doing it for them.'

'This is becoming ridiculous,' said Strang, though his eyes had the look of a fox that is running out of cover.

'That just left me,' said James.

'You always did take yourself far too seriously,' said de la Mere.

Nat had been struggling to contain her hatred for the drab, shifty men in front of her. James was striking the right note, and she wanted to let him finish. But listening to their evasions and denials was unbearable.

'He didn't know anything about Operation fucking Anemone,' she said furiously. 'It was just a stupid word. He didn't find out until we got to Algiers.'

'I don't follow,' said Strang.

'Oh, you follow just fine,' Nat said. 'Clive told Manni Hasnaoui to get James killed and he had to find out why. That's when he went looking for Anemone. That's how he discovered about al Bidayat. If you'd left him alone, none of this shit would have come out. You could have dug a deep hole and buried it.'

'Quite true,' said James. 'Until I spoke to Hasnaoui, I assumed you were monitoring al Bidayat, rather than funding it.'

'The very idea that MI6 would authorise— '

'We're not talking about MI6,' said James. 'We're talking about Iain Strang, Nigel de la Mere and Clive Silk. Three men facing certain disgrace.'

'I know nothing about this,' said de la Mere. 'It was Clive who spoke to Hasnaoui – went to see him in person, as I recall. He's always had a thing about you, Palatine, ever since Kosovo. This begins to make sense.'

'You fucking sent me to Algiers, and you told me exactly what to say!' said Silk.

'And Strang told *him* what to say,' said James. 'The point is, your superiors sent you so that they could deny it.'

Silk clambered to his feet and stumbled over to James, fists clenched by his sides, face scarlet. 'So what fucking difference does it make? Anemone is over and you, you always were a *cunt*.'

James stood and faced him. 'The difference is— '

'Every move I make, you're there with your public-school sneer, showing off your scars and calling me an office boy. Fuck you, Palatine. I've worked my way up from nowhere. I've only ever done what's best for my country, and you— '

James took Clive by the lapels of his jacket and dumped him back into his chair.

'Nigel, why don't you take Clive up to bed,' said Strang, 'while I finish with James.'

De la Mere was already on his feet, staring contemptuously at Clive. The two men gathered their cases and towed them off across the lobby.

'I blame myself,' said Strang. He'd managed to freshen up the grin and haul it back into position.

'Me too,' said Nat. 'Fish rot from the head down.'

'I should have throttled Anemone at birth – it would have been a kindness. I'm ashamed to say one part of me was quite keen to see Silk preside over a cock-up.'

'It wasn't Silk who got everything wrong,' said James. 'It was you.'

'Yet here we all are, safe and sound,' said Strang smoothly. 'Do you know who paid Zender to steal the IPD400?'

'You don't?' said Nat. 'Wow, you have some dreary spy-work ahead of you.'

'It makes no difference,' Strang said quickly. 'So, Dr Palatine, the corpus of British intelligence is manacled to the bed and awaiting your pleasure. What exactly is your pleasure?'

'I haven't decided,' said James. 'But there's no hurry, is there? Think I'll take a nice holiday.'

'Let's resolve things here and now, yes? End it properly?'

'What would you suggest?' said Nat.

'For a start, I'd like you to come and work for us at MI6, Ms Kocharian. And we might confiscate the IPD400 from Grosvenor, put it out of harm's way.'

Nat and James looked at each other, then stood up.

'Just remember this, Strang,' said James. 'I have the Anemone files. So behave.'

*   *   *

They left the Director-General of MI6 to stew and got the concierge to open the hotel shop. They bought a swimsuit, trunks and plastic beach shoes. When they got back to the lobby, Sir Iain Strang had gone.

'He ran off screaming into the night,' said Nat. 'It's awful for them when someone else gets hold of one of their secrets. They shrivel up and go mad. What will you do with them?'

'I don't know. I can't prove they tried to kill me, not unless I can get Hasnaoui in court. As for Anemone, it can sit in the archive for fifty years, along with all the other skeletons.'

'You're not going to the press?'

'Thing is, Nat, leaving them dangling, not knowing what's going to happen to them – that's the cruellest thing I could possibly do.'

'Bad man,' said Nat.

They set off for the harbour. When they reached the narrow gangway that led to the moorings, Nat stepped ahead of him. *Even the way she walks makes her desirable,* James thought. The composed energy, the neat, even roll of her hips. And yet her feet were slightly splayed – a hint of the duckling… The insight brought a powerful, almost melancholy urge to protect her, to shield her from all the harm the world had shown it could inflict.

They found a fishing boat preparing to sail. James asked the captain how much to drop them off the coast of Spain and the captain gave them a suspicious look and waved him away. James persisted and they arrived at a price. The captain showed them to a narrow berth in the bows which they had to share with two barrels of diesel and a dismantled winch.

'This must be the honeymoon suite,' said Nat.

It was a burly vessel and its way with waves was to bludgeon them aside. They spent the night chattering in each other's arms, listening to the slaps, thumps and shudders that marked their progress north. At ten, the coast of Spain came into view. They changed into their swimming things and stepped up onto the sun-warmed deck.

'What are the currents like here?'

'For boat, no problem,' the captain said. 'For swim, I no try.'

The coast was about half a mile away. A small town sprawled from the back of a bay a little way over to the east. They went to the side of the boat and slipped into the water. It was calm with a gentle swell. The boat surged away to the south and they listened to the crew joking behind them, their voices startlingly clear across the undulating blue-green surface of the sea.

'What day is it?' asked Nat, enjoying the feel of James's limbs in the cool water.

'Sunday. The day of rest.'

'Rest?' said Nat. 'No chance. Race you to the shore.'

James watched her body ripple through the water. She's a swimmer, too, he thought. I'll never catch her.

Epilogue

Sunday Tribune, **16 December 2006**

The Home Secretary today announced the surprise resignation of Sir Iain Strang, Director-General of the foreign intelligence service MI6. Sir Iain, 53, has held the post only since June 2004. A graduate of Manchester Grammar School and the University of Nottingham, his appointment was intended to herald a new departure for the Oxbridge-dominated SIS, which has come under fire in recent years for what critics perceive as its archaic methods and inflexible approach. Sir Iain Strang was not available for comment.

Books & Bookselling, **5 January 2007**

HarperCollins publishers have been forced to cancel publication of Nigel de la Mere's MI6 memoir *Secrets in the Blood,* following pressure from SIS lawyers. 'By the time we'd cut out everything we were told might breach the Official Secrets Act,' said spokesperson Nicky Talbot-Gray, 'there wasn't much left to publish.'

Intelligence Today, **20 January 2007**

MI6 staffer Clive Silk has swapped the high-pressure environment of MI6's Strategic Projects Office for the quieter life of SIS archive, where he will take the role of Digital Librarian. Silk had previously boasted involvement in a number of innovative MI6 operations and had been identified in government circles as a high-flyer. 'The importance of the Service archive cannot be overstated,' Silk said, 'and it's a place I've always wanted to spend part of my career.'

A Note on the Western Sahara

When Natalya Kocharian arrives at the compound for the first time she asks Claude Zender where they are and he describes the Western Sahara in the term allocated to it by the United Nations: a Non-Self Governing Territory. Nothing could be more expressive of the fate of its indigenous people than this ambiguous and irresolute designation.

The Western Sahara, which lies between Morocco to the north, Mauritania to the south, Algeria to the east and the Atlantic Ocean to the west, is one of the most inhospitable and sparsely populated regions in the world, with no natural sources of fresh water and temperatures regularly exceeding 50° Celsius. The indigenous population of Sahrawi nomads are descended from Arabic and Berber tribes, who subsisted on camel herding and other trading activities associated with the ancient caravan routes that criss-cross the region. In the 1600s the coastal territories fell under the control of Spanish slave traders; during the following centuries it became a centre for commercial fishing. In 1884 the Spanish formally declared it a colony, named the Spanish Sahara.

In 1975, as the slow and painful unravelling of European colonial empires entered its endgame, conflicting claims on the territory came to a head. The Algerian-backed Polisario (the *Frente Popular de Liberación de Saguía el Hamra y Río de Oro*) had spent the previous two years fighting the Spanish occupation, and their cause was bolstered by a ruling from the International Court of Justice that supported their right to self-determination. King Hassan II of Morocco responded by organising an extraordinary mass demonstration known as the Green March: on 6 November, some 350,000 unarmed Moroccans marched south into the Spanish Sahara, escorted by 20,000 soldiers. Eight days later, Spain, Morocco and Mauritania signed the Madrid Accords, carving up the territory between the two African nations. The Polisario were not party to the negotiation.

During the sixteen-year war that followed, the Polisario defeated the Mauritanians to the south, advancing at one stage as far as the capital Nouakchott, and fought a successful guerrilla campaign against the Moroccan army. The Moroccan response was to construct a 2,600-kilometre wall of sand and rock, two to three metres high and studded with bunkers, forts, radar stations and airfields. Completed in 1987, the Wall splits the territory from north to south and confines the Sahrawi population to a strip along the Algerian border, now called the Free Zone. In 2004, the Wall was manned by an estimated 160,000 Moroccan soldiers. Needless to say, the fisheries and newly developed phosphate mines all lie to the west of the fortification, under Moroccan control, while the area to the east has the dubious distinction of being the longest continuous minefield in the world. The war has driven tens of thousands of refugees across the border into Algeria, and the Free Zone itself now has a population of barely 30,000.

In 1991 the Polisario and the Moroccans agreed to a ceasefire, to be supervised by a UN force with the acronym MINURSO. A referendum was planned. And since then? Not much… The Moroccan government incentivises its citizens to migrate south, hoping to ensure that, should the referendum ever take place, the result will go their way. In 2003, US Secretary of State James Baker attempted to resurrect the process, but without success. Fighting breaks out sporadically, international support for one side or the other is offered or withdrawn, there are protests and speeches and demonstrations. Meanwhile, the Algerian refugee camps grow larger and are now home to as many as 165,000 people.

The plight of the Western Sahara is in large part caused by greed: the phosphate mines and fisheries are valuable, and surveys have indicated there are exploitable oil reserves, too. But perhaps the laws of commerce will also impose a solution. Reports uncovered by Wikileaks in 2011 suggest the Moroccans subsidise the region to the tune of $800 million per annum, one of the largest per capita aid programmes in history. In the capital city Laayoune, for example, water is supplied by desalinisation plants and sold at less than 1 per cent of the cost of production. Without these subsidies, the region is probably not economically viable.

After so many decades mired in the backwaters of international diplomacy, it must be time to end this grim stalemate. It is a powerful testament to humanity's resilience and resourcefulness that there is an indigenous population in the Western Sahara at all, and no one's interests are served by prolonging the cruel, stubborn and profligate occupation of their lands. The Moroccans should bow respectfully and withdraw, leaving this barren and beautiful place to those who for centuries have made it their home.

The above is a summary of the situation in the Western Sahara, which provides the backdrop to Little Sister. *However, the events and characters depicted in this book are entirely fictional, and no resemblance to any real events or characters is intended or implied.*

Acknowledgements

Many thanks to Philippa Harrison, Henrietta Heald and Tom Penn, who toiled through an early and disgracefully long draft of *Little Sister*, and gave me the advice and encouragement I needed to continue.

The following people read later drafts: Sophie Carlisle, Louise Colonna, Toby Farrell, Simon Gillis, Stephen Graham, Margaret Halton, Antony Harwood, Charlotte Hobson, Will Hobson, Adam Kean, Maddy O'Bryen, Stefanie O'Bryen, Jemima Reynolds, Rupert Rumney, Miranda Swan and Wynn Wheldon. Many thanks to you all for your helpful and gracefully worded comments, generous good humour and occasional yawns.

Thanks to all my children, Nell, Maddy and Louis, for not teasing me too much about the fact that I was devoting my life to this long and distracting task.

My wife Emma falls into all three of the above categories, and many more besides. Her patience, unwavering faith and astute editorial advice have underpinned the writing of this book from start to finish, and I dedicate *Little Sister* to her.

About the Author

Giles O'Bryen is married with three children and lives in London.